I0673084

PERFECTLY TORTURED

BY
KRISTINE MASON

Copyright © 2016 Kristine Thompson

All rights reserved. Except for use in any review, the reproduction or utilization of this work in whole or in part in any form by any electronic, mechanical or other means, now known or hereafter invented, including xerography, photocopying and recording, or in any information storage or retrieval system, is forbidden without the written permission of the author.

This is a work of fiction. Names, characters, places and incidents are either the product of the author's imagination or are used fictitiously, and any resemblance to actual persons, living or dead, business establishments, events or locales is entirely coincidental.

Print Edition

ISBN 13: 978-0-9861617-7-3
ISBN 10: 0-9861617-7-2

Edited by Tessa Shapcott
Cover design by Elle J Rossi of EJR Digital Arts

For Faye...
I wish your story would have ended differently.

Acknowledgements

Thank you Jamie Denton for the hours of listening and dealing with my *moments*. Thanks also to Tessa Shapcott for your editing skills, Elle Rossi, from EJR Digital Art for working with me on my covers and Sherry Fundin for helping with yet another story. As always, special thanks to my husband and kids. You guys experienced the brunt of my *moments*. Finally, thank you Marco Polo, who not only brought me soap and made sure there wasn't a fire in my hotel room, but sounded just like Vlad.

PROLOGUE

I think my mask of sanity is about to slip.
—Patrick Bateman, *American Psycho*

Tallahassee, Florida
October 20th, 3:21 p.m. Eastern Daylight Saving Time

"WHAT ARE YOU *waiting for?"*
Liam Forrester glanced in the rear view mirror. The demon sat on the center of the SUV's backseat. Her long, dark curly hair was slicked back in a severe bun. Her green eyes glittered with sadistic amusement and stood out against her heavy black mascara and eyeliner. Her lips, stained red and matching her dress, slid into a smile.

"You're not supposed to be here, Adeline," he said. Fear gripped him, but excitement twisted him from the inside out. She'd promised to stay away from him. Nearly two months ago, while he'd bathed in the blood of his victims, she'd assured him that he was free. Afterward, he'd retrieved the backpack he'd hidden in Atlanta, Georgia, then had moved to Tallahassee, Florida, where he'd taken a job, found an affordable apartment, and bought a car. Adeline would not ruin what he now had—a steady income, the promise of a normal life.

He'd kill again before he would allow that to happen.

Hatred burned through him. For her. For the wicked cravings hollowing out his stomach, making room for what he knew could come...what he knew he shouldn't allow. He looked away from the mirror and toward the small house tucked behind the tall

Florida pine trees. "Go away."

"*I can never leave you, lover.*"

Which meant he could never stop killing. The hairs along his skin rose. "Then where have you been?"

"*Cute. You* have *missed me,*" she said on a chuckle. "*Where've I been? I never left. I'm in your heart, in the blood pumping through your veins. I'm in your mind, Liam. I hear your thoughts, I know your fears, and what excites you. We're so much alike, lover. I know you're just as hungry as I am. So, again, what are you waiting for?*"

He ignored the pangs shooting through his stomach. "I'm nothing like you," he said, determined to leave and prove to her that he wasn't the man she *thought* she'd created. His hand shook as he reached for the gearshift. When her taunting laughter filled his head, he curled his fingers and dropped his fist in his lap, leaving the SUV in PARK.

"*Then why have you been sitting at the end of this woman's driveway?*"

"Because it's against store policy for employees to use their personal vehicles to deliver or pick up equipment from customers' residences."

"*You're a terrible liar. Tell me the truth. You were trying to decide how to go in there and…take.*"

"I wasn't," he denied with vehemence. Since fleeing the House of Archer, where Adeline and that sick prick, Rodney, had imprisoned him—filling him with drugs, torturing his mind—his wounds had healed. His body only held a few minor scars from the time he'd spent there. After he'd given Adeline what she'd wanted, killing the old couple he'd come across during his escape, the darkness that had been threatening to take over his mind had gone away.

Most of the time.

"*Come on, Liam. You know you want to go in there and take. Imagine how good she'll feel.*"

As Adeline's seductive voice washed over him, he did imagine, just as he had the moment Bella Johnson had walked into the tool rental department at The Home Zone, asking to rent a carpet cleaner. She'd looked so damned much like Adeline that he'd thought his mind had fractured again, that the psychosis could be returning. Then Bella had spoken. Her voice wasn't purposefully seductive like Adeline's, but sultry with a sweet Southern tang. During the rest of his workday, he'd replayed their interaction dozens of times. Last night, he'd lain in bed picturing her with him. Naked. Her creamy skin glistening with perspiration and flushed from sex. He fisted his hand tight. Her blues eyes wide, frozen with terror, with shock. Her mouth gaping open on a silent scream.

Adeline laughed. *"Yes,"* she hissed. *"That's how I picture her, too. How did you kill her, Liam? Tell me, lover. Did you choke the life out of her? Or did you cut her?"*

"She's not dead."

"No dip, silly. For someone who lived with multiple personalities, your lack of imagination surprises me."

He'd had no problem fantasizing about killing Adeline. Maybe if he'd been given the satisfaction of ending her life, she wouldn't be in his head—haunting his dreams, keeping him awake at night reliving the hell she and Rodney had put him through. Reliving the murders, how killing those old people and tasting their blood on his lips had quieted her...

"Let's make her dead, Liam," Adeline continued. *"No one will know. They* don't *know about you, or me and Rod. Even your sister doesn't have a clue."*

Kiera. He closed his eyes and pictured his sister's familiar smile. She was such a good person, and he didn't want to disappoint her any more than he had. "I can't do it. Not like this."

"Fine. We'll come back later."

He shook his head. "It's not right."

"If it wasn't right, then it wouldn't feel so good, so liberating. It's been too long, lover. Don't you miss it?"

"No."

"The power." She let out a throaty moan. *"Feed me, Liam. Give*

us what we both need."

"No," he repeated. He'd starve the bitch. He'd deprive her of what she craved, even if he longed to watch the life burn out of a person's eyes. Even if he ached to release his hatred and rage for Adeline and Rodney. As a tool rental technician, his job kept him busy. But there'd been slow days, when the hours had dragged by and his thoughts had drifted. Adeline didn't think he had a good imagination? She must've been sleeping when he'd been considering what kind of damage he could cause to the human body with a forty-two-inch bolt cutter.

He flinched when his cell phone rang, picked it up and looked at the screen, at Bella's number. Two days ago, he'd memorized her number and address after she'd left the store with the carpet cleaner. He still couldn't come up with an excuse why, or explain what his intentions had been when he'd driven by her house after he'd gotten off work that night, or why he'd followed her while she'd run her errands the next morning.

She'd called the store yesterday afternoon, upset because her car, a little blue hatchback, had broken down and was still in the repair shop. Since her car wouldn't be ready until later in the week, and she had finished with the carpet cleaner, she'd worried about paying for additional days on the rental. After she had explained her problem, she'd then asked if he would be willing to swing by her house, pick up the steam cleaner and return it to the store.

He hadn't been lying to Adeline. Because of liability reasons, it was against store policy for him to pick up equipment from a customer's house. Once he'd explained this to Bella, she'd replied, "What if I wanted to be more than a customer?"

"Answer the phone, Liam. Tell her you're here and that you can't wait to kill her," Adeline said, laughter in her voice.

Ignoring Adeline, he answered the phone. "Bella? Hi."

"Hey, Liam," Bella greeted him, and he loved the way she pronounced his name LEE-yum. Would the pronunciation change if he shoved his way into the house, uninvited, wielding a razor-sharp switchblade? "Is that you I see sittin' at the end of my drive?"

He glanced toward the house, which reminded him of a double-wide trailer, only a little fancier with wood siding and a covered porch. Between the tall pines he saw her waving to him from the top step. "Yeah, sorry. I was just finishing a call. I'm heading your way now."

"Great. See 'ya in a sec."

He set the phone on the passenger seat and looked in the rear view mirror. The corner of Adeline's mouth curled as she cocked a dark brow. "Go away," he ordered.

"That's *the girl you masturbated over this morning in the shower? She's a little beneath you, don't you think, Lee-yum?*"

His face heated as he shifted the car into DRIVE. "There's nothing wrong with her."

"*Nothing wrong…yet. After all, she's still alive.*"

"And she's going to remain that way. I'm taking the cleaner, and leaving."

"*But she wants to be more than a customer,*" Adeline reminded him. "*I think you should go for it. Take a little piece of that trailer trash.*"

"She's not trash," he seethed, and tried desperately to control his anger.

"*Take, lover,*" Adeline said, her voice coaxing. "*Let her spread her legs wide for you. Fuck her with that big cock like I know you can. Remember how I rode you? Remember how good it felt to be inside me?*" She let out a breathy moan. "*Remember how much you wanted to wrap your hands around my throat as you came?*"

He pressed on his thickening erection and tried to control his body, but he couldn't stop the images surfacing… Of Adeline—of Bella—riding him, large breasts bouncing, moans escaping from her throat, ecstasy crossing her face. He hated her. Hated that he hadn't been able to control his desire for her, that he'd loved fucking her. She'd taken part in strapping him to a bed, had tortured him by keeping his eyes taped open, and had forced drugs into his body. He'd wanted her dead, had wanted to kill her himself.

"Now you can," Adeline reminded him, and pointed toward the front porch.

As he brought his vehicle to a crawl, dark, demented desire settled on his soul. He stared at Bella, lust heating his blood, his skin. With the exception of how she dressed, Bella could be Adeline's twin. Instead of the faded jeans and T-shirt she wore, he imagined Bella the way he'd last seen Adeline… *Her low-waist, frayed denim shorts barely covered her hips and crotch. Her white shirt was unbuttoned and tied at the waist, revealing a patch of her stomach and lack of a bra.*

"Mmm. I remember," Adeline said. *"You were so hard for me."*

He'd been painfully aroused by Adeline. Despite hating her, he'd enjoyed her body. He would enjoy Bella's body as well, and immediately pictured…taking.

But only if she was willing. He was a killer, not a rapist, and knew all too well what it was like to be held down, to be powerless, to have his body used.

Adeline laughed. *"Oh, stop. You loved every minute of it."*

"Fuck you," he muttered, and brought the car to a stop at the apron of the gravel driveway.

"No. Fuck her, then kill her. Please, lover. It's been too long."

He ignored Adeline and got out of the SUV. Bella gave him a shy smile and twirled a dark curl around her finger. Her smile grew as her gaze shifted over him, before meeting his eyes.

"The little twat wants us," Adeline whispered.

Me, he countered. *She wants me. There is no us.*

"No one will ever know. I'll show you how, just like before. It'll be so easy, lover. Remember how much you loved the way the blood tightened your skin when it dried?"

His head hurt as Adeline continued to talk, encouraging him to be bad, violent, cruel and merciless. He tried to ignore her and keep his attention on the subtly sexy woman waiting for him.

The hunger pangs pierced his side. They'd been bad before,

but not like this.

He glanced toward the planter near the door. He could easily smash it over Bella's head.

"Wait until you're inside and you've had her."

He hadn't had sex since Adeline, and could use a good lay.

"It's going to be so good, lover. Feed us."

"Thanks so much for helpin' me out," Bella said when he reached the bottom porch step. "I really appreciate it."

"I'm hungry. Give me what I need."

He mentally shook off the nagging bitch. "No problem," he said, moving up the steps. "I'll take it to work with me this afternoon and make sure you're not charged. But you have to promise not to tell anyone about this, or I could lose my job."

"You're the only one who knows I've even rented the carpet cleaner," she said with a grin, and reached for the screen door handle. "So this is our little secret. Besides, I thought we were going to be friends?"

"See? No one knows. Go with her, Liam. Give us what we need."

"I'm still new in town and could use a friend," he said, following her inside. When he noticed the metal coat rack in the small entryway, his vision momentarily swam. He stared at Bella...*shock, pain and horror registered in her eyes...blood spurted from her nose and mouth, flowed from her face and dented head...*

"You okay?" Bella asked, and touched his arm.

He smiled and closed the door behind him. "I'm just a little hungry."

PART I

"We all go a little mad sometimes.
Haven't you?"
—Norman Bates, *Psycho*

CHAPTER 1

Three months later...
Crystal Creek RV-Trailer Park, Everglades City, Florida
Tuesday, 3:11 p.m. Eastern Standard Time

HARRISON FAIRCLOUGH SLOWED to a jog, his mood darkening as he approached his trailer. "What are you doing here?"

"Is how Harry greet all guest?" Vlad Aristov leaned into the fold-up lawn chair and crossed his tree trunk legs. "Or just Vlad?"

"Get out of that chair. You're too big for it. I already told you that—after I had to buy new material to re-web the frame."

When the Russian stood, his blond head nearly brushed the trailer's angled awning. "Vlad have long memory, Harry do not."

Harrison had no problem with his memory. The problem was forgetting. He pulled his shirt over his head and used it to wipe the sweat off his forehead. "Golly gee, Vlad, sorry I've lost my etiquette. Care for a spot of tea?" he asked, reaching for a bottle of water in the mini-fridge he kept outside the trailer. "Maybe a pastry, or a cold bottle of *I don't have time for your shit?*"

"That one."

"One fucking what?"

Vlad cocked a brow and narrowed his eyes. "That two."

"Two tits? What the hell are you talking about?"

"Potty jar. Harry owe three dollar."

Apparently, his mouth had become so offensive to a few members of their team that Lola, their ever spectacular and know-it-all leader, had set up a swear jar. Who he'd offended, he hadn't a clue. But he had his suspicions. He narrowed his eyes at the alligator-loving Russian and only suspect on his list. "The swear jar only counts when we're at Polina's. Otherwise, I can say whatever the *fuck* I want, especially in *my* house."

"Fine. Talk like filthy toilet. Vlad no care."

He was about to point out the ridiculousness of the 'filthy toilet' remark, when a dark sedan slowed at the four-way stop sign half a dozen trailers from his. "Shit."

"That make four. Vlad tired of Harry—"

He held up a hand and turned his back on Vlad to get a better view of the car's driver. Damn it. It looked like he'd be leaving Everglades City earlier than planned. That was okay. He was ready to make a move anyway. The questions he had weren't going to answer themselves.

"It's Nick Wagner. Go inside the trailer. Stay there until he leaves."

"Vlad have confusion. Detective Nick not know Harry and Vlad. Vlad now worry for Asian Lola."

Wagner's visit had nothing to do with Lola and everything to do with him. "Nick and his partner know we work for Ryan and Lola at the boat shop. They just don't know we moonlight as Lola's agents."

That was what Lola had told him, but the detectives didn't have a high case resolution for being stupid. Harrison suspected the men knew about Above the Law, the underground criminal investigation agency Lola headed, but continued to turn a blind eye for their own gain. Last year, while working their first case, Lola had been forced to 'align' ATL with Collier County Detectives, Nick Wagner and Jerry Tennyson. ATL had stopped a killer, and the two detectives had legitimately cleaned up the mess the agency had made. Since then, they'd worked a few cases for the detectives. Cases that had called for the use of people who weren't afraid of getting their hands dirty while skirting the law. There'd also been times when ATL had needed the long arm of the law to ensure an arrest had been made. End result: the detectives got their criminals, no questions asked, and left ATL to do their thing.

"Moonlight? Vlad no—"

"Just go. And I mean it. Stay inside until I get rid of him." Harrison didn't want the detective to suspect Vlad was involved in what he'd been doing—his extracurricular activities had nothing to do with ATL. The Russian hadn't a clue. His boss, Lola Tam, and her fiancé, Ryan Monahan, didn't know, either. He'd figured they, along with the other members of their team, would find out eventually, just not this soon.

When Nick parked in front of the trailer, Harrison tossed his damp shirt over his shoulder and finished his water. He'd been careful not to leave a trail behind, so Nick had nothing on him. He still wanted Vlad out of sight, and couldn't risk having any suspicion fall onto the Russian. The former hitman was not only wanted by the U.S. government, but the Russians and Interpol. If captured, he wouldn't just face prison, but the death penalty.

Nick stepped out of the car. "How's it going? Harrison, right?" he asked, and offered his hand.

Harrison kept one hand on the empty water bottle, and the other on the shirt. "Can I help you?"

"You work for Lola."

"And Ryan."

Nick nodded. "Right, at Cap'n Ryan's Airboat Tours. You handle their website and book tours, and blah, blah, bullshit." Nick moved either side of his sports coat—revealing his gun holster—and rested his hands on his hips.

"That's right. I do quite a bit of blah, blah, bullshit for them."

The detective shook his head and gave him a wry grin. "Don't fuck with me. I know what you did, and who you are."

"So what? It's no secret, and I've done my time."

He'd guarantee that all Nick knew was that he'd been convicted of cyber robbery, and had served four years for hacking into a bank and shifting money from customer accounts to the one he'd set up for himself and his brother, Mickey. As for the rest—the bombings, the murders he'd unknowingly facilitated because he'd helped stop the bastard behind the terrorist attacks—he'd only served a couple of months. Thanks to heavy arm-twisting from Ian Scott, the owner of CORE, ATL's legitimate 'parent' company, the FBI had made his involvement with the bombings disappear. He still couldn't vote, or carry a weapon, but at least he wasn't rotting in prison.

"Time for *hacking*." Nick stabbed a finger toward him. "And if you choose to be stupid and *hack* into the Collier County Sheriff's network again, I'm coming after you. Without my badge. Understand?"

Harrison tossed the empty water bottle into the blue box Everglades City supplied for recycling and blew out a breath. "Look, man, I don't know what the hell you're talking about."

"I'm talking about using my ID to access confidential files and federal databases. Did Lola put you up to it?"

"Lola?" He played dumb. He'd been using Nick's ID to gain information. The last time he'd logged in as the detective had been three days ago. But he'd come down with another bitch of a headache—the worst one yet—and must've made a mistake. Thank God the mistake was with Nick, and not the Georgia Bureau of Investigation. He doubted they'd simply drop by and threaten him. Nope, he'd find his ass back in prison. "Like I said, I don't know what you're talking about."

"The hell you don't. The only reason I'm not pursuing this is because I want to continue the relationship I have with Lola."

Harrison lifted a brow. "Does this relationship include her fiancé? Ryan doesn't seem like the sharing type."

Nick chuckled and shook his head. "You're an asshole."

"Tell me something I don't know."

"How about that I'm going to talk to Lola about you? I want you off her team. Otherwise, I will sever ties and—"

"Well, hey there, detective. Fancy meetin' you here." Barney Newton, ATL's Jack-of-all-trades and fellow resident of Crystal Creek RV-Trailer Park, waved as he power-walked toward them. "It's a good day for fishin', if you're interested. I was just droppin' by to see if Harrison wanted to go out on the boat," he said, nodding toward the park's docks.

Barney lived two lanes over. Normally it'd take the sixty-something war veteran a solid twelve minutes to reach Harrison's trailer from his. When he'd been on his run earlier, Harrison had also seen Barney dozing on a lounger outside his trailer, and knew the old man had already been out fishing this morning. With the way Barney was hauling ass—and not carrying a rod or tackle box—he'd guarantee the fishing trip was a load of crap. Vlad had probably called Lola, who must've contacted Barney to diffuse a potential 'situation'.

"Thanks, but I'll take a rain check." Nick gave Barney an easy smile. "I'm usually at the bar on Sundays. Stop by and I'll buy you a few beers."

Nick was part-owner of a popular bar and grill located in Bonita Beach. Harrison had hacked into that website, too. If the detective wasn't already suspicious of him, he'd recommend that Nick and his business partner invest in a more secure hosting site. "I'm off most Sundays, and I like beer," Harrison said to be a dick.

Barney walked between him and Nick to grab a bottle of water from the fridge. "Nick has a nice place right on the beach." He wiped the beads of sweat trickling from his thick graying curly hair, as well as around the black eye patch he wore—because of an injury from his time during the Vietnam War—and grinned. "Ain't nothing like drinkin' a cold one and watchin' them pretty girls in their bikinis."

"I didn't think cops could get a liquor license. Isn't that a conflict of interest?" Harrison asked, not caring about Nick's personal business. He just didn't like being threatened, even if the detective had every right to come after him. "Do the people you work with know about this?"

Nick adjusted his sunglasses and faced Harrison. "I'm sure you already know the answer." He glanced to Barney. "Don't be a stranger."

Once Nick drove off, Vlad burst from the trailer. Barney dropped the bottle, spilling water onto the artificial grass Harrison had installed along the front, and clutched his chest. "Judas Priest, boy! What in the Sam Hill is wrong with you, jumping out at me like a daggone albino gorilla?"

"There's such a thing as an albino gorilla?" Harrison asked, hoping to keep Barney talking and Vlad silent. He wasn't in the mood to deal with another one of the Russian's temper tantrums. "Or is that one of your made-up stories, like the albino alligator?"

"Ain't you ever heard of Snowflake, the world's only albino gorilla?" Barney wiped his wet hand on the front of his pants. "And albino alligators do exist. Just not in the Florida Everglades." With a sigh, he tossed the empty bottle into the blue bin. "I'll be glad to educate you on the various species of animals with the rare albino gene, after you tell me what has Vlad lookin' as mean as my ex-wife scoopin' up a pile of cat shit."

"If you think this is bad," Harrison began, "you should see Vlad's face when he's cleaning up after his gator."

Barney laughed and shook his head. "Hell, that's gotta be a sight. Hey, Vlad, how many times have you checked your gator's turds to make sure it wasn't a daggone human body part?" he asked, and laughed harder.

"Vlad have no laughter."

"Oh, c'mon, boy. I was just jokin' with you. I know you don't feed Polina people."

"You wouldn't want to be a squirrel, though," Harrison said, heading for the trailer door when he saw Lola's car turn down the lane. The RV Park was ten minutes from the boat shop. Lola must've broken several traffic laws to get there. He could understand why she'd be concerned about Nick stopping by without contacting her. ATL was her baby. Without the cooperation of the Collier County Sheriff's Offices, the agency could go under, people could go to prison.

Vlad blocked him. "Where Harry run?"

"I'm getting a shirt. Get out of my way."

"To cover ink blemish?"

"Ink what?" Barney asked.

Harrison maintained eye contact with Vlad. "He's talking about my tattoo." The Russian had been furious when he'd showed up at their house with his skin inked, bitching that only gangsters and prisoners marked themselves. Vlad didn't buy into the idea that people expressed themselves with tattoos of quotes or symbols. Harrison couldn't care less what people did to their own bodies. Pierce them, tat them…who was he to judge? He'd leave that for Vlad, the over-sized, over-opinionated, pain in the ass who had no filter.

Barney nodded toward the approaching car. "Vlad, quit playin' mother hen and let the boy get a fresh shirt before the lady gets here. And what do you care about Harrison's tattoo? Hell, I got one." He pushed the sleeve of his shirt to his shoulder and revealed a faded tattoo of the bald eagle clutching the American flag. *U.S. Marine* had been tattooed above the drawing, and *Semper Fi* below it.

Vlad glanced at Barney's arm, and stepped aside. "Fine. Vlad no want Asian Lola to see Harry vulgarity. Barney have reason to put ruin on body, Harry do not."

Barney frowned and let go of his shirtsleeve. "Why do I feel like he just insulted me?"

"Because he did. Now maybe you'll get why I moved out," Harrison said, and went into the trailer. He hadn't moved out of Polina's Paradise—ATL's headquarters and the house he'd been sharing with Vlad since they'd come to Florida over a year ago—because of the Russian. He'd moved out because he was afraid of the darkness shifting through him, consuming him, filling him with rage, rotting his brain with thoughts he couldn't always control.

"That day good fortune in camouflage," the Russian called through the screen door. "Vlad never so happy."

"Boy, you lost me," Barney said. "What's this talk about wearin' camo?"

After Harrison had pulled a fresh shirt over his head, he stepped back outside. "He's talking about a blessing in disguise."

He stared at Vlad and wondered what the Russian would think if he knew the truth, that the move *was* a blessing, a way to make sure he didn't kill the man in his sleep. He didn't want Vlad dead. Hell, that had been why he'd wanted Vlad to stop smoking and to set his alligator, Polina, free. But there had been too many nights where he'd woken outside Vlad's door, a knife or an unloaded pistol in his hand, murder on his mind. What scared the hell out of him was that he still couldn't be sure if he'd been asleep in the first place, or if he'd been having…episodes. Loss of time. Loss of memory.

Loss of his fucking mind.

"Sorry," Vlad began, an edge of sarcasm in his tone, "word do not roll from off Vlad tongue right way."

"Vlad, cut off his tongue."

Harrison's head buzzed. His ears rang. Over the internal noise, a car door slammed. He turned just as Lola climbed out of her vehicle. Her image faded, grew fuzzy.

He watched helplessly as the Russian used his thumb and index finger to open the scissors. When he rested both blades on either side of Mickey's tongue—

"Explain why Nick was here." Lola's demand snapped him back to the present.

He wasn't being held prisoner in the swanky offices of a billionaire, and he certainly wasn't about to watch Vlad cut the tongue out of his brother's mouth. His twin brother. No, Mickey was dead, and if he'd been ordered to, Vlad would have killed Harrison, too. Yeah, Vlad had no idea what a blessing his move to the trailer truly was, and how much the Russian's life depended on it. For months, bad memories had been filling his head and feeding the darkness within him. Memories of growing up on the streets with only his twin for a friend, of his drunk-ass mom, the beatings from her boyfriends, stealing, prison…Vlad resting scissors on his brother's tongue.

"Hello?" Lola called with annoyance. "Am I invisible?"

Harrison wiped his hand along his mouth, releasing the tension in his jaw. He packed the memories back in the suitcase he'd created in his mind, then zipped it shut. He'd open it again another day. When he was alone and far away from here. When he could unleash the rage bubbling under his skin, waiting for that moment to burst. When there was no one around, he could hurt.

"Hey, Lola." Harrison finally acknowledged her presence, then glanced at Vlad and Barney, wondering why they hadn't spoken. The men weren't focused on their boss, they were staring at him. Vlad's eye's held anger, while Barney's were banked with concern. Harrison looked away from them. "Glad you stopped by, it saves me from calling you."

Lola narrowed her almond-shaped eyes at him. "About Nick?"

"Nope. I'm leaving."

She swept her long straight black hair over her shoulders, then using the hairband around her wrist, pulled the mass back in a ponytail. "Are you coming back?"

"If I can," he answered honestly. He didn't like the person he'd become. He wasn't cold by nature or had a loner mentality. He liked being part of a team, part of ATL. But until he could be sure he wouldn't snap and go on a homicidal bender, he needed to go.

"Does your leaving have anything to do with why Nick came here?" she asked, worry lining her brow.

"Not really."

"Harry lie. Vlad hear all thing," the Russian said with disappointment, then added, "Harry hack Detective Nick account."

While Barney let out a low whistle, Lola fisted her hands. "Why?" she demanded.

To keep from punching Vlad, Harrison rubbed the back of his triceps which were still sore from the pull-ups he'd done yesterday. "It's none of your business."

"ATL *is* my business, and it's *our* organization," she said, circling a finger to include all of them. "We can't have any issues with the Collier County Sheriff's Office. If you're hacking into their system, jeopardizing our agency, then it sure as hell *is* my business."

While she had a point, he didn't care. What he'd done wouldn't affect Lola or the others, not really.

"This is about what happened in Georgia, ain't it?" Barney sat on one of the folding chairs and let out a sigh. "'Splains a lot, don't you think?" he asked, and looked to Lola.

Her eyes widened with alarm as she approached and gripped his arm. "Why didn't I see this? How did I miss it?" She searched his gaze to the point he became uncomfortable. "The weightlifting, changing your hair, moving from Polina's, how you've been acting... I don't understand. I thought the doctor said you were fine."

Taking her by the wrist, Harrison removed her hand. "I work out because I like it." And because he needed to make sure he was in shape for what he might be up against. "I cut my hair because I was sick of it, and I moved out of Polina's because I was tired of dealing with Vlad and renting from you. Forget about Georgia, I have." He hadn't, and knew he never would. But he couldn't have Lola and the gang fucking with his plans.

"Vlad tell Asian Lola from start," the Russian began, "Rodney Archer need kill."

Harrison agreed. For his part in the kidnapping and drugging, Rodney had definitely deserved killing. As for Adeline? He stopped himself from thinking about the dead woman before the darkness grabbed hold of him.

"Vlad, we've been over this." Lola sat in the chair next to Barney's, her shoulders slumped slightly. "If I'd let you kill him, it would've been murder."

Vlad shrugged his massive shoulders. "Vlad have murder many bad man. Asian Lola separate hair."

"I'm not *splitting hairs*. We're talking murder and the chance that you or any other member of our team could go to prison." She set her elbows on her thighs and her head in her hands. "Rodney confessed to kidnapping and murder, and will spend the rest of his life in prison."

Anger shot through Harrison. "A confession wasn't needed. GBI had enough evidence to convict him. What we needed was information on Liam."

Right after he'd been captured, Rodney, the lying piece of shit, had retracted the statement he'd given to ATL. He'd admitted to the kidnappings and murders, and Adeline's part in it all. Liam, he'd later claimed, had never existed.

Lola leaned back in the chair. "As far as the GBI and FBI are concerned, the case is closed. If Ian gave us the go-ahead, you know I'd use every resource possible to find Liam." She shook her head. "We're not even sure if that's his real name."

"That's the name Mel heard."

"And you were both drugged," Lola said with exasperation.

Rodney and Adeline had also been drugging Liam, experimenting on the man and several others they'd kidnapped from homeless shelters, just as they'd experimented on him and Mel. But Liam had been at their plantation house longer. How long, Harrison couldn't be sure. At this point, it didn't matter. What did was finding him. Rodney and Adeline had been attempting to take normal people, then turn them into psychopaths so they could fix them. Liam had killed one of Rodney and Adeline's test subjects before he'd escaped. Had the experiment worked? Had they turned Liam into a psychopath, into a killer?

Had they succeeded with him, too?

He ran a hand over his damp hair. "You weren't drugged and you saw him as well."

Barney nodded. "The boy has a point. How can three people see a guy that don't exist?"

"Not helping." Lola gave Barney a sidelong glance before looking back to Harrison. "I know Liam is real. The bruises he left on my face certainly were. But because Rodney refuses to talk about the man, or admit he was being held in the house, the GBI and FBI refuse to waste money and manpower to go after a man who could've possibly been a scared victim running for his life." She let out another sigh. "Ian agrees, and he's my boss. So we drop it. Period."

He gave her a mocking smile. "Great idea. Let's wait until Liam kills someone."

"There's no reason to be like this to me. It's not my decision."

"Who told Mel to stop investigating Adeline?"

She pursed her lips and glared at him. "I did. The woman was dead. Rodney had confessed, and Ian wanted to make sure ATL stayed under the radar."

Which was why the only two known survivors, him and Melanie, whose names had never been released to the press, had conveniently died right after Rodney's confession. Ian had wanted no links back to CORE.

"There were too many agencies involved," she continued. "Too few agents Ian could trust to keep quiet about us. Too much risk. I'm not going to apologize for wanting to keep my people out of prison."

"Are we done?" Harrison asked. There was no point in arguing with Lola. He was leaving anyway.

"Not quite. Vlad said you hacked Nick's account. I'd like to know why." She cocked a brow. "I have the right to know. Like I said, we can't have any issues with the police."

"There's nothing to tell. Vlad misunderstood," he said, hoping Vlad would keep his mouth shut. Lola was a bright woman. She knew he'd had it bad over the Archer case, and would figure out that he was using Nick's ID. He'd rather she came to that conclusion after he'd left town. He didn't need the members of ATL intervening with his plans and trying to stop him. "Nick was thinking about having his bar's website updated, and joked about having to hack into his own account to remember his password."

She frowned. "Really? So Nick came to your trailer to hire you to do his website? I don't believe you." She slid her gaze to Vlad. "You sounded very concerned when you called me."

Vlad reached into his pocket and withdrew a pack of cigarettes. "Vlad make mistake. Mince of word have confusion for Vlad."

Lola nodded, and turned to Barney. "Did you hear anything?"

Barney chuckled as he used the folding chair's plastic armrests to rise. "I heard Nick invite me to his bar for a beer." His bones cracked as he stretched his back. "Vlad, are you still cookin' for me, or do I have to order in a pizza?"

Vlad stared at Harrison. He gave him a smug grin as he lit a cigarette. "да." He nodded. "Vlad make хотдог for Barney."

"Well, hell, boy, that sounds awful fancy. Should I wear a dang tie?" Barney asked with a smile.

Harrison went to the fridge, then took out another bottle of water. "Don't get excited about the meal. He's making you hot dogs, probably the same kind he feeds his gator."

"Vlad make also макароны с сыром," the Russian said, and took a long drag from the cigarette.

Fuck if he didn't want to knock the damned thing off Vlad's face with the bottom of his running shoe. The bastard knew how much he hated the smoking, and that he had a no-smoking rule at his trailer. "And that's macaroni and cheese, which he also feeds to his gator." He opened the water bottle and looked to Barney. "You might want to order in."

"Nope. I could use the company. Plus, I'm gonna help Vlad clean the pistols. With this new guy of Ryan's comin' in next week, I want to make sure he's got what he needs." When Barney met his gaze, the old man's eyes no longer held amusement, but accusation. "You should join us."

Shit. Barney knew about the missing weapons. "I'm not supposed to be around guns. I'm a felon."

"Right," Barney replied, dragging out the single word.

Lola cleared her throat and stood. "Thanks for trusting me, guys. It means a lot." She started for her car, then quickly pivoted and stalked back toward him. "I thought we were friends," she said, and shoved his chest. "I thought you had my back just as much as I have yours." Tears misted her eyes, but she blinked them back and took a deep breath. "I don't know what's going on with you. If it has something to do with the drugs you were given, we can get you help."

"Help for what?" Harrison asked. "You saw my medical report. The drug was out of my system within days." But the damage had already been done to his brain. The question he needed answered—was it permanent?

"Then what else is it?" she asked, her tone a combination of helplessness and frustration. "Is it because we didn't pursue Liam? Is that why you're mad at me?"

"I'm not mad at you."

"Could've fooled me. There's been a few times I've caught you looking at me with murder in your eyes."

He scoffed. "What the hell are you talking about?" Lola was good people. Even though she was younger than him, she'd always treated him as if he were her kid brother. She'd also treated him with respect. He could never hurt her, had never wanted to hurt Vlad. Until he'd been kidnapped, tied to a bed and had his eyelids taped open, there'd only been one man he'd wanted dead, and Vlad had made that happen. He wasn't a killer. Not by nature. But maybe by nurture? Rodney and Adeline had filled his veins with their drug. They'd forced him to watch violent, gory videos, and made him listen to Adeline's recorded voice. God, he could hear her now—suggesting to act on the darkness, to embrace it and let it swallow him whole.

So seductive. So tempting.

He took a step back and brought the cool water bottle to his forehead. *Concentrate on the present.*

But he couldn't. Adeline had taken the goodness from him, had taken his freedom, his fucking pride, and had shit all over it. But the bitch was now dead. If only Rodney was, too.

"Why are you leaving?" Lola asked, forcing him to regain his focus. "If you're not mad at me, is it the job? Are you unhappy working for me and Ryan? Are you quitting?"

He looked to the other men, who both started at him with concern, then to Lola. "No. It's the best gig I've ever had," he answered honestly. "I just need a break."

She touched his arm and searched his eyes. "But for how long?"

"Don't know. I'll send you a text."

With a nod, she stepped back. "Will you need me to deposit money into your bank account?"

"I'm good." He probably had more money than Lola. While the Norfolk PD had recovered the majority of the money from the bank job he'd done with his brother, they hadn't gotten it all. That cash had earned interest during the four years he'd been in prison. When he'd been released, he'd kept quiet about the account, not even telling his brother who would have likely blown his share on gambling. After his brother's murder, he'd helped Vlad make a new start, but he still had a sizeable account. With close to one hundred grand in the bank, and no debt, he didn't need to work for Lola and could take an extended break from ATL.

"When do you plan to leave?" she asked.

"In a couple of days." Another lie. But he didn't want Lola sending over anyone else to try to talk him out of going, or to push him about his reasons for leaving.

She crossed her arms. "So that's it?" She shook her head. "I know you're lying to me about Nick. And based on how you're still bitter about the Archer case being closed, I think that has something to do with your leaving. You don't want to tell me? Fine. I get it. You clearly look at me as more of a boss now than a friend."

That wasn't true, but he wouldn't disagree. They'd been friends before he'd started working for her and ATL, and he knew when she was trying to force an argument. He didn't want to fight her. Hell, he didn't want to leave the Everglades to find Liam. He wanted to go back to the way things were before he'd volunteered to let Adeline kidnap him.

Now he was lying to himself. Even before what had happened to him in Georgia, he'd been growing restless—why, he still didn't know—and taking his frustrations out on Vlad.

"Since that's the case," she continued, "as your boss I'll leave you with this...take the time you need. If I'm put in a position where I need to cover your ass, I'll do my best. But if whatever you're up to puts any member of ATL at risk with the law..." She looked away for a few seconds and let out a deep breath. When she met his gaze, the disappointment in her eyes didn't surprise him. They were friends, and he did trust her. But if Nick came after him, he didn't want her involved or at risk. "Just be careful."

Wishing he could unleash the burden he'd been carrying, and tell her and the others his fear, he watched her go. Before her taillights disappeared, Vlad pushed past him to snuff out his cigarette in the gravel lane.

"Vlad looks spittin' mad." Barney came alongside Harrison. "I ain't so happy, either."

Barney's chastising tone momentarily blurred his vision with rage. He didn't need any shit from the old man or the Russian. "I'm sure you'll both get over it."

"And I'm sure Lola would like to know about the pistol missing from Polina's."

"So tell her," Harrison said, and didn't bother to look at the man. He'd taken the Glock, along with several boxes of ammo. He couldn't care less if Barney told Lola about the missing supplies. What would she, or any of them, do about it? Call the cops on him?

"Tell her I think you took 'em? Boy, I don't think you want me doin' that."

Harrison had been threatened one too many times in his life. Before the rage within surfaced to the top, he finally looked at the old man. "Barney, I like you. It'd be a good idea if you left. Take Vlad with you." Because right now, he hurt and wanted them to hurt. To feel his pain, the agony twisting in his brain, screwing with his thoughts. Making him hungry for something he couldn't identify.

Barney's eyes widened with shock, before they narrowed with curious understanding. "What is it, boy? Why are you leaving? Are you chasin' ghosts, or are you runnin' because they're chasin' after you?"

He hated that the man was so damned perceptive. Between that, the chastising, the threats, right now he hated Barney. Hated him to the point he wished—

"Harry!"

The Russian's shout, the anger and urgency in his voice, had Harrison blinking and bringing the water bottle back to his lips. When he saw Barney staring at the way his hand shook, he threw the plastic bottle toward the lane. "Leave," he said, frightened by his own thoughts, that how being agitated and provoked had elicited them. What if he'd been alone with Barney? What if he'd slipped into the darkness and hurt his friend? He didn't hate Barney and would never want anything bad to happen to him.

"Harry right. Barney go." The Russian turned his back on the old man and faced Harrison. "Come to Polina later. Vlad make хотдог."

As Barney walked past him, he set a hand on Harrison's shoulder. "You still want me to look after your trailer while you're gone?"

Harrison nodded. "Take what you want from the fridge before it goes bad."

The old man sighed. "Take care, boy. I hope you find whatever it is you're lookin' for, or shake whatever's got its claws into you."

As Barney's words rubbed him raw, reminding him of the mission he'd soon embark upon, he wished he could show the man his gratitude for sticking by him, and apologize for being a dick. That would be the right thing to do. He knew it, felt it. But he'd have to care enough to do either. Still, they were friends, and an apology wouldn't kill him.

"Sorry, Barn," he said, the lie easily rolling off his tongue. "I'll stop by and see you when I get back."

Barney nodded. "We all got ghosts. You gotta learn how to control them before they control you."

Harrison watched the Vet walk away. He didn't doubt that Barney had ghosts. The man had an easy smile and a story for just about everything. There had been times, times when the light in Barney's eyes would dim, as if there were more to one of his stories. He'd never questioned him then, and wouldn't question him now. Barney was right. They all had ghosts.

"Barney do not mincemeat words. Vlad have many ghost, too."

He glanced to the man who at one time would have killed his brother and him on command, the man who had killed for him. "Why didn't you tell Lola the truth?"

The Russian shrugged his shoulders. "Vlad worry for Harry. Yet Vlad need for Harry to…how to say…patch? No, not good word. Recovery?"

He cracked a smile. Vlad, despite aggravating him at times, was honest and uniquely aware of people. Of him. "No, man. That word works."

"Vlad wish Harry would not go by self. Liam…Liam could be bad man. Since Harry not killer, Vlad do not see how this work."

"Who said I was going after Liam?"

"What other ghost chase Harry? Adeline? Vlad have said—"

"I know what you said." Harrison raised a hand. "Better to have dick sucked than cut," he mimicked Vlad's voice. "This has nothing to do with Adeline. I just need…recovery. Once I have that, I'll be back."

"Harry sure Vlad cannot help?"

"I'm sure."

"The Glock and ammo?" The Russian grinned. "Do Harry think Vlad so simple? Vlad know." His smile fell. "Vlad know too why Harry leave Polina Paradise."

Shame had Harrison wanting to glance away, but he held his friend's gaze. They'd been through hell together, and Vlad was like a brother to him. "Yeah?"

"да. Vlad sleep not like baby in diaper," he said with a sad, half-smile. "Vlad still do not believe Harry killer."

His throat tightened. "Make sure your gator doesn't bite off your new roommate's arm," he said, when he knew he should be thanking Vlad. He didn't believe he could be capable of hurting anyone, either. He *wanted* to believe he was stronger than the darkness, but still needed proof. Distance.

The Russian started to walk away, but stopped before he reached the gravel lane. "Harry?" he called over his shoulder. "Vlad learn it sometime best to leave lying dog to sleep."

He couldn't let this sleeping dog lie. While he didn't know if chasing after a killer was the smartest move, at least he knew where to start.

CHAPTER 2

One week later…
Thomasville, Georgia
Saturday, 3:36 p.m. Eastern Standard Time

HARRISON HUNG ALONG the fringes of the thick pine woods. Crows circled above a rundown house, their black bodies standing out against the gray sky. He glanced around the small yard, to the derelict shed missing planks of wood, to an outhouse peeking from behind overgrown bushes, to the weeds overrunning what looked to have once been the driveway. A rusted metal pole rose from the ground where maybe a mailbox had once stood.

He looked back to the house. The night they'd escaped the House of Archer, he'd only caught a quick glimpse of Liam. The man had been rushing from the attic, down the smoke-filled stairway to the second floor. He'd estimated Liam to be about his height and size, maybe a little thinner. Liam's hair had also been a similar color to his, but maybe a lighter brown. The dark smoky haze that had been filling the stairway and attic had made it hard to tell. But the one thing he'd been certain of was the man's injuries. His face had been bloodied. As if someone had taken a whip or belt to him. Melanie had agreed. She'd gotten a better look at Liam right before the bastard had smashed her head into a door, then again when he was fleeing the room of the man he'd just killed.

It had been more than five months since that night, and Harrison had spent more hours than he could account for studying a thirty-mile radius of Rodney and Adeline's plantation house. Liam had been hurt. He'd been drugged. He would have needed shelter, food, time to heal. Which had been why Harrison had spent those hours examining aerial views of the states of Georgia and Florida. Although he and Liam had been held in Bower, Georgia, the Florida border was within ten miles of the plantation house. But he'd chosen to start with Georgia, concentrating on the backwoods, on places where he'd discovered rundown houses which were possibly abandoned.

Perfect places to hide, to recover.

Just like this one.

Even though it appeared as if no one was in residence, he kept his body low and behind the boughs heavy with leaves, and his eyes on the crooked porch and broken windows. Before he'd left the Everglades, he'd mapped each area for potential hiding places. The first three he'd found with ease, but they'd been empty, and had showed no sign of having been occupied in years. After getting lost and hiking for half the day, he'd located the fourth only to be chased off the property by three dogs and a guy with a shotgun. Yesterday, self-doubt had messed with his head. At that point, he'd already spent five days searching for any sign that Liam had survived and in what direction he might have gone. He had started to think the whole idea was stupid, and just another sign that he was no longer right in the head. But determination had him returning to the backwoods of Georgia, and caution had him ready for anything. If someone was living here, they probably weren't interested in uninvited visitors. People lived off the grid for a reason.

The wind picked up, pressing leaves against his cheek. The smell of rain hung in the air. If he didn't want to get caught in a storm, he'd have to be cautious and quick. He checked the knife sheath along his ankle—a gift Mel had given him prior to moving back to Tallahassee to live with her husband, Cash. He couldn't use the knife as well as Mel, but he liked knowing it was there.

A rumble of thunder had the circling crows flying toward the trees, and him moving across the tall grass and weeds. The screen door off the porch bounced lightly and squeaked on its hinges. He froze, stared hard at the door, then realized it was only the wind moving it. He continued forward, scanning the front yard, the house. When he reached the porch, he hesitated. Several of the floorboards looked rotted, and the porch's roof had a sharp slant to it. If the wind blew any harder, he wouldn't be surprised if the thing caved in on itself. Careful of his footing, he stepped onto the porch, then peered into the narrow window of the shotgun-style house. With the exception of the dim light filtering in from the windows, the interior was dark. The rooms he could see were messy, as if they'd been ransacked.

He released a deep breath. No one was here.

The screen door bounced again, a little harder because of an extra gust of wind, and he realized the screen on the lower half had been torn. The mesh flapped outward, as if an animal had created its own doggie door or someone had put a foot through it. When he reached the door, he nudged it with his boot. The main door stood open, so he edged inside, glancing from left to right, then straight ahead to another open door, which he assumed led to the back.

Another rumble of thunder made the old house shake as if a train were barreling through it. Although not interested in hiking back to his Jeep in a storm, he pulled a flashlight from his jacket pocket and walked deeper inside the house. He slowed his steps when the light touched on a broken tobacco pipe and the wooden matches strewn around it. Unease crawled up his spine. Neither looked old or weathered.

He moved the beam around what he assumed had been a living room. When the light caught a flash of shiny silver, he swallowed back his unease and walked toward it, careful not to step on the stuffing from the ripped couch cushions, or the faded floral drapes torn from the window. He stepped over a pile of dirt and a dead fern, a wooden stand, and then around a smashed picture frame. After pulling a single glove from his pocket, without bothering to put it on, he used it to grab the metal. Keeping the flashlight on it, he lifted the silver object.

He staggered back, dropping the flashlight and catching himself before he fell on his ass. Heart beating hard, his stomach tightening with fear, he quickly scrambled to his feet and looked around the small room. After a few deep breaths, he picked up the flashlight and aimed it at the floor. At the round silver ball jutting from a human bone.

His mind worked fast. The person who'd lived here could've died in the house, of natural causes. If this person was an off the grid recluse, why would anyone check to see if they were dead or alive? The guy he'd run into two days ago had been living in a house no better than this one. Aside from poor dental hygiene and vintage tattered clothes, he hadn't looked as if he was hurting for company. Then again, his focus had been on the shotgun pointed at Harrison's head. As for how the bone could have found its way behind an overturned end table? He glanced away from the bone and looked to the screen door.

Doggie door.

Fucking nasty.

He left the bone on the floor and used the flashlight to search for the rest of the deceased. When he reached the kitchen, he stopped mid-step. "This wasn't natural," he murmured, his skin prickling with disgust, with fear. Not for who did this. He wasn't afraid of Liam. He was afraid of becoming him.

More thunder rumbled, shaking the house again, drawing his attention to the dishes on the counter. He flashed the light toward them, toward the grease caked on the wall and wood-burning stove. To the cast iron frying pan on floor. To the large, dark-brown stain next to it. He used the light to follow the trail leading from the stain, which looked as if someone had dipped a large paintbrush in whatever had been on the floor, then dragged the bristles. Stomach clenching with dread, he leaned over to see what the trail led to, then jerked upright and sucked in a breath.

This still might not be Liam's handiwork.

He flashed the beam back onto the human skull. Long frizzy

gray hair still covered the top of the skull where pale leathery-looking skin clung to bone. The eyes were gone, the mouth was open and the lips shriveled, revealing broken or missing teeth.

He glanced back to the skillet, then to the red and white plaid curtain attached below the old farmhouse sink. More dark-brown stains marred the fabric, reminding him of BB pellets with tails. He wasn't a criminalist, but one had come to talk with the ATL crew last summer. CORE agent John Kain had spent a week teaching them the different aspects of a crime scene. The idea behind the sessions had been to help them make sure they didn't screw with crime scene evidence that legit investigators might need to close a case.

What he was looking at now wasn't death by natural causes. Someone had beaten this person—a woman, he assumed—and left a cast-off of blood when they'd swung the murder weapon. The frying pan?

He shifted his gaze across the room. More dark-brown stains were smeared on the wall leading back into the hallway. Careful where he stepped, he walked toward them, then followed the blood pattern—the arc along the wall in the hallway, the spray on the ceiling. He looked to the floor. More stains. More trails. Then another large spot, as if the person had bled out. Since it looked as if the woman had died in the kitchen, there must have been someone else in the house with her.

He remembered the pipe, pictured an elderly man smoking it, and being surprised by his attacker. Exhaling, he tried to control his rage, his worry, the fucking fear. Instead, he focused on the killer. How would Liam have done it? *Had* Liam been the killer?

The distance from the House of Archer to this place was nearly fourteen miles. To go undetected, Liam would've had to walk through the woods. Since Rodney and Adeline had taken his shoes, he assumed Liam would have been either barefoot or wearing socks. Fourteen miles wouldn't have been easy to manage without sturdy boots. By the time Liam had reached this place, he'd have been in pain, hungry, thirsty…desperate.

Harrison looked at the arc of dried blood on the walls, the spray on the low ceiling.

Liam had been manic. Frenzied.

Careful where he walked, Harrison returned to the front door and put his back to it. Put himself in Liam's bare feet.

The broken pipe and scattered matches were on the floor and to the right. Liam could have rushed into the house, caught the man by surprise. With what? He stared at the bloodstains.

Mel's switchblade.

Son of a bitch.

She'd said that Liam had taken it from her, then had smugly thanked her for the souvenir. So Liam could have easily overpowered the man, stabbing him, causing the spray and arc of blood. Harrison looked down the hall, imagined the man yelling out, the old woman coming around the corner to investigate. Her eyes would have rounded with shock and horror as Liam dropped the old man to the ground, stepping over him to get to her.

Harrison wiped a hand down his face and released a shaky breath. In a way, he hoped the person who had killed these people was Liam. Otherwise that meant some other sick bastard was out there.

He shook his head. The closed door to the left caught his attention. This was a single story house. A shack, really. The door had to lead to a bedroom. Liam had been injured, his face had been bloodied, and if he'd walked here, he would have needed to recuperate. He'd needed the perfect place to hide, to recover...

Using the glove, Harrison turned the doorknob, then nudged it open. The room smelled stale. Here, the window was intact. With the exception of missing bed linens, and a few pieces of women's clothing on the floor, the room was in decent shape.

Harrison looked over his shoulder and into the living room where he'd found the bone with the metal attachment. If Liam had stayed here, he could have taken the man's clothes, or worn them while he'd cleaned his own. Since he hadn't found any other skeletal remains, and the house had been left open, he wouldn't be surprised if animals had trashed the place and made off with various body parts.

He shifted his gaze back to the bed. Liam would have been able to recover quite nicely here. Since the sheets were missing, maybe carrying some of his blood, his hairs, he could have burned them. But if he'd spent time here, he had to have left a part of himself behind.

With disgust and hatred spurring him, he left the room and went back to the kitchen. He checked the sink again. The couple of dishes left there were clean. Determined to find something that could indicate Liam had been here, had eaten, had recovered, he opened the few upper cupboards.

Nothing.

He spun in a circle, noticed the red and white plaid curtain hanging on the wall where he'd discovered the head, then went to it. Ignoring the skull, he shoved the material aside and smiled. "Gotcha," he murmured as he took inventory of the small pantry. There were dozens of empty, open Mason jars with residue left inside them. He flashed the light on the jars, one in particular catching his attention. Keeping his gaze on the faint trace of dried blood coating the glass, he put on the glove, then pulled the jar from the shelf.

During the short time Harrison had been held captive by Rodney and Adeline, they hadn't fed him. Liam had been at the plantation house longer than him, and chances were he would have been hungry when he'd reach this place. After killing the couple, he would have searched for food. Harrison carried the jar to the kitchen table, then set it there. And it looked as if Liam had been too hungry to bother to wash his hands.

Using the pocket fingerprint kit he'd also swiped from Polina's Paradise, he lifted the print from the jar. After he put it back in the pantry, he did another walk through the house, this time taking pictures with his cell phone. When he circled back to the kitchen, a clap of thunder shook the house yet again, warning him that it was time to leave.

Still searching for additional signs that Liam had been here, he exited through the backdoor. A small refrigerator, about the size of the one he kept outside of his trailer, was to his right. Next to it was a couple of homebuilt generators. The porch groaned. Hoping the planks wouldn't cave, he looked to his feet, then took an immediate step back.

"Damn it." He dragged in quick short breaths as he stared at another human skull. Now he knew for certain there had been two people living in the house. What had happened to the rest of their bodies, he didn't want to know.

When he made his way down the steps, he noticed logs stacked along the back of the house, and that about a dozen or so metal fuel cans were stored under the porch. He bent near them and inhaled: diesel.

He faced the yard. The dead couple had a weatherworn chicken coop. To the right of it was a wooden lean-to with a log and wire fence separating it from the building and taking up part of the yard. Further down was a sizeable garden, overgrown with weeds. He approached the chicken coop, saw that it was empty, then turned to the fence connected to the lean-to. Bones were scattered throughout the fenced area. He moved closer. One of the skulls had horns. Although he'd grown up in the city, he'd seen farm animals at the petting zoo. He'd guarantee those were the remains of goats and pigs. Liam would've had plenty to eat. He could have stayed here for months, or he could've left after a few days. Now the question was, where had he gone?

As a light drizzle fell, a shiver ran through him. He zipped his coat, felt to make sure his phone and fingerprint kit were secure and dry, then started back toward the front of the house. Out of the corner of his eye, he glimpsed movement from the bushes near the chicken coop. Bristling, he quickly pulled the knife from its sheath. He faced the bushes, but took slow backward steps as the muzzle of an animal pushed through the leaves. When the coyote emerged, followed by another, he unclipped the Glock from his belt holster. Screw the knife. If these animals had been the ones who'd disposed of the bodies, they had a taste for human flesh.

The coyotes stayed near the bush, even as two more joined them. He'd been to the shooting range three times a week for the past four months and was confident he could kill each one of them. Since he suspected they'd made a meal out of the old folks, he'd enjoy it. But the animals stayed put. So he kept moving backward. When he reached the entrance into the woods, relief eased some of the tension in his shoulders, especially when the drizzle turned into a downpour, accompanied by thunder and lightning. The coyotes disappeared back to wherever they came from, and he began the one-mile hike back to his Jeep.

As he took to a jog, he considered his options. If he notified the local authorities, crime scene investigators would process the house. They would find the fingerprint, and go from there. If the fingerprint belonged to Liam, and the man wasn't registered in any federal databases, the case would go cold. Since there wasn't any evidence that Liam had walked to the old house, he couldn't see the FBI and GBI becoming involved, especially because Rodney Archer had made no claims to them that the man had even existed.

On the other hand, the fingerprint could be linked to the killer and an arrest could be made. While he wanted Liam put away for what he'd done, he wasn't ready for the man to be imprisoned. He wanted to find Liam, watch him, know and understand him. How else could he come to understand himself? Could he snap? Could he ambush an old couple? Stab them, beat them?

He slowed his pace when he reached an incline, then took his time to make it down the muddy hill without falling on his rear. When he reached the bottom, he ran the rest of the way to the Jeep. But as he drove through the storm, reaching Tallahassee's city limits just before dark, regret and his own stupidity had him shaking his head. The Mason jar. The fingerprint. He shouldn't have left them behind. If the authorities processed the house, they'd know someone had been there before them. The evidence would be in the faint dusting he'd left on the jar.

He pulled into the parking lot of the hotel where he'd been staying the past five days. Disappointed with himself, with his rash decision to lift the print, it still didn't change his agenda. He also had options.

He had a detective's ID.

Two weeks later…
The Hampton Club Apartments, Tallahassee, Florida
Saturday, 8:36 a.m. Eastern Standard Time

KIERA FORRESTER SWIPED sweat from her forehead before it traveled down the bridge of her nose, then gave a casual wave to the hottie who'd moved into the Club four days ago. Of course each time she'd seen him, it had been while they'd been running in opposite directions along the community's extensive jogging trails. Like now, she'd been a sweaty mess. He'd been, too. But he wore the sweaty look much better. Especially when he was shirtless, like today. God, she just wanted to lick him. Take him into the shower and trail her tongue along his chest, along the tattoo on his right pec, his stomach muscles, that sexy V that ran from his hip bone and dipped into his athletic shorts.

She blew out a breath. Like that would ever happen. There would be no tongue-trailing. Well, maybe if he was interested and she actually had the nerve to do it. She waved to another runner, this one a woman. A very pretty woman in her mid-twenties, with golden skin, blonde hair, flat abs and breasts that didn't require two sports bras to keep them from flopping. She was one of many who lived at the Club, hitting the jogging trails or the gym in their skimpy, sexy, fashionable athletic apparel. When the weather warmed, Kiera would bet they'd lounge poolside in tiny bikinis.

Those women were the reason she'd been putting in extra workouts. She didn't want to be blonde, and wasn't built to be skinny, but they'd inspired her to look after herself, to put her needs first. Now that her brother was finally settled, she was ready to date. Before she could put herself out there, she needed to be comfortable and feel sexy in her own skin.

Kiera made her way along her favorite stretch of the path, enjoying the cool morning air, the lake, and the wooded area that reminded her of home. Florida was a far cry from Aurora, Colorado. Everything here was so beachy, even if she lived forty minutes from one, and she missed the mountains. But Tallahassee had been where her brother had chosen to move—why, she still didn't know.

When he'd disappeared last August, she'd been scared out of her mind. She'd found his empty pill bottles in the mulch behind the shrubs alongside her house. That hadn't been the first time Liam had tried to hide pill bottles after flushing the contents down the toilet, and he'd been known to take off for a day or two. But when he'd left, she had always known where he was staying—the local shelter, the Lutheran church located downtown, or the twenty-four-hour diner near the edge of the city. She'd been unable to find him at any of his usual haunts, so she'd checked with not only the Aurora police, but Denver's too, and in other neighboring cities. When she hadn't found him in a hospital or morgue, she'd feared the worst. She picked up her pace, trying to outrun the worries that had kept her up night after night.

When a cramp seized her side, she slowed and tried to catch her breath. There was nothing to agonize about anymore. Liam was safe. He was settled. Where Liam had been, what he'd done prior to moving to Tallahassee, she wasn't sure. Right now, there was only one thing that mattered to her—he was back on his meds.

She slowed to a jog when she reached the area near her building. The pretty blonde she'd passed earlier stood just ahead, her foot propped against a tree, her lithe body bent over her thigh...and talking to the hottie new guy. Which, of course, confirmed there would be no tongue-trailing along his chest and abs...along that V.

Damn.

She glanced away from the couple and started for her apartment. This was her first Saturday off in five weeks, and she planned to find out what the good people of Tallahassee did for fun on the weekends. Liam had invited her over for a Sunday barbeque, so tomorrow was covered. She'd received a flyer earlier this week advertising that the Club's board was throwing a luau at the community pool. All residents were welcome for a five-dollar cover. A gathering like that would be a great way to meet more of her neighbors. But, she'd much rather hang out with the ones she'd lived next to in Aurora. She also missed her old job. Her grocery store. Her bank and post office.

By the time she neared her building, she'd come full circle. She'd started her run feeling down, homesick. In the middle, she'd had a few naughty thoughts about the hottie, then positive thoughts about her brother and living here, only to go back to feeling homesick.

An hour later, after a shower and a couple cups of strong coffee, her mood had brightened. She'd always been a positive person, even when nothing positive had been happening in her world. Instead of being homesick, she needed to embrace Tallahassee. Make the grocery store, bank and post office *hers*. Drive around and get lost. Maybe stumble upon a park or a diner that could become *her* spot. Then later, she'd check out the party at the Club's pool.

She grabbed the keys to her Chevy and headed out the door of her garden apartment. Instead of looking at this move as a sacrifice, she needed to look at it as a new beginning. Her apartment was affordable and had all the modern upgrades she hadn't been able to give her house in Colorado. The cost of living here was better, and obtaining her temporary Physical Therapist license had been a breeze, as had finding a job. She actually liked working at Tallahassee's Mercy Memorial hospital much more than the assisted living facility in Aurora. The pay was higher, the people were nicer, and, with the exception of being stuck with the Saturday shifts, her new boss and co-workers hadn't once made her feel like the newbie. Liam was her only family, so being near him was important to her, more important than little things like getting used to shopping at a new grocery store.

Several little brown lizards zipped across the sidewalk. Surprised, she dropped her keys and took several steps back. As she rubbed the goose bumps along her arms, she shivered and watched the lizards chase each other around the trunk of a palm tree.

There were plenty of things she could accept about living in Florida, but lizards weren't one of them. She bent to scoop up her keys.

"Did they try to attack you?" a man asked, amusement in his voice.

She looked over her shoulder and had to use her fingertips to maintain balance. Face-planting the cement in front of hottie new guy was not an option. "Bared their teeth at me," she said with a grin, and putting to use the yoga classes she'd taken in the fall, she rose to her feet with ease.

Hottie smiled. He had a nice smile. Shy but confident, and oh, so sexy. "Yeah, you gotta watch out for them. They've been known to take off limbs."

"I'll be sure to keep my machete handy." When her cell phone vibrated from inside her purse, she ignored it. Instead, she clutched the strap and tried to maintain eye contact. Hottie's hazel eyes had her a little off-balance. There was intensity in them, along with…appreciation. Maybe? "How do you like living here?" she asked, not ready to walk away, but not knowing where to take the lizard conversation next.

"Good, so far. How about you?"

"Good, so far." She gave him a quick grin. "I've only been in Tallahassee for a couple of months."

"You've got me beat. I've only been here for a couple of weeks. Where'd you move from?"

"Aurora, Colorado. It's just outside Denver. You?"

"Norfolk, Virginia."

She could ask him why he'd moved, but didn't want to play twenty questions or come off as nosey. Yet, she still wasn't ready to walk away. She hadn't dated in a long time and had missed male companionship, missed rough caresses, hot kisses, skin to skin contact. She glanced at Hottie's graphic tee and the way it stretched across his chest, his biceps. Skin to skin with him would indeed be nice.

"What made you leave Denver?" he asked.

"My brother moved here. He kept going on and on about how great Florida is, so I decided to come for a visit, and then only went back to Colorado to pack my things and sell my house." All true. She'd just left out the part when she'd begged Liam to change his mind and come home, where the doctors who knew and understood him could monitor his therapy. But he was a grown man, and had assured her he was under medical care. "What about you?"

"It doesn't sound like my story is much different from yours. I came down here to do a job for a friend, then decided to stay."

Oh, her story was way different. She'd guarantee Hottie didn't have a schizophrenic sibling. "What kind of job?" she asked now that they were playing twenty questions anyway.

"I'm a web developer. Mostly I create websites. I work from home, but when my buddy who lives here asked me to build him a website, I used it as an excuse for a working vacation." He gave her another shy smile, and held her gaze for a heartbeat. "I'm glad I did."

Her cheeks heated as her thoughts drifted to what he looked like without a shirt.

He let out a chuckle. "I mean, you can't beat the weather, right?"

"Right. I can't complain. If I was back in Colorado, I certainly wouldn't be wearing shorts."

"Well, I didn't mean to keep you," he said, but made no move to go about his business.

"I was just going to run errands. No biggie."

He looked down for a second, before meeting her gaze again. "Are you going to the pool party?"

She shrugged. "I thought about it."

He nodded. "I did, too. If you're going to be there, then I'll do more than think about it."

She couldn't have stopped the smile splitting her face if she'd tried. "Do you want to meet there at a certain time?" she asked, then added, "Since you're doing more than thinking?"

When Hottie chuckled, the sexy rasp had her imagining the two of them doing more than going to a pool party. "Yeah, I'm definitely doing more than thinking," he said. "How about I meet you right here at six? We'll head over together."

"I like the way you think. Six is perfect." She held out her hand. "I'm Kiera Forrester."

"Harrison Fairclough." He took her hand. "I'm looking forward to getting to know you."

Donut Scene, Tallahassee, Florida
Saturday, 9:57 a.m. Eastern Standard Time

"JUST DO IT, lover."

Liam ignored the hungry bitch and stared at his cell phone screen. He knew damn well Kiera was off the entire weekend. He needed to talk to her, needed to hear her voice to help him control the demon trying to control him.

"You don't need your sister. You need that woman. She'll feel so good, lover."

He looked away from the motel, from the woman standing outside of Room Twelve, smoking a cigarette and arguing with someone on her cell phone. *No,* he told Adeline. *I don't want her. I don't need her.*

Her seductive laughter filled his head. *"That's what you said last week, and look how well that turned out."*

That was a mistake. After nodding to the old man passing through the donut shop then out the door, he set his empty Styrofoam cup next to the napkin containing the crumbs from the glazed cruller he'd just finished. His weakness, his hatred for

Adeline, momentarily blurred his vision. He drew in a deep breath and tried to rein in his emotions, his needs. His hunger. *It won't happen again. We're leaving.*

"We're going to kill her," Adeline said before he could scoop up the cup and napkin. *"You* need *to do this, Liam. If you don't give her to me, then I'll take—"*

Stop! Liam grabbed the garbage from the table, then quickly stood and threw it in the trash.

"I can't. I'm hungry," Adeline nagged as he exited the donut shop. *"You are, too. You're starving, craving a taste."*

The piercing to his temple traveled deep in his head, as if an invisible icepick was being driven through his skull. *No. You're wrong. I'm happy. I'm in a good place in my life.* Without glancing toward the woman standing outside the motel room, he walked across the street to the convenience store on the next corner. The pain in his head grew worse and had him stopping in front of the store. Wincing, hoping to not draw attention to himself, he faced the glass storefront.

"There she is," Adeline taunted him as he watched the reflection of the woman in the glass. *"She's just like the last one. Petite. Sexy. Dark curly hair. Just like—"*

Don't say her name. He turned away from the reflection. Even though he wanted to run, he kept his pace casual as he headed for the next street where he'd parked his car.

"Then give us what we both want."

No.

He glanced around to make sure no one was watching him, that no one was aware of the inner battle being waged inside of him. Of the demon bitch in his head.

"You know how to quiet me. You know what I need."

Liam reached his SUV, quickly unlocked it, then climbed inside. "It'll never be enough," he muttered, and slammed the door shut.

"You're right, lover. I'm not going to lie to you."

He glanced in the rear view mirror. Today the bitch wore her hair down. Like the woman he'd watched outside the motel room, Adeline's curls framed her face, hid her shoulders. Also like the motel woman, she wore no makeup. "I know what you're doing," he said, and nodded. "I'm not going to fall for it again." She'd pulled the same bullshit last week. Changing her appearance to mimic the woman he'd...

"Fuck," he shouted. He slammed his fist into the roof of the car. Memories of the woman he'd killed washing over him like a warm rain shower.

"Remember how hot her blood was against your skin?"

He turned the ignition. "Shut. Up." Without looking in the rear view mirror, he pulled out onto the street.

"The sound of the pipe cracking bone."

The hairs along his arms rose. His fingers, his flesh, tingled as his mind replayed the thwacking sound.

"So powerful."

Yes, very powerful.

"So fucking satisfying," Adeline said on a groan.

Only because he'd pictured her skull making that thwacking sound when the tire iron hit it.

"Satisfy me, lover. Satisfy yourself."

He reached the main street where the donut shop and motel sat parallel. The woman from the motel room was marching to her car. There was determination in her steps. Anger in the way she tossed those dark curls over her shoulder as she got into her car, an older beige Toyota Camry. Someone had pissed her off. Boyfriend? Husband?

"Probably her pimp or drug dealer. She's trash. No one cares about her."

Someone had to care. She was someone's daughter, maybe a mother or a sister.

"Living out of a shitty motel room. Driving a rusted out piece of shit car." When he glanced in the mirror, Adeline added, *"You know I'm right. You know what you have to do."*

"I don't have to do a fucking thing for you," he said, easing the SUV onto the road.

"*Then why are you following her?*"

"I'm not. I'm going home."

"*Are you sure you want to do that? Remember, you're just as hungry as I am. Going home won't be good.*"

For once, Adeline was right. He couldn't go home, not like this. And his shift at The Home Zone wouldn't start until one.

"*Plenty of time.*"

"No."

"*You know you want to,*" Adeline whispered. "*The tire iron was satisfying. Didn't it take the edge off?*"

He glanced to the bitch in the mirror, then back to the car in front of him. The motel woman's car. He let another vehicle in between them. "It's wrong."

"*Is it?*"

"You know damn well it is. I'm not like you," he said, remembering how Adeline had told him about how she'd killed a person. How she'd enjoyed tasting the blood that had sprayed onto her lips.

"*You're exactly like me. You've just been in denial. But now I've set you free. You're welcome, lover*"

He gripped the steering wheel, but never lost focus on the motel woman's car and followed her onto Interstate 10, heading eastbound. "I'm not free. You're still with me."

"*But you know how to make me go away, don't you, lover?*"

He did know. On some level, it didn't bother him. Some days he was just as hungry as Adeline. Today happened to be one of those days. Which was why he'd left the house early. He'd had to get away, to leave before he'd done something he would actually regret. The people he'd killed…he'd known it was wrong. He just hadn't cared. Their deaths, their blood, fed the bitch, quieted her, kept her out of his head. Curbed her appetite, and his. Adeline was right about one thing—with killing came power.

"*Yes,*" Adeline hissed. "*That's it, lover. The power is amazing. Knowing you control life or death, pain or pleasure…that kind of*" *power is amazing. And it's only for the lucky ones to experience. People like you and I. Because we can, we do. There's no reason to worry about what's right or wrong, about morality. That doesn't apply to us."*

"I have a conscience," he replied, never losing sight of the motel woman's car.

"No, lover," Adeline said, her tone almost sympathetic. *"You've been brainwashed by society. You no longer have a conscience. You have me. You know what I did to you."*

He'd moved back to Tallahassee to be closer to where Rodney Archer was being held for murder and kidnapping at the Thomas County Jail in Thomasville, Georgia. Tallahassee wasn't too far from Thomasville, and he'd figured it was safer to live here than in a community where he'd killed two people. He'd also decided he liked Tallahassee, liked the idea of starting fresh. But he'd followed every story written about Rodney. Before he'd bought a used laptop, he'd clipped articles from newspapers and magazines. He did know what Rodney and Adeline had done to him, to the others that Rodney had buried in the barn.

"He fixed you."

Liam laughed. "Fixed me? He got rid of one set of voices and left me with you." He sobered and gripped the steering wheel tight. "Fixed me," he muttered. "I saw the article about the drug you two used. It damages the brain." He stabbed a finger against his head, and glared at Adeline in the rear view mirror. "It takes away empathy, morality."

She gave him a mocking smirk. *"Your conscience."* She let out a sigh. *"Are we going to do this every single time we kill someone? It's beginning to get old. Simply accept what you are and own it. Embrace it."*

But he wasn't born a killer.

"Of course you were. You just needed me to show you what you truly are. Embrace it," she repeated. *"Admit that you're enjoying yourself. You could have turned this car around at any point in the past twenty minutes. Yet here we are, stalking our prey."*

A road sign indicated that a rest stop was one mile up ahead. He'd exit and wait there until the motel woman put distance between them. When he was comfortable enough to get back on the road, he'd turn around at the next exit.

"Embrace it, Liam," Adeline coaxed, her whispered words echoing in his head.

To do as she suggested would mean he'd lose the last link to the man he'd been before his time at the House of Archer.

"You're still the same man. Only now you're more powerful, stronger. Those doctors thought they knew what was best for you, and they were wrong."

Dead wrong. He hadn't taken any medication since leaving Colorado. Not even an aspirin. Despite the hungry bitch, he was lucid, functioning better than ever. Before Rodney and Adeline had 'fixed' him, he couldn't hold a job or sustain a relationship with anyone other than his sister. Now he had—

"Power. A real life," Adeline said, her voice growing stronger, louder. *"Don't you want to keep everything you now have?"*

"Yes, damn it," he shouted, hating her because she was right. Because he knew death was the cost to maintain his current lifestyle, to hang onto the power.

And not his.

"Give her to me, lover. Give yourself what you know in your heart you want. She's perfect."

"That's what you said about the last one."

"And now she's perfectly dead," Adeline said on a laugh. *"This one will be, too. You have no choice, lover. It's either her or—"*

"Don't! Don't you dare say her name." He glared in the rear view mirror. "Understand?"

Adeline cocked a dark brow. *"Then kill the woman. Kill her, Liam. Kill her. Kill her,"* she repeated, screaming the words over and over until they were echoing over themselves, filling his mind, cramming it with hatred and rage.

She wanted the woman dead? He wanted Adeline out of his head so he could think straight. The same thing had happened at the old couple's house, as well as last week and the month before that. Adeline wouldn't shut the fuck up, wouldn't stop demanding and ordering him around. Fine. Fuck it. He'd feed the hungry bitch's appetite.

Once he'd made up his mind, her screams turned to a feathery whisper. His head ached as he watched the motel woman's car exit to the rest area. The rest area where he'd planned to stop to keep from following and eventually killing her. He smiled. It was as if she was asking for it. Tempting fate. Playing Russian roulette. When he briefly considered staying on the interstate and leaving the rest area behind, the whispers turned so shrill, he winced and gripped his skull.

With his head pounding, he exited the interstate. The whispers returned. Breathing hard, he grasped the steering wheel with both hands and followed the woman's car. While she parked near an outdoor vending area at the back of the building, he continued to drive to the side. There were three public entrances into the building, one on either side, and one at the front. He'd noticed a solid door, marked 'Employees Only' at the back near where she'd parked. The lot behind the building was set up for semis and RVs, and was empty. There weren't any cars near his, but he'd seen at least four when he'd pulled into the rest area.

The familiar hunger pangs returned. The whispers grew frantic. Though the words had become unintelligible, they carried a sense of urgency. He got out of the car. Through the building's large glass window, he watched a middle-aged couple exit the front and head toward their car. He started for the back. As he rounded the corner, he immediately saw the woman. She'd left a soda on the hood of her car, had the passenger door open and was leaning inside. She was digging around the interior with her left hand, while holding her right hand outside the vehicle, a cigarette dangling between her fingers.

Her body was nothing like Adeline's. Where Adeline had been curvy, this woman had stick legs and arms, and no ass. But he wasn't interested in her body. He was interested in feeding the bitch and getting on with his day.

The woman pulled out a handful of garbage—fast food wrappers, empty cigarette packs, soda cans—from the car, then jerked back when she saw him. She smiled. "Cleanin' day," she said as she walked over to the trashcan.

He fished in his pocket for change. "My car is worse," he replied, and after taking a Coke from the vending machine, he glanced to her cigarette. "I quit a few weeks ago. But I've been driving for hours and could sure use one. He pulled dollar bills from his front pocket. "I'll give you two bucks for one smoke."

She grinned as she took a drag. "Two dollars? That's crazy. You can buy a pack for seven."

"I don't want a pack. I just want to take the edge off."

With a shrug, she walked toward her car. "I get it. Lord knows I've tried quitting a bunch of times. Hang on. I gotta grab a new pack from my purse." She switched the cigarette to her left hand, used the right to work the lever on the side of the front passenger seat, then shifted the seat forward. She turned her head, took another long drag, then exhaled and tossed the cigarette onto the asphalt. As she swiveled back into the car, the whispers grew louder.

A shiver of anticipation chased up his spine. He quickly scanned the parking lot and building, then looked back to her scrawny backside.

"Kill her. Feed me, lover."

He clenched his fist, his teeth. They'd never been lovers. The slut had used him. She'd taken away his control, had left him powerless. She'd pushed drugs into his veins, drained his body, his mind. But it wasn't enough. She was still taking from him. Still controlling him. She claimed to have freed him, from the voices, from the fringes of insanity, but she hadn't. Instead, he'd become a monster. Dragged into an abyss where madness equated pleasure, where murder kept him sane.

He hated her for it.

He stared at the woman's skinny ass, pictured Adeline's round soft cheeks, how she'd used his body for her own twisted amusement, and shoved the woman in the rear, knocking her off balance and to the floor of the backseat.

"Hey!" She kicked her legs. "Get off me!"

Before she could kick him in the face, he grabbed her by the foot and calf, then twisted. The woman let out an agonizing howl and tried to reach behind her. With her head behind the driver's seat and pressed against the mat, she couldn't reach. But she was damned loud. He gave her another shove, sliding her lower body onto the backseat and trapping her head. She was practically doing a headstand. He reached down, grabbed her by her mass of thick curly hair and pulled. When her face came into view, he slammed his fist into her cheek, then her jaw. Her body went limp and she released a low moan. He let go of her hair, then closed the door behind him.

He grabbed her by the hair again, and positioned her so that she was seated. Her head lolled to the side. Blood trickled from her mouth, from where the skin along her cheek had split, and she was already beginning to bruise. He touched her other cheek. How he wished he'd been able to make Adeline bleed.

"I love the pain."

Adeline's seductive tone washed over him. Arousing him.

"Kill me, lover."

His cell phone rang. He drew in a shaky breath and pulled it from his front pocket. After he saw who was calling, he put the phone back. She would have to wait until he was finished here.

"Help." The woman's ragged whisper had him snapping his gaze to her.

"There is no one who can help you."

Tears spilled down her face. "Why?" she asked, and he realized he might've broken her jaw.

He moved her curls until they framed her face, just as Adeline's had when she'd been riding him, taking her pleasure from his body. "You look like someone I hate," he said, yanking on one of those curls, causing the woman to gasp. "But I'll make it fast."

Her eyes filled with acceptance before she closed them. "So merciful," she muttered with heavy sarcasm.

"Not at all." He gripped her by her swollen jaw, causing her to wince and cry out. "I just need to call back my fiancée."

CHAPTER 3

The Hampton Club Apartments, Tallahassee, Florida
Saturday, 5:33 p.m. Eastern Standard Time

HARRISON STARED AT his reflection in the mirror, hating what he saw.

He had a date with a killer's sister. Hell, he didn't plan to go on just one date with her. He planned to seduce her. Insinuate himself into her life in order to get closer to her brother.

He was a dick.

After smoothing cream along his jaw, he began shaving. Kiera was nice. Yeah, he'd seen plenty of pictures of her through social media, along with her driver's license photo, so he'd already known she was pretty. He'd figured it wouldn't be a big deal to date her for a few weeks, then once he'd had what he needed he would disappear. She'd go her way, he'd go his, and Liam would go to prison. He'd not only make it so the police wouldn't know he was the one who'd led them to Liam, but Kiera wouldn't either.

On paper, the plan worked. After he'd used Nick's ID to run the fingerprints he'd lifted from the Georgia house, and Liam's name matched the prints, he'd researched the man. His prints hadn't been in the system because he was a criminal, but because he'd been institutionalized at one time for a mental disorder. Schizophrenia. According to Liam Forrester's files, he was harmless. Delusional and paranoid, but otherwise a model patient—if he maintained therapy.

When Harrison had discovered Liam was living in Tallahassee, instead of letting Mel and Cash know he was in town, he'd holed up in his hotel room, researching, planning. When Mel had found Liam the night they'd escaped the House of Archer, Liam had told her they'd fixed him. Rodney had later said that the drug he'd given Liam—a drug that would counteract the one he and Adeline had been pumping into their victims—had cured Liam's schizophrenia, and that the only voice he could now hear was Adeline's.

Rodney Archer was an asshole. A pompous prick who liked to think he shit roses. If what Rodney had said was true, he hadn't *cured* Liam, he'd just switched around the voices in the guy's head.

Which gave Harrison hope. *He* wasn't schizophrenic, so Rodney and Adeline's drug—he assumed—had affected him differently than Liam.

Now that he knew about Liam's history with mental illness, he wished he'd handled the evidence he'd discovered at the old couple's house differently. As with too many times in his life, he'd been impulsive. Rather than using his head, he'd let his emotions and fears drive him. He'd tried to right his mistakes, though, and had gone back to the house with the intent to remove the jar he'd dusted, then he had planned to call the police and tip them off about the double homicide. Unfortunately, the house had been burned to the ground. Arson, according to investigators. Which meant he had to find another way to prove Liam was at the plantation house, and that he'd killed the old couple. Because if he gave the cops an anonymous tip now, emailed them photographs of the crime scene, along with the print he'd lifted, they could eventually find out Nick's ID had been used to run Liam's fingerprints.

He rinsed off the razor, then reached for a towel. He wasn't just a dick. He was an idiot. If Nick was questioned about why he hadn't reported the suspected murders of two people, let alone their body parts, he would be shoved into a tight corner. He supposed the detective could play dumb, say that his ID must've been stolen or the system hacked. But any decent Internal Affairs agent could look at who Nick associated with, at his call records, at the cases he and his partner had worked over the past year and find that there was something…off. He didn't have any beef with Nick or his partner, they were all on the same side. He also didn't want what he was doing to expose ATL.

He rubbed a hand down his face. He was a selfish piece of shit who could ruin the lives of everyone he cared about. But the damage was done, and he had a date with a killer's sister.

The guilt infusing its way into his chest was a good sign that he wasn't the monster he feared. It had been a while since he'd felt any type of remorse, and he'd worried it was the drug. In a way, he wished the guilt would disappear. It'd make tonight and the next few weeks easier.

Once he'd found out Liam had a sister, and that Kiera Forrester had recently joined her brother in Tallahassee, he'd researched her as well. What better way to get to know Liam than through his sister? He'd discovered he and Kiera were the same age, where she'd gone to school, that she was a physical therapist, and made about eighty-five thousand dollars last year. He'd used social media, hoping to learn her likes and dislikes. When he'd first seen pictures of her, he'd thought she was pretty. But those photos hadn't done her justice. They hadn't captured the unique blue of her eyes, which were more gray than blue and very striking. Playful, yet guarded. Her smile was sweet, especially when it grew big enough to reveal a couple of cute dimples.

Turning away from the mirror, he reached for the bottle of ibuprofen. He'd always had a thing for redheads. There was no reason. He just did. From her pictures, he'd thought Kiera's hair was brown. He'd thought wrong. When he'd stopped her outside her apartment building, the first thing he'd noticed was her curvy ass. The second, the way the sun hit on the auburn highlights streaked through her dark shoulder-length hair. Her hair had a wave to it, looked thick, soft, and had him wondering what it'd feel like against his chest.

He dry-swallowed the ibuprofen, then considered chasing it down with a beer. But he didn't want to meet Kiera with alcohol on his breath. His goal for tonight was to make a good impression, and hopefully walk away with plans for a second date. He'd rather stakeout Liam's place, and follow him around, than use his sister. The problem was where Liam lived and worked. He'd be easily noticed outside Liam's residence, and he didn't want to draw attention to himself either by sitting in the parking lot of The Home Zone, or loitering around in the store for hours. Plus, he had zero patience for stakeouts. He didn't like to sit and wait, he wanted to make something happen.

And he wanted to make something happen between him and Kiera. He pulled a white V-neck T-shirt over his head, tucked it in the waistband of his khakis, then slid into a plaid short-sleeve button-down, rolling up the sleeves two times and leaving the front unbuttoned—just like the guy at the store told him to do. After he'd decided to try to date Kiera, he had taken a look at himself in the hotel mirror. His wardrobe consisted of worn jeans or shorts, and graphic T-shirts. Wanting to give Kiera the impression he had his shit together, he'd decided to go to the mall and do something he hadn't bothered to do in years—buy clothes. If the clerk at Nordstrom worked for commission, he'd made a killing that day by helping Harrison pull together clothes that were nothing like his preferred slacker-chic style.

He finished buckling his belt and checked his reflection. Maybe Kiera liked faded jeans and T-shirts. Maybe she couldn't care less how he dressed because she wasn't interested in him as anything more than a neighbor. His experience with women wasn't good. He'd never had a steady girlfriend, or dated much. He'd never really had much of an opportunity. Growing up with no money, no father and a mother whose only interests where alcohol and her abusive live-in boyfriends, he hadn't really cared about dating. All he'd cared about was his brother and finding ways to make money. Spending time in juvie, then later in prison, also hadn't helped in the romance department. Wasn't he a fucking catch?

He ignored his nervous stomach and pulled a light-weight jacket from the closet. The last time he'd kissed a woman was over two years ago. It'd also been the last time he'd had sex. The only other woman who'd touched him since had done so without his permission—assaulting him, humiliating him. He turned away from the mirror and grabbed his wallet off the dresser.

Adeline was dead, and he couldn't change the past. Besides, he'd destroyed his dignity long before Adeline had entered his life.

And Kiera would never know. She'd never know he was a criminal, that he wasn't worth her time. For the first time in his life, he could pretend to be the man he wished he could be—honorable, successful…worth loving.

He shoved his cell phone and wallet into his back pockets, and left the bedroom. Next to Polina's Paradise, this apartment was the nicest place he'd ever lived. But he still liked his trailer and living near the water. He liked that he owned it outright, and that he didn't have to worry about answering to the bank or a landlord.

When he entered the kitchen, he checked the time and saw he had only five minutes before meeting up with Kiera. His nervous stomach tightened up, and he drew in a fortifying breath. He thought about the skulls he'd found in the backwoods of Georgia, the blood spray, the pools of dried blood that had been on the floor, and snagged his keys off the kitchen counter. As he left the apartment, locking the door behind him, the guilt that had been nagging him began to fade. Kiera was the sister of a killer. He had to keep reminding himself of that, and remember he was lying to not only help put a murderer in prison, but potentially save himself from walking down the same dark path as Liam.

He exited the building and immediately shoved Liam from his mind. This evening wasn't about him, but about winning over Kiera. If she ended up not wanting anything to do with him, he'd have to find another way to get close to Liam. The problem was, if he knew of another way, he would've already done it.

The temperature in Tallahassee was cooler than Everglades City. By the time he reached Kiera's building, the chill in the air had him slipping into his jacket and wondering who'd had the brilliant idea to throw a luau in February.

The door to Kiera's building opened. Rays from the dying sun kissed her head, bringing out the auburn highlights he loved. But Kiera's hair color didn't matter to him because her smile stole the show.

"Did you run into any traffic on your way here?" she asked, her eyes teasing.

"Three lizards and a squirrel. Not too bad." He nodded to the small cooler she carried. "Was I supposed to bring something? The flyer didn't say."

"I emailed one of the women who's putting on the luau, and asked about BYOB. Apparently they forgot to put that in the flyer, but they did have it on the website."

He thumbed behind him, and toward his building. "I have beer back at my place. It'll only take me a few minutes to grab it."

"Save it. I brought a six pack of wine coolers for us."

"Good choice," he said, catching the amusement in her eyes. "Only real men drink wine coolers. Personally, I'm partial to peach-flavored."

She laughed as he took the cooler from her. "Then I hate to disappoint you, because I was just kidding. Water and soda are provided, so I packed beer."

"Thanks. I owe you."

"No, you don't." She slipped a lock of hair behind her ear, exposing the side of her neck. "I'm glad I don't have to go to this by myself."

"So you're using me for company," he said, while wondering if she liked being kissed along the neck. If so, did it give her goose bumps?

She let out a heavy sigh. "You discovered my secret."

He grinned. "It's not much of a secret since you flat-out told me. But I do think you'll owe me for this."

"I don't know how you figure. I did bring beer, and you were the one who asked me to go with you."

Damn it. Why couldn't she be boring, unlikeable and ugly? "Actually, you asked me. All I asked was if you were thinking about going."

"You're right. I did suggest we go together." The corner of her mouth slid into a grin, drawing his attention to her dimple. "I'm normally not that forward."

Based on how outgoing she'd been so far, he doubted that. "I'm not sure if I believe you," he said, holding open the gate to the community pool. "But I'm glad you asked."

She paused at the entrance. A light breeze lifted her hair, and carried her scent. He inhaled. Damn, she smelled fresh, as if she'd just gotten out of the shower, and had him wanting to take her to bed and mess up the sheets.

"I'm glad you suggested coming," she said, then entered the pool area.

He ignored Kiera's protest as he paid their luau fee, then they went in search of a table to claim. "How about that one?" he asked, pointing to the table furthest from the DJ and food.

"I think the point of the luau is for residents to mingle," she said, walking with him toward the table.

He had no interest in knowing anyone here but Kiera. The blonde who had stopped him after his morning run had been the one who'd told him about the party. With the way she'd acted, he'd been under the impression that she'd hoped to meet up with him later. She was attractive and seemed nice, but he had an agenda to keep, and a woman to seduce.

He held out a chair for Kiera and set the cooler on the concrete. "I'm mingling with you."

She held his gaze for a moment, her gray-blue eyes holding appreciation, and maybe wariness. "We're both new to the area. We should be making friends."

"I already have friends. But they're all dudes."

She glanced away, a pretty shade of pink flushing her cheeks. "So you're looking for a friend who's a girl."

"I already have a friend who's a girl. But she's married to one of the dudes."

Chuckling and shaking her head, she looked at him and gave

him a wry grin. "So you're looking for a girlfriend."

"Nope." He bent and lifted the lid of the small cooler. After he opened, then handed her a beer, he said, "I'm hoping to get to know you. Not to sound like a stalker, but I saw you the day I moved in, then every morning since along the jogging path. I think you're pretty and you have a great smile. I'm not looking to make friends here tonight. I want to see more of your smile."

Her dimples deepened as her smile grew.

He wasn't lying. Kiera was very attractive and he did want to get to know her. If circumstances were different, he doubted he would've had the nerve to be so bold. Hell, he wouldn't have bothered to even try to date her. She was out of his league. A law-abiding citizen, a good person who'd never been in trouble, and who donated to charities. But circumstances *weren't* different. He wanted access to her brother, and he'd use her, play on her emotions and trust to get what he wanted. He'd rather be the dick who used a woman, than deal with the guilt of letting a murderer kill again.

"Stalker, huh?" She ran her fingertip around the rim of the beer can. "I'm not sure what to do with that."

Run.

Liam Forrester's house, Tallahassee, Florida
Saturday, 9:49 p.m. Eastern Standard Time

THE SHOWER CURTAIN billowed before sliding open. With his eyes still closed, his head under the hot spray, he let out a groan when a soft hand cupped his erection. "I was wondering when you were going to be home."

"I left you a note. Didn't you see it on the kitchen table?"

He opened his eyes and stared down at Bella. His beautiful sweet Bella. The woman he loved and fought from killing. "I saw it." He turned so that she shared the water, and ran his hand through her wet curls. "Why didn't you go during the day, or tomorrow morning? You know I don't like it when you're out at night by yourself. There're too many crazies out there."

She wrapped her arms around his waist, pressing her naked body against his. "*You're* crazy for being so darn overprotective. I've been livin' by myself for a long time and managed just fine. Besides, I stopped in at the restaurant to see if anyone wanted me to pick up their shift. No one was willin' so I took advantage of this beautiful day and went to the park, then came back here to get some gardening done." She rubbed his erection again. "And why would I want to waste my Sunday morning runnin' errands when I could be spending it with you?"

"You have a point," he said, then kissed her. As her tongue stroked his, memories of the scrawny motel woman flipped through his mind like a fast-moving slideshow. Her broken jaw hanging open, the way the whites of her bruised eyes turned a demonic red from ruptured capillaries. The fear, the power.

He gripped Bella's hips, digging his fingers into her soft flesh. When she left out a soft whimper, he eased back and stared into her trusting eyes.

"Is it that time again?" she asked, and placed a hand along his cheek.

He nodded. If he spoke, he wasn't sure he could control the words. Killing the woman, then having to go to work had been a bad idea. He'd spent the day standing behind a counter, helping dumbasses try to figure out what tools to rent or showing them how to use them. If only the man who'd asked for instructions on how to use the stump grinder knew that he himself had been staring at that piece of equipment for days, wondering what it would do to a human body. Same went for the woman who'd rented the small rototiller for her garden. Five months ago, he'd killed two people in a day. It had been quick, and he'd taken no pleasure from it. All he'd wanted to do was shut Adeline up…feed the bitch. Today, he could have gone for two again. He could have fired up that rototiller and done some serious damage to the woman who'd rented it. Killing the motel woman hadn't been satisfying enough. It'd been enough to get Adeline out of his head, but it hadn't curbed *his* appetite. It hadn't taken away the hunger pangs.

"Talk to me, baby," Bella said, taking his chin in her hand. "Where are you?"

After they'd dated for a few weeks, and she'd told him she loved him, he'd admitted the same. He understood love and what it meant. The problem was there were too many days when he had fantasized about killing her. How could he want to destroy someone he loved?

"I'm here with you," he managed, his fingers still digging into her hips.

She winced, then her gaze probed his. "I feel like you're thinkin' hard, or trying to fight it. You know, the white noise."

Once they'd professed their love for each other, he'd admitted that he'd been diagnosed with schizophrenia. He hadn't planned on telling Bella. But he knew Kiera would not only question him, but question Bella—ask if he was taking his meds or having delusional episodes. Kiera was a good person, the one person in the world he trusted with his life. But he could never tell her why he no longer needed the medication. If he did, she'd know. She'd know he'd been a victim. She would demand justice for what Rodney and Adeline had done to him. That would be okay, except he had killed. The moment he'd been freed from his bindings, he'd killed a man, then he'd gone on to kill the old people. His sister could never know he was a monster. Bella couldn't either. But she understood that he sometimes fought demons.

"I am," he said, his heart racing. The pent-up frustration, the anticlimactic letdown he'd experienced after killing the motel woman had his body tense, on the verge of...something. "Help me."

"I'll give you what you need," she whispered, a tear slipping down her cheek. "Just like last time."

He pressed his erection against her stomach. "Why?" How could she want what he wanted? His Bella was sweet, not dark, dirty and twisted.

"Because I love you."

After shutting off the water, he pushed a wet curl from her face. "I love you, too. Now go get the ropes."

Mile Marker 125, Interstate 10, Tallahassee, Florida
Saturday, 10:19 p.m. Eastern Standard Time

DETECTIVE SHARON LARSON parked at the rear of the rest area, about fifty feet from the crime scene tape. Thirty minutes ago, her eyes had been burning from exhaustion, and she'd been wrapping up for the night and preparing to go home to an empty house. To the unwanted memories and reminders.

Too bad the welcoming distraction meant another dead body.

She killed the ignition, then exited the car. Her partner and best friend, Bernadette Richie, who had already been on her way home when the call came in, met her outside the crime scene perimeter. "Why are we here?" Bern asked. "This isn't our stomping ground."

Sharon had asked their lieutenant the same question when he'd notified her of the homicide. "Russ thinks there might be a connection to last week's vic."

"And we think last month's murder is related to that one," Bern said, her voice filled with frustration.

"Don't remind me." Sharon looked from the car, a Toyota Camry, to the building door specified for employee use only, to the vending machines. She glanced over her shoulder toward the back parking lot, and scanned the dozen or so semis parked for the night. "We need to introduce ourselves," she said, lifting the badge dangling from around her neck as she nodded to a couple of uniformed officers.

The crime scene unit was already processing the area. Since it was dark, and the lighting at the rest area was limited, halogen lights had been brought in and set up around the car. She noticed only a few yellow markers in the parking lot, which meant that the majority of the evidence was either in the Camry, or with the killer.

A repeat of last week's murder victim, and the one before that.

"No intro needed," Bern said, and nodded to Lyle 'Jak' Jakowski.

Good. Jak was a friend, had gone through the academy with her and her husband, and was a topnotch detective. When he looked away from the Camry and noticed them, he waved them over.

"Sharon, Bern," he greeted them, his expression grim, his eyebrows drawn together in a deep V. "Glad you two are here."

Bernadette's eyes widened slightly. "You requested us?"

Jak nodded and ran a hand along his thinning hair. The habit momentarily took Sharon back to another place and time. To when Jak'd had a thick head of hair, and they'd all been young cadets ready to take on the criminal world. "Yeah, I heard about the Morrison case and thought it might be linked to this one."

"How was the victim killed?" she asked, her thoughts quickly shifting to Morrison Apartments, located near Florida State University—a solid forty-minute drive from the rest area. The victim, Jennette Salvetti, a thirty-two-year-old substitute teacher, had been found dead in her car—twenty feet from her ground floor apartment.

"Based on the bruising around her neck and the broken blood vessels in her eyes, it looks like strangulation. But we didn't find rope or cord."

"So you're suggesting someone choked her with their hands?" Sharon shook her head. There was no link between their cases. "That screams personal to me."

"Agreed. Jennette Salvetti was killed with a tire iron," Bern informed him. "At this point, we don't have any leads indicating she knew her murderer."

Jak stepped closer. "I know. Just pop your heads inside and tell me what you see."

The worry in his shadowed eyes intrigued and concerned Sharon. Jak wouldn't have asked her and Bern out here if he hadn't seen a connection between their cases. Which meant they could be dealing with a serial killer.

She slipped on a pair of gloves and, without a word, walked over to the passenger side of the car. The halogen light was aimed at the backseat of the Camry and directly on the dead woman.

Tell me what you see.

"Dark curly hair," she said to Bern, who leaned close to her. "Just like Jennette."

"And Carla."

Carla Rodriguez had been found in the bushes off the walking path at Juniper Park, which was located ten miles south of Morrison Apartments. Carla also had dark curly hair, but she'd been older than Jennette and their current victim. She'd also been stabbed.

Bern pulled out a flashlight, then aimed it at the areas the halogen lights couldn't reach. "Purse is on the floor mat. Doesn't look like a robbery." She flashed the light to the front of the car, where a sunshade covered the interior windshield. Had the killer put it in place before or after the murder?

Sharon inhaled through her nose. "It smells like Jennette's car."

"And cigarettes. It's got me craving one."

"It's been five years."

"Five and a half," Bernadette corrected her. "But you're right. It does smell the same. Musty."

Sharon's chest tightened as she met her partner's worried gaze. "Wet," she said, peeling off one glove and praying she was wrong. "Shine the light on the woman." Once Bern did as she asked, Sharon reached over and touched the dead woman's clothes. "Dry."

"Try the seat."

When her fingers met with the fabric, the nausea rolling though her stomach was almost as bad as after one of her chemo treatments. "It's wet."

"Shit."

Sharon stared at the woman—at her battered face—and a piece of what was left of her heart broke. It wasn't fair. The dead woman was probably twenty years younger than her. At fifty-three, Sharon had plenty of life to live. But without treatment, her oncologist claimed she had maybe six to nine months. And while her health issues were terminal, the victim's was terminally criminal. She gave the woman one final glance. "Let's go talk to Jak."

"We need more than wet clothes or car seats to tie the victims together," Bernadette said as they walked back over to the detective.

"Well?" Jak asked when they reached him.

"The seat material beneath her and the bottom of her clothes are still wet." Sharon removed the glove from her hand and pocketed it with the other. "Did you find any bottles, cans, jugs?"

He shook his head. "Nothing. Did you notice the front seat is perfectly dry? It's as if the guy hosed her down after he killed her."

"We found the same in Jennette Salvetti's car," Bernadette said, zipping her jacket. "Her clothes were still wet, though. Do you have an estimated time of death for the deceased?"

"Or a name?" Sharon asked. She'd always hated referring to the victim as the dead person or deceased, or by a case number. For her, it took the human element out of the equation.

Jak pulled out a small notepad. "Wendy DeMarco. ME thinks she's been dead ten to twelve hours, putting her murder between ten a.m. and noon."

"Then the car seat shouldn't still be wet," Bernadette said, plucking the same thought from Sharon's head.

"He came back," Sharon said, a chill sliding over her as she met Bernadette's worried gaze. "Just like Jennette. He came back and doused her with water."

"And they all have the same look," Bern said. "Dark-brown or black curly hair."

"But they were killed differently. Stabbing, bludgeoning, strangling."

Bernadette pushed her short ash-blonde bangs to the side, a

gesture she made when she was thinking, brainstorming. "Different ages, different ethnicities and the locations have no rhyme or reason to them."

"No sexual assault, no robbery or sign that they were hired hits."

"But they were all washed. Why risk coming back to the scene?" Bern asked.

Jak cleared his throat. "Did you two forget I'm standing here?"

Sharon gave him a half-smile. "Sorry. We're convinced we have two murders that are linked, but no concrete evidence," she said, then told him about Carla Rodriguez. "She was bone dry when she was discovered, but there was hardly any blood on her, and she'd been stabbed eight times. The blood evidence that was recovered was watered down."

"As if someone had cleaned her." Jak looked to the Camry. "I knew about the Morrison murder, but not about that one." He faced them again. "Once CSU is finished, and the body is removed, they're taking the car back to the lab and giving it a check. Were any foreign fibers or hairs found at your two crime scenes?"

Sharon nodded. "A hair was removed from the cuff of Carla Rodriguez's yoga pants. It wasn't human. CSU thought it was canine."

"Carla didn't own any animals, but she was also found off a trail people use to walk their dogs," Bernadette added.

One hair. That had been all they'd had. One hair, eight stab wounds, and a clean body. No murder weapon, no indication of a struggle, no damned reason for the thirty-nine-year-old mother of three to have been brutally killed. "We had the hair sent to a veterinary forensics lab for testing anyway," Sharon said, her memories fading from Carla's body to when she and Bern had met with the woman's husband. No matter how many years she'd been on the job, telling a family member their loved one wasn't coming home would never be easy. But telling George Rodriguez his wife was dead, while he'd stood in front of a sixteen by ten canvas photo of their beautiful family…that had hurt her more than the day her oncologist had informed her she was dying. She no longer had a husband, she had no children, hardly any family left. All she had was Bernadette, her cat and her job.

"We're ready to move the body," a CSU investigator told Jak.

Jak gave the investigator a nod, then rubbed his eyes. "It's going to be a long night," he said with a sigh.

Of that, Sharon had no doubt. "I noticed a windshield sunshade covering the interior window. I'm assuming that's why it took ten to twelve hours before anyone found her?"

"Yeah, a rest stop employee called it in about an hour after he arrived for his eight o'clock shift. He thought she was sleeping, until he took a closer look."

"What about the other employees?" Bern asked. "It only hit seventy-two today, but someone had to think it was odd that there was a woman sleeping in her car all day."

"Florida Department of Transportation is providing me with a list of who worked here today."

Sharon glanced to the back entrance. "I don't see any security cameras."

"Unfortunately there aren't any." Jak looked toward the car, and she swore the lines on his face deepened as Wendy DeMarco's body was removed. "Anyway," he began, looking away from the scene. "A cigarette butt matching the brand we found in her purse was located just outside the passenger door. We had the trash bag from the can near the back entrance retrieved from the dumpster. CSU recovered a few items that appeared to have come from her car. None of it worth much of anything."

"Jak," a uniformed officer called as he made his way from the parking lot. "I've got a guy from FDOT asking for you."

"Have him meet me inside." As the officer walked off, Jak said, "I have to go. Thanks for coming out. Do you two want to get together tomorrow and go over what we have for all three murders? I should have the autopsy by then, and hopefully interviews with whoever was working here today."

Sharon looked to Bernadette, who nodded. "Absolutely," Bern said. "If you need help talking with any other witnesses, let us know."

"Will do." Jak started for the rest area employee entrance, then stopped and turned. "Sharon, you never finished what you were saying about the dog hair. Was the lab able to get a breed?"

"Yeah, the hair belonged to a Siberian Husky."

CHAPTER 4

Liam and Bella's House, Tallahassee, Florida
Sunday, 12:57 p.m. Eastern Standard Time

KIERA SCRATCHED GINGER, Liam and Bella's adorable, six-month old Husky, along her back. "I love her," she said to her brother. "I'm jealous. You know how much I love dogs. But I'm just not home enough."

"Are you allowed to have pets at the Club? By the way, calling your apartment complex 'the Club' sounds so pretentious."

"Tell me about it. And yes, you can have pets."

"Get a cat."

"I'm allergic, remember? I'll just puppy-sit for you guys."

"Hired." Liam grinned. "So did you go to the luau at *the Club*?" he asked, stressing 'the Club' with a haughty tone.

"I did."

His brows rose. "Really? Bella and I had a bet going. Now I guess I owe her a back rub."

She wrinkled her nose. "TMI."

"Whatever. So how was it?"

Fantastic. "Nice," she said, and couldn't help smiling.

"Nice, huh? I know that smile." He sat on the grass next to her. "Kiera found a boyfriend," he sang in a teasing tone.

"Shut up." She threw a few blades of grass at him, which caught Ginger's attention. When she bounced around Liam, he fell back and acted as if the little dog had knocked him over. Laughing, she lay next to him and stared at the cloudless blue sky. She missed moments like this. When they could just...be. Like when they were kids. Before Liam had changed. Before their parents had died.

Before the burden.

"Who's the guy?" her brother asked while evading puppy licks.

"His name is Harrison."

Ginger plopped between them, and Liam turned his head toward her. God, he looked so much like their father: same hair color, brown eyes and smile. She'd inherited their dad's hair color, too. Other than that, she was the spitting image of their mom.

"Did you meet him at the party?" Liam asked.

"No," she said, then told him about how he'd caught her attention, about seeing him on the jogging path, then their 'sort of' date last night. She rolled to her side and propped her head on her hand. "You know me. I can have fun in a box and find something in common with just about anyone."

He grinned. "I remember the fort we made out of the refrigerator box, so yes, I do know you can have fun in one."

"It was a kickass fort."

"Totally badass."

She stroked Ginger's fur. "I would love for Harrison to come hang out in my kickass, badass fort," she admitted.

"Seriously? You just met him."

"I know. The thing is, I've never met someone I have so much in common with. It's almost a little creepy."

"If he's a creeper—"

"No, *he's* not creepy, it's just weird. When we were hanging out together last night, I was amazed by how he's into so many of the same things I am." She rolled onto her back. "I don't know. It's been a while since I've dated, and I'm in a new place. I'm probably attracted to the idea of having someone."

At least that had been what she'd told herself all morning. After giving herself permission to sleep in, she'd cleaned the apartment, taken care of a few bills, then prepared the potatoes she'd promised Liam she'd bring today. Through it all, she'd tried not to overthink last night. She'd done it anyway. She was very attracted to Harrison. During her morning runs, she'd already had mental sex with him. Many, many times. After spending the evening talking with him, she could still picture them having sex. But more than that, she could see them as a couple.

"That doesn't sound like you," Liam said. "You've never gone out with a guy just because."

"I've also never lived anywhere but Aurora."

"So because you've moved you're desperate for companionship?" He let out a breath. "Well, that doesn't make me feel too guilty."

She turned her head and looked at her brother. "I chose to move."

"So you could keep an eye on me."

"No. Because you're the only family I have."

When he met her gaze, she suddenly saw them back in time. Back to that refrigerator box fort. To when everything was simpler. "I'm glad you moved here. I feel guilty for that, but I'm glad you're here anyway."

She was and she wasn't. She'd uprooted her life for Liam. When they'd been living in Colorado, there'd been many times when she'd been forced to change plans, change boyfriends and even jobs because of him. But this was different. She'd had to sell her house, move to another state and start all over again.

On the flip side, being in Tallahassee kept her close to Liam. Those months when she couldn't find him had been hell. The definition of 'loose cannon' was Liam Forrester. Unpredictable, sometimes uncontrollable, he could be a danger to himself and definitely others.

"I can't complain about the weather, that's for sure," she said to keep the conversation light. She didn't want him feeling guilty for her choice. They were both grown adults, and she owned her decisions.

"Or the new guy," Liam added.

Her stomach filled with butterflies. "Or the new guy. He's taking me to dinner Tuesday. Hibachi." Her favorite, and apparently Harrison's, too. He also liked to watch horror movies, listened to country music and loved doing anything outdoors. She probably couldn't have found a better match using an online dating service. "He's new to the area, too," she continued. "It'd be fun to have someone to explore the city with me."

"Well, I hope this guy catches on fast that you're awesome."

"I'll let you know how it goes." She sat up and glanced toward the back of the house. "I should see if Bella needs help. She's been in there for a while."

"And I should light the grill," Liam said, rising.

Ginger rested her head on Kiera's leg and looked up at her with ice-blue eyes. "Who's getting to be such a big girl?" she asked the puppy, who rolled onto the grass exposing her white belly for a rub.

"If you start telling me she's answering you, I have some pills that'll help with that."

She looked up at her brother and chuckled. Liam had been through so much. It amazed her that he could joke about his problems. What amazed her even more was how far he'd come in the past six months. He'd gone from paranoid schizophrenic to average Joe.

"I've been practicing the art of zoolingualism." She stood, then walked with him toward the deck, the puppy following behind. "You should hear the conversations I have with the little lizards outside my apartment building."

He grimaced as he pulled off the grill cover. "I'm still getting used to them. Can you tell the lizards around here to stay out of my house? I found a couple of dead ones by the back door. I think they run in when one of us is letting Ginger in or out."

She picked up the glass of iced tea she'd left on the patio table. "Gross. But I'll take a lizard over spiders or roaches. Do you remember how bad they were at Aunt Rosaleen's?"

Liam chuckled and looked toward the house when the patio door slid open. "Hey, honey. I was wondering when you were coming out to join us," he said to Bella.

"I was makin' the salad and checkin' on the yummy-lookin' potatoes Kiera brought." When Bella wrapped an arm around Liam's waist, Kiera watched the couple. Liam hadn't had a girlfriend since he'd been diagnosed with schizophrenia, and that girl had been an athletic blonde who was into snowboarding and hiking. Bella was plain, but pretty, and very petite. Standing next to the woman, Kiera felt like a giant.

"What'd I miss?" Bella asked.

"We were just talking about our Great-Aunt Rosaleen," he said. "She lived in Colorado Springs in a house built in something like 1900."

Kiera nodded. "I think that's exactly when it was built." Just thinking about the tiny, spooky old home made her shiver. She hated her aunt's attic, but hated the dark basement even more, especially the old coal room. There were just too many places the boogie man could hide.

"But you two grew up around Denver, right?" Bella asked.

"Aurora," her brother responded. "I'll have to take you there for a visit. The beach doesn't have anything on the mountain views."

"I'd like that." Bella hugged him closer, then stepped away. "So what made you guys think about your aunt?" she asked as she pulled a couple of the plastic chairs away from the house, and offered one to Kiera.

"Bugs and lizards." After Kiera took a seat, she brushed white puppy fur from her black leggings and decided she'd never wear dark colors to her brother's again. "When our parents would take us to visit her, she used to give us a nickel for each roach or spider we killed."

"Oh, good Lord, that's disgusting." Bella half-laughed and wrinkled her nose. "I wouldn't do it for a dollar."

"I was eight and Kiera was ten. Smashing bugs provided us with hours of entertainment."

"Yeah, and it was an easy way to earn a buck," Kiera said, thinking back to how she'd spent her dollar on a couple of packs of grape Hubba Bubba bubble gum.

"That'd mean you killed twenty bugs." When Bella sat down, Ginger hopped onto her lap. "I don't know, it almost sounds like child abuse. I can't believe your parents thought that was okay."

Kiera hid her irritation with a smile. Their parents had been good people. Their mom was a soft spoken, kind woman who would do anything for anyone in need. When their dad was medicated, he'd been wonderful to be around. He'd had a great sense of humor and a quiet strength that had always given her comfort.

"What's the big deal?" Liam asked, his tone amicable, but his eyes narrowed. "So we killed a few bugs for an old lady. It beat the shit out of having to sit in her smelly living room and listen to her Andy Williams records."

"I'm not makin' a big deal out of it," Bella said as she continued to pet the puppy. "It just doesn't sound like something I'd let my kids do."

"Let's just drop it," Kiera suggested. She'd seen her brother lose his temper more times than she could count. With the way he glared at Bella, and tensed his shoulders and jaw, she worried he'd explode on his fiancée. And over what? Their short stint as exterminators?

"Sure." He nodded and turned toward the grill. After he lit the burners, he glanced over his shoulder at Bella. "Don't ever say anything about our parents again."

Bella held his gaze. "Sure, hon," she replied, her tone cautious.

"At least they weren't white trash like yours," he continued.

"Liam, enough." Kiera stood. "Don't be a jerk."

He closed the grill's lid, then faced her. The anger in his eyes faded to regret. He looked to Bella. "I'm sorry. I didn't mean what I said. You lost your parents, too, and had no one." After taking Kiera's hand, he gave Bella a sad smile. "Thank God I had my sister with me."

Kiera's throat tightened. Not because she was touched, but because she sometimes hated herself. Sometimes she wished he had been in the car with their parents the day it had gone over a cliff. Not because Liam's mental illness had been a burden. She loved him and wanted to help him, to see him go back to being the man he'd been before the mental break. No, she resented her brother for forcing her to keep his secrets. Secrets that ate at her, haunted her…made her want to be an only child.

He let go of her hand and went to Bella. After kneeling in front of her, he touched his fiancée's face, then her dark curly hair. "Forgive me?"

"Of course." Holding the dog, she leaned forward and kissed him. "I love you." After Liam stood, Bella said, "I'm gettin' hungry. I can smell Kiera's cheesy potatoes from out here. Why don't I get the chicken ready while the grill is warmin' up."

Ginger hopped off Bella's lap, then ran out into the yard. Bella had a nice piece of property. According to Liam, pine trees made up most of the six acres. A small pond was hidden behind those trees and sat at the back of the property. Liam had once told her that he'd explored the area often, and that those walks were good for his mental health. He'd then told her what he liked the most about the property was all the places he could hide a body. While she'd known he was joking, as the keeper of his secrets, she hadn't found the comment funny.

When the patio screen door closed, Liam stepped next to her and also looked out at the yard. "Looks like I'm going to have to put up a fence for Ginger," he said as they watched the dog run with a stick she'd just found.

"Looks like." She sighed. "Why'd you get so nasty toward Bella?"

"I didn't like what she implied about Mom and Dad. They were great parents."

She hadn't liked Bella's comment either, but it hadn't warranted Liam's reaction. "What have you told her about them?"

"I told her I inherited my crazy gene from Dad, and that Mom was a saint to put up with us." He chuckled and dropped an arm around her shoulder. "Don't worry, Big Sis, your secret is safe with me," he said, giving her a gentle squeeze before releasing her. "Tell me more about the luau?"

While she'd rather think about Harrison and how much she'd wanted to kiss him last night, she didn't like the way Liam had hinted that *she* was the one who should worry about secrets. "It was fine." She followed him to the grill. "What did you mean by *my* secret?" And where the hell had the sweet guy she was laying on the grass with gone?

He opened the grill, then turned the burners to low. "The grill's ready when you are," he called to Bella. When she shouted back that she'd be right there, he closed the lid and faced her. "If the cops find out what you know, you'll go to prison." The smile he gave her was one she hadn't seen in nearly ten years. Demented, and without humor.

Before she could process it, Bella came outside carrying a plate filled with raw chicken breasts. "Here you go," she said, setting the plate on the table next to the grill.

Liam blinked several times, then frowned. He looked from her, to Bella, then to the grill. "Where's Ginger?"

Bella shifted her gaze to the backyard. "Chompin' on a stick. I'm sure she'll be right by your side the moment she smells the chicken cookin'." She touched Liam's shoulder. "I'm headin' back in to finish up the salad. Do you need something to drink?"

"I'm good," he said, still frowning as he began placing the chicken on the grill.

Something was off with Liam.

"Let me help you," Kiera said to Bella. Once they were in the small kitchen, and Kiera was slicing the watermelon she'd brought, she tried to decide how to approach Bella. She and her future sister-in-law had discussed Liam's medical history before. Kiera had wanted Bella to understand how imperative it was that Liam take his medication and meet regularly with a therapist. Now she wanted to know if Bella was giving Liam the proper support he needed to enjoy life.

"Can I ask you something?" Bella set a bowl in front of Kiera, and began putting the cut-up watermelon inside.

"Sure," she said, wondering if Bella was just as concerned about Liam.

"First, I'm sorry about what I said. I didn't mean to sound like I thought you had bad parents."

Although Bella had irritated her earlier, she'd been around the woman enough to know she wasn't cruel or insensitive. If anything, Bella reminded her of her mom. Accepting, quiet, a little shy and very kind. "It's okay," she said, giving Bella a reassuring smile.

"It's not okay. I really upset Liam. Which brings me to my question—why won't he talk to me about your parents?"

Because he killed them.

Cash and Melanie's House, Tallahassee, Florida
Sunday, 3:43 p.m. Eastern Standard Time

"LOLA'S LOOKING FOR you." Melanie Scarlet Maddox, aka the Ice Cream Lady, set her beer aside and leaned toward Harrison. "She's called or texted me four times in the past week. And don't get me started on Vlad. The big goof has been worse than Lola."

Harrison leaned back in the patio chair and watched as Mel's husband, Cash Maddox, grilled pork chops. Their German Shepherd, Dolly, rolled toward Cash. "Did Dolly get a new set of wheels?" he asked. During his time with the Army, Cash had been an explosive ordnance disposal specialist. Dolly had served with him. When they'd been stationed in Iraq, she'd lost her legs saving Cash's life, and now rolled around in a custom-made wheelchair.

"Yes, Jude made a new chair for her and gave it to her for Christmas."

Jude Kendrick was not only a gruff giant, but Cash and Mel's partner in their car repair and repo business. He'd had little interaction with Jude while he had been working the Archer investigation with Mel, but had gotten to know the guy during the months since. Jude was solid. The same went for the other men who worked for Cash and Jude. They'd been dicks to him when they had all first met, but had grown on him. Or maybe he'd grown on them.

"You're ignoring my question," Mel continued.

"You didn't ask me a question."

She narrowed her blue eyes at him. "You're right. I didn't. But you knew exactly what I meant. So go ahead and play dumb." She shrugged and raised the beer bottle to her lips. "I'll just let Lola and Vlad know you're here in Tallahassee."

She wouldn't. When he'd first met her, she had honestly scared him a little. Mel was a gorgeous woman who knew how to use a knife in a fight, could chop a car and hide a body. Once she'd let him get to know her, and met the woman hiding beneath the sexy, badass veneer, he'd learned he could trust her as much as he trusted Vlad. The day they'd been drugged and taken to Rodney and Adeline's plantation house of horrors had been the day that he'd realized just how much Mel meant to him. He would have died trying to save her life that night, because the world would be a boring place without her in it.

"Don't believe me?" she asked when he hadn't commented, and reached across the table. "Fine. I'll just get my phone."

"If you tell anyone I'm here, then I won't tell you about my date with Liam's sister."

Her eyes widened and lit with excitement. "You found Liam? You're sure it's him?"

When he nodded, the relief on her face was the best gift he'd had in a long time. Since Mel had unknowingly set the killer free, the guilt had been weighing her down. When she and Cash had come to the Glades to spend Christmas with her daddy, her mood swings had yo-yoed several times. Cash had confided to him that there were days when she'd withdraw into herself, or he'd catch her crying. Because Mel was the type of woman who would tell depression to go fuck itself, he and Cash both agreed her issues stemmed from what had happened within the rotting walls of the House of Archer.

"Lola doesn't know?" she asked.

"Doesn't know what?" Cash set the plate of grilled chops on the patio table, and glanced from Mel—who'd looked to the concrete—to him. "Why do I feel like I just walked into a conversation that's none of my business?"

Mel met Harrison's gaze. He had no issue telling Cash about Liam. The man would die for Mel, and Cash had risked his life to save his butt. Plus, he might need Cash's help. "I think he should know."

She gave him a small appreciative smile before sliding her chair back. "Let me go grab the potato salad from the fridge. You can tell us everything while we eat."

Cash handed him a heavy-duty paper plate, then a roll of paper towels. "What's Mel talking about?"

He tore off a couple of sheets from the roll. "I found Liam."

Cash's face grew stony. "Where?"

Hell if he'd tell the man. Liam had smashed Mel's head into a heavy wooden door and left her to die in a burning house. Cash would not only die for his wife, but he'd kill for her, too. He didn't want Cash doing time for murder, and would rather see the state of Georgia give Liam a death sentence. The problem was, he had to find a way to put Liam on the authorities' radar without involving Nick or ATL.

"I'm not telling you. Mel would feed me to her daddy's gators if I let you go after Liam."

Cash sat across from him. "You're more scared of Mel than what I might do to you if you *don't* tell me?"

Harrison used his fork to place a pork chop on his plate. "And you're not worried how she'd react if you did something to me?"

Cash looked as if he was considering the outcome, then shook his head. "Nope. I know how to rock her world."

"Oh, my God," Mel gasped. "Cash Maddox, you did not just say that." Mel stepped outside, then set the bowl of potato salad on the table.

"Say what?"

"Don't you start playing dumb with me, too. I could hear everything you two were saying through the kitchen window."

Cash placed a pork chop on her plate, then did the same for himself. "Well, that *is* what you told me last night."

She grinned. "I did, didn't I?"

"We need to change the subject," Harrison said, not bothering to hide his irritation. "I'm not in the mood for the Mel and Cash porn show." The shocked look on their faces should've had him apologizing. But he honestly didn't care. Although he was concerned with how Liam's escape had continued to affect Mel, she was doing just fine. She was back in Tallahassee with her husband, back to work at the garage she and Cash owned, doing what she loved with the man she loved. Meanwhile, he'd been stuck in a swamp, alone. Dealing with the darkness, the living nightmares, the worry over losing his mind.

"I don't know what to say to that," Mel said, genuine hurt in her voice.

"I do." Cash glared at him. "Go fuck yourself."

Harrison shook his head. Cash was such a barbaric asshole. "You got it, man." He pushed his chair back and stood. "Thanks for the beer."

"You're seriously leaving?" Mel asked.

"Uh, yeah."

"You still have to tell us about Liam."

He looked at their yard. They had a nice piece of property, a swimming pool, a cool dog, rocked each other's worlds…he didn't have to do shit for them. "Some other time."

Mel stood, then gripped his arm. "What is wrong with you?"

"Nothing."

Cash put a spoonful of potato salad on his plate. "Bullshit."

Mel nodded. "What Cash said. You've been so dang weird lately. I don't know what to do with you." She tugged on his arm. "Why are you being mean?"

He couldn't look at Mel. He didn't want to see if her eyes held the same hurt that was in her voice. "I'll text you tomorrow."

Her gipped tightened. "Vlad told me he's worried about you. He said you haven't been right since you were drugged."

"Doesn't say much coming from a man who refers to himself in the third person."

"There you go again, being mean. I know you can be a little sarcastic, and I know you and Vlad have had some issues, but plain and simple—you're being a bad friend."

He finally met her gaze. The concern in her eyes lifted a layer of the darkness cloaking him. It also scared him. He didn't want to be mean, or alienate his friends. At the same time, he didn't want to go back to how he'd been before Rodney and Adeline had fed him their drug. He no longer wanted to coast through life. While he'd enjoyed working for ATL, the gig wouldn't last forever. Rodney and Adeline might have screwed with his brain, but their drug had also enlightened him. It had forced him to accept and face his dark side, the envy and resentment he hadn't realized he'd possessed. He'd come to know that he wanted more for himself. If he survived to sixty, he had no intention of living with a former Russian hitman and his alligator.

"I have episodes," he admitted.

"What do you mean?"

Harrison looked to Cash, who nodded toward the chair he'd just vacated. Mel no longer worked for ATL, and Cash had only associated with the agency because of his wife. In the months since the drugging, Harrison had talked with Mel, had visited the couple, and trusted them. Mel knew what had happened to him, had endured his humiliation right along with him, but she didn't know about the darkness. Neither did Vlad, Lola or any of the ATL team. Maybe it was time to talk, to tell the truth.

To get some help.

"I don't know what else to call them," he said, then sat back in his seat. "I don't know if I'm sleepwalking, or if I'm awake, but there've been times when I've come to standing outside Vlad's bedroom door…holding an empty gun or a knife."

Cash set his fork on the paper plate, then pushed his chair

back. "I know guys with PTSD who've had blackouts." He lifted the lid of the cooler they kept outside, then pulled out three beers. "What happened at the plantation house was traumatic."

Anger settled over Harrison, dragging the darkness with it. He glanced to Mel, who shook her head slightly. The imploring look in her eyes told him she had kept what happened to him between them.

"I've researched the disorder," he said, the anger fading quickly. "It's possible, but I think it's the drug they gave me. I think it damaged me." He opened the beer Cash set in front of him. "I feel like Jekyll and Hyde. I'm fine, then I'm not. I feel like the drug tapped into a dormant side of me, the side that doesn't give a shit about anything or anyone."

"Do you feel that way now?" Mel asked. "Answer honestly."

He held her gaze. Mel wanted an honest answer, and she deserved it. "I have no problem walking out of here now and dealing with this shit on my own. I don't need you, or ATL." He lifted the bottle to his lips. "But I like you guys, so I'd rather stay."

"You're being an ass," Cash said.

"I know."

"For whatever it's worth, I don't mind. Just watch what you say to my wife and we'll be good."

"I'm so glad my husband is *good* with my best friend quite possibly being a psychopath." Glaring at Harrison, Mel scooped potato salad and slopped it on his plate. "I'm even happier to know that you like me enough to allow me to help you deal with your *shit*." She gave herself a dollop of the salad, then pushed the bowl to the center of the table and smiled. "Well, this is turning into a fine dinner."

After taking a long drink, Harrison set the beer on the table. "You consider me your best friend?" he asked, guilt creeping into his chest.

Tears misted in her eyes. "Of course. Why do you think I was upset when I found out you were in Tallahassee and didn't bother to call me? You didn't have to stay at a hotel. We have plenty of room here."

"I needed time."

"For what? To deal with this Jekyll and Hyde thing on your own?" She shook her head and sliced into her pork chop. "You know, I thought Vlad was just bein' his goofy self when he called complaining that 'Harry not Harry', but now I see what he meant."

"I didn't say I wasn't still me," Harrison said, growing defensive as he dug into his meal.

"Right." Cash pointed his fork at him. "He's Harrison on steroids. What are you benching?"

"I'm not taking steroids."

"Didn't say you were. All I'm saying is that you're you, just bigger and badder." He forked a slice of meat. "Almost makes your pompous name cool."

Harrison laughed. His name had been a running joke between Cash and the guys he worked with at the garage. "And you think I'm the ass."

"I'm glad the two of you are having fun," Mel said.

"Come on, baby." Cash leaned over and rubbed her arm. "I'm just trying to lighten it up a little." He looked to Harrison. "But seriously, man. Why were you staying at a hotel? And don't give us the needing time crap."

After another bite and a sip of beer, he finally said, "Because I screwed up, and I was trying to figure out a way to fix what I did."

Mel pushed her plate aside. "What did you do?"

"You can't tell anyone. Not Lola, or even Ryan or Shane." Mel had grown up with Ryan and Shane Monahan, and was still tight with the brothers. If she talked about this with either of them, he knew it'd get back to Lola.

"I know how to keep a secret," Mel said.

This he also knew, and he respected her for keeping his. Because he trusted her and Cash, he was here, on the verge of telling them the mess he'd made and how he planned to fix it. "Even though Rodney and Adeline's drug was out of my system within forty-eight hours, I still kept having the same symptoms—dark thoughts, bouts with so much frickin' rage I'd lock myself in my room. When the episodes started happening, I knew it had to be the drug. I've never had issues with headaches, but I get them all the time now, and they're usually connected to my dark times." He reached for his beer. "I don't know what else to call those times when I disconnect from my regular self and turn into a total prick."

"Did you see a doctor?" Mel asked.

"No doctors. No more needles. No trying to explore my head and see what's going on in there. Rodney and Adeline did enough of that."

The sympathy in her eyes irritated him. She'd been victimized, too. Fortunately, they hadn't given her as much of their poison.

"When Rodney's case was closed, I decided to find Liam. I needed to know if Rodney and Adeline had succeeded."

Mel dragged in a breath. "You want to know if you'll turn in-to a monster."

He nodded. "So I conducted my own investigation," he said, then explained how he'd theorized where Liam could have gone after escaping the plantation house. "I think he walked through the night, until he ended up at a house I found deep in the woods. The place was miles from a main road, even the dirt one was difficult to get to." He looked to Cash's empty plate, then to Mel's half-eaten meal. "Are you finished eating?" When they both nodded, he opened his cell phone to PHOTOGRAPHY, pulling up the pictures he'd taken at the dead couple's house. "This is what he did." He handed Mel the phone. "I think coyotes got into the house and disposed of the bodies. All but a femur and two skulls."

Cash stood and moved behind Melanie, who held the phone so they both could view the photos. "When were you there?" he asked.

"Two weeks ago."

"And no one else knows about this?"

"No," Harrison said, then told them about finding and lifting the fingerprint. "This is where I screwed up. I should've taken the jar with me."

Cash sat back down. "Why?"

"When I left the house, I went straight to the hotel, then uploaded the print into IAFIS—you know, Integrated Automated Fingerprint Identification System."

"We know. We watch Forensic Files, and I used to be a secret agent," Mel said with a half-smile as she handed him back his phone. "Because I'm familiar with IAFIS, I also know you have to be in law enforcement to access the database."

"Right."

"And you're not in law enforcement."

"Right again."

"You didn't hack into the system, did you?"

"God, no. I did it legitimately...with a stolen ID."

Cash chuckled, while Mel rolled her eyes. "Not so legit, man," he said. "Who's ID?"

"Nick Wagner's."

"You didn't." Mel leaned back in the chair and rubbed her forehead. "That's really, really bad."

"Who's Nick Wagner?" Cash asked. Once Mel had explained about the detective, Cash looked at him. "Now I see where you messed up."

"If I made a call, investigators would find the print, see that someone had already tried lifting it once, then see that Nick Wagner had uploaded that same fingerprint into IAFIS."

Mel pushed her blonde bangs aside. "Nick would be questioned, and whoever questions him could discover his activities with ATL." She blew out a stream of air. "Yeah, you messed up. But we can fix this. Let's go back to the house and get the jar."

"Once I found out the fingerprint belonged to Liam Forrester, I did go back. Liam's a paranoid schizophrenic. He's had no criminal history, but was in the system because he'd been institutionalized after a psychotic break. I figured how the drug affected him might not be the same as how it affected me."

"He told me Rodney fixed him," Mel began, "and that all the voices were gone, but hers."

"Right, Adeline's. And that's one crazy bitch you don't want in your head."

"Wait." Cash held up a hand. "How is having only Adeline's voice in his head any different from how he was before they kidnapped and drugged him?"

"I don't think it's any different at all. I think Liam is probably just as schizophrenic. If anything, I think they made him worse. None of the records I found indicated that Liam was violent."

"He about put my head through the door before snapping a man's neck. Now he's killed two people." Mel looked out into the yard. "I wonder if he used my knife on them."

Anger flashed in Cash's eyes. "Don't start. You didn't kill those people. Based on those pictures, Liam would've probably killed them with whatever he could find."

She cleared her throat, then smiled at her husband. "I know. I just can't help feeling sad and guilty about it." She turned to Harrison. "But I'll feel good once he's in prison."

"Yeah, about that. Two days after I found out everything I could about Liam, I went back to get the jar. Someone burned the place."

Concern lit Mel's eyes. "What?"

"Liam knows." Cash glared at him. "He's following you. And you could lead him here, to Mel."

Cash was such an alarmist. "Take it easy. Liam didn't burn down the house. I know for a fact he was either working or at home, because *I* was following *him*."

"The entire time?"

"No. But according to the Thomasville investigators report I found, the fire was in full blaze at around five in the evening— when Liam was working a shift at The Home Zone."

Mel's face contorted in disbelief. "The house sat intact for over five months. You go there and two days later, it catches fire? That's awfully coincidental."

"I agree. But I still don't think my being there has anything to do with the fire which, by the way, investigators have ruled as arson. When I was there, I saw a couple of generators that looked homebuilt. There were also about a dozen five-gallon cans of diesel, and a ton of logs piled along the back of the house. The report I found said an accelerant was used throughout the house and along the logs. And, surprise, the diesel cans were empty."

"And you still don't think the fire has anything to do with you being at that house?" Cash rubbed Dolly's head when she rolled next to him. "Face it, man. Someone knows about you."

"Did you hear about the woman they found at the rest area last night?" he asked.

"Yeah," Mel said. "They found her in the backseat of her car."

"How about the woman who was murdered at the Morrison Apartments?" The guilt over his mistakes made his head hurt. "If I had called the authorities the moment I confirmed the fingerprint belonged to Liam, they'd be alive."

"You think Liam killed those women?" Mel asked as she reached for her cell phone.

"I do. I think there might be another. A woman was killed in Juniper Park about a month ago."

Mel stared at her phone's screen. "No name or picture of the woman from the rest area, but...wow." She met his gaze, as she handed the phone to Cash. "The other two have dark curly hair. Just like Adeline."

"That doesn't mean anything." Cash slid the phone toward her. "And how do you know what the woman they found yesterday looks like? Or that the murders are related? The police haven't even implied as much."

"Because I can get into just about any system I want." He wasn't being arrogant, just telling the truth. "I know the detectives assigned to the first two murders, and I know that they're joining up with the detective working the rest area case."

"You used Nick's ID, didn't you?" Mel asked with disappointment.

"No way." Harrison learned his lesson the hard way, and now had to deal with the dark cloud of death hanging over him. "That was all me." He turned his attention to Cash. "And what I know is that this last woman also had dark curly hair."

"Were they all killed the same?" Mel asked. "It didn't say in either article I found."

"No. All three were killed differently, but the last two were found in their cars." He held up a hand before she spoke again. "I know, not much of a connection. But here's why I think it was Liam…the police found evidence that the bodies were washed."

Cash shrugged. "So?"

"The victim from Morrison Apartments… One of the detectives noted that her clothes and the seat of her car were saturated when she was found—six hours from the estimated time of death. Suggesting that the killer came back to clean up his mess."

"Or that he has someone doing it for him." Cash ran a hand over his short hair. "That's a stretch."

"How else can you explain the fire? According to the Thomasville local paper, Delford and Dottie Dougal had lived like recluses for more than thirty years. The only time they came to town was for an occasional supply run or a doctor's appointment. It wasn't unusual to not see them for months, so I get why no one checked on them. But who would know about them besides locals?" Frustrated because he knew by the looks on Mel and Cash's faces they thought his theory was shit, he pushed back the chair and stood. "Another drifter besides Liam? I hiked through miles of those woods. Guess how many people I ran into? None."

"I get where you're coming from, honey," Mel said, motioning for him to sit back down. "You have proof Liam killed the couple. Call the detectives. Show them the pictures you took and the fingerprint. You have evidence of a crime scene at your disposal. Give it to them and tell them about Rodney and Adeline."

Mel had lost her mind. "You do realize how many laws I've broken, right? And let's not forget that there's no evidence that Liam was ever at the plantation house with us. They're not going to believe me."

"Ask Nick for help."

"So I can expose ATL. We've been over this." The ache in his head grew worse. "Let's just forget I told you guys about this."

"It's kind of hard to forget," Cash said. "And how are you going to feel if another woman dies? 'Cause, buddy, that'll be on your head. You know that, right?"

"Cash, don't," Mel said in a censuring tone.

"It's the truth. You've been beating yourself up for setting Liam free. Now we can turn him over to the police. Even if there's no proof he killed the three Tallahassee women, he'll go down for the old couple."

"I'm not ready to go to the police," Harrison said, his temper rising, his head throbbing, his thoughts darkening. Cash was a dumbass. If it wasn't for Mel, he'd tell the man to shut the fuck up and stay out of his business. "And if he goes to prison now, we may never be able to prove he has someone helping him, or give justice to those three women. Have you thought about that?" He grabbed his phone and keys off the table. "I'm going home."

"Harrison, wait." Mel quickly stood and blocked him. "I get where you're coming from, and I agree with you." She looked over her shoulder at Cash. "Sorry, but he's right about those three women. Now that I think about it, the pictures you have, the fingerprint…it might not be enough to prove Liam was the one who killed the couple."

"Okay." Cash nodded. "I guess I can see your point."

The same point he'd just made, but whatever.

"So, you're the man with plan," Cash said. "Let's hear it."

He didn't need Mel or Cash's help. Not really. He'd thought maybe Cash and his boys from the garage could help with keeping an eye on Liam, but wasn't ready to bring that up yet. Cash would need that to be *his* idea. For now, he'd stick with his original plan, and the one he'd already set in motion.

"I'm going to date Liam's sister."

CHAPTER 5

Five days later…
Lake Talquin State Forest, Tallahassee, Florida
Friday, 11:33 a.m. Eastern Standard Time

"THE LAKE IS beautiful," Kiera said, a catch to her breath as she stopped at the top of the hill. "This was such a great idea. Thank you for thinking of it."

Harrison stared at her profile. The pretty smile crossing her face was beautiful. The lake? If he hadn't had to walk a couple of miles over sand hills, through swamps and the forest, he'd have a different opinion. The outdoors wasn't his thing. He'd grown up in the city. Camping was something you did in a cabin. He might own a trailer back in Everglades City, but it had the same amenities as a regular house. And hiking? Well, it wasn't that bad. He did like being active, but mostly he liked letting Kiera take the lead on the trail and staring at her rear.

He was going to burn in hell.

Kiera was nice, sweet, funny, and everything he could want in a woman. If her brother wasn't a serial killer, she'd be perfect. Too perfect for him, of course.

He moved next to her. A lock of her auburn hair had escaped from her ponytail. He tucked it behind her ear, then trailed his finger down her arm and took her hand. "Thanks for exploring it with me."

She turned her head and looked up at him. The acute interest in her eyes sent his heart racing. Her sexy smile had his brain telling his body, "No." They'd had their first date Tuesday, and since then they had met every morning for a run, and every evening for either dinner or a couple of drinks. He'd kissed her—nothing major, and definitely no tongue. But, damn, if those sweet kisses weren't almost as good as sex. It had been so long since he'd been with a woman, he supposed any physical contact would, as Cash liked to say, *rock his world.*

But he couldn't *be* with this woman. He wasn't that much of a jerk. He was using her to get to her brother, not for sex. Plus, he wasn't sure how he'd react if he discovered that Kiera had been covering up for her brother.

"There are a lot of things I'd like to explore with you," she said, and keeping her gaze locked on his, rose to her tiptoes, then kissed him like they'd been kissing throughout the week. Not a quick peck, yet nothing long and lingering. The press of her soft lips against his was becoming familiar, necessary. Since he'd never had a girlfriend, or dated much, he sometimes felt like a virgin around Kiera. He knew what to do, knew what he liked and how to please a woman, but being with her without being with her was a level of intimacy he didn't know how to handle.

"More swamps?" he asked with a grin.

"This Colorado girl could do without that. The beach would be nice. I've only been once since I moved here."

Kiera didn't seem like the bikini type. While she had the body for one, and she was outgoing and confident, he'd noticed her shy side, especially when it came to her body. She covered up her sexy curves with too many layers of clothes, hid her large breasts by wearing loose tops. Even her kisses were shy. Shy and so fucking sweet. He wanted to devour her. Force her to reveal the uninhibited wanton existing beneath the good-girl façade.

She glanced back to the lake. "Unless you're not into the beach."

He closed his eyes for a brief moment. When he was around Kiera, the darkness never crept in, and neither did the anger. He also hadn't had a headache since Sunday afternoon when he'd been at Mel and Cash's. He didn't know what that meant. But he did know for certain that the times he'd spent with her, even if he was with her for the wrong reasons, have been the best days of his life. The dark desires rushing through him now had nothing to do with the damage the drug had done to his brain, and everything to do with Kiera. He wanted her. Badly.

"I'm sorry, I didn't mean to put you on the spot with the exploring comment," she continued, her tone rushed, agitated. "I'm not trying to make more out of our...us. Let's just forget I said anything and hike back."

When she started to pull her hand from his, he held her still. "You didn't put me on the spot. I love the beach." She kept her eyes averted. He bent to meet her gaze. "What are you doing?" he asked.

"I'm showing you that I'm feeling a little insecure."

He grinned at her honesty. "Because I didn't say anything right away?"

"Ah, yeah." She nodded. "In a roundabout way I was trying to tell you I like being with you and your reaction, or lack thereof, showed me you're not as certain. It's not a big deal. We just met."

"If it wasn't a big deal, you wouldn't be upset."

She turned and faced him. "You're right."

"I am?"

"I just said I like you."

He held both of her hands and inched closer. If he leaned in slightly, her breasts would touch his chest. "I like you, too. I didn't answer your question about the beach right away because I was trying to decide if you'd wear a bikini or something else. That had me thinking other thoughts, and about other things we could explore."

Her pupils dilated, her gray eyes darkening to slate. As she shifted her gaze to his mouth, her lips parted. They were tempting, and he was a fool to think he could feel nothing for this woman. He'd had sex with willing partners. Consensual, no-strings, vanilla sex. There'd never been an, *I love you*, or even an, *I like you*, exchanged. Beyond a friend, no woman had ever said those words to him. He hadn't realized how much he wanted to hear that he was liked, loved, that someone other than a gator-loving Russian and a knife-wielding ice cream lady cared about him.

Knowing he shouldn't, he touched her cheek. He wanted to touch her, to hold her, to pretend he was the Harrison Fairclough he'd introduced to Kiera. The man who had his life together. The entrepreneur who made a good legit salary, who knew how to treat a lady, and who didn't lie or steal.

"Since you're not saying anything," he began, growing bolder, moving closer until her breasts pressed against his chest. "I must've put you on the spot."

The corners of her mouth turned up in a smile as she leaned her head toward his. "I didn't respond because I was too busy picturing exploring." She brushed her lips along his. "But maybe you meant exploring the city or the local library, and I need to hose off my dirty imagination."

Just hearing the word 'dirty' coming out of her mouth had his mind spinning, imagining her naked, pinned beneath him on his bed. Despite being aroused by her, he chuckled, and took a step back before he kissed her the way he wanted. They were in the woods, where anyone could come along. And after hiking all morning, he could use a shower. "You should probably keep the hose shut off. I believe the state of Florida has a rule about water conservation."

"Good idea." She grinned and, still holding his hand, started for the hiking trail. They slipped into the easy conversation they were having before their stop at the lake. Nothing too personal, but more of the 'getting to know you' talk, which was still new for him.

After spending the past three days listening to her talk about her life in Colorado, her job, hobbies, likes and dislikes—all of which he'd been aware of from the research he'd done prior to meeting with her—it made sense why being around her had become familiar, comfortable. She had yet to talk about her brother, other than to say he was engaged and worked at The

Home Zone. Harrison hadn't pressed the subject, either. Maybe because he selfishly wanted to keep pretending they were a normal man and woman, embarking on the beginnings of a relationship. Except every night after hanging out with her, he'd gone back to his apartment to research Liam and what the detectives knew, which wasn't much at this point. And once he'd shut off his laptop for the night, he'd crawl into bed and go back to pretending. Pretending the life he'd created in Tallahassee was real. That the apartment was just a stepping stone until he was ready to build or buy a house, that he was in the market for a wife.

After they'd finished hiking the five-mile trail, he drove them back to their apartment complex. Because he knew what she liked, he kept his Jeep Wrangler's top down and the radio tuned to a country station. He'd never been a fan of country music. Actually, he'd hated it. But he'd told Kiera he loved country, so he'd been forcing himself to listen to various bands and artists. The music was growing on him, and he sometimes caught himself humming a random song. Between the music and the wind, they fell into a companionable silence.

When he glanced over, he caught her mouthing the words to the song on the radio. She looked cute and easy-going, so relaxed and happy. Because she was with him? Because they'd had a great morning together? Wanting to believe it was real, he reached over and took her hand. She looked at him and smiled, then belted out the chorus of the song. He attempted to join in, screwing up the words and having a good time doing it.

When they reached the Club, he wished he had a reason to stall, to keep her with him for a little while longer. He didn't want to go back to pretending, to remembering why he was with her in the first place, or the consequences once she found out the truth.

In the end, she would know everything. Or would she? Why would she have to know he would be the one behind her brother eventually going to prison? Why couldn't he continue the lie?

Because she deserves better.

She did. In the end, walking away would be the right thing to do. He'd like to exit her life without her knowing the truth, but if she found out about him and his lies, he would deserve her disgust and hatred. With that last thought in mind, he parked the Jeep, then killed the engine. After he climbed out, he pulled her pack from the back, then walked with her to her apartment.

"Do you want to come in for lunch?" she asked as they entered the building.

"I thought you had to work later."

She opened the door to her ground floor apartment. He didn't like that she was on the lower level. The security at the Club was good, but if someone was determined enough to get inside her place, they could.

"No, I have a mandatory meeting. Of course they'd hold it on a day I'm not working." She stepped inside, leaving the door open for him to follow. Her apartment mirrored his, only his was on the second floor and he had a balcony that faced the lake. "I don't have to be there until three." She set her keys on the kitchen counter, then turned and opened the refrigerator. "I have lunchmeat," she said, then looked over her shoulder and wagged her brows. "And Doritos."

He laughed and set her pack on the floor. "Now I really know you like me." During their first date he'd discovered her addiction to Doritos. She'd even admitted to having dozens of recipes which included the tortilla chip. What had been awesome about that moment was he hadn't known that little quirk about her from his research. And each day he'd learned new things about her. Dark water and basements scared her. She believed in psychics and ghosts. She was right handed, but swung a bat and golf club with her left. Little things that never came up during his search into her background. Little things that had him looking at her as more than a killer's sister, or a means to an end.

"I don't share my Doritos with just anyone," she said, opening the pantry and revealing several bags, spicy nacho and cool ranch. "But if you don't eat any, I won't."

"Why's that?"

She pulled a bag out and opened it as she approached him. "If you have to ask, then you've never kissed anyone after they've eaten Doritos," she said, circling the bag in front of him. "Smell the goodness."

Chuckling, he snatched the bag from her, then held it behind his back with one arm, and pulled her to him with the other. "I don't want Dorito kisses."

"Should I ask what kind of kisses you'd prefer?" she asked, twining her arms around his neck.

He was in over his head, and had no idea what the hell he was doing. Leading her on, leading himself on? "Probably not," he said anyway, and pressed his hand against the small of her back. Whatever he was doing felt good, and right. She fit perfectly against him.

"I'm kind of curious." She ran the tips of her finger along the base of his neck, the subtle touch giving him goose bumps. "You seem to like to kiss. You've kissed me every night since our first date."

"It's only been a few days since our first date," he reminded her, while remembering each and every one of those kisses.

"Multiple times during our dates," she continued as if he hadn't spoken. "They've been sweet kisses."

"Only sweet?"

She shifted her gaze to his lips before meeting his eyes again. "Sexy."

"That's more like it."

"Tame."

"I've been a gentleman."

"And if you weren't?"

He dropped the Doritos behind him, then gripped her ponytail and gently tugged until his lips brushed her ear. "You'd be naked, and my mouth would be on every inch of your body." He pressed an open-mouthed kiss along her neck and below her ear. "Would you like more detail?"

When she nodded, he ran his hand from the small of her back

down over her rear. "I want to taste you." He rocked her along his thigh. "I want to kiss you while you're moaning. I want to wake up in the morning and smell you on my skin. Then I want to kiss you all over again." He dragged his mouth along her jaw until he reached her lips. "I want to slide my tongue over yours," he murmured. "I want to show you how much I want you, but I'm afraid it'll be too much for you to handle."

"Sounds like you're challenging me," she said, a slight hitch to her breath when he pressed her against his thigh.

"Just telling you the truth," he replied, for once being honest.

"I love honesty." She jabbed an imaginary knife in his chest. "So I'll be honest. I want everything you want. I'm just not ready yet."

He held her still against him. "I would never push you into something you weren't ready for."

She slid her hand from his neck to his jaw and gave a smile that melted his insides. "I know. I really like you, Harrison. Because I do, I'd like to take things, physical things, slowly."

"I'll take things at whatever pace you need," he said, meaning it. He shouldn't be messing around with Kiera anyway. Even though stripping her naked and fucking her against the wall was at the forefront of his mind, she was right to be cautious, and was doing them both a favor. Sex would only lead to more guilt.

"Would it be selfish of me to still want a kiss?" she asked, while brushing the pad of her thumb along his lower lip.

"Not at all." He rubbed his hand along her spine until he cupped the back of her neck. "Kiss me at your pace."

That shy smile returning, she tilted her head slightly. She rubbed his lower lip again, then keeping her eyes on his, kissed him. Once. Twice. Then she closed her eyes and licked his lower lip. He opened for her, sighed when her mouth covered his. God, it'd been so damned long since he'd *really* kissed a woman. The puff of her warm breath against his skin, the touch of her tongue against his, tentative, sensual…he wanted her to stop. Not because she was too good for him, but because this, her kiss, her sweet goodness, would become a faded bitch of memory.

He welcomed the darkness, a reason to escape. But it just wasn't there. Not when he was with Kiera.

She kissed the corner of his mouth and looked up at him, her gaze searching his. "Kiss me back." Leaning forward, brushing her lips along his, she murmured, "Kiss me."

He opened his mouth and captured her lips. Slowly glided his tongue along hers and brought their bodies completely flush. Kissed her deeply, kept his urgency, his desire, under control. He ached to hold her as the man he could've been, if he'd been given the right opportunities. But he wasn't that man, and she deserved better.

With regret, he ended the kiss and pressed his forehead against hers. "I need to go."

"So no lunch or Doritos?"

He forced a smile, and pushed the hair that had fallen from her ponytail away from her cheeks. "Another day." When he stepped away, he glanced to the bag of chips on the floor, and the few that had escaped.

"Don't worry about them. I'll clean it up."

Not knowing what to say, he walked to the door. "I'll call you."

She held his gaze. The disbelief in her eyes cutting him to the core. "Sure."

"Why don't you believe me?"

"Who said I didn't?"

"The way you're reacting right now."

She walked toward him, then stopped a few inches away. "Does knowing I won't have sex with you today, or anytime in the near future, bother you?"

He took her hand and brought them closer. "I want to have sex, but that doesn't mean I don't want to keep seeing you."

She pulled her hand away. "Then next time kiss me like you mean it."

In an instant, he had her pinned against the door, her breasts against his chest, his mouth against her ear. "Being with you has been the best thing that's happened to me in more years than I can count. I don't want to mess it up." He gently nipped her earlobe. "You're so special," he said, meaning it. Maybe he shouldn't give a shit that her brother was a killer. Maybe he should ignore it and find happiness with this woman. She liked him. Maybe she could eventually love him. Or maybe he was just a pathetic fool.

He eased back. When he saw the tears misting in her eyes, that imaginary knife in his chest twisted. "I'm going to go home and take a shower. If you're free later, I'd love to take you out, or do whatever you want." He dragged in a deep breath. "Why do you look like you're going to cry?"

"I've never been special." She pressed her hand along her nose, sniffed and looked away. "I, ah, don't really want to go out to-night."

He'd gone and screwed it up anyway. With disappointment settling over him, he nodded. "I understand."

She looked at him. "I meant, I wouldn't mind hanging out here...with you. We could watch a movie. Or—"

He kissed her. Not the way he truly wanted, but hopefully enough to let her know that she *was* special, and that he wasn't with her for sex. "What time should I come over?"

"I'll text you after my meeting."

As he was about to leave, he turned. In two strides he stood in front of her, cupped her head, knocking her loose ponytail free. "I meant what I said. Your pace. I think we could have something, so unless you tell me to get lost, I'm not going anywhere."

She rested her hands on his chest and searched his eyes. "I think we do have something."

Unable to resist her lips, he kissed her. "I'm looking forward to later."

They said their goodbyes, then he headed for his apartment. He could have severed his relationship with Kiera today. The opportunity was there. After spending most of the week with her, he'd realized that going through the sister to get to the brother would take more time than he'd planned. Honestly, he didn't need Kiera. He had his computer, access to what the Tallahassee detectives knew, and, if he approached Cash the right way, maybe he could use the guys from the garage to help monitor Liam's movements.

So why hadn't he just ended it? Why tell her he wasn't going anywhere when he knew he would? When he knew he'd leave?

He entered his empty apartment, thought about his empty trailer, his empty life, then slumped on the couch. Because Kiera truly was special. And when he was around her, there was never any darkness.

Wilkes Street, Tallahassee, Florida
Friday, 2:13 p.m. Eastern Standard Time

WHY THE HELL wasn't she answering the phone?

"Because your sister doesn't give a shit about you," Adeline whispered. *"She's too busy with her new boyfriend and job to care about your problems. Your hunger."*

He set his cell phone on the passenger seat of his SUV. His manager should have never called him in to do deliveries. If he hadn't, Liam would have never met the woman. It didn't matter that he couldn't remember her name. All that mattered was what she looked like. *Who* she represented.

"Oh, dear, lover. You're starting to give me a complex."

He glanced in the rear view mirror. "Are you just now seeing a pattern?"

"I am. Do you think the police are?"

"I don't see them knocking on my door."

"Yet."

He ignored her and stared at the woman's yard as he drove past it. Now that he thought about it, her last name began with a T. Tor-something.

"Liam, you're not listening. You can't take, not from this woman."

He half-laughed. "This coming from someone who's always hungry. 'Feed me. Feed me, Seymour,'" he begged, imitating the plant from *Little Shop of Horrors*.

"Seymour? Lover, I think you might need to take some time off."

"Shut up, Adeline. It's from a movie. I'm not sure if you're aware, but there are more entertaining things to watch besides beheadings and bloody massacres." Before images of the videos Adeline and Rodney had forced him to view took root in his head, the woman, Tor-something stepped out of her house, a kid in tow. He didn't remember there being a child at the house earlier.

"I wouldn't make fun of me."

The warning tone in Adeline's voice had him looking in the mirror. Today, she wore her hair down. Her dark curls framed her face. When she'd been alive, he'd never touched them, but had felt them along his stomach when she had taken him in her mouth. He'd love to feel those curls run through his fingers now. Yank them from her pretty head until her scalp bled.

"I know what I'm talking about. I didn't get away with murder for being stupid and…predictable."

He stopped at the four-corner intersection, then turned right. "I'm not stupid."

"But you're predictable. Think outside the box, lover. Didn't you notice the neighbor just next door?"

The blonde. She'd come outside while he'd been helping Larry deliver Mrs. Tor-something's new stainless steel refrigerator.

"All great innovators think outside the box. And no one would call you predictable if you took from her."

"I don't know. It's so soon after the last woman." Too soon. He'd killed the motel woman just six days ago, the apartment woman a week before that, and the woman in the park a month earlier. He didn't want this to become a weekly habit.

"Slow down. There she is, in the backyard."

He brought the SUV to a crawl, and pulled along the curb. The houses on this street were mostly two to four unit rentals, with limited parking. He'd been through this area before during past delivery rounds and was familiar with it. Between the university and the nearby hospital, the people who lived on this particular street were transient, moving in and out of the various duplex and quadplex buildings. The Tor-something lady's neighborhood was different, more suburban.

He parked the car, and looked between the lots to the blonde's backyard, at the short, white picket fence that wouldn't be able to keep a large dog in, or him out. A little puff of fur bounced near the blonde as she began plucking a few weeds from the nearby flowerbed. Between the little dog and little fence, the woman looked vulnerable, easy to take.

"Think outside of the box, Liam. Don't be predictable."

He swallowed hard. Killing was becoming too easy. Once he fed the bitch, she demanded more. When would it be enough? When would it stop?

"Feed me. Give us what we both want."

"This isn't what I want," he said, hatred churning low in his stomach.

"Then why do you crave it, too? Why does the hunger twist your gut, make it feel as if it's eating itself?"

He sucked a breath in through his nose. He'd been asking himself that from the moment he'd killed the Dougals, and was convinced it had to be due to the drug they'd fed him. When he'd first met Bella, it had been almost two months after he'd killed the old couple. Adeline had pushed him to take Bella. He'd fought the hungry bitch, and had been certain he'd lose. Because he *had* craved the rush, the power. But the moment Bella had invited him into her home, a calm had settled over him. She looked so much like Adeline, yet she was the polar opposite. For several months, he'd been able to keep Adeline under control, keep his and Bella's time with the ropes limited. But just shortly after Kiera had moved here, Adeline had grown restless, had threatened Bella, threatened Kiera, nagged him to give her what she'd wanted until he'd finally caved.

Adeline's laughter filled his head. *"Don't you dare place all the blame me. Why do you sometimes lie awake at night staring at your* precious *Bella, picturing a chain choking her neck, blood dripping from her nose and mouth? Why, Liam?"* She scoffed. *"You need to kill, to feed off the vulnerable, eat their fear, possess their terror, fill your belly with their souls, and your mind with power and knowledge. We both know there's nothing more powerful than taking a life. When you fantasize about killing Bella, then resist, do you feel that power? That knowledge that you could snap her neck at any given moment? Maybe you should drive away, then go home to your precious Bella. Kill her, Liam. Show her your power."*

He grabbed the gold and garnet Florida State University baseball cap Bella had given him for Christmas, then slammed it on his head, tugging the bill low. Wearing jeans and a gray T-shirt with the FSU logo, he could be anyone. A fan, a student…a killer. After checking for traffic, he opened the door and exited the SUV.

"Where are you going, lover?"

Shut up, he told her, while trying desperately to block images of his hands around Bella's slender throat. He loved her. She would be his wife, and give him the chance at a normal life. He couldn't let Adeline get to him, push him into doing something he would forever regret. He needed to keep the hungry bitch at bay, and only knew one way how.

"She's going inside."

I know.

"Make sure no one is watching you."

He glanced to the backyards neighboring the blonde. The Tor-something woman had a six-foot privacy fence. The blonde's other neighbor had created a natural fence with tall hedges. Neither of the two quadplexes to his right had garages, and there were no cars parked beneath the carports, same went for the duplex to his left. Was it possible the residents of those buildings didn't own cars, or they'd parked in the street? Absolutely. The windows of the building immediately behind the blonde's house were closed, and he could hear the faint hum of a window unit air conditioner coming from the duplex. Without knowing if anyone was home, he considered coming back when it was dark.

"No, feed me now," Adeline shouted as if she were a bratty three-year-old demanding a toy.

You need to shut the fuck up. He leaned against the brick building and behind a tall, flowering bush. His head hurt. Her shouts, her constant nagging, was like having nails hammered into his skull.

"No, lover. Now you listen to me. You have to do this now. You have to kill her. You can't come back here. If you do, you'll have to lie to Bella and make up an excuse for leaving. You don't want Bella questioning you."

He didn't. He didn't want to be trapped in a lie, or for her to ever know the truth. That she was sleeping with a monster.

"You have forty minutes before you need to be at the store to work your regular shift. You won't be off work until eight-thirty. By that time, the people living here could be home. If the blonde has a boyfriend or husband, he could be at the house. Now is the only time, Liam. Kill her."

He pushed off the brick wall, and rounded the bush, stared into the blonde's backyard.

"Kill, kill, kill," Adeline goaded him, her voice, now shrill and provoking. As she repeated the word, she filled his head with suggestive images…the blonde's eyes bulging as she gasped for air, blood seeping from her stomach like water coming out of a crack in a dam.

He couldn't go to work with blood on him, and wouldn't risk taking the time to clean himself at the woman's house. When he reached the Tor-something woman's privacy fence, he hid behind it, then edged slightly to view the blonde's yard one last time. Still empty.

With anticipation knotting his stomach, and the prospect of the kill heightening his excitement, he hopped the fence, and ran across the yard. When he reached the covered patio, he realized the blonde hadn't closed the glass patio door leaving only a flimsy screen slider as a barrier.

Adeline groaned, the sultry sound sent a chill down his spine and made him hard. *"Yes,"* she hissed. *"Take from her."*

I will not violate her. He pressed on his thickening penis. He wouldn't deny being sexually aroused by thoughts of killing the woman, but he refused to rape her. That was Adeline's MO, not his. Unlike Adeline, he didn't need to rape to feel powerful. The snap of a neck, the release of a final breath, the last beat of a heart—all because *he* had made it so—was the embodiment of power.

Ready for that power, he slid open the screen door. It barely whispered as it moved along the tracks. Good. The little dog might be a yapper, and he didn't want to alert the blonde. The surprised look on their faces, the shock widening their eyes—that was one of his favorite parts.

"Mine, too," Adeline said, her tone breathless. *"Oh, yes, mine, too. You have to make this time last, lover. Drag it out, make me come."*

He'd love nothing more than to take his time, but he wouldn't give Adeline the satisfaction. On this, he most certainly held the power. While a quick kill left him dissatisfied, as if he was chasing an orgasm, or on the brink of one only to be drenched with cold water, it was necessary. He controlled how, who and when he fed the bitch.

He stepped into the kitchen. Unlike the Tor-something woman, the blonde's kitchen was a flashback to the early nineties, and the white appliances looked to be just as old. Other than the hum of the dishwasher, the house was quiet. He left the kitchen, stopped in the living room, which the blonde had tried to modernize with updated furniture and paint, but there was no denying the ugly sculpted brown carpet. He glanced to the right, then the left. There were two wings to the house, which one should he choose?

When Adeline giggled, he couldn't help grinning. He'd never been into hunting. His grandfather had, and had tried to take him out a few times. Ironically, he'd hated the thought of killing a living creature. What he hadn't realized was that he just hated the thought of killing an animal. While trying to decide which wing to take wasn't even close to defining a true hunt, it had him thinking what it might be like to really stalk his next victim. And there would be another. Until he could find a way to get rid of Adeline, of that he had no doubt.

A door closed from the right. Knowing he didn't have much time, he quickly made his way toward the hallway entrance off the living room. The carpet kept his steps quiet. When he neared a doorway, voices reached him. At first he thought she was with someone, until a car insurance commercial aired.

"What are you waiting for?"

Hunger pangs seized his stomach. His heart rate accelerated, his breath became shallow. The pain in his head disappeared, leaving him with clarity, with only one thing on his mind.

Killing.

He stepped into the room. The blonde was sitting on the bed folding clothes, her head down. The puffy dog was curled on the pillow. It lifted its head and barked. The blonde looked up and gasped, the shock crossing her face thrilling him. But it was the utter horror in her wide eyes that pleased him even more. He would remember her face, her eyes later. Tonight, when he was with Bella, he would take his time and mentally kill the blonde all over again.

The blonde threw the clothes she'd been holding at him, and rushed off the bed. He caught her by her hair as she stumbled over the clothes basket, then punched her in the face. Bone cracked. Her body went as limp as a ragdoll's. He looked down at her face, at the blood oozing from her nose and down her lips and chin. Her eyes rolled back as if she was fighting to stay conscious.

"Don't worry. I'll be quick," he told her.

"No! Don't kill her yet. I need blood," Adeline pleaded, her tone sultry-sweet, when he knew it was all an act. Adeline only knew cruelty and manipulation, bloodlust and pain. *"Please, lover. I need to see her bleed. If you do, I'll leave you alone."*

"Liar." He dropped the woman onto the floor. The little dog ran to the edge of the bed, whimpering, its tiny tail between its back legs. He ignored the animal and went into the bathroom attached to the bedroom. He scanned the small space, saw a large brush, curling iron and hot pink blow dryer on the counter. As the woman moaned, he grabbed the blow dryer and walked back into the bedroom. The dog had pissed the bed, and had burrowed its head into the pillows, as if it couldn't bear to watch its person die. Would Ginger care if someone was trying to kill him or Bella? Would Ginger care if *he* tried to kill Bella?

He let the cord dangle. Instead of thinking about his dog, he focused on blocking out Adeline. The savage bitch was suggesting ways he could kill the blonde with the blow dryer, sick, vile ways that didn't appeal to him. He didn't mind the blood or bone cracking, but too much gore made his stomach sick.

The woman gripped the hem of his jeans. The sudden, unexpected movement startled him. Without thinking, he took the blow dryer by the cord and swung it like a bola. The plastic connected with the woman's jaw, knocking two teeth from her mouth. Her eyes wild, her face bloodied, she cried out, planted her hands onto the carpet and pushed herself upright.

Damn it. She wasn't going to go easy.

He kicked her in the stomach. She dropped, then immediately started to rise again, but he was on her back in a heartbeat, wrapping the cord around her neck and pulling, tugging until her spine curved unnaturally inward, her stomach and chest several feet off the carpet. As her face grew a violent shade of red, and her eyes watered, she clawed back at him.

"You fool. Why are you playing with this pathetic woman? Show her you're in control." Adeline snorted. *"You think you're powerful. Maybe you're the one who's pathetic. Kill her right fucking now."*

Enraged that Adeline would call him pathetic when she was nothing without him, he held the cord taut with one hand, then reached into his back pocket and pulled out the switchblade—a souvenir from his time at the House of Archer. "You want blood?"

He pressed the button which opened the blade. "You want death? You want to be fucking fed?" He yanked the woman's head back until her spine cracked, then slit her throat. "Choke on it," he said, then shoved the woman's face forward. Her head bounced off the carpet. Blood oozed from her neck and spread along the ugly brown carpet fibers. Breathing hard, he looked down at her, met her dead eyes, and wondered what was the last thing she'd thought of as she'd taken her final breath. Him? A lover? Her little dog?

"Thank you, Liam. You've once again impressed me."

"I don't care." He checked the time on the digital clock sitting on the nightstand. He had ten minutes at the most before he would need to leave. He glanced to his jeans, noted there was no blood on them, then stood. He stepped around the dead woman and went into the bathroom. There he used a towel to wipe off the switchblade, before placing it back in his pocket.

He stared at the cracked blow dryer, at the black cord. Could his fingerprints be lifted from the rubber? Not willing to find out, he quickly unraveled it, then twined the cord around the dryer until it no longer dangled. The only souvenir he'd kept with him had been the switchblade. It symbolized his time with Adeline and Rodney. The blow dryer wasn't a keepsake, it was evidence. Adeline was right, he needed to start thinking outside the box.

Certain he'd left nothing else of himself behind, he left the bedroom and entered the living room. A noise floated from the other wing. Hoping he didn't have to kill a witness and arrive to work late, he quickly crossed the living room and moved into the hallway, his focus on the opened door to the right. Prepared to take care of business swiftly, he retrieved the switchblade. Without hesitation, he rushed into the room. He came to a sudden halt as he stared at the baby in the crib.

Now he knew what the blonde had been thinking about when she'd taken her last breath.

CHAPTER 6

Cash's Auto Repair and Detailing, Tallahassee, Florida
Friday, 4:06 p.m. Eastern Standard Time

HARRISON WALKED THROUGH the open bay of Cash's garage. Reese, one of Cash's mechanics, rolled out from beneath a Dodge Charger, and grinned. "What's up, man? Are you finally ready for me to teach you how to change your oil?"

Since buying the Jeep Wrangler from Cash, Harrison had been trying to learn how to make minor repairs on his own. Computers, he understood. He could take apart and rewire a hard drive, hack and build backdoors into high security systems, and make his movements untraceable. Cars were a challenge to him. But he'd learned how to change the head and tail lights, replace the windshield wipers, put in a new battery, and to change and rotate the tires. An oil change was next on his list of must-learns.

"Not today. I'm looking for Cash."

Reese sat up and whistled, his gaze on the other opened bay. Harrison turned as Sully, another mechanic who also worked as a repo man, pushed a sweet motorcycle into the garage. "Nice bike. Do you know how many chicks I could get riding that thing?"

"The only female who would chase after you is your mother, and that'd be with a baseball bat," Sully said with a lopsided smile.

"Yeah, Mama doesn't like me riding motorcycles. I'm thirty-three years old and she still treats me like I'm three." Reese chuckled. "The woman makes me crazy."

"But she makes the best pot roast. You need to get us an invite for dinner."

Harrison watched the exchange, and envied the camaraderie between the two men. All the guys who worked at the garage had, at one time or another, served together in the Army. He envied Reese even more for having a mother who gave a crap about him, and who would cook him a meal. He envied their sense of family.

If Vlad heard his thoughts, the Russian would probably say, "Harry have family in Vlad." Or something like that. Within months of becoming a part of ATL, he had considered the team a surrogate family. Whether they were working a case or not, they looked out for one another, had spent holidays together, and every other week, they'd made it a point to get together for dinner—and not just during an investigation. Since returning from the House of Archer, he hadn't gone to all the dinners, and had missed a couple of holidays. Not because he didn't care, but because he cared too much. Those people liked him and accepted him for all of his faults. But he didn't want to test their friendship, or lose their trust. If they knew about the darkness, the episodes, the painful headaches that had always followed, they might look at him differently. Lola could suspend him from future cases. Then what?

"Is that the BMW HP2 Sport?" Cash asked from across the garage.

Sully parked the motorcycle. "Yep."

"Any problem?"

"Nope. When Jude and I approached the guy, he took one look at Pete sitting in the truck, then just handed over the keys."

"Good." Cash nodded to Harrison and grinned. "What's up? Lookin' for Mel?"

Harrison started for the office. "No, I was looking for you."

"Well, you found me. Come on in," he said, leading him into a room with three desks, bookshelves, filing cabinets and a big bed for Dolly, who was currently sleeping.

"What about the paperwork?" Sully asked.

"I'm busy. Give it to Jude," Cash called, then chuckled as he took a seat at the empty desk. "I hate filling out paperwork. I'd

almost rather worry about someone taking a bat to my head."
Cash had originally planned to sell his portion of the repo business
to Jude, but he and Mel discussed it and had decided they'd
remain investors. The only condition was Cash had to promise
Mel he would no longer go on repo jobs.

"So you miss it?" Harrison asked, sitting where Mel usually
did.

"Sometimes, but I'd miss my wife even more if she left me
again." Cash leaned back in the chair. "What's going on? Did you
come to learn how to change your oil?"

"No." Harrison scratched the back of his neck, unsure how to
approach Cash.

"Do you need to do something to our website?"

"No, I can do that from my apartment."

"You do know that I've been hit in the head with a bat a few
times, right? Make it easy on my brain and tell me what's up."

"I wanted to talk to you about Liam." That wasn't the main
reason for coming to Cash, but now that they were sitting across
from each other, it seemed like a stupid idea to even think about
asking the man for advice on women. "I think we should monitor
his movements. I wanted to know if your guys would be willing to
take shifts and help me follow him."

"You want to tail a paranoid schizophrenic."

A pulse beat hard at Harrison's temple. "I'd also like to keep
an eye on his fiancée and sister."

"The little five-foot nothing Liam is marrying and the woman
you're dating?"

The pulse turned into a dull throb. "Fuck it." He scraped the
chair back and stood, waking up Dolly.

"Settle down, man," Cash said, his tone good-natured, his
gaze wary. "Talk."

"About every stupid idea I just gave you? I'm good."

"They're not stupid, just not viable."

"Viable? Was that recently one of the vocabulary words from
your 'word of the day' calendar?"

"You know, I like this dickhead Harrison, just not when it's directed at me. And, for your information, feasible was yesterday's word of the day. Viable was the synonym. I like using it because it sounds more badass."

Harrison laughed and took a seat. The creeping darkness retreated. But it remained on the fringe, waiting, stalking. "Sorry, dude. I didn't mean what I said."

"Then why'd you say it?"

"I don't know," he answered honestly. "When I left your house on Sunday, I kept asking myself what happened or what was said that caused me to go off a few times."

"Did you find any answers?"

He shrugged. "Sometimes I think it's the aftereffects of the drug, other times I think it's the real me just tired of keeping his mouth shut." He leaned forward. "I've spent my whole life being directed by someone, and taking all kinds of shit. I know your mom basically abandoned you, and I don't take what you went through as a kid lightly, but I wish my mom would have left me and Mickey."

"That's your brother?"

"Twin."

"Where is he?"

"Dead." Not wanting or needing Cash's sympathy, he held up a hand. "I loved my brother, but he was bad news. Leading me into all kinds of get-rich-quick deals that involved stealing other people's money. Did Mel tell you I did four years for robbery?" When Cash shook his head, Harrison said, "It wasn't easy, and made the times I was in juvie look like preschool. Once me and Mick got out, I got a legit job washing dishes for a restaurant. Since it paid shit, I took on two other jobs. Mickey didn't. He kept looking for the easy way, and it got him killed."

"That's how you hooked up with Vlad and CORE."

Harrison nodded. "For years I did the wrong thing, let myself be pushed into directions I knew I shouldn't take, and didn't have the balls to walk away."

"Being poor makes a man desperate."

"You were poor. Instead of robbing people, you joined the Army. I couldn't because of my juvie record. Because I couldn't lead, tell Mickey no or stand up for myself, I made bad choices." He let out a breath and looked to the concrete floor. "Those choices will follow me to my grave."

"Why are you tripping down memory lane? You're not that kid anymore, and if I thought you were a piece of shit, you wouldn't be sitting in my office or associating with my wife." Cash reached for the can of Coke on his desk. "Do you think what you do for ATL is the wrong direction?"

"It's the best job I've ever had. I'm useful, I have purpose."

"So I'm back to asking you…what's the problem?"

"I want what you and Mel have. I want a wife and a house. I want a job I can talk about, not one that could put me back in prison or get me killed." He ran both hands through his hair, then looked up at Cash. "This lie I'm currently living, where I have my own business, goals, a woman who likes me…it's awesome. I'm getting a taste of what normal people have, and I want more."

"Why can't you have your own business building websites or doing graphics? The Internet gives you anonymity—before you ask, I got that word two weeks ago."

Regret brought back the headache. "I didn't mean to make you feel stupid."

"Let it go and think about what I said. Why can't you have your own business? You already own the trailer. If you want out of ATL and the swamp, sell the trailer and come here. Set goals for yourself, buy a house, settle into the community, find a nice woman."

"I have," Harrison admitted, his stomach shrinking in on itself.

"The serial killer's sister?" Cash shook his head. "Who was the last girl you dated?"

"Does doing shots and having sex on my buddy's couch a few times a week count as dating?"

Cash frowned. "Depends on how many weeks."

Harrison thought back to that time, to when he and Mickey had been too reckless and foolish to see that the choices they were making in their youth would affect their future. "I don't know, two, two and a half."

"I guess that'll work. So how long's it been?"

He pictured Hailey, the girl he'd been *dating*. She'd had pierced eyebrows, a ring in her nose and one through her tongue. Her hair had been dyed black and pink, and she'd had a few bad tattoos on her ankle and wrist. He'd known her since elementary school, when her skin had been untouched by a needle, and her hair had been a pretty golden-brown. But she'd gotten into drugs, which had been why he'd stopped doing shots and having sex with her on his buddy's couch. Drugs had been one thing he'd never done, and the only time he'd been on any had been when Adeline and Rodney had strapped him to a bed.

"Ten years," he finally answered.

Cash's eyebrows rose. "Ten years?"

"The girls I dated before that…it was pretty much the same thing. We had sex a few times, then went our separate ways."

Cash leaned forward and rested his hands on the desk. "Why did you really come to see me?"

"I told you, I wanted to talk about Liam."

"You're one of the smartest guys I know. Don't patronize me by playing stupid. It's about the girl. You like the sister."

"She's nice."

"You like her and you want dating advice." Cash smacked his palm on the desk and gave him a triumphant smile. "I'm right, aren't I?"

Cash's enthusiasm had him relaxing. Now he wished he'd just come right out with it and had asked him for dating tips. "Unfortunately, yes. I'm thirty-two years old and I have no dating experience."

"Well, buddy, you're not going to get any advice from this guy."

Harrison started to smile, until he realized Cash was dead serious. "What the hell, man?"

"Okay, I take that back, I'll give you some advice. Ready? Cut fucking bait. You don't need to date Liam's sister, you need to turn the evidence you have over to the police."

Harrison waited for the darkness, for the anger to settle over him, but it didn't. He'd already told himself everything Cash was saying now, and he couldn't be mad at the man for being honest.

"Look," Cash continued, "we've been through some serious shit together. We haven't known each other for very long, but I consider you more than just Mel's friend. You're mine, too. Seeing this woman is a mistake. Nothing good is going to come from it. When she finds out about you—"

"She doesn't have to know. When I have evidence that won't affect Nick or ATL, I can tip off the police anonymously."

Disappointment settled in Cash's eyes as he scrubbed a hand down his face. He let out a strained sigh. "Then what? You'll comfort her as her brother goes to trial and is later sentenced to death? We're in the state of Florida, man. We've got us the death penalty. Are you going to comfort her then, too, hold her in your arms and dry her tears, knowing you're the reason he's being injected and put to death?"

At that moment, Harrison hated Cash. And it had nothing to do with his head not being right. "Thanks for the advice. I'd prefer if you'd keep this conversation between us."

Cash stood the same time he did. "You don't want her to know, because you know what you're doing is wrong. Come on, Harrison. This isn't you. I just listened to you complain that you've spent your whole life following the wrong people and making the wrong choices. You need to break the mold. That woman isn't the only one out there."

"Kiera could be the one cleaning up after her brother." He didn't believe that, but it served as a good excuse to keep seeing her.

"And wouldn't it just suck to know that you've fallen for a

woman who's enabling a serial killer to keep on killing." Cash sat back down, then pulled a file from the drawer. "Catch you later."

Harrison stared at the man for a moment, then left the office. He said goodbye to the guys, then made his way out of the bay and to his Jeep. As he drove back to the Club, bits and pieces of his conversation with Cash replayed in his mind. He knew Cash was right about everything they'd discussed, and he wanted to not care. He wanted to keep seeing Kiera for his own selfish reasons that had nothing to do with Liam.

By the time he reached the apartment complex, he'd made up his mind to take Cash's advice and *cut fucking bait*. Kiera not only didn't deserve to be in the middle of her brother's mess, she deserved a good man, not a fuckup like him.

As he pulled around the parking lot, he saw her climbing out of her Chevy. She waved to him. Since he was driving past her, he had no choice but to stop. "Hi," she greeted him, a pretty smile on her face as she approached his Jeep.

"I thought you had a meeting?" he asked, then noticed the front of her light gray shirt was wet. "What happened to your shirt?

"It was cancelled last minute," she said as she tugged at the hem of her shirt and glanced down. "While I was already out, I stopped at the store and picked up a few things for us. I thought I'd make dinner."

Bail. Tell her you forgot you'd made plans with your buddies.

"You know how I buy the gallon jugs of water?" she continued.

He did, she didn't like the waste involved by using plastic bottles of water.

"Well, I accidentally dropped one when I was loading my car. It splashed up on me." She shook her head. "I'm such a klutz."

No, she was cute, and sexy, and he really wanted one more taste of her lips.

"So? Dinner and a movie at my place?"

"What time?" He was going to go to hell anyway, he might as

well enjoy every reason why.

The Beechum Residence, Tallahassee, Florida
Friday, 7:42 p.m. Eastern Standard Time

DETECTIVE SHARON LARSON met Bernadette on the sidewalk. The sun had already set, leaving the sky a deep plum. The tall street lamps running along Wilkes Street revealed the crowd that had gathered on the opposite sidewalk. The red and blue lights from police cruisers flashed across their frightened faces, on the concrete and green lawn. From within the ambulance, a baby cried. Knowing that the six-month-old had been in the house while his mother was murdered made Sharon's skin crawl.

Hatred settled in her stomach. During the years she'd been on the job, there'd been times when she had wondered how she could hate an unknown person so passionately that she would dream of vengeance, of torturing the nameless, faceless man or woman the same exact way they'd killed their victims. This person deserved death. Remorse, penitence, finding Jesus…that didn't work for her. If you took a life, you deserved to pay. And she wanted the man behind the murders plaguing her city to pay with his life.

"Hi Sharon. Bern." Officer Gary Underhill, a patrolman who used to fish with her husband, called them over.

"Hey, Gary," she said. "Who was first on the scene?"

"Kirk Simpson." He nodded to his right. "He's at his cruiser with the victim's husband."

Sharon and Bernadette both looked toward the vehicle. A man, who looked to be in his late twenties or early thirties, paced the back end of the cruiser, his head down, his arms crossed. "The husband found her?"

"Yeah, and I think we can rule him out. He was at work until five, then went to dinner with clients, and was home at ten after seven."

"You've verified this?"

"I called his boss at home. He was also at the client dinner."

Sharon shifted her gaze to the white car in the driveway, a Nissan Altima. Nothing flashy, nothing that screamed money.

"What's the victim's name?" Bernadette asked.

"Julie Beechum. Twenty-eight. The husband is Patrick Beechum, also the same age. The baby you hear is their son."

Sharon looked to Patrick Beechum, and realized that, with every pace, he stared at the ambulance. "Why isn't the father with his son?"

"You don't want to interview him?"

"Christ, Gary," Bern muttered.

"What?" he asked, looking at each of them.

"Let the man go to his baby. We'll talk to him later." When Gary started to walk toward the cruiser, Sharon said, "Wait. Let me."

The deceased wasn't going anywhere, and she wanted to quickly speak with the husband before she walked the scene. "Mr. Beechum? I'm Detective Larson, and this is Detective Richie."

The man was wearing wrinkled tan trousers stained at the knees, a long-sleeved button-down shirt, rolled at the elbows, and a loosened tie. He stopped pacing and, still hugging himself, pressed his fist to his chin. Tears streamed down his face as he shifted his watery gaze toward the ambulance again. "My son...can I go to him? They said they're going to take him to the hospital. I need to be with him. Julie..." His face crumpled, but he dragged in a deep breath and kept it together. "Julie wouldn't want him to be with strangers."

"I understand. And I'm sorry for your loss." Death at any time was difficult to accept. To lose a loved one to sickness or disease was hard. But Sharon knew from experience that having the person you love suddenly ripped from your life was even harder. She immediately thought about her husband, but before Alan's smile filled her head, she said, "I want you to be with your son, but I need to ask you a few questions first." She touched his arm, gave him a reassuring squeeze. "Patrick, we will do everything we can to find who did this. I need you stay with me for a few minutes longer."

When he met her gaze, she had to harden herself to his misery, to whatever internal struggle he was facing. She had to block out the baby's cries, to remember she had a job to do and to keep her emotions locked away. She would cry for these people later.

"What happened when you came home?"

He blinked a few times, then looked over her shoulder at the house. "I had dinner with clients. I, ah, was anxious to see Julie and tell her I landed the account I've been chasing. It's big money for the company, which means I'm getting a big bonus." His eyes filled with more tears as his chin trembled. "She's been so patient. Our house needs updating, and with the baby and Julie having to quit her job to stay home with him...we just didn't have the money to redo the kitchen. I was so excited about telling her it was finally going to happen." He wiped his nose and cleared his throat. "I walked into the house. Nicholas was crying. Everything was dark. Even the dog didn't...Julie's dog. I forgot about—"

"Don't worry, Patrick. We'll make sure the animal is taken care of," Bernadette said. "Please continue so we can get you to your son."

He let out a shaky breath. "I was immediately concerned. Julie would never let Nicholas cry. But then I thought she might be in the shower." He looked to the darkening sky and shook his head. "Thank God I went to look in on her first. Our bedroom was dark, but the light from the bathroom was on Julie. She was...she was on her stomach. There were clothes scattered on the floor. Blood around her head." He choked back a sob. "Her eyes were open. I put my head down next to hers and stared into her eyes, praying she would blink. But she didn't. She didn't."

Imagining the scene, Sharon's throat tightened. "You didn't touch her or move her?"

"I touched her hair, then her cheek. She used to love when I touched her cheek. She said that's what all the heroes in the romance books she reads do." He swiped at his eyes with both hands. "Heroes don't let their wives die."

"What did you do next?" Bernadette asked. Thankfully. The man was making it very difficult to keep her emotions in check.

"I ran to my son's room, pulled him from his crib, then got out of the house and called 911. I didn't know if whoever hurt Julie was still there, or how long she'd been that way…I didn't know what to do. So I sat on the front stoop rocking my son and lying to him by telling him it was all going to be okay."

Sharon had the urge to pull the man into her arms and tell him he was right. He wouldn't be okay for a long time and the pain never went away. "Patrick, do you have family you can call?" she asked instead. "You need to be around people who love you and Julie. I can have an officer place those calls for you."

"I'd rather it be from me." He met her gaze. "You'll find who did this?"

"We won't stop until we do," she promised. "We'll want to talk to you again, to discuss anyone who might want to harm Julie."

"There's no one. Everyone loved her."

Not everyone.

"Go to your son. We'll be in touch."

After Patrick walked off, Bern let out a deep breath. "Wow. I almost lost my shit. That was awful."

"I know. Now we get to see what he saw." They made their way into the house. CSU investigators were there, processing the scene.

One of the investigators, Dana Wong, noticed them and walked over. "This sucks," she said.

"Hi," Bern said.

"Hi, this sucks." Dana pointed to the left. "The baby's room is down that hall. I've got someone in there now, but so far nothing. He either didn't know the baby was there, or draws the line at killing children." She turned her back to them and faced the opened patio door. "Possible point of entry. The glass door was open, the screen door closed. The garage door was locked and, according to the first officer on the scene, the husband claimed to have unlocked the door when he arrived home. There isn't a single print on the screen door or glass door, but fingerprints are all over the front and garage door."

Sharon looked to the fingerprint dust along the front and garage doors. "He cleaned up after himself."

Dana turned to the left. "The master bedroom is located on this side of the house," she said, leading them across the living room and into a short hallway. "Here you go."

When Dana stepped to the left, Sharon stopped. Bern came up beside her. "Julie's a blonde. I don't know whether to be relieved about that or not," her partner said, then stepped around a crime scene marker.

Sharon didn't know how to react, either. If they could prove the three murders they'd been working were related, they had themselves a serial killer. Since this one didn't fit with the others, that meant they had some other sick prick to find. "How was she killed?" she asked as she slipped on a pair of latex gloves.

Dana stepped around spilled laundry and crime scene markers, then crouched next to the deceased. She pulled the woman's matted hair aside, and Sharon remembered what her husband had said about touching her hair and face, and how much she'd loved it.

"The marks and bruising along her neck indicate she'd been strangled with a cord, but we haven't found the one he used on her." Dana lifted the woman's head, exposing a gash along her neck. "Ultimately, he slit her throat. The kitchen knives have been checked. At this time, it doesn't look like any are missing, and so far we've found no blood evidence."

"He came prepared," Bern said. "Do we have a time of death?"

"Not yet. ME is on his way. But based on rigor, I'm estimating sometime between noon and three."

Bern touched her own neck as she looked around the room. "What are the stains on the bed?"

"Dog urine. The Beechums have a Teacup Poodle. The dog is

tiny and weighs around six pounds. When the first responder arrived, he said she was huddled on the pillow, shaking. The poor thing probably couldn't get down."

"Was the dog injured in any way?" Bernadette asked.

"Not that I'm aware. Apparently animals are off limits, too."

Sharon moved closer, touched Julie's cheek like the heroes in one of her romance novels. Her skin crawled again, this time with fear. "He beat her, but there's no blood."

"Press on the carpet by her body," Dana encouraged.

She met the investigator's gaze, saw the dread in her eyes and didn't want to do anything else but leave. "It's wet?"

Dana nodded. "As if someone dumped a couple of buckets on her. Only they didn't use water, they used hydrogen peroxide."

The cleaning of the victim and the dark curly hair had been the only links they'd had. But with Julie Beechum being a blonde, and hydrogen peroxide having been used instead of water, their link was now threadbare. "Who else has been in this room?"

"Myself and Jimenez. Officers Simpson and Underhill, the husband, and I think that's it."

Sharon thought back to Patrick Beechum and looked to her partner. "I noticed a stain at his knees, but didn't put it together. If he knelt next to his wife and the carpet is soaked, his pants would be, too."

Bern nodded. "We need to make sure he doesn't share that with anyone."

"Do you think this victim is related to the others?" Dana asked.

"In your experience, how often are victims' bodies cleaned?"

"Point taken." Dana stepped into the bathroom. "I think he used a blow dryer."

Sharon stood, followed Dana and Bernadette into the bathroom and began opening cabinet doors and drawers. "There isn't one here. We'll need to ask Patrick where Julie kept hers and what it looked like."

"The marks along her neck reminded me of an appliance cord.

I've already made a note for the ME."

Sharon slipped off the gloves and exited the bathroom. "Any foreign hairs?"

"I didn't find anything on the victim. Once her body is removed I'll vacuum the room," Dana said, her tone patient, tolerant.

"Sorry. I'm not trying to do your job."

"I know, Sharon. I want this guy just as badly as you. There's something disturbing about knowing a child slept just down the hall while his mother was brutally murdered. I keep wondering how you grow up dealing with that."

"At least he has the chance to grow, and he's too young to know," Bernadette said. "Come on, let's talk to the neighbors."

Once they were outside, Gary informed them that, so far, two people had come forward to talk about the last time they'd seen Julie Beechum alive. Autumn Torgenson, who lived to the right, and Marlene Cramer, who lived across the street. According to Gary, neither woman had seen Julie since around one that afternoon when she'd gone outside to sign for a package. Autumn Torgenson had said that Julie had walked over to inquire about the delivery Mrs. Torgenson received from The Home Zone, then she'd rushed back home because she'd left the baby in his Pack 'n Play. Marlene Cramer had been watering her flowers when she'd also seen Julie, and confirmed witnessing the woman sign for a package, then quickly talk with Mrs. Torgenson, before hurrying back into the house.

Sharon thumbed toward the side yard, then pulled out her flashlight. "Let's take a look out back." As they walked between the Beechum and Torgenson homes, she said, "Okay, so we know she was alive at one. If Dana's right, Julie was killed sometime between one and four. We need to get her phone records, check her emails and online activity. I think we can narrow down that window even more."

"We need to find the murder weapon," Bernadette said, moving her flashlight along the grass.

"A blow dryer and a knife. I wonder if it's the same knife used on Carla?"

"I'm wondering what this guy does for a living. Time of death for all of our victims has been either in the morning or early afternoon."

"Does he plan his next murder, stalk his target or is he opportunistic?" A wave of dizziness hit Sharon. She immediately crouched until it passed. "The knife could be his," she said, a little breathless. "The tire iron he used on Jennette was, according to her boyfriend, hers, and the blow dryer...I've never heard of a killer bringing one to commit a crime."

"Sharon, hush." Bernadette knelt next to her. "Stop talking, stop thinking. Let me drive you home. I'll take things from here tonight and you can get back on it tomorrow."

"I'm fine. It's just the medication. I don't think I ate enough before I took it."

"I've been with you all day, you've hardly eaten a thing."

The nausea had been so bad lately, the thought of food no longer appealed to her. "I used to love to eat," she said. "And Alan loved to cook. He swore I married him for his lasagna." She chuckled at the memory. "I was half in love with him the day he fixed the dish for me. By the time I cleaned my plate, I was not only easy, but ready to say I do."

Bern touched her cheek. "I'll never stop looking for who killed him. I promise you."

Because she wouldn't live long enough to do it herself.

The bastard who'd shot her husband in the back had never been found. Alan's case had grown cold, but it'd never been forgotten by anyone from the Tallahassee PD. Bernadette had suffered by her side, along with the men and women who'd loved Alan and those who'd never had the good fortune to know him. She would love to die knowing who the murderer was and see him sentenced to death. But it had been three years since the shooting, and she was running out of time.

"Thank you." She rested her hand over Bern's. "I think I'm

okay now. Help me up. I'm interested in the buildings behind these houses."

Bernadette took her hands and helped her stand. "Those are apartments. Duplexes and quadplexes."

When they entered the backyard, Bern waved to a CSU investigator who was checking the back flowerbed. They continued walking through the yard, darting their flashlights over the grass until they reached the short white picket fence.

"How easy would it be to park on the street and hop the fence?" Sharon studied the buildings. "This guy doesn't live here. He probably doesn't even live anywhere near here."

"I get that same feeling. Everything is so random. And why go from killing women with dark hair to a blonde?"

"The bigger question is why come back to clean the victim?"

Bernadette stopped. "Bigger than that…are we dealing with the same guy?"

"I don't know." Sharon stepped over the picket fence. She was so tired and drained, she was having a hard time thinking straight.

"I think we should get a couple of officers and start going door to door," Bern suggested. "Starting with the duplexes and quadplexes. It's my understanding that a lot of the people who live along this street attend the university or work at the hospital. Students and medical staff usually keep odd hours. Maybe one of the residents saw something today."

Sharon's upper lip and forehead grew sweaty, her chest became heavy and her nose itched, likely from whatever plants were nearby. She rubbed her itchy nose, only to end up with a tickle in her throat. "Wouldn't that be ideal," she said, suddenly breathless as they walked toward the well-lit carport of one of the quadplexes.

"It would." Bern grinned and glanced at her. Her eyes widened and her face fell. "Are you okay?"

"I told you I'm—" Sharon covered her mouth with her forearm and began coughing. She had a moment of panic when she couldn't catch her breath. When it passed, she ran a shaky hand along her mouth, and realized Bernadette was still staring at her.

"What is it?" she asked, breathless, her voice raspy, her throat sore.

Bern grabbed her forearm and angled the flashlight to Sharon's jacket. "You're coughing up blood."

Liam and Bella's House, Tallahassee, Florida
Friday, 8:36 p.m. Eastern Standard Time

LIAM TUGGED AT the restraints around his wrists and ankles. He desperately wanted to break free, grip the soft dark curls brushing along his stomach and thighs. "Stop. This isn't right."

She tossed her hair to the side and licked his penis. "You always say that, but if it wasn't right, then you wouldn't be this hard for me," Bella spoke the words he'd instructed her to when he'd first realized what he'd needed to in order to keep from killing her. The murders had been too quick, too anticlimactic. But they'd always stayed with him throughout the day, replaying in his mind, making him want more. Making him want to kill again.

After giving the head of his erection a final suck, Bella leaned back on her heels. She hid her sexy body with a loose tank top and panties. While he'd love for her to wear exactly what Adeline had been wearing the last time she'd come to his prison to fuck him— no bra beneath an unbuttoned blouse tied at her waist, and shorts so short they could be underwear—he wouldn't request it. Bella wasn't Adeline, no matter how much he'd wanted her to be, and, as it was, this had to be uncomfortable for her.

"Do you want to see my breasts?" Still unknowingly attempting to play the role of the woman who'd once tortured him, she slowly removed her tank top, then held her breasts. "Would you like to suck these?"

"Yes," he said, his voice hoarse, strained. He'd desperately wanted to take Adeline into his mouth—her nipples, her sex.

She leaned forward, her breasts barely touching his chest. "Will you bite me?"

"Yes."

She gave him what he knew was a forced smile. "That's why

you're not allowed a taste," she said, pushed her underwear over her hips, then clumsily rubbed her heat along his thigh. "Do you want me to fuck you?" she asked, unable to look him in the eyes.

Guilt tried to join the party, but he wouldn't allow it. He needed this, need to be in touch with Adeline, to pretend she was on top of him as he relived what he'd done to the blonde.

"Yes," he finally said. *Then I want to kill you.*

She guided him inside her. Her brow wrinkled slightly as a small smile crossed her pretty face. "Yes," she hissed, sounding so much like Adeline.

"Tell me I'm a good subject," he said, watching her.

"You're such a good subject. Your big cock pleases me. If you make me come, I might let you go."

Bella would never win an Oscar, but he'd give her a nod for trying. It didn't matter. He didn't need his fiancée to become Adeline. He just needed enough to finish what he'd started earlier today. Only he hadn't wanted the blonde, he'd wanted her neighbor. He'd wanted to wrap the cord around that woman's neck, look down at her dark head, see Adeline clawing, struggling for life.

Bella groaned as she moved over him. He stared up at her, at the dark hair framing her face, at her flushed chest and hard nipples. Then he closed his eyes and went back to the house on Wilkes Street, only instead of the blonde woman, or even her neighbor, Adeline was in the room.

"Do you want me to free you?"

Bella's breathless voice mingled with Adeline's. He was caught between the House of Archer, the house on Wilkes Street and his home, here with Bella.

Her fingers scraped along his chest. "Keep pleasing me and I'll find a way to set you free."

He squeezed his eyes shut, heard the snapping of the blonde's spine, felt her hot blood along his fingers as he slit her throat. As his orgasm neared, he opened his eyes and looked up at Bella. Disappointment cut through him like the switchblade had cut through the blonde's throat—quick, unforgiving. Anger surged to the surface. He pulled at the ropes, hoping for give, hoping to break free so he could wrap his hands around her throat and squeeze every last breath from her body.

"Don't untie me," he panted.

"Will you hurt me?"

He closed his eyes. "Yes."

Images commingled. Adeline, the videos she'd forced him to watch, the blonde, the other women he'd killed...Bella. His sweet Bella. How easily he could kill her, do to her everything he'd fantasized about doing to Adeline. As he envisioned her riding him as she was now, he pictured gripping her throat, then using his souvenir on her. Her blood would be warm. There would be no washing it away. It would stay with him. It would finally free him.

On a harsh groan, he came. With his release, the satisfaction he'd been seeking as he'd killed the blonde finally overpowered him, draining him, nourishing him, feeding his hunger. For now.

Breathless, Bella fell forward. She kissed his chest and reached for the rope around his wrist.

"Don't."

She rested her palm on his chest, her chin on her knuckles and searched his eyes. "You won't hurt me."

"Just give me a minute."

"Is it the white noise that makes you need this?"

"Yes."

"What would happen if the white noise came and I didn't have you tied up?"

I'd kill you. "I...the sex would be too rough. I don't want that for you. I never want to hurt you." He didn't. Even though she wouldn't have been his first choice in a woman, he loved Bella. She was a little simple and lacked certain manners, but she thought he was the shit, and could cook and keep a clean house.

She leaned forward and kissed him as Adeline never had, trusting him with her tongue and lips. As she kissed him, she loosened the ropes along one of his wrists, then did the same to the other.

"See? We're all good," she said, then scooted down and released his ankles. When she finished, she climbed back in bed and pulled the covers over them. "It's still early. You're not thinkin' about falling asleep on me, are you?"

With his body sated, and his mind clear, that had been his plan. This moment was the first time he'd had his head to himself since Sunday when his sister had come over for dinner. Living with Adeline was hell.

"No," he said anyway, and he kissed her head. "What did you have in mind?"

She pushed up on her elbows, and gave him an excited smile. "I thought we could talk about baby names?"

"Baby names? Why would—" He quickly rolled her onto her back, fear and excitement pumping through him. "Are you? Are we?" Since he'd been diagnosed with schizophrenia, he'd thought his life was over, that he'd never be normal. Have a wife, job...kids. This couldn't be true. Couldn't be happening.

She wrapped her arms around his neck and nodded. "I am, we are, and I hope you're as happy as I am."

He couldn't stop smiling. "We're having a baby." He kissed her. "I'm going to be a dad." He kissed her again, then pulled back and stared into her trusting eyes. "Thank you. This is what I want."

She hugged him. "Me, too. Other than loving you, it's all I've ever wanted."

As he held her, he pictured Bella round with his child, then he imagined life after the baby was born.

And saw Bella...her dead eyes, blood around her head. Their baby in the crib down the hall...

PART II

"All good things to those who wait."
—Hannibal Lecter, *Silence of the Lambs*

CHAPTER 7

Three weeks later...
Kiera's Apartment, Tallahassee, Florida
Friday, 5:21 p.m. Eastern Standard Time

TOMORROW MARKED THE fourth week since the night she and Harrison had gone to the luau together. So much had happened during those weeks, she sometimes needed to stop and take it all in, tuck special moments into her memory bank to look back on later.

Kiera untied the sash of her robe, then let the plush material slip from her shoulders. The lapels gaped open as she pushed her fingers through her hair. She'd taken her time to add loose thick curls, and had kept away from the hairspray. Harrison liked to touch her hair when he kissed her, and she wanted it to be soft for him, even as she hoped there would be more than hair touching tonight. She thought by now he would have at least copped a feel, caressed her breasts through her shirt, slipped his hand between her thighs and rubbed her there through her shorts or panties.

She slid her hand over the small swell of her stomach, then shrugged out of the robe. When they'd gone to the beach, he'd seen her in a forgiving tankini. Would he look at her naked, curvy hips and think she should lay off the Doritos? Was she ready to find out?

With a sigh, she picked the robe up off the floor, then began dressing. She could probably have a body like the slim women she'd see at the Club's pool or on the jogging path. While she'd been trying to cut back, making Doritos a special treat rather than a daily necessity, she enjoyed food, and wasn't one of those people who ate to live. She worked out regularly so she could have her Doritos and enjoy the empty calories of a beer or mojito, or whatever adult beverage struck her fancy.

As she stepped into the pink polka dot panties she'd recently bought with Harrison in mind, she realized her body wasn't the issue, but an excuse. Harrison had told her from the start that he would take their relationship at her pace. She'd appreciated that. Past boyfriends had pushed too quickly, and she'd allowed those relationships to become sexual before she'd been ready. But she couldn't place all the blame on those men. She'd probably misled most of them into thinking her need for physical contact meant sex. It hadn't. She'd wanted affection. To be held. To feel strong arms around her so she could allow herself to momentarily let go of the burdens she carried.

After adjusting the black lace along the edges of her bikini underwear, she put on a black strapless bra. She looked in the mirror and decided Harrison would like what he saw. Eventually, though not tonight. The panties and pretty bra were for her. They made her feel sexy, feminine, and she liked imagining Harrison's reaction to them.

Because that was safe.

She let out another sigh and reached into the closet for the strapless dark-pink dress she'd owned for months but had never had the confidence to wear. T-shirts and loose, lightweight sweaters were more her thing, and she only brought out the occasional tank top when she exercised or if the temperature had spiked. The panties and bra might be for her, but the dress was for Harrison. Maybe he'd cop that feel she was hoping for and yet was nervous about at the same time.

He should have never let her take the lead. She was incredibly attracted to him, loved kissing him, loved when he hugged her or would lie with her on the couch when they watched TV or just talked. While she was certain sex with him would be fantastic, taking that final step to intimacy would take their relationship to a different level. She was already half in love with him, maybe more like three-quarters of the way, but wasn't ready to fall head over heels.

She wasn't ready for him to meet her brother.

Yes, Liam was in a great place. For the first time since they were teenagers, he had his life together. Even when they were in high school he was all over the map when it came to friends, sports, part-time jobs, what he wanted to do after graduation. She'd thought he was sometimes either a little weird or simply trying to navigate through puberty and into young adulthood. Later, after his first psychotic break, she'd realized just how wrong she'd been. That she'd been in denial. He hadn't been her weird little brother, he'd been unbalanced and dealing with the voices.

But now Liam had a fiancée he planned to marry in May, a house, a dog, a job and a baby on the way. Kiera had never thought she would be an aunt, let alone watch her brother marry. She should be thrilled, ecstatic for him, only she wasn't. Bella, the baby, they would become extra burdens for her. Two more people to worry about, two more people to watch over and keep safe.

Because it was a cooler evening, she put on her favorite faded denim jacket, then the brown leather cowboy boots she'd had for years. She completed the ensemble with a pair of gold hoop earrings and called it good.

When she gave her reflection a quick glance, she liked what she saw, but hated the worry burning inside her. She should tell Harrison about Liam, though not the whole truth. God, no. She wanted him to be three-quarters in love with her, too. Not disgusted by her cowardliness. But Harrison should be aware that Liam had some...mental issues. She'd learned the hard way with past boyfriends that she should have been upfront. Instead, she'd kept the dirty secret to herself, until it'd blown up in her face and caused breakup after breakup.

Since she didn't want her relationship with Harrison to end, it was only fair that she told him the partial truth about her brother. He was a *harmless* paranoid schizophrenic. And if being with a person whose family had a history of mental illness was too much for Harrison to handle, then he'd never get to see her pink polka dot undies and bra.

She left her bedroom just as a knock came at the door. As always, when she knew she would see Harrison, butterflies filled her stomach. She opened the door with a smile. "Hi," she said, then kissed him once he stepped inside. "You look great." She ran one hand along his charcoal blazer, the other along his white button-down shirt, and imagined unbuttoning it and kissing his chest, kissing the tattoo on his right pec. As the fantasy played out, his subtle cologne, a woodsy blend she enjoyed, tickled her senses, made her want to act on her urges to skip dinner and speed up the pace of their relationship.

He placed his hands on her hips and bunched the material of her dress in his fists. "You're beautiful," he said, kicking the door shut and kissing her neck.

Goose bumps rose along her skin when he hit that spot just below her ear. Her nipples hardened. She clenched her thighs to alleviate the ache building between them. It didn't help. Neither did the way he hiked her dress higher, until it was almost mid-thigh.

With one word, she could have him out of his dark blue jeans and boots. She could give them what they both wanted. Or she could break the pattern she'd been repeating for years. Trust Harrison with some of her burdens before trusting him with her body.

He let go of her dress, smoothing the material over her hips, then kissed her before stepping away. Either he sensed a shift in her, or he didn't want to pressure her into going any further physically. Whatever the reason, she was glad he'd put space between them. She knew herself, and knew she could continue to put off the conversation about Liam because she'd done it many times in the past.

His gaze drifted over her. "What does the top of your dress look like?"

"Pink, like the rest of it."

The corner of his mouth slid into a sexy grin as his hazel eyes darkened. "You know what I meant. Can I see you with your jacket off?"

The flutter in her belly moved to her heart, which began to beat rapidly. "Sure. There's not much to see," she said, slipping out of the denim jacket.

He kept his gaze locked on hers and took a step toward her. He stood close without touching. "Why haven't you worn a dress before?"

She forced herself to maintain eye contact when she desperately wanted to look at his mouth, lean in and kiss him. Tell him to take the initiative and rip the dress off her. "I don't know. I have several in my closet."

He brought his fingertips to the bodice of the dress, then hovered them where her full bare skin met pink cotton. If she drew in a deep-enough breath, his hand and fingers would connect with her breasts. When he grazed the tip of his fingers along her skin, she let out a breath instead.

"It's probably a good thing you haven't worn anything like this." He traced his index finger along the bodice, dipping it slightly when he reached her cleavage. "Because right now, all I can think about is what's beneath this dress, and how easily I can access it."

"Do you want to see?" she asked, unable to help herself. It'd been a long time since she'd had sex, since hot male breath had brushed along her nipples, since rough hands had kneaded her flesh.

He stilled his hand and kept his intense gaze on hers. "Do you want to show me?"

He was forcing the pace to remain hers. The reminder brought her back to her burden. To how she'd allowed herself to be hurt when past relationships had ended. And she *had* allowed that to happen. If she'd been truthful with her boyfriends before she'd become too invested in them, she would have never been hurt.

"I want that and more," she admitted. "But we have a dinner reservation."

Instead of showing his disappointment, his eyes held approval. As if she'd passed a test. Which made little sense. He leaned in and kissed the corner of her mouth. "Your pace, baby," he said, then retrieved her jacket and helped her into it. "Let's go have a drink at the bar while we wait for our table."

Yes, they needed out of her apartment before she changed her mind. When they reached the Jeep, she was grateful to see he'd put up the top. The air had a chill to it, and she'd much rather have Harrison's big hands mess up her hair than the wind. Once they were driving out of the complex, he reached over and took her hand. She loved that he didn't mind holding hands. In her experience, most men weren't into it.

With her body still humming from the way he'd tempted her in the apartment, she rested his hand on her knee, then slid it up the hem of her dress, settling his warm palm on her thigh. "My bra is black."

His fingers dug into her skin. "And?"

"My panties are pink. They have little black polka dots on them and are trimmed with black lace."

"Are they damp?"

Her sex, slick with desire, pulsed. "Yes."

"Good." He pulled his hand free, then gripped the steering wheel. "Because you have me so hard I can't think straight."

When he rolled down the window and blasted the air conditioning, she laughed. He did, too. From there they fell into comfortable conversation. And as he talked about his day, as if she hadn't discussed her underwear and he hadn't told her he had an erection, she fell a little more in love with him. He was patient, smart, sweet and sexy. And he genuinely cared not only about her, but about them. She didn't want to lose that, or him. She also didn't want to be hurt. But better to deal with the hurt now, while she was eighty percent in love with him, than later, when she was so far deep, she needed him to breathe.

Forkista's Cantina, Tallahassee, Florida
Friday, 6:58 p.m. Eastern Standard Time

AFTER THE HOSTESS had seated them for their seven o'clock reservation, Kiera excused herself to use the restroom. Once she'd left, Harrison picked up the menu and pretended to look. He already knew what he wanted to eat and it wasn't on these pages. Just when he'd thought he had a handle on how to deal with their relationship, she had to go and get her sexy on, to the point where he couldn't concentrate on anything. When they'd been sitting at the bar, he'd wanted to lean close, slide his hand up the skirt of her dress and find out just how wet she was for him.

He obviously hadn't and likely wouldn't, even if she wanted him to once they reached her apartment later. She was hiding her brother from him. One of the reasons he'd wanted to go at her pace was because it lessened some of his own guilt. When he'd first starting seeing her, he'd done so to use her to get to Liam. With the hope of gaining some kind of evidence he could give to the police, he'd pictured striking up a friendship with the man. Anonymously, of course.

While he had no right to be disappointed that she hadn't trusted him enough to talk about Liam, it bothered him anyway. Her lack of trust had been the other reason he hadn't wanted to have sex. He'd never had a real relationship with a woman before. So far, being with Kiera was the best thing that had ever happened to him. She made him want to be a better man, set goals and reach them.

He wished Cash hadn't been such a righteous prick about his relationship with Kiera. He'd like to ask him how he'd known Mel was *the one*. After he'd gone against Cash's advice, not cutting bait and continuing to see Kiera, his buddy had warned him to never bring the subject up again. While he understood why Cash hadn't wanted to discuss Kiera, things had changed. There hadn't been a murder in three weeks. Liam, according to his bank and work records, had been living like a regular guy. Either this was the calm before the storm, or he'd been given the golden ticket. Liam had killed the couple in the woods, he knew that for a fact. He couldn't prove Liam had killed the four women who had been murdered over the past two months. He'd thought there was a connection because the first three women had dark curly hair like Adeline's. But when the detectives had discovered the fourth victim was a blonde, and that her body had been cleaned with hydrogen peroxide rather than water, they'd loosely connected her to the others, and he'd begun to question himself.

Did he believe that after Liam had escaped the House of Archer his state of mind had been psychotic? Absolutely. Liam had also been held at the plantation house longer than him and Mel. The drugs had to have affected the man more than they'd affected him. Plus, Liam was schizophrenic. Liam had no criminal history, no history of violence. Harrison wasn't excusing the murder of the old couple, but it could be that Liam had killed because he'd been momentarily out of his mind, that the darkness had gotten to him. He might have left the Dougals' home in the same state he'd been in before Rodney and Adeline had kidnapped him. Even now Liam could be thinking back to what he'd done, regretting it, wishing he could right it without going to prison. Was it Liam's fault that Rodney and Adeline had scrambled his brain and created a monster?

He set the menu down and picked up one of the glasses of water at the center of the small, intimate table. He couldn't even bullshit himself. No wonder Cash was still mad at him for dating Kiera. He was being selfish and needed to own up to it. He didn't know what it was like to be in love, but the thought of never seeing Kiera again made him ache almost as much as the day his twin had died. He didn't want to experience that loss, to not be able to see her smile, hear her laugh, talk to her, kiss her. He wanted to tell her the truth, that her brother was a murderer. But exposing Liam would expose him, and his questionable intentions.

The conflict weighed heavy on him. He knew she liked him. How much, he wasn't certain. So he knew, in the end, they would both be hurt. The *better to have loved and lost, than never loved* thing didn't work for him. He was tired of being on the losing end, chasing dreams that were just out of reach.

Kiera approached the table. He noticed several guys appreciating her curves. Unlike Cash, it didn't make him jealous. She was going home with him.

But how long will she stay?

"How does the menu look?" she asked after she was seated.

"Good. Mel and Cash come here a lot. They both said you can't go wrong with the smoked pork chops or the blackened grouper."

"Both of those sound great," she said, opening her menu.

When their server came to their table, they gave her their drink orders and declined an appetizer. While the server took care of their drinks, Kiera suggested they order what Cash and Mel had recommended and share the different dishes. He loved the idea, or maybe it was that he loved that they'd fallen into that comfortable-couple mode, where they could share food, a glass, a fork.

A bed.

God, he was a bastard to want what he shouldn't have. A woman he didn't deserve.

Once they had their drinks and had placed their order, Kiera looked to the silverware resting on the white tablecloth, her brow slightly puckering. "So what are your plans for the rest of the weekend?"

"Whatever you'd like to do."

She glanced up and smiled, but there was concern, hesitation in her eyes. "My brother and his fiancée invited me, us, over for a cookout tomorrow. I didn't know how you'd feel about that."

"About meeting your brother?" he asked, keeping his cool. This was what he'd been waiting for. The last time he'd been close to Liam, the man had bloody welts on his face, and he'd just finished slamming Mel's head into a door and snapping a man's neck. "Why wouldn't I want to meet him?"

"Well, some people might look at that as another step in a relationship."

"I'm going at your pace, so if you'd like me to meet your brother, I'm all in."

He'd expected her face to soften with relief. Instead, the pucker between her brows deepened. "I…ah, yeah. I think it would be good for you to meet him. I mean, he's a part of my life. A big part, since I moved here to be near him."

He leaned forward and reached for her hand. "Say what's on your mind." He knew what she wanted to tell him, and didn't see the point in allowing her to be upset over it.

She met his gaze. "My brother was diagnosed with schizophrenia when he was twenty."

When she didn't go on, he asked, "Why do you seem nervous about telling me?"

She let out a deep breath. "Because Liam can be an issue. When he's not medicated, he has these paranoid delusions that are sometimes so out of hand, it's caused problems for me with my jobs, my friends…boyfriends." She glanced to the table again. "I don't want him to cause a problem for us."

If only she knew. "Why would your brother affect us?"

"You know how in the movies they'll show the schizophrenic guy talking about the government coming after him? Well, that's not fiction. It's real. I've lived it. Last June I suspected he wasn't taking his medication or seeing his therapist. He started to fall back into his old routines and was fired from his job at the grocery store. The sad thing was, he'd been training for a management position. By the end of July, I would hear him in his room talking on a cell phone he didn't own. He would use the TV remote to contact the secret agents he was working with to bring down the other secret government agency he was convinced was trying to harm American citizens."

She took a sip of her berry mojito, then gave him a wry, sad smile. "He went missing in August. He'd taken some clothes, not much. The money I knew he had stashed, and the two hundred dollars I keep for emergencies. I found his empty pill bottles buried in the mulch behind the bushes on the side of my house." She squeezed his hand and held his gaze. "I was so worried. I filed a missing persons report, spent hours driving around the places he liked to go. Then in October he called me and said he was here."

"Did he say where he'd been?"

"No, but I'm not sure if he knows for certain. When he's not getting the right medicine and therapy, he loses touch with reality. He could've thought he was in China, when he was really in Philadelphia. Or chasing government spies through the streets of New York City, when he was actually in Cleveland. All he told me was that he'd wound up in a homeless shelter here, and that one of the workers helped him see a doctor who gave him the medication he needed." She shook her head. "The details are sketchy. A part of me wants to know exactly what happened to him, the other part of me doesn't." She took another drink. After setting the glass on the table, she touched her forehead. "He has a scar that runs from here to here." She moved her fingers down along her cheek. "He didn't have it the last time I saw him in Colorado, and he doesn't know where it came from."

"That's scary."

"What scares me now is that he has his life together and I'm terrified he's going to stop therapy and take off again. Only this time, he wouldn't just be leaving me to worry, but a wife and a baby."

"Baby?"

"His fiancée, Bella, is pregnant. She's only about nine weeks along and isn't due until late August."

The guilt Harrison had been trying to hold back unleashed itself, making his head ache, his stomach twist. If he'd found a way to alert the authorities, Bella wouldn't be pregnant with a monster's child. Because of him, his mistakes, his fear of the darkness inside of him, a number of lives had been and would be affected, and not in a good way. Liam possibly killed three women, maybe four, he still wasn't sure. And how would Bella manage without having Liam to help support her and their child? According to his research, she waited tables and occasionally tended bar at a restaurant. He knew enough about the restaurant business to say with confidence she couldn't make more than thirty grand a year. His biggest regret would be Kiera. Once again, her brother's mental illness would affect her life.

No, his choices, his secrets would be what would hurt her.

"Is Bella aware of your brother's condition?" he asked.

She nodded, then gave their server a smile when she set their plates in front of them. After promising to bring them another round of drinks, the girl disappeared.

"Bella knows," Kiera began, slicing the grouper and putting two thirds of it on his plate.

He cut the pork chop in half. "I thought we were splitting the food."

"I'm not as big as you, so don't give me all of that," she said, guarding her plate.

No, she wasn't. She was the perfect size, the perfect shape. The funny thing, he'd never been called big—ever. When Mickey had still been alive, Harrison had always been the tall lanky brother. When he was around Vlad, at six-one he was still considered the Russian's 'little' buddy. But even Ryan, Shane and Cash looked small next to the blond giant. Since his time at the House of Archer, he'd probably put on about twenty-five pounds of muscle. Not because he was all about getting ripped. After a month into the nutrition and lifting program he'd created, he'd realized it was about control. He controlled what happened to his body. He would never allow another Adeline, or even a frickin' Honey Badger, to control him again.

"I guess we'll be taking some of this to go," he said, slicing into the pork. "Back to Bella...unless you don't want to discuss it anymore."

"It's fine. I brought it up."

He scooped a forkful of the rosemary mashed potatoes. "If

Bella knows, can't you have her make sure Liam's getting the therapy he needs?"

"I've stressed how important it is, and she agrees. She says she's doing it, so I have to believe her. What am I going to do? Ask her every time I see her, or nag her about it?"

"Has she commented about any changes in him?"

Kiera shrugged as she sliced her meat. "Liam can sometimes become…angry when the subject of our parents comes up." She lifted the fork to her mouth. "They died in a car accident about a week before Liam's first psychotic break," she said, then took a bite.

He knew from his research that Edmund Forrester had driven himself and his wife off a cliff, killing them. A murder-suicide, according to the Arapahoe County Sheriff's Office. He hadn't put the timeline together, though. If Liam's break had happened after the crash, that meant Kiera had been dealing with her brother's illness alone. She couldn't have been more than twenty-two or twenty-three then. When he'd been that age, he'd been following his brother into trouble and on his way into prison.

As she talked, he pictured her finishing college, while caring for her schizophrenic brother. There'd been life insurance split between her and Liam. She didn't tell him, he knew that from his research. But there hadn't been much, and because Kiera's parents had taken a second mortgage, the siblings couldn't count on the sale of the family home, either.

"Liam's half of our inheritance went fast," Kiera continued. "I couldn't tell you how many hours I spent online or on the phone, trying to get government aid to cover his doctors, therapists and prescription drugs. I used my inheritance to pay off student loans and as a down payment for a house. I wanted to make sure Liam had a stable environment." She pushed her plate forward and he noticed she'd mostly picked at her food, or had shoved it around her plate. "Sorry, I didn't mean to make this all about me."

She was a loyal woman and he had the utmost respect for her. "I'm glad you told me. What you've gone through with your brother is a huge part of your life."

"Thank you," she said, then reached for her drink. "If knowing I have a little crazy in my family is a problem, I totally understand."

"I'm going to pretend you didn't say that," he said, disappointed that she'd think he'd walk away because of her family members' past. Hell, he knew her brother was a killer and he still wanted to be with her.

"Sorry, but you wouldn't be the first guy who's walked away."

"If I go anywhere, it'll be because you want me gone." When she glanced to her drink, he leaned forward. "Hey, look at me." She met his gaze. "I grew up poor," he began, then told her about his mom, her boyfriends, and that he'd never met his dad. "Does the fact that my mom was the worst mother ever, and that my dad wanted nothing to do with me and my brother make a difference to you? Don't lie."

"Of course not. How is it your fault that you were raised...I see what you're doing," she said with a smile.

"Good. Don't ever assume something about me, or how I feel about you. If you want to know, just ask."

Their server approached. After they declined coffee and dessert. He paid the bill, then walked her to the Jeep.

"It's still early. Do you want to catch a movie or go find a band to watch? I thought I saw The Big Rig Rogers are playing over at Swingles this weekend." The Big Rig Rogers was a local country band. Four weeks ago, if someone told him he'd be listening to country music and enjoying it, he wouldn't have believed them. Now he was downloading songs and keeping his radio dialed to the local country station.

"Only if you want to," she said.

After she slid into the passenger seat, he closed her door, then made his way to the driver's side, wishing she'd never brought up Liam. Yeah, he'd wanted her to talk about her brother, but he realized he really didn't need Kiera to get to Liam. He needed to work smarter. To think of other ways to link him to the murders…murders that he might not have committed.

"I'll do whatever you'd like. We could sit in a box and I'd still have fun with you." He shoved the key into the ignition, then noticed she was staring at him, an odd expression on her face. "What'd I say wrong?"

"Nothing. It's funny, my brother and I joke too about how we can have fun in a box. Clearly not in the way you might mean." She gave him a sad grin, then leaned back in the seat and looked out the windshield. "Sometimes I think back to when me and Liam were kids and I miss the boy he once was." As he backed out of the parking spot, he saw her wistful grin. "Remember how I said I have a little crazy in my family? Well, I should probably mention that my dad was schizophrenic, too. The car accident that killed him and my mom…investigators thought my dad caused the accident while he was having a psychotic episode."

Harrison took her hand and drove them toward their apartment complex. After the heavy conversation, he couldn't see them going to a club to watch a band, and would rather take her home where she could deal with the emotions he was sure were churning through her. He'd stay, if she let him. He'd asked for this. He'd wanted her to talk about her brother. Most of what she'd told him he had read about while researching Kiera and Liam. But to hear the heartbreak in her voice, to see the sadness in her eyes…

"I'm sorry," he finally said. For everything she'd lost, and for what he would still take away from her.

"It's okay. Their death can't be undone, and Liam will never be that boy again."

"You two were close?"

"Very. My dad's symptoms came and went. When they were bad, he never left the house. So we never had friends over, or left the house, either. According to my dad, someone might've snatched us. We'd miss school, parties, whatever sport we might be playing. But Liam and I had each other." She rolled her head toward him. "You've never mentioned your brother until tonight. Are you close?"

"Twins." He gave her hand a gentle squeeze. "Mickey died about two years ago."

"Oh, God. I'm so sorry. And I've been going on about Liam."

"I'm glad you told me. I feel like it was something you needed to say."

"I know we haven't been seeing each other long, but I thought you should know before...we grew a little closer. I don't want Liam to come between us." She let out a nervous chuckle. "I think I need to stop talking."

He drove through the entryway leading into the Club's complex. "Why, because you're telling me the truth?"

"Because maybe I'm being presumptuous about our relationship."

"Do I need to write *I'm not going anywhere* on Post-it notes and stick them all over your apartment as a reminder? You're not being presumptuous. I don't know what kind of guys you've dated in the past, but adults discuss adult things."

Not that he had personal experience to back up that fact. But he'd been around enough couples to understand the workings of a relationship. From what he'd learned, honesty and compromise were big-ticket items. There could be love, but if there wasn't trust, and neither person was willing to give, there'd be no future, or a very unhappy one.

He parked the car, then killed the ignition. "It's a nice night. Do you want to go for a walk?"

She brightened. "Absolutely. I've wanted to go by the lake at night, but not by myself."

After he'd helped her from the Jeep, he took her hand and led her toward the jogging path. "Smart. There're a lot of bad people in this world."

"I know. It's sad. It's also why I own a gun and have a conceal and carry permit."

He didn't bother to mask his surprise. "I didn't see that coming." He honestly hadn't stumbled across that fact during his research.

She nudged him with her shoulder and walked closer. "There're a lot of crazy people, too. Remember, I lived with one."

When they reached the lake, he led them to a wooden bench. "Are you afraid of your brother?" he asked, not to have additional information he might be able to give the police, but because he cared. When he'd lost his brother, there'd been an emptiness he couldn't explain. Even now there was a part of him that had been lost and buried with his twin. He might never have more with Kiera than now, or the days or weeks before he found a way to expose Liam, but knew if something happened to her, there'd be emptiness. He knew he'd lose another part of himself.

She stared out at the lake which had a spotlight shining on the water fountain at the center. "I love my brother."

"That's not what I asked you."

After taking their joined hands and resting them in her lap, she shook her head. "I don't think Liam would ever hurt me. But there was a time when I worried he might hurt someone else during one of his breaks with reality. Maybe I was overdramatizing things by getting a gun and learning to shoot. I don't know. I think mostly it was my way of taking back some control." She turned her head slightly and met his gaze. "Since Liam's first break, I haven't had a moment of peace. I was searching for answers, doctors, money to pay for bills...juggling my career, trying to have a normal social life, all while trying to keep an eye on Liam. Don't get me wrong. There were a couple of good years when Liam even moved out and got his own place. But then the symptoms would return, or he stopped therapy." She let out a slow breath. "The gun, taking self-defense classes...those were things I could control and use. I guess they made me feel less vulnerable, if that makes any sense."

Harrison thought back to the day he'd watched his brother die. How the bastards had put a knife in his hand, put a gun to his head and forced him to hurt his twin. Before his throat tightened with the pain, the loss, Adeline's image emerged, replacing sadness with hatred. He understood vulnerability more than Kiera could ever know.

"It makes absolute sense," he said, wrapping an arm around her and pulling her close. "I was there when my brother died." She'd been honest with him, and had trusted him with a part of herself. She deserved the same from him. "I'm not going to sugar-coat it, me and Mick, we used to get into a lot of trouble. Trouble caught up with us and…Mickey was shot."

She turned into him and laid her hand on his chest. Her eyes were filled with tears. For him? Mel had cried for him. Because he'd been violated, humiliated and she hadn't been able to stop it. He selfishly wanted to believe the tears slipping down Kiera's face were because she cared so much about him, it hurt her to know about his loss. He was a jerk for even thinking that, but didn't care. She'd become special to him, and he wanted to be special to her.

A couple of raindrops fell on them. One hit her cheek and mingled with her tears. He wiped it with the pad of his thumb.

"I didn't tell you that because I wanted you to feel bad for me," he said, wishing they could stay like this for just a little while longer. He'd never been a nature guy until he'd spent time out-doors with Kiera. For more than a year, he'd basically lived in the swamp. Vlad had loved it: the sounds, the animals, the plants. He hadn't. But being with Kiera had taught him to appreciate those things. He wanted to stay on this bench with her and talk. Hear more about her childhood as the frogs croaked, the insects sang and the water fountain showered the lake. Then later, he didn't want to go back to her apartment and just kiss her goodnight. He wanted to kiss her in the morning, too. He wanted to hold her all night, sleep next to her, feel the rise and fall of her chest beneath his arm as he held her close.

"But I do feel bad," she said. "When it comes to our brothers, we've both suffered in different ways." She looked up to the sky, then closed her eyes when the rain fell harder. As he was about to suggest they head back to her apartment, she met his gaze. "I still have mine." Her chin trembled slightly. "And I wish I didn't."

CHAPTER 8

H ARRISON PRESSED HIS lips to hers. Nothing sensual, but a connection. As if he were letting her know whatever she said next, or whatever she felt, was okay. But it wasn't okay. She shouldn't wish her brother was gone. Not dead, just out of her life.

She wrapped her arms around him and kissed him. Wishing she could swallow back the words, while relieved that she'd finally admitted one of her darkest secrets. The others, Harrison or anyone else could never know. She'd been a coward when it had come to her brother, and accepted the label she'd given herself. But she didn't have to accept the life she'd been living. In and out of relationships and never truly happy, because she'd been living in the shadow of Liam.

Harrison pushed her wet hair from her cheeks and drew back. "Let's get out of the rain." As he took her hand, they began walking down the jogging path. Most people would probably run, especially when thunder rumbled in the distance. They didn't. She wasn't sure what to make of it. They had a ton of things in common, which was nice and made them compatible. More than that, he knew her so well. As if he could crawl inside her head, gauge her mood, know when to back off and when to push. Her connection to Harrison was strange and beautiful. Strange because it terrified her that she could come to deeply care for someone in a short amount of time, and beautiful because she could finally be herself, be secure in her emotions for him, for how he felt about her.

Still acting as if he was in no rush to get out of the rain, he wrapped an arm around her and kissed her cheek. She pressed into his wet clothes. They stuck to his lean, hard body. His broad shoulders and strong arms gave her the security she'd been searching for since her parents' deaths. When he held her, confidence replaced the vulnerability that had driven her to purchase a gun. In that moment she'd realized that she had allowed herself to become another one of her brother's victims. And she hoped being honest with Harrison was the first step in taking her life back. She needed to lose the guilt, take control of her goals, allow herself to dream again and to be happy.

"I'm not going anywhere, unless you want me gone."

The moment the words had been spoken, she'd gone from three-quarters in love with Harrison to all the way. From the very beginning, he'd made his intentions and attraction for her clear, yet he'd considered her feelings, showed that he was a patient man and had never pushed her into making their relationship physical. She'd wanted to be with him, make love, but how could she give her heart to him and open hers if she wasn't honest. She'd rather he know the kind of person she was now, while her love for him was still new, rather than later, when losing him would tear a hole in her and bleed her dry.

Lightning splintered just as they reached the door to her building. Once they entered her apartment, she looked down at the puddles they were leaving on the tile floor in front of the door. "Let me get some towels," she said, kicking off her boots.

"That's okay. I'll go back to my place."

So much for not going anywhere. She fought the hurt, tried to force a smile, but failed. This was supposed to be about her and Harrison. She was supposed to be happy and able to fall in love without having her brother's shadow or his psychotic episodes interfere. And while Liam was living it up, preparing to marry, have a baby, she was still dealing with the problems, the fucking burdens he'd created. "I get it. I'm a bitch for what I said, but I don't care. That's the truth," she said, letting the anger, the years of pent-up frustration go.

"I'm not judging you."

"Then why are you leaving?" She held up a hand. "Honestly, I think it's better I don't know. I'm emotional right now. Telling you my sad, pitiful tale has left me drained. So save your reasons for leaving for another day, or save the Post-it notes and don't call again."

The shock in his eyes made her want to backtrack, take the words and rearrange some while leaving out others. But she couldn't. They hung in the air and she had to own them.

She shivered, and began to peel off the soaked denim jacket. "Close the door behind you," she said, then left the room. When she reached the bedroom, she flipped on the light and caught her reflection in the mirror. What the hell had happened to the woman who'd stood here just a few short hours ago?

Gone were the thick curls she'd hoped Harrison would touch, now her wet hair was plastered to her head. Although she hadn't worn a lot of makeup, her mascara had run, creating a smoky eye effect that might have been cool if she'd intended it. Gone was the excitement, the confidence and hope. Over time, they'd come back, and she'd learned a valuable lesson.

Keep her secrets a secret.

When she heard the front door click, she removed her hoop earrings. As she turned toward the bathroom, Harrison filled her doorway, looking hurt and angry.

"I thought you'd left," she said, taking a step back.

"No. I locked the door. Did you really think I was going to leave it unlocked while you were back here by yourself? I don't care if you own a gun or can throw a wicked punch. If someone wants to hurt you badly enough, they will. Especially if they have the element of surprise."

"Thank you for the public service announcement."

"Sarcasm doesn't work on you," he said, taking a step forward. "Bitchy doesn't, either."

"Clearly you don't know me very well. I can do both bitchy and sarcastic very well."

"You're also not very good at losing your temper."

"Would you like me to show you how good I am?" If he pushed her, he would find out just how horrible she was at losing her temper. Confrontation wasn't her strong suit. When she yelled out of anger, her voice would grow so glass-shatteringly high it would embarrass her into silence. But she'd rather not argue, and wished he'd just leave and let her deal with the regret of opening up to him.

"Not today." He stepped into her bathroom, then opened the narrow linen closet. "My plan was to go to my apartment and change, then come back here." He pulled out a couple of thick bath towels and approached her. "I thought you wanted to still hang out, and I didn't want to do it in wet clothes."

"Now I feel stupid. I'm sorry." Embarrassed by her behavior, she reached for one of the towels he held. But he tossed one over his shoulder and unfolded the other. "Can I have one of *my* towels, please?"

"I don't want you to be sorry or feel stupid. After everything you told me, I should have said from the start that I was going to come back." He used the towel to dry her hair. "I'll always want to come back to you."

Her heart pounded a little harder. He kept telling her he wasn't going anywhere, and now he was telling her he'd come back to her. She'd fallen in love with him in four weeks, and until she'd experienced that need—the desire to be with him, to stay connected emotionally, intellectually and physically—she wouldn't have believed it was possible. Was that what Harrison was trying to tell her?

"Where would you go?" she asked, then began unbuttoning his shirt.

"Hopefully nowhere." He gently wiped the mascara smudges around her eyes. "But a few minutes ago you were giving me the boot."

She opened his shirt, then took the towel from his shoulder and rubbed it along his chest. "I jumped to conclusions. I was worried you thought less of me because of what I said."

"You're honest, and you're human. Right or wrong, we all feel in different ways at different times in our lives." He moved the thick material over her shoulders. "I don't think I'm good enough for you, but I want to be."

She looked up at him. "Why would you say that?"

"Because I've made choices in my life I'm not proud of."

She didn't care about his past. She cared about now, and the future.

"I want to be honest, too," he continued, gliding a hand over her arm, then to her hip where he fisted her dress. "I'm dying to touch you." He hiked the hem higher. "I want to take off your clothes and dry off every inch of your body, then make you wet for me."

To keep from groaning, she pushed his shirt over his shoulders and kissed the compass he'd had tattooed on his right pec. She was already wet for him and aching to rid them both of their clothes.

"But I think I should tell you something first."

She brought the towel to his chest again. "This isn't confession time."

He gripped her hips and pulled her close, the intensity, the worry in his eyes making her ache in a different, unpleasant way. She didn't want him to hurt or to worry she would judge him.

"I know that, but how can I *not* give you a part of myself. You were honest and you trusted me enough to put your feelings out there. I trust very few people. I want to show you that you're one of them."

Her eyes grew moist. No man had ever spoken to her about trust and giving part of themselves. His words frightened and thrilled her. She'd longed to be with a man who she could count on and love, a man who would be there for her no matter what. Harrison could be that man—and it scared her. It scared her that she might end up loving him too much. But he spoke of trust, and she had to trust that if he committed himself to her, if he eventually said he loved her, it was the truth.

She kissed his chest again. "You didn't judge me, I would never judge you."

"You might." He glanced away, and inhaled deeply. When he met her gaze again, he said, "I spent four years in prison for cyber robbery. I'm an ex-con with a felony record." He let go of her dress and dropped his hands to his sides. "That's a lot different than wishing you no longer had a brother, but I think it's only fair that you know."

She hadn't expected a prison record, but at least he wasn't a murderer. At least he wasn't a coward like her and had the nerve to admit the truth. "Thank you for telling me."

"That's it? Don't you want to know the details?"

"You promised to dry off my body, then make me wet. We can discuss details later."

She gasped when he gripped her by the upper arms. "I'll keep my promise, but I need to know how you feel. I'm a criminal. A thief. I stole money. Doesn't that bother you?"

"Of course it bothers me. But are you that man now?"

"No."

She broke free and gripped his shirt, pulling him closer. "Four years is a long time. That's high school or college, days you'll never get back. Do you want me to push you away because you feel like you should still be punished for choices you've made?"

"Maybe. It bothers the hell out of me to think about how you were graduating from college and dealing with your brother on your own, while my brother and I were getting sentenced."

"Your brother was involved, too? You said the two of you got into a lot of trouble."

"He was always the man with the plan," Harrison said, his tone bitter. "I could have walked away."

"Why didn't you?"

"Because I was tired of working three jobs to make ends meet. I had computer skills, but I was self-taught and couldn't find a decent paying job. I couldn't join the military because I have a juvenile record...I told you, me and Mick were trouble."

"But Mickey's gone and you're not that guy." Suddenly irritated with him, she let go of his shirt and stepped back. "Why am I convincing you that you're worth caring about, when you should be trying to convince me that you're great for me, and that we could have something great together?"

"I shouldn't have to convince you."

"You're right, but you also shouldn't stand there and tell me how horrible you are."

"I never said I was horrible."

She shrugged. "Prison is pretty horrible. Having a juvenile record isn't so great."

The corner of his mouth tilted in a wry grin. "I'm loyal and a hard worker. I'm neat and always clean up after myself. I don't expect the woman I'm with to cook for me or do my laundry. I earned my associates degree in computer science while I was in prison. I make a good salary and have money in the bank. I can cook. One bite of my homemade salsa will have you ripping off my clothes."

"Is this a tested fact?"

"Not yet, but my salsa makes me want to rip off my clothes, so it's just a wild guess." She laughed as he looked to the ceiling. "What else..." He met her gaze, ate up the distance, but didn't touch her. "I'm crazy about you. That night at the luau, I meant what I said. I wanted to know you and see your pretty smile. I've gotten to know you, and I have your different smiles memorized, but it's not enough. I want more of you." Like he had before they'd gone out, he ran the tip of his finger along the bodice of her wet dress. "And I don't mean sex."

He wanted her heart. She didn't need to hear him say the words. He'd said enough. "So does this mean you won't be drying off my body, then making me wet?" she asked, attempting to lighten the heavily emotional conversation. "Because if you're not in the mood for that, I'd like to take off your clothes, dry off every inch of your body and make you hard."

He slid his finger from her cleavage to her chin, and tilted it up slightly. "I'm already hard."

"And I'm already wet." She tugged his shirt until it fell to the floor in a heap. "We should do something about that," she suggested, taking care of his belt.

While she undid his jeans, he unzipped the side of her dress. The bodice gaped. He took the material and moved it down her body, bending to the floor and out of her reach until she stood there in nothing but her black strapless bra and polka dot pink panties. He sat on his heels and ran his hands up over her legs and hips. "You're more beautiful than I imagined," he said, leaning forward and kissing her thighs. He rose to his knees and, at the same time, moved his hands over her rear, cupping her bottom and drawing her close and off balance.

She ran her fingers through his short hair to keep steady, and shamelessly pressed her pelvis forward. She wanted her panties off and his mouth on her.

He grinned against her thigh and looked up at her. "Take off your bra," he said, sliding his fingers beneath the lacy waistband of her underwear. As she unhooked the strapless garment, he kept his hungry gaze on hers and slowly tugged down her panties. They hit the floor the moment her bra did. He shifted his attention to her lips, her breasts, then he closed his eyes and pressed his mouth along her stomach, then lower still.

She gripped his head when his warm tongue slid across her labia, then sucked in a breath as he started to rise, kissing her stomach, the skin below her breasts. When he reached her nipple, he brushed his lips along its taut peak, then flicked his tongue against it. She shuddered. Before she could hold him close, encourage him to do more, he kissed his way up, along her collar bone, her neck, to the sweet spot behind her ear before sifting his hands through her wet hair.

His breath fanned along her mouth. "You taste so good," he murmured against her lips, and rubbed her bottom. "I need more." He lifted her leg, opening her, then he picked her up off the floor as if she weighed nothing, and took a few steps to her queen-sized bed.

The moment he sat her on the edge, she gripped the waistband of his jeans and looked up at him. She loved how dark his eyes had turned, how he stared at her with longing and…concern. Was he worried over how sex would change their relationship? Maybe he feared she'd come to her senses, reconsider his past and walk away? Or maybe she was misinterpreting him, and he was as nervous as her. She'd never taken sex lightly. Sure, she thought about it a lot and had fun fantasizing, but when it came to the actual act, she'd always been in a relationship. And she wanted this relationship to work.

She tugged both the denim and cotton of his underwear a few inches over his hips. "The first time I saw you running without your shirt, I couldn't stop thinking about this." She skimmed the tips of her fingers along the sexy line of muscle that started near his hip bone and dipped into his jeans.

Before she could finish shoving down his jeans and underwear, he ran his hand along her hair, then gripped a fistful. He tilted her head up, bent and kissed her. Pressed her against the mattress until her rear dangled off the edge. As she tried to use her tiptoes to scoot her lower body onto the bed, he moved his thigh between her legs, holding her in place and keeping her from sliding off.

"I've got you," he said, easing back. He looked so sexy standing over her, his gaze following the path of his hand…along her cheek, her neck, her breasts, where his large palm cupped one, then the other. When he captured her nipple between his fingers and gently squeezed, her breath caught and his eyes met hers. Keeping her half on the bed, he bent forward and took the peak into his mouth. He sucked, causing a tug low in her belly. She speared her hand through his hair, encouraging him to her other breast, but he knelt between her legs instead. As he rested her hamstrings on his broad shoulders, keeping her rear high in the air, she rose to her elbows. Then dropped her head back when he swept his tongue along her labia. He kissed her sex, hot, open-mouthed. When he wrapped his arms around her upper thighs and spread her, she couldn't stop the groan escaping from her throat. He moved his tongue along her sex, penetrating, then withdrawing, circling her clit, teasing her, driving her so close to the pleasure her body craved.

His hands moved from her thighs to cup her bottom. He kept her lifted, spread her labia with his thumbs and made her insane with his lips and tongue. As if he couldn't get enough of her, as if he was a starved man. As if this might be his only chance to touch and taste her.

The fleeting thought disappeared as he flicked his tongue over her clit until her orgasm shot through her, tensing her body with pleasure, clearing her head of all thoughts but one—Harrison.

Harrison kissed her inner thighs, then moved her fully onto the bed. She looked so damned perfect lying on the rumpled comforter. Even with the taste of her on his lips, her scent on his skin, he couldn't believe this was happening. That he'd allowed it to happen. He should have bolted the moment he'd had the chance. Instead, he'd said everything he could to convince her to accept him in her life, to seduce her into thinking they could have a future. He hadn't been lying. He was crazy about her, except, now what?

Pretend Liam wasn't a killer? She'd been through so much because of her brother, and he would put her through more. By doing everything he could to see Liam go to prison he would betray everything she'd told him today, and her trust.

Unable to resist her soft curves, he rested his knees on the edge of the bed and moved his hands over her hips. He needed to find an excuse to leave, even if he didn't want to go.

She reached up and feathered her fingers through his hair. "Take off your jeans," she said, her voice breathy, her face still slightly flushed, her eyes so fucking loving it was killing him.

He helped her scoot away from the edge of the bed so she wouldn't slip off and onto the floor. "I don't have a condom," he said. Thank God. He needed to kick his ass back to his apartment and figure out a way to handle the situation. Only this wasn't a *situation*. This was him screwing with someone's life.

She gave him a shy, playful smile. "I do," she said without a hint of apology, which turned him on even more. Smart women were incredibly sexy. "Most men I've dated usually forget about protection. I'm glad you're not like most men." When he didn't respond, she sat up, and turned into him. Her breast pressed against his bicep, as she slid her hand to his erection beneath his jeans. "Unless this is where you want to stop tonight."

He had another chance to bolt. Tomorrow, he could tell her he had to go out of town, then stay with Mel and Cash. He could stop the hurt before it happened.

As she rubbed him, kissed his shoulder, and her nipple brushed his skin, driving him insane with lust, tomorrow seemed decades away. He turned his head, sought her lips, kissed her, then murmured, "Where are they?"

"Linen closet. Top shelf."

After another kiss, he went into the bathroom, grabbed the box, then returned to find her sitting on the edge of the bed, her legs spread just enough to expose her sex. He stood in front of her. Feeling like a virgin, he kept his hands steady as he opened the box and pulled out a packet. When she kissed his stomach, his lower abs, it took everything in him to remain still, concentrate on the wrapper, not on what she was doing.

But thoughts, dark ones, drifted through his mind like a hazy, drunken memory. The plantation house. The ropes around his wrists and ankles. The tape holding open his eyelids. Mel, her blue eyes wide from the tape, her mouth gagged, her hands and ankles bound, the tears streaming down her face, her muffled cries.

His heart lodged in his throat when Kiera, inch by agonizing inch, pushed his jeans and underwear over his hips. When she cupped his testicles with one hand and stroked him with the other, he tried not to think, but to feel. As he tore the wrapper and looked down his body, he saw dark curly hair brushing his skin.

He blinked several times before the urge to lunge back, to

strike out at her took control, and sifted his hand through Kiera's damp hair. "Put this on for me?" he asked, keeping the irrational irritation from his voice. Kiera hadn't assaulted him. Adeline had. She'd humiliated him by forcing Melanie to watch as she took him in her mouth against his will. Kiera was only trying to pleasure him as he had pleasured her. He understood this, and knew the difference between what was happening now—consensual sex between a loving couple—and what had happened at the House of Archer.

But it didn't prevent the dark thoughts from invading the moment, from leading his mind astray. Because as much as he'd hated Adeline, he'd wanted the woman at the same time. That night he'd fought for control, never giving her the satisfaction of making him hard and at her mercy. No one knew the truth, but him. With the drugs they'd been pumping him with, the woman's sensual voice ringing in his ears, and the way she had sucked his dick, he'd wanted her.

Kiera took the wrapper from him, then took him in her mouth. He tightened his hold on her hair, forced himself to not jerk away, to enjoy what she was doing to him. But he couldn't stop thinking about that night, the humiliation of being sucked off by a psychopathic slut in front of his friend.

"Harrison," Kiera murmured, bringing him back to now. Her gaze held desire, not judgment. "We're learning each other's bodies. If you don't like something, you have to let me know."

"I love what you're doing to me. It's been a long time since I've been with anyone and you're making it hard for me to stay in control."

She grinned as she stroked him, then she kissed the head of his penis. "I'd like to see you lose a little control," she said, and began rolling the condom down his length.

Once there was a shield between his erection and her sexy mouth, he relaxed. He wasn't being fair to her and had to get out of his head. This was Kiera. He trusted her, cared about her and needed to show her she meant something to him.

He lifted her toward the center of the bed, then sat on his heels next to her. "Are you sure about that?" he asked, tugging her hair until her neck arched back.

Her eyes glittered with excitement and she smiled. "Give me what you've got."

God, she was killing him. With a chuckle, he bent and pressed his lips along her neck, dragging them to the place below her ear which, when he kissed her there, always gave her goose bumps. When she squirmed and let out a soft giggle, he massaged her breasts, gently tugging her nipples, turning her giggles to groans. As he moved his hand to her neck, he kissed only her lower lip, the corner of her mouth. Sex with his past partners had always been fast, minimum foreplay, and hard fucking. There'd never been any talking, never a question of what either he or the woman he was with had liked. He wanted to talk to Kiera, to tell her how much she turned him on, to see if dirty words made her blush or made her wet.

He moved his hand from her neck along the valley of her breasts until he reached her sex. "Do you remember the day we went hiking at the lake," he asked, rubbing his fingers over her labia but never penetrating.

"Yes," she said against his lips.

He pressed a finger into her heat. "Do you want to know what I was thinking about?"

She gasped. "Yes."

He worked a second, then third finger between her slick folds. "I was thinking about the way you kiss. Shy kisses that are so sexy, I wanted to devour you." He pumped his fingers and looked down the length of her body, loving the way she undulated her hips against his hand. "I stood by that lake thinking about the woman behind the sweet kisses, the girl next door smile and layers of clothes." He pressed deep, held his hand still while rubbing her clit with his thumb. "You want to see me lose a little control?"

Her forehead wrinkled slightly as her eyes closed and her lips parted with a whisper of a moan. She nodded, pressed her hips forward and back, trying to ride his hand. Her inner muscles gripped his fingers. He'd already tasted her passion, now he wanted to feel it wrapped around his dick.

"I want the same," he said, flicking his tongue along her lower lip. "Show me what you like, tell me what you want."

"Make me come."

He smiled. "Like that?" he asked, working his hand slowly, while still rubbing her clit.

Her legs fell open. She reached for him, holding his head in place. "More," she demanded before kissing him. He swallowed her moans as he drove his fingers deep, then wanted to let out a triumphant shout when she came.

He didn't think he'd ever been this hard, and knew he wouldn't last. After quickly rolling on top of her, he pinned her against the mattress, then thrust.

Her body hugged his, drew him deep. She was so damned tight and he wished they could be skin on skin. In another lifetime.

He moved over her, trying to go slow when he wanted to slam into her body and do as she'd wanted—lose control. But his pleasure was about hers. With her body primed, he hoped he could take her over the edge with him one more time. Feel her orgasm, know that he could give her ultimate pleasure. Make her body come apart.

She met his thrusts, scraped her fingers along his chest. He glanced to her face. Her cheeks were flushed, her lips parted, and her gaze was locked on where they were joined. "Do you like watching me fuck you?" He loved it, thought it was incredibly hot.

She skimmed her fingers down his chest, then around his hips and grabbed his ass. "Next time we'll do it in front of a mirror," she said, with a sexy as hell smile. "So I can really watch."

"And I want to watch you come again." He leaned in for a quick kiss, then raised her left leg over her shoulder and rocked hard, fast and deep. Warm and wet, her muscles gripped him. His mind fogged as his body tensed and the sweetest sensation shot through him, gripping him by the balls, releasing the tension from his body. He let out a harsh breath as she groaned his name. Seconds later, he fell forward, careful not to crush her.

While he tried to regain control of his heart rate and breathing, she ran her hands along his back. When he pushed to his hands and stared down at her, the smile on her face made him want to howl at the moon. He leaned in for a kiss, then said, "That wasn't too out of control."

"I guess you'll have to try harder next time," she said, her eyes teasing as she brought her hands to his chest.

He grinned and kissed her again. "I guess I will."

Before he could slide free, she traced his tattoo with her fingertip. "Why a compass?" she asked.

"To remember where I've been and not lose track of where I'm going." Only he *had* lost track. The moment he'd decided to use Kiera, he'd strayed from the path he'd been taking, and now wasn't sure what direction to travel. Be honest with Kiera, or continue to lie? Stay with ATL, or remain in Tallahassee and start a new life?

"I love that," she said, and touched his face. "Will you stay with me tonight? No pressure."

If it were possible, he'd stay with her every night. "I sleep naked. Is that a problem?"

"Nope." She chuckled. "If we're confessing...I'm a bed-hog. Will it bother you if I'm sprawled over you?"

"Will you be naked?"

"Absolutely."

"Then I guess I'll be staying the night."

After he kissed her again, he went to the bathroom to get rid of the condom and wash his hands. She met him at the door looking cute and rumpled in a fluffy bathrobe that matched her eyes. "I'm not sleepy yet," she said. "What about you?"

"Are you naked under that robe?"

When she nodded, he stepped forward, then kissed her cheek. "Popcorn and a movie?"

She grinned. "I'll meet you on the couch."

As she left the room, he went in search for his underwear which he found easily, and thankfully dry. He stepped into them, picked up his wet clothes to hang in the bathroom, then glanced at the bed. The guilt he expected didn't take root. Maybe because he deserved a little happiness, or maybe he was just a dick.

CHAPTER 9

Tallahassee Police Department, Tallahassee, Florida
Saturday, 10:01 a.m. Eastern Standard Time

D ETECTIVE SHARON LARSON exited the TPD building and
fell into step with Bernadette. "You drive," she said to her
partner, and handed over the keys. She'd been off work since the
pulmonary embolism she'd experienced the night of Julie
Beechum's murder. The moment she'd started coughing up blood,
Bern had notified the EMTs still in front of the Beechum residence, and they'd taken her to the hospital, where the embolism
had been discovered in her lungs. During the time she'd been on
sick leave, she hadn't driven as much as usual. Just last week she'd
started to venture out to the grocery store which was only a few
miles from her home.

Bern took the keys. When they reached the sedan and climbed
in, her partner sat for a moment and stared out the windshield.

"Forget something?" Sharon asked.

"No, but you did."

She wracked her brain, then opened her leather binder and
leafed through it. They had a list of addresses, phone numbers
where they could reach witnesses who had either already been
interviewed once, or who were new on their list. She also had her
weapon, phone, purse... "Okay, I give. What'd I forget?"

Bernadette let out a long breath. "I've known you more than
half of my life." She faced Sharon, the tears in her friend's eyes
taking her by surprise. Bern wasn't a crier.

"What's wrong? Did something happen I don't know about?"

"Yeah, my best friend is keeping secrets from me."

Sharon closed the binder. "I'm not keeping anything from you."

Bernadette shoved the key in the ignition. "Then it must have slipped your mind."

"God, Bern, I don't know what the hell you're talking about. Spit it out already."

"I had to hear from Jacoby that the cancer has spread into your lungs," Bernadette said, accusation in her eyes as a tear slipped down her cheek. "Why would you tell him before me?"

"Because we work for him and he needed to be aware of my medical issues." Sharon's throat clogged with tears she refused to shed. Cancer could go fuck itself. She was done crying over it, over why the disease had to invade *her* body. But she would cry for Bern and the pain she'd caused her friend. "I'm sorry. I asked him not to say anything. He must've assumed I told you."

"A clear mistake."

"I'm sorry," she said, her voice rising. "I'm sorry that I didn't want to make you worry any more than you already do."

"Turn it around," Bern shouted back. "You would be furious with me if I didn't let you in, if I didn't ask for help. My God, you won't even let me hug you."

Because she was hurting Bernadette, the tears fell anyway. She quickly wiped them away. "I don't want your sympathy and I don't want you to feel bad."

Bernadette sniffed and also swiped her tears. "As partners, we've sworn to always have each other's backs. We've seen horrible things that have made us both fall into each other's arms and cry. We've dealt with the pain of having to tell a victim's mother that her son wasn't coming home. Ever. I never left your side after Alan died and I still swear to you, I won't stop looking for his killer. After everything we've been through—good and bad—you can't let me grieve with you."

Her eyes burned as more tears clouded her vision. "Grieve."

"Yeah, grieve. You're a fighter, and probably the strongest per-

son I know. But we both know how this is going to end." Bernadette's chin trembled. "Please don't shut me out. When you're
gone, I'll still be here. Thinking about you, wondering if I could
have done more, been a better friend." She choked back a sob. "I
don't want there to be any regrets."

"Blunt Bernie," Sharon whispered the nickname her husband
had given her friend the day he'd met her. "I'm sorry. I wasn't
thinking about what you would live with when I'm gone. I was
selfishly thinking about me and how much I don't want to see
your sadness."

"Too bad. You're going to see it anyway. Because I am sad,
and angry." Bern pressed her head against the headrest. "So
damned angry." She turned her head, and released a shaky breath.
"I don't know what I'm going to do without you."

Sharon didn't know what to say, and hadn't considered the
impact her death might have on the people who knew her well.
She had, just not to the extent that had her suddenly reconsidering
another round of chemo. "When Alan was killed, it left a hole in
me. There were days I didn't want to live, days I didn't know what
to do with myself. But I had you. And I'm going to be here for
you for as long as I can, so there won't be grief, just good memories. Right?"

Bern lifted her head and nodded, then turned the ignition.
"We should take that cruise we've been talking about for what, six
years?"

She reached into the glove box and pulled out a stack of mis-
matched fast food restaurant napkins, then passed Bern a few.
"Make good memories. I like it."

"Good. We'll book it today."

"Today? I think we should talk about—"

"Today." Bern took her hand. "Today," she repeated. "Should
doesn't work anymore. No more of this passive I'll get around to it
BS. We're going. Period."

"You got it." She grinned. "We need tans."

"No kidding. It's sad we live in Florida, but have to go on a

Caribbean cruise to get some sun."

Sharon reached over and touched Bernadette's forearm. "You're my best friend, Bern. I'm sorry I was afraid to tell you the truth. I didn't do it to hurt you."

"I know." Bern gave her hand a squeeze, then reached for the gear. "Are we ready to do this?"

"I've been sitting around the house for three weeks thinking about these murders."

"I'll take that as a yes," Bern said, backing out of the parking spot. "I've kept you up to speed on the results from Julie Beechum's autopsy and crime scene."

The woman's murder had only one similarity to the other three—she'd been cleaned. But even that similarity couldn't link Julie to the other murders. Those victims had been doused with water. In Julie's case, the killer had dumped hydrogen peroxide over her body, making it more difficult to extract DNA evidence. Including the killer's. Sharon finished wiping her nose, then crumpled the napkin. "We have a serial killer."

"Jacoby doesn't disagree, but he did refer to Julie as the outlier." Bernadette exited the parking lot, then headed east. "I get where he's coming from. The first three victims had a similar look and water was used on their bodies. Either the killer wanted to see if blondes were more fun and learned a thing or two about forensics, or we've got a different guy."

"Do you still agree that he's an opportunistic killer?"

"The ME confirmed that the cord used around Julie's neck matched the make and model of the blow dryer her husband said they owned. Jennette was killed with her own tire iron. I don't feel like he comes prepared."

"Except for the knife. He obviously brought one with him when he murdered Carla."

"Right. And there wasn't a knife missing from the Beechum residence, or one with her DNA on it."

Sharon stared out the window. "Then why not just use it every time? Why not just make it quick?"

"Since there's no sign of sexual assault, maybe the kill is how he gets off."

She nodded. "The first time was impulsive. He'd been in the park, saw Carla walking alone and went for it."

"The impulsive trait is what scares me. I don't think he watches his victims for very long."

While Sharon had sat alone in the house she'd once shared with her husband, trying to finally learn to crochet, then giving up on it, she'd considered this. "It makes sense that he might've seen Jennette, then followed her to her apartment complex." Jennette had worked in the pharmacy at the local grocery store. She'd taken ill the morning of her murder and had left late morning. "He could have seen her there, or have been leaving at the same time and picked her."

"Because she had dark curly hair? Then where the hell does Julie fit? And what about the victim from the rest area? Did he see Wendy DeMarco on the interstate and follow her?"

While that was highly possible, it bothered Sharon that he'd been brazen enough to not only kill her at a high traffic location, but in broad daylight. She opened the leather binder, worn from years of use. "Has anyone gone back to the hotel where she was staying?" Wendy had been in Tallahassee hunting down her ex who'd violated custody orders and had taken their children from her. According to her bank records, she'd had little money. The attorney working for her had said she'd spoken with Wendy at about ten a.m. the morning she'd been killed, and had stated that she'd believed Wendy was still at the motel during their conversation. Wendy's cell phone records confirmed that fact, which meant the attorney was the last person to speak with Wendy before she'd died. They, of course, had considered the ex, but he'd had an alibi.

"I went again last week. Same story from the manager. She was only there for a day, and he didn't see anything out of the ordinary." Bernadette made a turn. "I flashed her driver's license photo at the convenience store next to the motel, then across the street at the donut shop, the bar, the pawn shop and the tattoo joint. A couple of people remember seeing her, but nothing more."

Sharon leaned into the seat and rested her head back. "We need a sketch of our killer. I'd take a drawing of a stick figure, as long as we could at least get an idea of race, height, and if the guy had hair."

Bern chuckled. "If one of us was the sketch artist, that's about all they'd get."

"Speak for yourself. I can draw."

"Okay, Picasso." Bern grinned, then slowed at a red light. "Prove your artistic skills and go to paint nite with me."

Bernadette had discovered that the pub near her occasionally held a 'paint nite' where, for a fee, you were provided the canvas, equipment, art instructor and wine. After a three-hour session, you could walk out a little tipsy carrying the masterpiece you'd painted. "Deal. Sign us up." After their earlier conversation, Sharon wanted to embrace every moment she could with her best friend. When she was gone, she wanted Bern to only have good memories. "For the record," she continued, "I think Julie Beechum is the key. She's different. Maybe he realized he was becoming predictable."

"So he went for a blonde over a brunette. What about the hydrogen peroxide?"

She blew out a breath. "No clue. Still, how is it we have four bodies all showing signs that the perp tried to clean up after himself?"

Bernadette pulled into the parking lot of The Home Zone. "I don't know. I don't even know if talking to the two guys on our list is worth our time. But I feel like we need to be doing something."

The few leads they'd had, had gone dry. When they'd looked over the Beechum case again and focused on the neighbors, they'd noted that the woman next door, Mrs. Autumn Torgenson, had mentioned seeing Julie, just as a couple of men had arrived to deliver her new refrigerator. The purpose of their visit was to discover if these men had seen anything the neighbors had missed. A jogger, a person on a bike, a random car on the street. In Sharon's experience, neighbors noticed out of the ordinary stuff. But if a delivery truck and the new item their neighbor was receiving had distracted them enough, they could have missed the jogger, the person on a bike, the random car on the street. The killer lurking in the shadows.

As they exited the sedan, Sharon zipped her jacket. Last night's rain had brought with it cooler temperatures, but the sun should take them from the low fifties to the low seventies by mid-afternoon. Thinking about warmer weather, seeing gardening equipment displayed outside the home improvement store, had her considering what she'd plant in her vegetable garden this spring. Then she wondered if she should even bother. There was a good chance she could be gone by the summer or too sick to tend the garden.

The thought infuriated her, and her conversation with Bern slammed home. She wasn't dead. Her death was inevitable, but she was here and she should be enjoying the time she had left. Go on the cruise with Bern, grace her home with drunken masterpieces and plant a big-ass garden.

"I should rent one of these for my garden," Bern said, stopping to check out the small rototiller. "It was so pathetic last year. I have no idea what to plant now."

"Get out of my head." Sharon said with a grin. "I was thinking the same thing."

Bern looked up and smiled. "We'll rent the rototiller and help each other." They continued into the store. "I want a fire pit, too. I haven't roasted marshmallows in years."

"You hate marshmallows."

"So, it doesn't mean I don't enjoy roasting them." Bern nodded toward the service counter. "Let's find the manager."

When they reached the counter, a young man approached, asking how he could help them. When they flashed their badges and asked for the manager, the man's eyes rounded. He made a call and after a few minutes, a tall, lanky man who Sharon placed in his fifties met up with them.

"Detective Richie," Bern said. "We spoke on the phone yesterday. You said the two employees who'd delivered a refrigerator to Autumn Torgenson on Wilkes Street would be working today."

The manager nodded and motioned for them to follow him. "Yes. Larry Winters called in about fifteen minutes ago. He just finished dropping off and installing a washer and dryer set. He knows to come see me when he gets back to the store. Should be any minute."

He led them toward a large open bay. A sign with Tool Rental Center was displayed over the top of the entrance. "It's a terrible shame about that woman," the manager said. "I spoke with my regional manager and she said to give you whatever help you need."

Sharon entered the rental center and glanced around the room. "We appreciate the cooperation."

A man in his late twenties or early thirties was kneeling near a piece of equipment, a concrete saw if memory served her right, wiping the blade with a rag. He looked over his shoulder. First at them, then the manager. He stood. "Hey, Darrel," he said to the manager, then smiled at them. "Are you looking to rent something today?"

"Not today. But we might be interested in a rototiller in a few weeks." Bernadette stepped forward and showed him her badge. "We're Detectives Richie and Larson. It's our understanding you helped deliver a refrigerator to a residence on Wilkes Street. This would be about three weeks ago."

"Yes, ma'am. Darrel asked me to come in early to help out."

"We'd like to hear about the deliveries that day." Sharon flipped open the small notepad she always had on hand. "Let's start with your name first."

"Sure. It's Liam Forrester."

Liam and Bella's House, Tallahassee, Florida
Saturday, 3:47 p.m. Eastern Standard Time

GINGER BARKED WHEN the doorbell rang, signaling his sister and her boyfriend had arrived. Liam remained on the back deck, figuring Bella could handle greeting their guests. He still needed a few moments to climb out of the funk he'd been in since the two detectives had stopped by to talk to him. He wasn't panicked or worried that they suspected him of anything, just rattled. Adeline had been right. He'd guarantee that if he'd gone after the Tor-woman, he wouldn't be getting ready to fire up the grill, he'd be at the Tallahassee Police Department being questioned for murder.

Even if they suspected him, what did they have on him any-way? So he'd been diagnosed with a mental illness. His record was otherwise clean and he'd never been in trouble with the law. He was engaged and had a baby on the way. He contributed to society by working and paying into the system.

He still hadn't liked the detectives coming into his place of business and asking questions. He'd been tempted to tell Bella about the brief interview, then had changed his mind. Knowing his fiancée and her love for crime shows, she'd think it was excit-ing that he could've been a key witness to a murder investigation. But what would his sweet Bella think if she knew he'd thrown the blonde woman's blow dryer in the pond at the far edge of their property? He hadn't wanted to bring the evidence home with him, but he'd had little choice. Although Tallahassee was basically surrounded by forests and state parks, he hadn't wanted to run the risk of someone seeing him toss the dryer into a lake or finding it in bushes along a trail. Had the blow dryer been black instead of hot pink, he still would have brought it home. He had a routine he followed. Driving out of his way to dispose of evidence would have left open gaps and his time unaccountable.

Ginger finally stopped barking when he tossed her tennis ball into the yard and she took off after it. The husky pup was the only one who knew his secret and had almost dove into the pond to retrieve the dryer. He half-smiled at the memory and at how he'd ended up throwing her sticks for the next hour after hiding the evidence.

While the dog chased the ball, he decided he should be social. After all, it had been his idea to invite Kiera and insist that she brought her boyfriend. When he'd realized that his sister was becoming serious with the guy, he'd thought a lot about her past relationships and regretted the trouble he'd caused for her. Today was about proving to Kiera that he wasn't that person any longer. There were no more government conspiracies or alien cover-ups. Hell, even Adeline had disappeared.

"I knew I'd find you by the grill," Kiera said as she opened the sliding door.

"Wait until you see what I'm cooking for you," he said, giving her a half-hug, then looking to the man stepping onto his deck. He held out his hand to the man. "Liam Forrester."

"Harrison Fairclough."

Harrison had a firm grip and a clean-cut look. First impression: the guy was all right. "I'm glad you could come over," Liam said. "Now we can put a face with a name."

"Same here." Harrison looked out into the yard. "This is a nice piece of property. You've got a taste of the country with the city only twenty minutes away."

"Ain't that the truth?" Bella came outside. "It's been in my family since the 1940s. This old house has been added onto over the years. I doubt it's even up to code." She touched her belly, which was still flat. "Me and Liam want to have a big family. We'd love to get this place fixed up and all modernized."

He took Bella's hand and drew her close to him. "That's right. Are you handy?" he asked Harrison. The man was cut and about an inch or two taller than him. But big and buff didn't mean he knew jack-shit about hammering a nail into a wall.

"I've put in flooring and done minor kitchen and bathroom remodeling." Harrison grinned. "YouTube and trial and error were my instructors."

"I never thought about watching YouTube."

Bella rolled her eyes. "Oh, boy. Thanks, Harrison. Now Liam is gonna spend all his spare time searchin' for how-to videos," she said with a playful smile. "But if it gets our bathroom remodeled before the baby comes, I'll suffer."

Contentment, a feeling he hadn't experienced since he was a young kid, warmed Liam as much as the afternoon sun against his back. He was going to be a father. While he worried their child could carry his schizophrenic gene, he still wanted this baby. He knew the signs, knew what to look for. If their kids showed any indication that they were like him, they could seek immediate therapy. Too bad Rodney hadn't bottled the drug he'd used to cure him. But the prick, as far as he knew, hadn't told anyone. If he had, local and government law enforcement agencies would be looking for him. They'd want to know what was done to him, maybe even experiment on him to see if Rod's drug had worked.

"Harrison's a computer guy," Kiera said, keeping him focused. "I think I told you he builds websites."

Bella started for the patio door. "About all I can do on the computer is check emails. I just started payin' my bills online. And don't try to get me to go on social media. That stuff scares me."

"Why?" Kiera asked.

"There're too many crazy people out there. I don't care if they say those sites are secure and that only people you want can see your profile. If someone wants to stalk you, they're gonna get away with it." She reached for the door handle and smiled. "On that note, what can I get y'all to drink?"

He and Harrison opted for the beer Harrison had brought with him, while Kiera decided to help with drinks and bring out the appetizer she'd made. As they waited on them to return, Liam started the grill. "Kiera said you're new to the area, too."

"Yeah. I love it here." Harrison walked toward the edge of the deck. "Is that your dog?"

Liam closed the grill and glanced to the yard. He chuckled when Ginger came barreling out of the shrubs, a stick that was about half the length of her body clenched between her teeth.

"That's Ginger." He whistled. Ginger stopped and looked in his direction, then took off toward the deck. "She loves to chew on wood. Fortunately she's been keeping that habit to what she finds outside and not the kitchen table."

Ginger dropped the stick when it snagged on the rails lining the stairs, and bound for Harrison as if she'd never seen another human. "She's cute." Harrison crouched and gave Ginger some love. "I hear Huskies have a lot of energy to burn."

"Oh, yeah. I wish I had a third of her energy. I'd probably already have the bathroom remodeled."

Bella and Kiera returned outside. While the grill heated, they sat at the patio table and worked on Kiera's spinach dip.

They ate, drank and talked, but Liam's mind kept drifting. To the detectives. To the blonde. To Adeline.

He studied his sister as she talked. Kiera was always an animated talker, spoke with her hands and had an expression for every mood. Today, she looked genuinely happy, and he wondered if she was falling for Harrison. So far he seemed like a decent guy. But what if they grew even more serious? What if they decided to marry? Would Kiera continue to keep his secrets, or would she tell her husband?

That would be a serious mistake. He smiled at something Kiera said, while thinking about how much concrete it would take to weigh down Harrison's dismembered body in the pond out back.

And Adeline had thought he'd needed her. That he didn't have the balls to deal with people. The crazy bitch had no idea. These past three weeks without her had given him many glorious moments of clarity. He'd been able to think straight—about Bella, his sister, the people he'd killed. With the hunger pangs now satisfied, he believed he truly loved Bella, enough that the urge to kill her no longer existed. When he looked at her, he no longer saw a carbon copy of Adeline. He saw his future. A future without ropes.

As for his sister, he regretted what he'd put her through, but there wasn't anything he could do about it now. He couldn't raise their parents from the dead. Nor would he want to—his mom had needed to go. After living with a schizophrenic for over twenty years, she knew what was happening to him, and knew what he was becoming. He'd seen her daily planner, the doctors' appointments she'd scheduled, and had to get rid of her before he'd ended up in an institution. After his first psychotic break from reality, he'd ended up in the hospital a week after their deaths anyway. But that had been okay. If their mother had still been alive, she would have begged his doctors to push drug therapy on him and keep him institutionalized, just as she'd done to their father on numerous occasions.

Kiera used to cry every time her father was sent on 'vacation' to the 'special place'. She'd once told him that if it had been up to her, she would have kept their dad home and taken care of him herself. He'd counted on that the day he'd rigged his parents' car and caused their untimely deaths. As the older sibling, Kiera had made it her duty to see to it that he'd received proper therapy, but had refused to place him in a halfway house or a mental facility.

Although he loved his sister, if she betrayed his trust he would punish her by killing her lover. She had no clue what he was truly capable of, but he would make sure she knew about Harrison's death. In gory detail.

No one betrayed him.

Adeline had. The slut had used him with the promise that she would free him. She hadn't physically freed him, the blonde woman he'd taken the switchblade from had. But Rodney and his drug had at least cleared his mind of the voices, the ones that had made him paranoid, wimpy and in a constant state of worry. The ones that had sometimes suppressed the memories of killing his parents. He supposed he owed Adeline a little gratitude. Her encouragement to embrace his dark side had given him permission to accept who he truly was, who he'd always been. Not a monster per se, just one crazy son of a bitch you didn't ever want to fuck with.

"So what made you decide to move to Tallahassee?" Harrison asked him.

He reached for his beer. "Kiera didn't tell you?" He decided to take the direct approach to discover just how much his sister liked the guy.

Without looking to Kiera, Harrison gave him a slight nod. "She told me you'd left Colorado unexpectedly, and why."

This must be love. Kiera had never told past boyfriends about his mental illness until he'd made it impossible to ignore. "The life of a mercenary can take you all over the country," he said with a grin, and looked to his sister. "I'm glad those days are over."

She smiled. "Me too."

"Me three," Bella chimed in as she stood. "My life changed for the better the moment I met Liam." She leaned down and kissed him.

"How'd you two meet?" Harrison asked.

"I was needin' a carpet cleaner and met him when I rented one from his work. I never could get that stain cleaned and ended up rippin' out the carpet of the back bedroom anyway. Lost my carpet, but gotta man." She grinned and squeezed his shoulder. "We'll have to come up with a more romantic story to tell our kids."

"I think it's a cute story." Kiera also stood. "Harrison and I met while I was being attacked by lizards."

Harrison chuckled. "Viciously attacked."

"Exactly," she said, picking up her boyfriend's empty beer bottle. "Need another?"

"I'm good for now. And you don't have to wait on me."

Liam was seriously starting to like this guy. He was direct, treated his sister nice, owned his own business. He just might stay out of the pond after all.

While the girls worked in the kitchen, he and Harrison grilled the beef kabobs he and Bella had prepared earlier—a favorite of Kiera's. After they'd eaten, and the sun had moved behind the tall pine trees, Kiera and Bella both pulled on sweatshirts, which was his cue to start a fire. When he told Bella that was his plan, she said she'd bring out the fixings for making s'mores, and asked him to gather sticks to roast marshmallows. Harrison and Ginger tagged along, following him to the pit he'd built several weeks ago.

"I have property envy." Harrison grabbed a few logs from the pile near the small shed Liam planned to repair next weekend. "I grew up in the city, so even a half-acre would feel like country living to me."

"I couldn't imagine living in the city. It's just not my speed." Memories of when he'd been in Atlanta, convinced he was working with a mercenary named Mitch were fuzzy. He remembered the bus depot, the paranoia, the filth…the kidnapping. "Do you think you'll make permanent roots here in Tallahassee?"

Harrison was grinning as he wrestled a stick from Ginger. "I don't have any desire to be anywhere else."

A vague answer, but Liam supposed he shouldn't have expected the man to proclaim his love for Kiera, or spell out his plans for the future. They'd only been dating a month.

Once the fire was lit, he and Harrison dragged lawn chairs around the pit. As the wood crackled and the blaze grew, Liam pulled his switchblade from his pocket, then began whittling one of the sticks Harrison had gathered into a fine point. Ginger must've tired herself out, because the active pup had slipped under his chair and now was snoring.

"Cool blade," Harrison said.

Liam glanced to the knife, to the way the orange glow from the fire bounced off the steel. "It's a souvenir." He applied the blade to the stick again. "Until last August, I'd never been outside of Colorado. If Kiera's told you about me, I'm assuming she told you about our father."

"She did."

"He was convinced people were watching him. Sometimes it was the government, for a while it was the mafia. He couldn't handle all the cameras in an airport, and he claimed using public transportation left him too vulnerable. So, I'd never been outside of Colorado until last August. My reasons for leaving might've been a little bat-shit crazy, but I ended up learning a lot about myself and taking control of my mental illness." He tested the point of the stick. "This switchblade represents that journey." He'd also used it to kill four people. If the police swabbed the switchblade would they find the DNA of the old people, the park lady and the blonde? Could they match the knife blade to the fatal wounds he'd given the two women? He should probably toss it into the pond along with the blow dryer, except it was handy to have around.

"Well, I'm glad you made that journey. If you hadn't, I wouldn't have met Kiera."

Yeah, he was seriously starting to like Harrison. He hadn't had a male friend who was real and not imaginary since he was a kid. Even then, he'd mostly hung out with Kiera. It'd be cool to have a buddy to grab a beer with, or to help with a remodeling project.

Liam reached for another stick. "I'd toast to that if we had a couple of beers." He glanced to the house. "I'd settle for a toasted marshmallow at this point."

"I was just wondering what was taking Kiera and Bella so long."

"I'll run up to the house and see what's keeping them."

Harrison stood. "I got it, man. Do you want me to grab you a beer while I'm up there?"

"That'd be great," Liam said, then watched Harrison head toward the deck. Ginger woke and crawled out from under the chair. He stroked the dog's fur. When she stilled and stared at the house, he followed her gaze.

The worry on Harrison's face as he ran from the house had him dropping the stick he'd been whittling and rising from the chair. He slipped the switchblade into his back pocket and met Harrison halfway.

"What wrong?"

"It's Bella."

His stomach dropped. Without another word, he took off.

When he reached the house, he found Kiera in the hallway leading to the bedrooms and bathrooms. "Where's Bella?" The concern in Kiera's eyes scared the shit out of him. And why in the hell was she carrying towels. "What are you doing?"

"She's in the bathroom. Liam, you need to remain calm."

His heart beat rapidly. "I am fucking calm," he said, walking backward down the hall. Then he called out for Bella.

Kiera followed him. "I need the keys to your car. We need to get Bella to the hospital."

She stopped him outside the hall bathroom where he could hear Bella's muffled cries. When he noticed his sister's eyes had misted with tears, his throat clogged. "Is it the baby?" he managed.

Kiera's chin trembled as she nodded. "Bella's bleeding."

CHAPTER 10

Cash and Mel's House, Tallahassee, Florida
Sunday, 2:42 p.m. Eastern Standard Time

HARRISON PULLED INTO Cash and Mel's driveway. His mind was still on Kiera, on everything that had gone down yesterday, along with what he would disclose to his friends. Since their discussion at his garage, Cash had turned into a jerk anytime Kiera's name had been mentioned. Mel, he knew, was just as obsessed as him, and wanted Liam caught and put in prison. She also knew he was still dating Kiera. If she had an issue with his and Kiera's relationship, she kept her feelings to herself.

He climbed out of the Jeep, then walked toward the front door. Their garage was open, and only Mel's Camaro was inside. Good. He didn't want to deal with Cash or have him start taking on the role of his conscience. He didn't need Cash piling any more guilt on top of what was already dragging him down. As he knocked on the door, his stomach tightened with regret anyway. He'd been as honest as he could to Kiera, but the deception that remained could destroy anything good between them. Sometimes he didn't care. He selfishly wanted what he wanted. For the first time ever he had a girlfriend who actually wanted to do more than just have sex and do shots. But then he'd remember the tears in her eyes as she'd talked about her past, her trusting gaze, her sweet kisses.

The door opened. "Hey," Mel greeted him with a smile. "Just in time. I need help getting Dolly strapped in her chair."

He entered the house and followed her into the kitchen. Dolly was in her dog bed, head up and panting. "Hi, girl," he said, then bent and rubbed the dog's head.

"She was sound asleep when Cash left, so he didn't want to disturb her." Mel wrung her hands and kept a worried gaze on the German Shepherd. "I used to have no problem doing it on my own, but her good legs aren't so good anymore and I don't want to hurt her."

"I've got it," he said, easily lifting the eighty-pound dog and securing her to the doggie wheelchair. Dolly licked his face, then rolled toward the patio door. "When's Cash going to be home?"

"I'm not sure. Maybe a half hour or so." She walked toward the patio door, then opened it and let the dog out. "Are you planning on being gone by the time he gets back?"

He followed her outside. "Why would you ask that?"

She lifted the lid of the outdoor cooler and pulled out a couple bottles of water. "I dunno. You two haven't been acting right for a few weeks. And the last time you came over, you didn't stay long and barely spoke to Cash."

That had been because Cash had pulled him aside to blow him shit about Kiera again. "Nothing is wrong on my end."

She sat in one of the chaise lounges near the pool, then slipped her sunglasses from the top of her head to the bridge of her nose. "How many friends do you have?" she asked, toeing off her flip flops.

"Enough." He sat at the edge of the neighboring lounger. "Why?"

"Well, I think you have about as many as I do, maybe less. That's not a bad thing."

"I came here to talk about Liam, not get all deep about friendship."

"Maybe I want to get all deep."

Irritation blossomed in his chest. "I said that I don't."

She turned her head toward him. "Is this where you're going to get all dark and brooding on me? Maybe tell me to frick myself."

"How is it you have no problem getting rid of a dead body, but you can't say 'fuck'?"

"Fine. I think you're being a fucking jerk."

He half-laughed and shook his head. "I don't need it. I'll see you around."

As he started to rise, she asked, "Do you love her?"

"No," he lied, and sat back down. "I take it Cash told you about our discussion?"

"You mean your argument? Not all." She grinned, then reached over and petted Dolly when the dog settled by her chair. "So she's expendable?"

His irritation morphed into anger. "I never said that."

"But isn't that how you've approached dating her? She's disposable. A means to an end. A way to get to her brother."

"I won't deny that I purposefully approached her—"

"With the intent to date her and get close to her brother."

Anger and guilt collided and made his stomach sick and his head ache. "When I came up with the plan she was a name, not a person."

"And because your life hasn't been so great, and you haven't had your share of women, you deserve to have a little fun at this girl's expense." She shrugged and adjusted her sunglasses. "She's related to a serial killer. So how could her feelings really matter?" She glanced at him again. "Are you ready to tell me to go frick myself yet?"

"Is that what you want?" he asked, disappointed with himself and with Mel. "Instead of going the passive-aggressive route, which, by the way, doesn't suit you, why don't you just put it all out there?"

She swung her legs over the side, sat up and faced him. "Fine. You've been dating Kiera for a month. Are you sleeping with her?"

"None of your business."

"You're right, it's not. But the Harrison I know has integrity. Are you going to tell me that Rodney and Adeline stripped that away from you? Are you going to blame the drug?"

"No," he shouted, and stood. "You don't think I feel guilty? Kiera's a great girl. And she likes me." He hit his hand to his chest. "I even told her I went to prison, and she still accepts me."

"So you gave her bits of the truth to offset the guilt."

"Get off your high and mighty fucking pedestal."

She stood. "Sorry, but from my pedestal you're looking like a total douche bag."

He waited for the anger, the headache that accompanied the dark thoughts. Instead, embarrassment swallowed him, made his face hot. "I just keep screwing up," he said, taking a couple steps backward. "If I'd reported the Dougals, I wouldn't have—"

"We're home," Cash called from inside.

"Wouldn't have what?" Mel asked.

We're home? Rather than get caught up with Cash and his buddies from the garage, he needed to get the hell out of there. Kiera wouldn't be back from her brother's for several hours. Since he'd spent the night and today with Kiera, he hadn't had time to check in on Detectives Larson and Richie, and wouldn't mind poking through their files.

The patio screen door slid open with a foreboding screech. "Look what cat drag into yard."

Fuck me. Harrison stared at Mel. With her sunglasses on, her eyes were unreadable. But the set of her jaw told him enough. She'd set him up.

He turned as Vlad stepped onto the patio. Part of him was relieved to see his friend, while the other part of him wanted the Russian to go back to the Everglades. Vlad knew him too well. He knew too much. He would disapprove of everything Harrison had done.

As Vlad walked across the patio, Harrison wished those dark thoughts, the reasons he'd escaped Everglades City, would fill his head now. He wanted to be angry, not relieved. He wanted to finish what he'd started, right or wrong, his way.

"How's it going?" he asked, because what else was there to say.

The Russian towered in front of him. "This all Harry have for

Vlad? How it go?" He shrugged. "Vlad go okay. New roommate. New job at boat shop. Misty still love of Vlad life. And Polina gain three pound."

He'd forgotten about the roommate and honestly couldn't re-call the guy's name. All he remembered about the man was that he was a former Navy SEAL and had served with Ryan. "What's the new job?"

"More like train."

"You mean you're training for a new job."

"That what Vlad say. Captain Ryan say Vlad make good boat captain. So, Barney have been—"

"You're joking, right?" Had Ryan lost his mind? Vlad could handle a car at any speed and in any situation. The man also had quick reflexes. So Harrison had no doubt that Vlad could handle an airboat. But to captain one...with passengers?

Mel giggled. "You're so goofy. It's just too cute." She tapped Vlad's arm as she walked past him. "Whatcha drinkin', honey"

"Why this goofy or joke?" Vlad looked to Cash who shrugged. "This no jokey joker. Vlad deadly serious."

"But you have to be friendly with customers," Harrison re-minded him.

"Vlad friendly."

"You have to tell stories about the Everglades."

"Vlad have story." He nodded and pointed. "Once upon time, there live alligator name Polina." He laughed, then gripped Harri-son's shoulder. "Vlad is jokey joker. Captain Ryan would have been drunk for to let Vlad run boat tour." Vlad pulled him in for a man-hug that about threw out his back. After he'd finished squeezing the life out of him, Vlad stepped back. "Vlad also lie. Misty have move on. She say Vlad no husband material."

"I'm sorry to hear that, man. I know you really cared about her."

"Yes. Vlad thought Misty love of life. But after break up, Vlad heart not broke. Yes, Vlad had sadness. But then Vlad won-der...was the love for Misty or for blonde with big titties?" Mel cleared her throat while Cash burst out laughing. "That should have been said in private, no?"

"Yeah, man." Harrison grinned, and slapped his friend on the arm. "It's good to see you."

Vlad studied him with his ice-blue eyes. "It is good to be seen by Harry. Vlad have worry you would not return to the Glades."

"I'm coming back."

"But will Harry come *home*?"

He'd been asking himself the same question for the past couple of weeks. "I'm not sure."

"Would you stay in Tallahassee?" Mel asked.

"I like it here."

Vlad helped himself to a water from the cooler. "What about job?"

He sat at the patio table. "Over the past couple of weeks I've designed a few websites."

"Rachelle said she's happy with what you did for the bar," Cash began, also taking a seat. "She plans on writing up a testimonial."

Vlad's brows furrowed with confusion. "What this about?"

"I also created a website for the guy who lives down the hall from me. He started selling fitness products on the side. Two of his buddies who are doing the same thing in other parts of Florida have already contracted me to design their websites."

Mel grinned as she sat next to Cash. "I'm really proud of you."

Ten minutes ago she was calling him a douche bag. But he understood why. He *had* fed Kiera bits and pieces of the truth.

"So Harry go legit?" Vlad settled his body in the chair diagonal from his. "No more ATL? No more chase bad guy?"

"I'm thinking about it."

"Why?"

"Why'd you decide to stop working for criminals and work for Lola?"

"Vlad go where Harry go," the Russian said as if this were a well-known fact. "That what best friend do, no?"

Racked with guilt, Harrison didn't know what to say. These past five months he'd been a jerk to Vlad, hoping to drive his friend away. Prior to that, he and Vlad had fought constantly—about the Russian's smoking, the gator, his annoying habits. Vlad had given him just as much hell, and had made it clear that living with him wasn't a stroll on the beach.

"Man, you've gotta cut the cord," Cash said to Vlad.

"What cord? Phone? Electrical? That very dangerous."

"He's talking about an umbilical cord," Harrison explained. "Which was a shitty thing to say."

"I wasn't being shitty. All I'm suggesting is that Vlad be his own man."

Vlad narrowed his eyes at Cash. "Repo Man think Vlad little baby in diaper? Make no mistake. Vlad have no problem living on own. Harry and Vlad…have joint."

Cash cocked a brow. "Look if you two want to smoke weed, that's your business. But don't be bringing it around here."

Harrison chuckled. "Do you mean bond?"

"да. Vlad also prefer cigarette to wacko tobacco," he said, and looked to Harrison. "Vlad pledge friendship to Harry. If not for friend, Vlad would work for another criminal. That no good. Vlad spend too much life wasted on corrupt man. Vlad owe Harry life."

Vlad had killed for him, and had helped him take revenge against the man who murdered his brother. After he'd escaped the House of Archer and was hospitalized, Vlad had spent the night at the hospital, never leaving his side. The Russian was a loyal friend who owed him nothing. He, on the other hand, owed Vlad an apology and an explanation.

"You said you know why I moved out of Polina's."

"да, it why Vlad keep door locked."

"Why didn't you say anything?"

"Vlad have demon, too. It mine to fight." The Russian leaned forward. "Harry have several demon, да?"

"Yes. Real and in my head."

"The fight in head is for Harry alone. But real demon can be slay."

"Don't you listen to him, Harrison," Mel said. "Killing Liam is not an option."

The Russian grinned. "Liam? Vlad suspect this what Harry search for. You have found man?"

"I not only found him, but I think I'm in love with his sister."

Vlad's bark of laughter startled Dolly. When Harrison didn't even crack a smile, the Russian sobered. "Harry serious?"

"As a Honey Badger on the hunt."

Vlad puffed his cheeks and blew out a breath. "That serious."

"Seriously stupid," Cash said. "I warned you, man. I told you to cut bait three weeks ago and focus on Liam, not the girl."

"Don't get all fired up, honey." Mel touched her husband's forearm, but stared at Harrison. "This is a delicate situation that requires some thought."

"What's to think about?" Cash asked. "Kiera is going to find out Harrison has been lying to her and drop his ass. So she'll not only have to deal with finding out her brother is a serial killer, but that her boyfriend used her to put Liam in prison."

"You've made this point clear, and so has your wife," Harrison said, growing tired of defending his actions. "You think I'm a dick, and Mel thinks I'm a douche. I get it."

The Russian held up a hand. "Vlad think this problem can be solved."

"How's that?" Cash asked.

Based on far off look in Vlad's eyes, along with his small smirk, Harrison knew the answer. "Kill Liam," he said.

"Exactly," Vlad said. "Kill Liam. Then Harry become shining knight who comfort sister in need of time. Harry secret stay safe, get girl, fall in love and make many baby. It perfect plan."

"The big goof has a point," Mel said with a shrug.

"He does," Cash agreed. "I mean, it's not like Liam's innocent."

Harrison stared at them. "You three are insane."

"Vlad say before, Harry not killer. But, would Harry kill for girl?"

"If it was a matter of saving her life, absolutely. But we're talking murder. Premeditated, by the way. I'm not going to prison for murdering a murderer."

"Thank God," Mel said with a sigh.

Cash nodded. "Yeah, I was starting to worry about you, man."

"You two just sat there and said it was a great idea."

"No," Mel began, "we agreed that killing Liam was the best way to save your relationship with Kiera. But it don't make it the best choice. There're others. And the more I think about it, I don't see why Kiera has to find out it was you who ratted out her brother. You can take that secret to the grave."

"Maybe. But I still need to give the detectives a reason to question Liam," he said. "I went to his house for a cookout yesterday."

Mel's eyes widened. "Oh. My. God."

"Yeah, having dinner with a serial killer is kind of weird," Cash added. "What's he like?"

Harrison shrugged. "Nice. Hospitable. Seems like he genuinely cares about his sister and fiancée. That all changed by the end of the evening, though. Do you remember how I told you Liam was going to be a father?" When Mel and Cash nodded, and Vlad gave him a blank stare, he quickly brought the Russian up to speed.

Vlad's blond brows drew into a deep V as he leaned back in his chair. "Vlad have change of mind. Vlad will kill Liam. It better for baby to not know such man."

"Actually, Bella had a miscarriage last night."

"That good fortune in camouflage," Vlad said with a nod, his facing relaxing.

Mel stared at Vlad for a moment. "Now I know I've told you before that's not how the saying goes. I swear you screw stuff up on purpose."

After living with Vlad for over a year, Harrison was convinced of it.

Vlad waved her off. "Vlad know it *blessing in disguise*. But that so…cliché. Now. Enough discussion of Vlad words." He focused on Harrison. "Is Liam cause of miscarry?"

"Not at all. He was visibly devastated. I'm telling you, the guy was a freakin' mess. Kiera was going to drive them to the hospital, but Bella insisted on staying home."

"How far along was she?" Mel asked.

"Maybe ten weeks?"

"That's tough," Mel said. "Unfortunately, I miscarried at eight weeks." When Cash took Mel's hand, she looked at her husband. "It just wasn't our time."

As the couple kissed, Vlad met Harrison's gaze, then the Russian rolled his eyes. "So, tell Vlad more about cookout. What the fiancée like?"

"Bella's a local. She's nice and, get this, she looks a lot like Adeline. Same long dark curly hair, similar build."

Mel tapped her manicured hot-pink nails along the glass table. "I think it's strange Liam plans to marry a woman who looks like Adeline, especially when he's killed three women who have similar hair color and style."

"*If* he killed those women," Harrison corrected her. "We have no proof. But Liam does own a Husky."

The Russian brightened. "Young Vlad once have Siberian Huskies, Annik and Bars." He grinned. "Дед use dogs to pull cart or sleigh on farm."

"What's a Дед?" Mel asked.

"Grandfather," Cash answered, and looked to Vlad. "Vlad told me about his grandfather. He was an admirable man."

Vlad's grin broadened. He had talked to Harrison about his childhood, too, and had every reason to be proud of the man who'd raised him. His grandfather, Maksim Aristov, had been raised on the family farm, fought for the Soviets in World War II, then afterward had gone back to farming. After Vlad's father had died, Maksim and his wife, Lizaveta, had taken in Vlad's mother, Polina, and had practically raised Vlad and his siblings.

"Anyway," Harrison continued, then explained to Vlad how forensic investigators had found a dog hair, specifically the hair of a Husky, on a woman who had been murdered nearly two months ago. He then went on to fill Vlad in on the subsequent murders. "But a dog hair isn't enough of a reason to contact the detectives and risk exposing Nick and ATL."

"Maybe Harry call Nick and find out?"

"No way. The guy was mad enough the last time I saw him. He's going to be pretty pissed off when he finds out I used his ID to get a hit off the bloody fingerprint."

"But the fingerprint is enough evidence to bring Liam in for questioning," Mel said.

"That I took illegally. I tampered with evidence and didn't report a crime. Then I kind of impersonated an officer of the law."

"You did more than kind of," Cash reminded him. "But if you contacted Nick and explained the situation, he might surprise you."

"Right. With a warrant for my arrest." Harrison shook his head. "There hasn't been a murder in over four weeks. I keep thinking that maybe I'm wrong about the women killed in the Tallahassee area. Maybe Liam had nothing to do with it and only killed the old couple."

Mel crossed her arms. "What about the dog hair?"

"It was *one* hair. And the victim was found in a park where people walk their dogs."

Cash mimicked his wife's pose. "Sounds like you're trying to come up with an excuse to let Liam off the hook. And why not? Those old people were recluses. No one cares that they were savagely murdered by a psychopath created in a lab by other psychopaths."

Anger, disappointment and loathing brewed in Harrison's stomach. Churning. Burning. "Go fuck yourself."

Mel gasped. "Harrison!"

He pushed back his chair and kept his gaze on Cash, who didn't look stunned, but ready to kick his ass. Let him try. He'd about had it with Cash and the constant digs—about the way he'd screwed up his personal investigation, about Kiera...he didn't need it. "Sorry, Mel," he said. "But I'm tired of your husband's bullshit. Everything that comes out of his mouth is negative and nasty."

"And true," Cash added. "That's why you're pissed off at me. You know I'm right."

Harrison stood. "You got it, dude. You're always right." There was no point in trying to argue with Cash. The man was stubborn and temperamental. There were days when he thought they were friends, and others when he didn't know what the hell to do with the man.

"Where are you staying?" he asked Vlad.

"Vlad stay with Repo Man and Ice Cream Lady."

"Well, I'd let you use my place, but I only have one bed-room."

"Why not shack up with the serial killer's sister and let Vlad have your place?"

"Dang, Cash." Mel stared at her husband as if he'd just sprung an extra head. "What's gotten into you?"

When Cash shifted his narrowed gaze from him to Mel, his face softened. "Sorry, baby, but I don't have any respect for cow-ards."

"Harrison is *not* a coward." She tossed her long blonde hair over her shoulder. "How could you say such a thing?"

"Mel, I don't need you to defend me." The toxic combination that had been brewing in his stomach boiled to the surface. Before he did or said something he might regret, and worried he'd be too tempted to punch Cash in the head, he edged away from the table. "Before I forget, last night, Liam used your switchblade to cut down a few sticks. He claimed the knife was a souvenir and repre-sents his *journey*. I plan on getting it back to you."

"I'll get it back for my wife."

"That's what this is about?" Harrison chuckled. "Mel warned me you were a jealous guy, but I never thought you'd be jealous of me."

"Is that true?" Mel asked.

Cash rubbed his eyes with one hand and let out a sigh. When he looked at his wife, he said, "No. I trust you, and I trust Harrison." He turned his head and glared at him. "It took months for Mel to get over what happened at that house. I still don't know what Rodney and Adeline did to you two, and as much as I want to, it's probably best that I don't. But now you're back, stalking the man who's caused my wife to wake up screaming, or crying, or a puddle of sweat. And what pisses me off is that you're getting soft. Since you've been seeing the sister, you've lost your edge. You're looking for reasons to stay with her."

"I know," Harrison shouted, pushed both hands through his hair and looked to Mel. "I never meant to cause you any hurt. I thought you'd want to be part of this because of everything that happened. But now that I think about it, I didn't really give you much of a choice." The way Mel had looked with her eyes taped open, tears streaking down her face, and bound to a chair filled his head and intensified the guilt. His need to go after Liam disturbed Mel, could destroy Kiera, and damage Nick's career. "I'm sorry. I've been selfish."

"You don't need to apologize, honey. I know you'd never hurt me. He has to be stopped. To be honest, I'd have been upset if you hadn't told me about Liam."

He waited for Cash to make a smartass remark, but he didn't. Instead, the former repo man walked to the cooler and pulled out several beers. He handed Harrison one. "I don't think you're a coward, but you need to get your head straight." After giving Mel and Vlad their cans, he sat down and nodded toward the empty chair. "I'm no criminal investigator, but I'm married to a woman who used to be, so that should count for something."

Mel chuckled. "Of course." She shifted her gaze to Harrison. "Come on and sit down. We need to figure out how to handle this."

"By 'this' you mean the messed up situation I created," Harrison said. Wanting to be with people who understood and accepted him despite his many mistakes, he took a seat.

"Liam killed the first two Tallahassee women before you'd found the Dougals," Mel reminded him.

"And now two other women are dead."

"Vlad have question," the Russian said, opening the can of beer. "Everyone know Vlad like blonde with big…" He cleared in throat. "Everyone know blonde Vlad type. Liam have type, too."

"So why deviate, right?" Harrison asked. "It's possible he didn't kill Julie Beechum. Not only did she have the wrong hair color, but her body was doused with hydrogen peroxide, not water."

"Still a little too coincidental." Mel said. "What's funny is me and Cash just watched a crime show where the killer used hydrogen peroxide to remove DNA evidence."

"Yeah, I remember that." Cash nodded, and looked at him. "Not to be a dick, but does your girlfriend watch those kind of shows? Don't forget, someone started that fire at the Dougals'." He lifted his beer. "I get you dig this girl, but what'll you do if you find out she's been cleaning up after her brother?"

"You're married to a former cleaner."

Vlad laughed. "Harry right. Mel not Ice Cream Lady for just selling ice cream cone to little kiddies."

Mel grinned. "Got that right. But there's a difference. I was doing a job."

"You were hiding evidence. Illegally," Harrison countered.

Mel turned to her husband. "He has a point."

Harrison set aside the unopened can of beer. "I don't think Kiera is covering for her brother."

"Harry must be honest with self. Would Harry cover for brother?"

He'd carved up his brother's stomach with a knife to save not only Mickey's life, but the others who were being threatened. "You know I would."

"So it settled. Kiera not off hook. Maybe Bella?"

"Yeah," Mel agreed. "The fiancée could be the cleaner. A desperate woman might do just about anything to keep her man."

He'd been more concerned with stopping a murderer than figuring out who was cleaning up after Liam. Or maybe he'd been ignoring a huge, looming possibility. Kiera could be covering for her brother. The day Julie Beechum had been found murdered, he'd run into Kiera in the parking lot of their apartment complex. Her shirt had been wet, and she'd claimed water had splashed onto it. He pulled out his cell phone and opened up a search engine.

"What are you doing?" Mel asked.

He quickly typed in the address for the Club and for Julie Beechum's residence. When the directions and distance popped up, he set the phone on the table. "I saw Kiera the afternoon Beechum was murdered. She had a meeting at work, then went to the grocery store. I saw her unloading her car, so I don't think Kiera's responsible for cleaning up after her brother."

A total lie. Kiera's meeting had been cancelled. Between the distances from Beechums' to the grocery store, then to the Club, it was possible she'd been to the dead woman's house. The day the murdered woman had been found at the rest area had been the day they'd gone to the luau. He'd seen her that morning, then later that evening. She'd been off that day, and had told him she'd run errands and had gone to a park. Could she have also stopped at the rest area?

"Then we'll have to look into Bella," Cash said. "Or, maybe you're wrong about the fire. Maybe Liam set it."

"*That* would make the most sense," Mel agreed. "Just because he'd clocked into work that day doesn't mean he didn't take an extra-long lunch break."

Harrison nodded, and wrapped his mind around the prospect. He had to shake the suspicion off Kiera, and hated himself for suspecting her in the first place. Kiera had opened up to him about her brother, and had admitted that he'd been a burden, that she wished he'd stayed missing. He could tell Mel, Cash and Vlad, but didn't want to break Kiera's trust.

"I ran the distance after I found out about the fire. From where Liam works, it would take him about forty-five minutes to reach the road that leads to the Dougals'. From there, he probably would have hiked to their place rather than risk leaving tire tracks. So figure another ten plus minutes to hike to the house."

"He'd need time to set the fire, then head back," Cash added. "So at the minimum, we're talking two hours to do the deed."

Harrison pressed his fingers into his shoulder where the muscles had grown taut. "It's not like I've been completely stalking the guy." No, he'd saved that for Kiera. "It's possible he'd left for a couple of hours and returned to work."

"Honestly," Mel began, "that makes sense to me. Think about it. Unless Liam told Kiera what he'd done, or *she* was following him, how would she know where to find the Dougals? Plus, doesn't she have a full-time job? And while I've seen desperate women perform desperate and dumb acts, covering up not just one, but a bunch of murders for a guy you just met, doesn't add up to me."

"Vlad agree. Ice Cream Lady make good sense."

The tension in Harrison's shoulders lessened. Not much, though. What was supposed to be a quick stop at Mel and Cash's to tell them about the cookout had turned into more than that. They'd forced him to admit the truths about Kiera he'd been avoiding, and Cash had opened his eyes, pointing out that he'd selfishly reopened Mel's wounds—wounds that hadn't even had the chance to heal. On top of all the emotional crap he hadn't wanted or been prepared for, Vlad was now in town. And he was good with that. The Russian knew him better than anyone. He knew his secrets, his mistakes and his faults, and still called him friend. Would Kiera? She might be okay with keeping his incarceration in the past, but what if she found out about Honey Badger and the work he'd done for the bastard...and all the people who'd died because he'd been forced to press a button? Would she call him a coward for carving into his brother's stomach to save lives, his included? What about ATL? He'd done things for the underground agency that should have him serving ten to fifteen in the Florida State Prison. For what he'd done during this *private* investigation, he could still go to prison.

He shook off the thought. "I need to go," he said, rising. "Vlad, let's get together tomorrow."

"Vlad have plan, but will call Harry."

"What plans?"

"He's coming to the garage with me," Cash said as if that should be answer enough.

"Okay. Then call me whenever." Once Harrison was in his Jeep, and making the fifteen-minute drive back to the Club, he focused on what he'd planned to do until Kiera came home. She'd promised to make him dinner, and he was looking forward to another one of her home-cooked meals. Mostly, he was looking forward to her company. If he were honest with himself, he couldn't care less if she'd been covering for her brother. But he was also a liar and a thief. Yeah, it'd bother him, but he'd guarantee his past would bother her, too.

Still.

What kind of fucked-up fantasy world was he living in? He'd never been in love, so how could he know he was in love with Kiera? She liked him, and he liked that. A lot. It felt fan-fucking-tastic to have someone care, to want to be with him, to consider him, to touch and kiss him. He loved every minute and didn't want it to stop. Just thinking about never seeing Kiera again made his insides sour. Especially if she walked away hating him. But Mel might be right. He could get his man and keep the girl without her ever knowing the beginning of their relationship had been calculated.

How? What had he missed? What had the detectives missed? There had to be something, one tiny thing, that would give him a substantial reason to direct the detectives to Liam. A dog hair wouldn't cut it. No one knew Liam had been at the House of Archer, so Mel's switchblade wasn't enough, either. But he'd bet the detectives would love to get a hold of that piece of evidence. If

Liam had used the switchblade on Carla Rodriguez and Julie Beechum, there could be DNA on that blade.

As he drove into the gated community, he reconsidered calling Nick. Based on the detective's mood the last time they'd spoke, he couldn't see that conversation going well. No, a call to Nick would be a worst-case scenario.

But a worst-case scenario would mean another dead body.

When he veered toward his building, he noticed Kiera closing the door of her car. She turned and waved. In that moment he realized his past didn't matter. The things he'd done, or been forced to do, the choices—good or bad—weren't important. What mattered was now.

Kiera could hate him for putting her brother in prison. But what would she think of him if he'd been able to stop another murder, and hadn't? Could she accept a man who would allow her brother to get away with murder?

He parked the Jeep. As he approached her, she closed her door and smiled. Sometimes her smile was cute and dimpled, other times it was sexy. Today, the smile she gave him was tired, and her eyes held relief. As if seeing him was what she'd been hoping for, what she'd needed.

After they'd left her brother's last night, she'd been visibly upset and unusually quiet. Suspecting she was worried how the miscarriage might affect Liam and his relationship with Bella, he hadn't pressed her. Instead, he'd crawled into bed with her and held her throughout the night. When Kiera wanted to talk, he'd listen. Even this morning, while she'd prepared a meal to take to Liam and Bella, she hadn't said much.

When he finally stood in front of her, he took the large tote bag from her hand. "Are you okay?" he asked, worried about her, and wanting her to open up and tell him what was going through her mind.

Her chin trembled, she pressed her lips together and nodded. She suddenly looked so small and vulnerable, he wanted to scoop her in his arms, toss her in his Jeep and drive. Run away with her and pretend her brother had never existed, start a fresh life, one that had the promise of a future with Kiera.

He wrapped an arm around her instead and kissed the top of her head. "Come on, let's go inside." Once they were in her apartment, he set the bag on the floor and pulled her close. When she gave him a stiff hug, he released her. "Did I do something wrong?"

A tear slipped down her cheek. "No. Liam did."

CHAPTER 11

"**W**HAT DID HE do to you?" Harrison stepped forward, his hands fisted at this sides, his face hardening and his eyes narrowing.

Kiera immediately went to him and placed a hand along his tense jaw. She didn't want him angry. She'd dealt with enough of that already today. "He didn't do anything to me. I'm sorry, I didn't mean to upset you."

"You're the one who's upset. You looked like you were about to cry when we were in the parking lot."

"I'm sorry."

He took her by the upper arms. "Stop apologizing and tell me what's wrong."

Now she wished she'd kept her mouth shut. She wanted to have fun and enjoy the rest of the afternoon with Harrison. Worried she would tear up again and, this time, start bawling, she didn't want to go into detail.

"Oh, he was just being a jerk," she said. "He's mad about the situation and took it out on me." At least that was what she'd kept telling herself as Liam had berated her, telling her the lasagna she'd made them wasn't fit for the dog, that she looked more pregnant than Bella had, that Harrison would never stay with her because she was an insecure, whiney, nagging bitch. What had hurt the most was when he'd told her that he wished she'd never moved to Florida, and better yet, that she'd been in the car with her parents the day it had gone over a cliff.

Harrison's expression was still hard and angry as he stared at her, his gaze demanding and intense. "What did he say to make you cry?"

"It wasn't what he said," she lied. "It was how he acted." She pulled free and walked toward the kitchen. "I shouldn't have brought it up, and I'd rather forget about it." She opened the refrigerator and reconsidered baking the lasagna she'd made earlier. "How about breakfast for dinner?"

"What happened to the lasagna?" he asked, coming around the small island. "I thought you made two trays?"

She had, one for Liam and Bella, and one for her and Harrison. "It's in here. I wasn't sure if you'd want it."

"Why wouldn't I? Did Liam say something about it?"

After closing the refrigerator door, she turned and faced him. "Not at all. It's just such a heavy meal, but I'll lighten it up with a salad."

"Or I can take you out."

"That's okay. We both just got home." And, damn it, there was nothing wrong with her lasagna, or her relationship with Harrison. As for looking pregnant, Liam knew she was weight-conscience. Even as a kid she'd been insecure about being a little thicker than some of the girls at school. If her brother had wanted to get even with her about something, or just be a jerk, he'd made chubby comments. But he hadn't employed those tactics since he was around fifteen. She wasn't whiney or a nag, and she refused to allow her brother to make her insecure and begin questioning herself.

She glanced at the clock on the microwave, then reopened the fridge. "I'm in the mood for a cocktail."

"Did you just check the time?" he asked, amusement finally lightening his tone.

After she pulled a jug of lemonade from the fridge and set it on the island, she opened the lower cabinet for the bottle of strawberry-flavored vodka. "I did." She grinned. "It's not quite five, but it's close enough."

"I can't let you drink alone." He grabbed a couple of glasses, then filled them with ice. "And I don't expect you to cook for me. I'll take care of the lasagna and salads."

She chuckled as she began mixing their drinks. "The lasagna just needs to go in the oven and the salad mix tossed into a couple of bowls."

He leaned in and kissed her cheek. "I will do all of that for you."

"My hero," she said, batting her lashes. "So tell me about Cash's. It had to be more fun than my brother's house." She'd been a little jealous when Harrison had told her he planned to hang out with Cash and his wife. Since moving to Tallahassee in December, she had yet to make any friends. There were a few girls at work she liked, but they were all married and had kids. The only thing they really had in common was their careers. She'd met a few women at the Club who had invited her out for drinks. They were fun, but had gone to college together and were a little too cliquey. Right now, the only people she could call friends were Harrison, Bella and…Liam. While she loved being with Harrison, she longed for female companionship. Bella was a nice person, but the only thing they shared was her brother.

"You're making me feel bad." Harrison said. "I told you I'd go with you."

He had offered, which had been sweet and supportive. Last night, her brother hadn't handled the miscarriage well, and Harrison was still a stranger to him and Bella, and she hadn't wanted to make anyone uncomfortable.

She walked around the island, then kissed him. "I know you did. Don't feel bad."

"I still do," he said, wrapping an arm around her and slipping a hand in the back pocket of her denim capris. "But I'm glad I went. My buddy, Vlad, rolled into town unexpectedly, so it was great catching up with him."

"Vlad? Is that his real name?"

"Yep. He's Russian. He's weird and inappropriate." He grinned. "You'll love him."

"Oh, you mean I get to actually meet him?"

His brows furrowed. "What do you mean?"

She rested her arms on his shoulders and clasped her hands at the base of his neck. "We've been dating for a little over a month, and I haven't met any of your friends."

His eyes filled with apology. "I'm a jerk."

"No, my brother is a jerk. I *was* starting to wonder if you were making up these people, or if maybe you're secretly married and trying to hide our relationship," she teased. Neither thought had ever entered her mind, but it had bothered her that he hadn't introduced her to his friends. Especially Melanie and Cash. It sounded as if he was tight with them, so naturally she'd hoped they could double date.

He chuckled. "Trust me, they're real." He moved his hand from her pocket and slid it inside the back of her T-shirt. "I'll see if Mel and Cash want to get together this week."

"And Vlad," she reminded him. "I've never met a Vlad before."

"You'll never meet anyone else like him," he said, caressing her skin. "So what days this week will work for you?"

"I'm scheduled eight to five every day but Tuesday, and I'm off this weekend."

"All weekend? Nice. We should go on a road trip. What do you think about spending the weekend in Pensacola?"

Butterflies filled her stomach. A romantic weekend away from reality. "I love that idea." She bent her head and kissed him. "I'll see if I can get out of work a little earlier on Friday."

He brushed her hair away from her face and tucked a chunk of it behind her ear. "It's okay if you can't. I planned on spending the weekend in the hotel room."

"So no beach?" she asked, loving his train of thought. She could easily picture an uninterrupted weekend in bed, and honestly couldn't care less if they went to the beach. Now that Harrison had helped her climb out of the mood Liam had put her in, she wanted to play. "That's too bad. I just bought my first bikini."

His gaze dropped to her breasts. "Really?"

"It's pink," she said, adjusting her legs until she practically straddled his thighs. She then leaned closer, making sure to brush her breasts against him, and pressed her mouth to his ear. "*Hot pink.*"

He slipped both hands under her shirt, then pushed the material up and over her breasts. "You should probably try it on for me," he said as he unhooked the clasps of her bra. "Let me help you get out of these clothes first."

Grinning, she pulled her T-shirt over her head, then tossed it on the floor. "Are you going to help me put on the bikini, too?"

The straps of her bra slid down her arms as her breasts spilled forward. He finished removing the bra, then leaned in and brushed his mouth along one of her nipples. "Now that you brought it up, I think I should." He undid the front of her capris. "Where's the bikini?"

"Bedroom. Top middle drawer." She moved between his legs so he could tug her capris and underwear over her hips. "I'll model it for you later," she said, reaching for the front of his jeans. "The bedroom is too far away."

His warm breath fanned across her nipple as he chuckled. "If you're not going to try it on for me, why am I getting you naked?"

She stepped out of the capris before she tripped, then walked backward toward the short hallway leading to the bedroom. "You do have a point. There really is no other reason for me to be naked on a Sunday. Especially when it's barely five o'clock."

His eyes darkened as he moved his gaze from her breasts to her sex. He pulled off his shirt. "I can think of a few." He stood, then followed her. When they reached the bedroom, he walked past her, and straight to the dresser. "I'll show you what they are after I see you in this," he said, pulling the hot pink bikini from the drawer.

With a combination of nervousness and anticipation, she stared at the bikini. Last week, while shopping for a new bathing suit, she'd seen the two-piece on a mannequin. The sales clerk had caught her checking it out, took one look at the one-pieces she'd planned to try on and shook her head. "Come on and show off the goods, sister," the clerk had said with a wink, and Kiera had decided, *what the hell?* She'd tried the bikini on and, to her surprise, had loved the way it had looked on her. But what if Harrison didn't?

Harrison had enjoyed her body Friday night and again yesterday morning. But this bikini modeling idea wasn't a good one. Their sexual relationship was still too new. The late afternoon sunlight streaming in from the windows was suddenly too bright. She had the urge to shut the blinds and make the room as dark as possible. Hide her body's flaws, the few unwanted dimples, the curve of her hips and DD breasts.

"Here, I'll take it," she said, holding out her hand. She'd take the two-piece and slink off to the bathroom. She hadn't tried it on since the day she'd been shopping, and could check her reflection before exposing herself to Harrison.

He stepped closer. "That's not gonna happen."

"Then can you at least close the blinds?"

"No one can see in here, so that's not gonna happen either." He stopped in front of her, his body only inches from hers. "Are you getting shy on me?"

"I...no. It's just really bright in here."

"Good. I get to look my fill."

She let out a nervous half-laugh. "There's a lot to look at, so this might take a while. Maybe I should have brought my drink with me."

He didn't crack a smile. Instead, he took her hand and pressed it along the front of his jeans. He released a breath when she rubbed his erection through the denim. "If I ever heard anyone say something like that about you, I'd think they were petty, mean and probably had their own insecurity issues."

"That's different."

"No it's not. I love your body. So it bothers me when you rip on yourself. I don't get it. You were fine when we were in the kitchen. What happened from then until now?"

"I had second thoughts about how I looked in the bikini. I don't want you to be disappointed." As she stroked him, she touched his hard abs. "I mean, you're solid and I'm...soft."

A half-smile curved his mouth. "In the perfect places," he said, gripping her hip. "I don't ever want you to be uncomfortable with me. So if you'd rather make the room dark and just have sex, I'm good with that."

Her cheeks heated. "I'm not hiding from you."

"Good." He removed his hand from over hers, and went to his knees. Keeping his gaze on hers, he held open the bikini bottoms. "Take your time. The view from here is beautiful."

Warmth spread throughout her. Not from embarrassment, but from the heat in his eyes. Using his shoulder for support, she stepped into the bikini bottoms, then prayed the elastic would be forgiving as he brought the material over her thighs and hips.

Instead of quickly putting them in place, he took his time. Peppered her skin with hot, open-mouthed kisses as slowly, inch by inch, he worked the bottoms up her legs. He stopped mid-thigh, left them stuck there, and slid his hands over her hips. His fingers dug into her, but rather than becoming self-conscience of having too much flesh, she loved the way he held her. Possessive, greedy, as if he couldn't get enough of her. When his warm breath blew against her dark curls, her sex pulsed. She ached for him to fill her, kiss her, make love to her.

"This part of you is so sexy." He kissed the slight muscle running from her right hip to her pubic bone, the same area that she loved on his body and had been fantasizing about licking. "When I first saw you in those pink polka dot panties, all I could think about was kissing my way to here," he said, and pressed his mouth against her sex. When his tongue slipped between her labia, she used his shoulders to steady herself. Then he kissed the small swell of her belly, and slowly slid the bottoms in place.

She pressed her inner thighs together. "You didn't need to put those on," she said as he picked up the bikini bra and rose to his feet. "I thought things were going just fine without them."

The corner of his mouth slid into a grin. "I did, too. That's why I'm looking forward to stripping you naked." He moved behind her. The hot pink top dangled below her breasts as he wrapped the string around her ribcage and tied it at the middle of her back. He palmed her breasts and kissed her neck, brushing his lips along that sweet spot just below her ear. "You barely fit in my hands." He shifted both of them until they faced the mirror above the shorter dresser. "Look at how hot you are."

With Harrison's big body behind her, his large hands holding her better than any bra she'd ever owned, she not only looked sexy, but he made her feel incredibly desirable...adored. At this point, she'd have sex with him in a room filled with mirrors and under florescent lights. The man had made his point. He wanted her, flaws, or what she'd perceived as flaws, and all.

He breathed against her ear, sending goose bumps along her skin. "Now let's see how hot you look in this bikini." He moved his hands from her breasts to capture the pink triangles. After he fitted them over her, he tied the string at the base of her neck.

She stared at her reflection. This was what she'd seen in the dressing room mirror. A sexy, desirable woman. "I was thinking about you when I tried this on," she said, meeting his hungry gaze in the mirror.

"What were you thinking about?"

She grinned. "You taking it off me."

Chuckling, he slid his hand down her torso, then pressed his fingers against her sex. "I plan to, and I think you need to try to get off work early on Friday so we have some beach time after all."

She pushed her rear against his groin. "I thought you wanted to spend the weekend in the room."

"I'll do that, too, as long as I get to see you in this again."

When he teased her nipple, she dropped her head against his chest, and reached behind to rub his erection. "Let's talk about this later."

"Good idea," he said, untying the string at her neck and back.

The top fell to the floor in a hot pink puddle. As she went to turn, he grabbed her hips, stopping her, then walked her a few steps toward the dresser. With his gaze on hers, he hooked his fingers through the edge of the bikini bottoms, then tugged them down. Once they were over her hips and revealing her dark curls, he moved to his knees. Exposed, uncomfortable, she turned to stop him.

"Hands against the dresser," he said, nipping the top of her right ass cheek.

"No, that's okay." Her rear wasn't her best feature, and she'd prefer to keep the hot moment hot.

"It's not an option."

She met his teasing gaze in the mirror. "Do I have any options?"

"Not really." He grinned. "Now, how about those hands on the dresser?"

Closing her eyes, reminding herself that Harrison desired her, flaws and all, she did as he asked. As the air hit her bare bottom, she tried not to tense, tried not to imagine what her rear looked like up close. Then his hot mouth was on her sex. She sagged to her forearms and raised her bottom in the air to give him whatever access he needed. Insecurity could go to hell. There was no place for that nonsense here. Not with the way her body was being loved.

Loved...a strong word, but she didn't care. She was in love with Harrison, and probably had been from the moment he'd told her he wanted to get to know her smiles. He might not love her, but he cared, and he treated her with more respect than any man she'd ever known. She trusted him with more than her body, and hoped what they had would last.

As he worked his mouth along her sex, dipping his tongue between her swollen lips, flicking it across her clit, her legs grew shaky. Her mind drifted from thoughts of everlasting love when he began kissing his way from her inner thighs, to the back of her leg, then along her rear and spine.

She heard his jeans hit the floor and opened her eyes. Met his gaze in the mirror when the head of his erection kissed her sex, then groaned when he filled her. The drag of his arousal, the deep connection, sent more goose bumps along her skin. She gripped the edge of the dresser and met each thrust…wanting the moment to last, and yet anxious for that ultimate pleasure she knew he could give her.

"I can't get enough of you," he said, his voice harsh, husky, and filled with emotions she wouldn't even try to decipher. Not now. Not yet. She'd thought she had known what love was until she met Harrison. But that had been when she was in college, when she was young, naïve, a dreamer. She still loved to dream, but understood reality. Damn if she didn't want this—them—to be a reality.

She wanted to say something, to tell him *enough* never needed to happen. With their relationship still new, and unable to find the right words to express her feelings, she pressed into him. Welcomed each thrust, the possessive grip of his hands as they bit into her hips until her orgasm rushed through her. Releasing a moan, she closed her eyes and welcomed the pleasure, rode out the waves of utter ecstasy. As her orgasm multiplied, he pulled out of her with a low grunt and released his passion at the base of her spine.

Their gazes met in the mirror. His eyes held no apology. Instead, she saw the possessiveness she'd felt in the rough grip of his hands, the deep thrusts of his hips.

He dragged in a breath, and still keeping his eyes on hers, kissed her shoulder. "Don't move," he said, then disappeared into the bathroom. Within seconds, he was cleaning her back with a hand towel. When he finished, he stood behind her, then traced the tips of his fingers along her ribcage. "I'm sorry I forgot the condom."

"I'm glad you remembered, because clearly I didn't."

A shy smile curled his lips and he looked away. She reached back to bind her arms around his neck. "What's that about?" she asked, surprised that he'd act self-consciously after not only forcing her to expose herself to him, but after giving them both a fantastic time.

"You're special." He wrapped his arms around her waist. "I guess sometimes I can't believe I'm with you…that a woman like you would want to be with me."

His past hit her, but didn't bother her. She'd spent her adult life carrying a secret only she knew, and living with a murderer. Harrison's four-year stint was nothing compared to the prison she'd been living in for the past ten years.

"I think you're special, too. I also think we deserve each other."

He turned her away from the mirror to face him. There was longing in his eyes, as if he struggled with believing her. She moved her hands along his broad chest and shoulders. He was a strong, confident, masculine man. The quiet vulnerability he allowed her to see made her heart ache, and at the same time deepened her love for him.

"We all make mistakes," she continued. "But not everyone grows from them. You have." He'd been raised in an abusive environment, had received little love and care, and had been forced to fend for himself. She couldn't begin to imagine growing up like that, and wouldn't think of condemning him for the choices he'd made. She'd been lucky enough to be raised by two loving parents. Even though her dad hadn't always been himself, there had never been any abuse, there had always been food on the table, and there'd always been hope for a better future. "I admire the man that you are and don't judge you for your past."

He kissed her. Tender and achingly sweet. As he deepened the kiss, intimately sliding his tongue along hers, she wondered if he would judge her if he knew her secrets. Would he condemn her for the choices she'd made and consider her a coward?

"Do you have anything else you want to model for me?" he asked as he moved his lips from her mouth to her cheek and rubbed his hand over her back and rear.

She reached between their bodies and stroked his arousal. "I was just thinking I'd like to see you model my apron. You did say you'd cook for me."

"Do you have an apron big enough?" he teased.

She focused on Harrison, the way he set a fire along her skin, and how sexy he'd look wearing nothing but her apron. She planned to be buried with her secrets, so there was no point dwelling on them. There was no point in allowing her brother, and what he'd saddled her with, to ruin the happiness and possible future she had with Harrison.

Liam and Bella's House, Tallahassee, Florida
Sunday, 6:39 p.m. Eastern Standard Time

"I TOLD YOU to kill her," Adeline said, her tone condescending and bitchy. *"You should have slit the useless twat's throat from the start."*

"Shut up!" He gripped his head, covered his ears and fought the throbbing through his skull. "You're the useless, *jealous* twat."

"Jealous? Of what? Good God, lover, your sweet Bella has nothing on me. She's so pathetic, she can't even carry your child."

Pulling at his hair, he jumped to his feet. He bent and grabbed a rock, a few sticks, then threw them toward the pond. "You're probably happy about that, aren't you? You get off on other people's pain."

"But are you really in pain, Liam? Be honest. Are you truly broken up over the baby?"

"How dare you question me?" He picked up a thick fallen branch and swung it like a Samurai warrior, whacking leaves off trees, cracking thin saplings, kicking up weeds and grass until the tip of the stick caught in the mucky mud at the edge of the pond. Releasing a frustrated cry, he kicked the branch, then fell to his knees. With a whimper, Ginger slunk away and hid in the tall grasses. His vision distorted by tears, he watched the dog go, then he looked to the treetops. The sky behind the pine trees was a combination of pumpkin vomit and purple unicorn shit. Bella loved when the sky took on these color hues, and thought it was beautiful. He saw no beauty in it today, and wanted no color. Instead, he craved the blackness.

"I never thought I'd get married, let alone have a child," he said between heavy breaths. "I wanted the baby. I wanted to be a dad."

"But you would've ended up like your father, so it's probably best the dumb twat miscarried," Adeline taunted him. *"Even worse, what if the child had ended up like you? A pathetic, paranoid schizophrenic who needed his sister to babysit him."*

"Fuck you. I'm not that man anymore." He looked to where Adeline sat on the crooked tree branch hanging over the water. Today, her hair was loose and wild, the way he loved it, and she wore a flimsy, pale-pink see-through sundress. Although the pines surrounding the pond cast eerie shadows along the water, there was enough sunlight behind Adeline to reveal the outline of her nipples and the dark patch of hair at the apex of her shapely thighs.

He hated that he wanted her. Given the chance, he would take her right here, right now. No woman had ever satisfied him like she had, not even Bella. Sex with Adeline had been dirty, had muddied his mind and soul with demented, dark thoughts of violence and murder, namely hers. More than that, she understood him, maybe more than he'd understood himself.

She hiked up the hem of her dress, spread her legs and dangled them from the tree. *"Then what kind of man are you, lover? The working man? The fiancé? The wannabe daddy?"*

"I'm all of those things."

"I wasn't finished," she said. *"Let's not forget murderer and psychopath."*

"I wasn't until I met you."

When she laughed, he turned away. *"How can you lie to yourself? Isn't it exhausting? Admit it, lover,"* she whispered in his ear, sending a chill through him. *"You were a killer before we met. I just helped you finesse your skills."*

He turned and faced her. She now stood inches from him, the light breeze moving her curls and adding to her sensual, forbidding allure. "I hate you."

"No, you hate yourself, and that's sad. I've never hated myself. I accepted me, and didn't give a shit what anyone else thought." She smiled. *"I kidnapped and drugged you. I used your body any way I pleased. I warped your mind, fed you lies until you believed me. I never killed out of vengeance or for a cause. I killed because I could, because I wanted to, and because I loved it. Why did you kill your parents?"*

"My mother was going to have me institutionalized."

She gave him a knowing smile. *"That's not the whole truth."*

Anger and guilt settled on his chest. "If you know the truth, then why are you asking?"

"Because you need to admit it out loud. Own your reasons, lover. What did your mother see? What scared her so badly that she chose to take preemptive measures? I mean, what the hell? You hadn't showed any signs of psychosis, you hadn't been diagnosed with schizophrenia…what had the bitch seen?"

His face heated. He didn't want to admit anything. He didn't want to take fucking ownership for what he'd done. Damn it, he didn't want to be like Adeline.

"Tell me," she whispered. As the two hushed words bounced through his head, tumbling over each other, running together in an echo, he saw the shock and disgust on his mother's face, along with the shame in her eyes. *"What did she see? Look, Liam. Tell me."*

He stared at his hands. Instead of seeing mud under his nails and dirt on his knuckles, he saw his fingers gripping a maroon and gold throw pillow that had gold tassels at each corner.

"Lift up the pillow," Adeline encouraged him.

He slowly raised his arms, and smiled. Great Aunt Rosaleen's lifeless blue eyes stared up at him. Her mouth gaped open, stretching her pale, paper-like skin.

"Why did you do it?" Adeline asked, but her voice had changed

and she sounded just like his mother.

"Because she was old and I wanted to know what it was like."

"Did voices tell you to kill her?" Adeline and his mom asked.

"No," he admitted. The pillow disappeared, leaving him with filthy hands.

"What about when you killed your parents?"

"I didn't hear any voices until after they died." His head began to throb again as Adeline grew louder, more demanding. He honestly couldn't remember much from that time, only that he'd hated his mother. "Why does it matter?" he asked, rubbing his temples.

"I suppose it doesn't. You're going to kill for me anyway. I guess I was hoping you'd take more pleasure from it."

The fine hairs along his neck stood on end. "It's been more than three weeks since I've fed you."

She grinned. *"No wonder I'm so hungry."*

He ignored his own cravings. "Where did you go?"

"Who said I ever left? You see, lover, I've never been one of those smiley, happy types. You're right about me, I take pleasure in other people's pain. I thrive on it. And if I can inflict the pain? I like to call that an orgasm of the mind."

"My happiness weakens you." Was that possible?

"You'll never truly weaken me," she said, her tone now harsh, cautionary. *"You're lucky I haven't completely taken over your mind, otherwise the twat would be dead. You do know how much I want you to kill her, correct?"*

"You've made it abundantly clear."

"You claim to love her, why? Why didn't you kill her that first day like you'd intended. And don't lie to yourself or me. You'd fanta- sized about her death. I saw the fantasy, then later watched you masturbate in the shower over it."

"Shut up," he warned her, but couldn't deny that Adeline was right. He'd had every intention of killing Bella the day he'd come here to pick up the carpet cleaner. But as he'd walked into her house, Adeline's demands had only made him want to defy her.

The hungry bitch wanted to control him, to be the only woman in his life. She didn't like Kiera, either, and would surface when his sister was around.

"She's poor, uneducated trash," she continued. *"You're so much better than her. I bet she got herself pregnant on purpose. She tried to trap you, which is exactly what those types of women do best."* Adeline's image faded with the dying sun. *"But she does look like me, doesn't she? I think that's why you keep her. It's me you want. Not her. When you're fucking the little slut, do you fantasize about me? When she ties you up, who do you see riding you?"* she asked, her whispers turning seductive and making him hard. *"Don't you want to go in there now and strip her naked? Punish her for not being me, for not being able to give you that baby you wanted so badly?"*

God help him, he did.

"How easy would it be? You can tie her up, keep her in your bed and do anything and everything you've ever desired. I'll be with you, lover. I'll help you fulfill every single one of your fantasies."

He saw the image Adeline painted, along with the fear in Bella's eyes and the terror on her face. He wanted it to be real. For the first time in weeks, the hunger pangs returned. He doubled over with them.

Ginger darted from the grass, came to his side and licked his face. The sun had completely vanished behind the tall pines, leaving only the dog's white fur visible. He pushed himself to his feet and stayed on the path that led to the open yard at the back of the house. As he walked, avoiding decaying logs and using his arms to protect his face from the tree branches creeping into the path, Adeline continued to whisper. Encouraging him to take what he wanted, to kill because he could, and because…he loved it.

As he reached the yard, a cramp seized his stomach. His head grew dizzy, causing him to stagger and slow his steps. But he pushed forward. Bella would be waiting for him, hurting over the loss of their baby. As the thought entered his mind, he waited for guilt to follow.

Nothing.

"There's no reason to feel any guilt. You're entitled to her. Take her, lover."

He stopped at the glass patio door. "I...love her."

"So? You loved your parents at one time, too, and your sister. I meant to mention this earlier, Kiera could be a problem. Have you thought about that? Would she tell her boyfriend about you?"

"She won't betray me."

"I think you should make it so she understands what will happen if she does."

He thought about Kiera, about what he'd said to her today, then once again waited for the guilt.

Nothing.

Good.

He gripped the wooden handle, then slid open the door. The zesty scent of Kiera's lasagna still hung in the air. He smiled when he remembered the look on his sister's face when he'd ripped apart the dish she had made them. She'd had tears in her eyes when he'd called her fat and pretty much told her he'd wished she was dead.

"She's a nag, and if she keeps coming around, she'll find out you're not taking your medication."

Which had been why he'd treated her badly. Kiera was too perceptive and knew him too well. At first, he'd been glad she'd moved to Tallahassee. Her voice and smile soothed him, reminded him of their childhood, of the good memories and the point in his life when he'd cared, truly cared about people. He could never hate Kiera and he really didn't want her dead. But if he ever caught her snooping in his medicine cabinet, he *would* make it so she wouldn't bother him again.

"Liam?" Bella called from their bedroom.

His balls tightened. The hunger pangs hollowed out his stomach.

"Mmm, yes," Adeline whispered. *"Take, lover. Bind her to the bed."*

She's still bleeding.

"So what? Cut her more. Bathe in her blood. Taste it on your tongue, and you'll taste power."

When he'd sliced the Dougal man, his blood had burst from his neck, splashing Liam in the face. The same thing had happened after he'd cracked the old lady with the cast iron frying pan. He knew what blood tasted like, and wanted to taste Bella's. He wanted that power over her. He wanted her exactly the way he'd wanted Adeline: incapacitated, at his mercy and begging for him to kill her.

"Because you can."

"Because I can," he repeated, and headed down the hall. With each step the fantasy became a reality. As he neared the opened door, he didn't see yellow paint on the bedroom wall, he saw streaks of Bella's blood. When he stopped at the threshold, Bella wasn't sitting in bed leafing through a magazine and wearing a sweatshirt and sweatpants. No, Adeline was naked, her arms and legs were stretched, her wrists and ankles secured with rope. Her black curly hair fanned across the pillow, capturing her tears, the blood oozing from her mouth and nose. Her body was covered in bruises, welts and cuts.

Adeline laughed. *"Go ahead and hurt me, lover. Kill me...kill me...kill her."*

"There you are," Bella said, looking up from the magazine. "I was wonderin' where you'd gotten off to." Ginger came into the room, and immediately went into her crate. Bella smiled. "I see you tuckered her out."

"Kill her. Make her suffer. Please, lover. Make me suffer."

Bella set the magazine on the nightstand, then tossed her hair over her shoulder. "You've been quiet since Kiera left. Is everythin' okay?"

He stared at her neck, pictured it bruised by his hands. As he remembered kissing her there, and the softness of her skin, the bruises faded, along with Adeline's *killing* mantra. Another cramp gripped his stomach, twisting it, demanding that he satisfy the craving.

"Honey, you're scarin' me," Bella said, moving off the bed. She walked toward him, then suddenly she stopped and put a hand low along her belly. Her eyes widened with alarm as she stared at him.

"What is it?" he asked, sickly hoping she knew what he wanted from her so she could run.

"I'm bleeding. Bad. I need to get to the bathroom before I bleed all over my sweats."

He grabbed her arm before she could move past him and gripped her tight.

Wincing, she looked from his filthy hand to his eyes. Her breath quickened. She licked her lips. "You're hurtin' me."

"I know."

Pity and pain filled her eyes as a tear slipped down her cheek. "Is it the white noise?"

He shot his other hand out and grabbed a fistful of her hair. Fighting Adeline, fighting the hunger, he yanked Bella's head closer. "I'm going out." He released her, and she took a jerky step backward, and hugged herself.

"Where are you goin'?" she asked, taking another step back.

He noticed the dark blood staining the inner thigh of her light gray sweats. The blood served as a reminder of what he'd lost, of the happiness he'd foolishly embraced. Before the anger sliced through the last shred of decency he possessed, he started for the door. "None of your business."

"What are you doing?" Adeline asked, her voice frantic. *"Liam, stop. She needs to die, she needs to fulfill your fantasies."*

"You're scarin' me," Bella said again. "Honey, please don't go."

Adeline filled his head with a piercing shriek, stopping him cold. *"Listen to her. Stay. Kill her."*

He glanced to his fiancée, ignored the blood on her pants, and the tears streaking down her cheeks.

"She wants you to stay with her," Adeline shouted.

"Keep the bedroom door locked. Don't let me in when I come

home, and don't come out until the morning. Understand?"

With a nod, Bella hugged herself tighter. "You'll be okay? You won't need the rope?"

He ignored Adeline's giggles. "Not tonight. I'll be fine."

She blinked a few times, then wiped her nose. "Should I be scared?"

"Terrified," he said, then slammed the door shut. He raced down the hall, grabbed the keys to his SUV off the kitchen counter, and rushed out the door.

"Well, that was stupid."

"Why is that?" he asked as he started the car.

"You had a perfectly good woman you could kill right in your own home. Where are you going to find another one on such short notice?"

"You said you were hungry." He glanced in the rear view mirror and met Adeline's gaze. "How about some fast food?"

CHAPTER 12

Crabby's Bar and Grille, Tallahassee, Florida
Monday, 5:39 p.m. Eastern Standard Time

DREADING HAPPY HOUR, Harrison helped Kiera from the Jeep. He now wished he'd never called Mel about meeting up for drinks. Although he was proud to show off Kiera, let his friends get to know her and find out what a great person she was, he didn't want to share her. Their time together was limited. He'd known it from the start. No matter the outcome, he wouldn't walk away from the mess he and Liam had created with the girl. Because in the end, he would have to be honest with her.

"Are you sure you want to meet my friends?" he asked as he took her hand. "They're just not right."

She laughed. "I grew up with crazy, so I'm sure we'll get along just fine."

"Sorry, I didn't mean—"

"Oh, stop it." She nudged him. "You're allowed to make crazy jokes around me. But if you make fun of dogs with underbites, I might take offense."

Chuckling, he leaned in for a quick kiss. "I wouldn't dream of it," he said, then held the door open for her. When they stepped inside, they made their way to the back of the restaurant where the patio bar was located. He spotted Vlad immediately. "See the tall blond guy smoking a cigarette?"

"The one that looks like the German bad guy from the first *Die Hard* movie?"

He supposed, if Vlad grew out his hair. "Yeah, that's Vlad.

The girl next to him is Mel, and next to her is Cash."

"My God, she's gorgeous. Why didn't you tell me?"

He stared at Kiera's profile. "Why would I?"

She met his gaze and smiled. "You wouldn't," she said, then moved to her tiptoes and kissed him. "Let's get a drink."

Vlad was the first to notice them walking toward the table. He didn't say anything to Mel or Cash. Instead, he gave him a big, approving smile. At that moment, Harrison hadn't realized how nervous he'd truly been about introducing Kiera. Last night, after the modeling show in the bedroom, they'd spent the evening fooling around, eating lasagna and drinking strawberry vodka and lemonade. She'd told him they deserved each other, but he knew otherwise. She was too good for him. Too trusting, too loving. And he could only hope that he was right, that a special woman like her would love him. A criminal, liar and thief.

"Harry," Vlad said, when they reached the table, and held out his hands to Kiera. "Vlad Aristov." He kissed both of her cheeks. "It is pleasure to meet Harry girlfriend."

Mel laughed. "You big goof. You've got to learn to master the English language. You make it sound like Harry's girlfriend is hairy."

"That not what Vlad say. And Vlad think Harry girlfriend beautiful."

Kiera laughed, too. "Thank you." She turned her attention to Mel and Cash. When Vlad finally let go of one of her hands, she reached across the table and introduced herself before he had the chance. "Harrison has told me a lot about you. I was looking forward to meeting you."

"Us too." Mel forced Vlad to sit. "Harrison mentioned you were a physical therapist."

Cash groaned and shook his head. "Don't start."

"What?" Mel asked, her eyes wide and innocent. "Your back has been bothering you since you stopped going for treatment."

Cash cocked a brow. "You're the reason my back has been bothering me."

When a simmering look passed between the couple, Vlad rolled his eyes. "Harry must help. Living with Ice Cream Lady and Repo Man have been hell on Vlad. The kissing and eyeballing…it all too much."

"Bring your stuff over in the morning."

"Or tonight," Cash suggested. "The guest room is close to our room."

Mel nodded. "It's true."

"This why Vlad have drove separate with bag packed."

"Oh, honey," Mel began, "we didn't mean to make you feel uncomfortable."

"It okay." The Russian stood. "Vlad must find more beer," he said taking the empty pitcher with him toward the bar.

"Harrison, I am so sorry," Mel said.

Cash shook his head. "No, she's not, and neither am I. Don't get us wrong. We like Vlad."

"Love him," Mel added. "But we can't live with him. So we figured since you and Kiera spend so much time together, maybe it wouldn't be a problem if he stayed with you. At least you're used to him."

"Were you guys roommates?" Kiera asked.

Harrison nodded, but kept his focus on Mel's apologetic gaze. "Vlad is always welcome at my place." The dark months after the kidnapping suddenly seemed so distant. The petty fights they'd had prior to his time with Rodney and Adeline were just that— petty. He'd already apologized to Vlad, but needed to again.

"Is beer okay, or would you like something else?" he asked Kiera.

"Beer is good."

"да. Beer is good." Vlad set two large pitchers on the table. "So, Kiera, come from Colorado?" he asked, pouring her a glass.

"Aurora, which is outside of Denver."

"I've never been west of Alabama or north of Georgia," Mel said.

"Ice Cream Lady have not see snow? That crazy."

"No, what's crazy is that people pay to vacation in snowy places and do things like ski. I just don't get what's so fun about putting on layers of clothes, then going out in freezing weather to exercise."

Cash nodded. "I'm with my wife. If you want an adrenaline rush, I could come up with other ways than tumbling down a mountain."

"Repossessing cars isn't a sport," Harrison reminded him, then chuckled when Cash gave him the finger.

"This true." Vlad nodded. "Do Harry girlfriend enjoy animals?"

Mel wrinkled her forehead. "What kind of questions are you asking the poor girl?"

"What the problem? Vlad want to learn more about Harry girlfriend."

"No, he's looking for another opinion about his gator." Cash reached for the pitcher. "I told you what to do. Set it free and get a dog."

Kiera turned to Harrison. "Are they talking about an alligator? As in, he owns one?"

"Unfortunately."

"Vlad have already made up mind. Polina must go." He smiled at Kiera. "Vlad breaking ice with Harry girlfriend."

Mel reached over and rubbed Vlad's shoulder. "I'm really proud of you. I know this has been a hard decision to make."

"Vlad capture in middle of crushing rock and brick wall. But it right to do. Plus, Vlad cannot bring Polina here away from swamp."

"Could we backtrack for a sec?" Kiera asked. "You seriously own an alligator named, Polina?

"That what Vlad say. Polina good pet."

"Hold up," Harrison said, no longer interested in discussing the gator. "You plan to move to Tallahassee."

"Vlad say that before." He grinned. "Vlad have job with Cash."

His temper rose as he turned his attention to Cash. "Vlad doesn't know anything about cars."

"He can drive one, and he's big and badass."

Mel looked to her husband. "I told you Harrison wouldn't like it."

"Of course I don't like it." He faced Vlad. "Do you have any idea how dangerous the repo business is?"

The Russian grinned. "Vlad have worse job. Harry know this."

He did, and he supposed Vlad would make a good repo man. Hell, he'd rather see Vlad repossessing cars and boats, than working for the Russian Mafia or a man like Honey Badger.

Kiera cleared her throat. "So the repossessing cars not being a sport wasn't a joke? Cash actually does that for a living?"

"Not anymore," Cash said. "Me and Mel own part of the business, though."

She let out a breath and reached for her beer. "I haven't made any friends since I've moved here. I think you've ruined me." She grinned. "After meeting you guys, anyone else is going to seem boring."

"Cheers to that," Mel said with a smile, and raised her glass.

Relieved Kiera accepted the kind of crazy he was used to dealing with, he joined the rest of the table in a toast. They finished the pitchers and ordered another round, along with burgers and wings. Kiera fit right in with them, as if she'd been around for years, rather than a couple of hours. Harrison could get used to nights like this, and was already used to the idea of permanently relocating to Tallahassee.

As they paid their bills and headed home, he realized he'd also become used to Kiera, to her kisses, to showering with her, sleeping next to her, and making love. He didn't want that to change, and wanted to remain a couple, build on their relationship, plan their future. But how?

He parked the Jeep outside Kiera's building. "I'm going to walk you in, then get Vlad settled at my place."

"Are you sure? I understand if you'd rather hang out with him tonight."

After helping her from the Jeep, he pulled her close. "I'll always want to be with you."

The tall lampposts revealed her shy smile. "I feel the same way."

His insides melted as he leaned in for a kiss.

"Vlad is third tire."

Kiera chuckled before he had the chance to kiss her. He pressed his forehead against hers. "Let me get the tire settled."

He and Vlad watched her walk into her building, then headed for his. The Russian nudged him with his elbow. "Harry finally have redhead, eh?"

"I don't *have* Kiera. I never will," he said, the good time they'd had tonight fading fast.

"Vlad never said never."

"No, you never say I, me, he, she…"

Vlad chuckled. "Harry still have sensation of humor. That good."

"I guess."

"Harry guess what?"

"Nothing, man," he said, leading Vlad into his building. Once they were in his apartment, he flipped on the light and headed into the kitchen, where he kept a spare key in one of the drawers. "The sheets are clean, so you can take the bed."

Vlad grinned. "Harry did have redhead."

When his cheeks grew warm, he turned away and opened the refrigerator. "There's not much here, but help yourself. I'll pick up some groceries tomorrow."

"Vlad will buy food after work."

He faced his friend. "Are you sure you know what you're getting into with this repo business? You know Cash should be in a wheelchair, right?" A couple of years ago, a repo job had gone bad. A guy had taken offense to having his truck repossessed, and Cash had ended up in the hospital.

"Vlad know. But what else is for Vlad?"

"You can stay in Everglades City and work for Lola."

The Russian came around the island. "ATL not same without Harry. The only reason Vlad join was because of Harry. So, it just would not be same. Also, Vlad do not like new guy."

"Why not?"

"He bossy and filled with arrogant."

Harrison cracked a smile. "You're a good dude."

"Vlad know and feel same for Harry."

"I'm sorry for being a dick."

"It okay. But Vlad wonder what will happen next?" He took a step forward and placed a hand on Harrison's shoulder. "Harry, Kiera is good woman."

"I know, she's too good for me."

"Why say that?" Vlad frowned, and crossed his arms. "Harry good catch"

"I *used* her. I've lied to her. And I'm the asshole who plans on putting her brother in prison."

The Russian shrugged. "There are worse thing in life. Remember, love is all that matter."

"You read the books Barney gave you for Christmas." Vlad loved to read, mostly self-help books, or non-fiction books about history. As a joke, Barney had bought him a few romance novels for his birthday.

Vlad lifted his chin. "Do not judge. And Vlad think it true anyway. If Kiera love Harry the way Vlad see, then sending serial killer brother to death row will not matter."

"What? Do you hear yourself?"

"Vlad have perfect hearing."

"So do I. It's my conscience calling." He headed out of the kitchen. "Kiera's waiting for me."

Vlad's chuckle stopped him. "Harry have not change like Vlad have thought."

"What's that mean?" he asked, facing the Russian.

"Harry always on defense, and always looking for easy way.

Vlad see nothing change."

"Your memory is warped." Irritated, he stepped forward. "Our first meeting was basically a kidnapping. You and Santiago held a gun to me and my brother's heads in order to get your boss's job done."

"Harry make mincemeat of words. Yes, it all true. Yes, Vlad was supposed to kill Harry and Mickey, but Harry miss Vlad point."

"Whatever your point is, make it. Because you're starting to piss me off and make me regret offering up my apartment."

"The truth will hurt."

Harrison scrubbed a hand down his face. "Just say it."

"Fine. Harry need stop playing victim."

Back in his other life, before the Russian Mafia had gotten to him, Vlad had been a heavyweight boxer. At this moment, Harrison would trade a physical blow from Vlad over the one his friend had just unleashed. Embarrassed, his face growing hot, he looked away and thought back. Memories spilled through his mind, tumbling over one another. His abusive childhood, stealing, juvenile detention, stealing some more, prison, working three jobs to live in a roach-infested shitty apartment because that had been all he and his brother could afford. His first meeting with Vlad, and knowing Mickey had brought them into something way over their heads. Through it all, he'd fought to survive, and it cut deep that Vlad thought otherwise.

"I'm no victim. I'm a fucking survivor. After all that we've been through, after the shit you've seen me do to stay alive, I can't believe you'd go there." He started for the door, but still too pissed off to leave, he turned around again. "And how in the hell am I playing the victim right now?"

"Because Harry already give up fight." Vlad moved forward and leaned into the kitchen island separating them. "Do not throw away towel in ring. Do not make up mind for Kiera. Vlad *have* seen Harry fight. Why not fight for what Harry know is right? Take offense attack and not easy way?"

The Dougals, the four victims he believed Liam had killed, their images filled his head. "Because I handled everything wrong and made too many mistakes when I *did* go on the offensive."

"Was Kiera mistake?"

"She's been the best thing that's ever happened to me."

"Vlad agree," he said with a sad smile. "But this about more than girl. Vlad see many change in Harry."

"Look, I told you I was sorry for how I acted before and after I moved out."

"It more than that. Vlad believe Harry unhappy in choice to work for ATL. Instead of quitting, Harry bitter like grapefruit."

For the first time in years, Harrison understood true relief. When he'd first accepted the job with ATL, even coming up with the name of their organization, he'd been gung ho and excited to not only be part of a team, but to be working on the right side of the law. Except, ATL wasn't supposed to exist, and the majority of the activities performed by him and the other agents had been more criminal than what had landed him in prison. He never wanted to see the inside of a prison cell again. After spending time with Cash and Mel, he realized he wanted out, and wanted what they had: a nice house, legit jobs, a solid relationship. With his current position at ATL, he'd never have those things.

The house he'd shared with Vlad had been the nicest place he'd ever lived, but Polina's Paradise had also become ATL's headquarters, creating a privacy issue. Now he owned a trailer. He made good money working for ATL, and was paid by the job. In between cases, he scheduled airboat tours for Cap'n Ryan and helped around the boat shop when he'd rather use his brain and computer to create web designs. While he'd rarely been alone and the agents had become his closest friends, he'd still been lonely. He'd watched as his friends had paired up with awesome women, and envied them, because what woman would want to date him.

The relief faded as all those thoughts collided into one—Vlad was almost right. "I'm no victim, but I've accepted my lot in life instead of changing for the better."

Vlad frowned. "Harry have change for better, never doubt that. Vlad have know many bad people. It experience that bad people stay bad, or go to prison or get killed. Not Harry, and Vlad proud to call Harry best friend."

"Thanks, man." Harrison let out a breath, looked at the clock, and thought about the woman waiting for him. "When I told Kiera about going to prison, her response was that she admires me because I've grown from my mistakes, and that she doesn't judge me for my past. But she thinks I'm a web designer." He ran a hand through his hair. "It's all so screwed up because I want to be the man she thinks I am."

"Harry is this man. Once serial killer brother gone, it easy as cake." He pushed off the island and crossed his arms. "Tell Vlad, did Harry need Kiera to get to brother?"

"No," he admitted. "But I used it as an excuse because I liked her and she liked me."

"It feel good to be liked." The Russian nodded. "Repo Man tell Vlad about argument with Harry. Vlad find it of interest." He also looked to the clock. "Harry should go to woman."

"Wait, why is my argument with Cash interesting?"

"When was argument?"

He shrugged. "I don't know. A few weeks ago, why?"

"Harry went after woman knowing it wrong, then argued point to Repo Man. Now Harry grieve for death of relationship while still in relationship. Why have Harry lost the fight now? What have changed in few weeks?"

Sometimes he hated Vlad. The Russian knew how to work his way inside his head and scramble it up with outlandish words of wisdom and broken English. He didn't want to answer Vlad's questions, not even in his own head. To admit the reason he was giving up, accepting the fate of his relationship with Kiera would only make losing her more difficult.

"I need to get going. Kiera has to be to work at eight. Let's grab coffee before you go into the garage."

His friend nodded. "That sound fine. But one more thing,

then Vlad stop…have Harry wonder what Kiera would do if Harry told truth?"

"Of course, I have. Why do you think this is such a huge problem for me?"

"Yes, it big problem. But what if Harry wrong?"

He opened the door. "I'll see you in the morning," he said, then stepped out of the apartment. As he made his way to Kiera's, he thought about what Vlad had asked, but quickly shook it off. Kiera was a smart, reasonable woman. She would agree that her brother shouldn't be on the streets, but there was no way in hell she would accept that he'd initially used her. Even if she did, what would she think of him once she'd learned about what Honey Badger had made him do? What about his position with ATL? As much as he wanted to be honest with her, he couldn't see the point.

When he reached her apartment door, his stomach twisted with self-loathing. He had given up on Kiera, and he was, in a way, grieving over the impending death of their relationship. Vlad had wanted to know what had changed over the past three weeks. He'd fallen in love with Kiera, and he loved her too much to hurt her. If that made him a coward, he didn't care. He didn't think he could bear the disappointment in her eyes if he told her the truth.

When she opened the door, then greeted him with a smile and a kiss, part of him wanted to run back to his apartment. Kiera was wrong. He didn't deserve her. But the other part of him never wanted to leave. That side of him wanted to pretend his alter ego hadn't existed, that the man standing in front of her was the real Harrison Fairclough. He knew better than anyone that reality was unavoidable, and that there was no place for fantasies in his life.

"Is something wrong?" she asked, closing the door behind him.

"No, everything is good."

"Are you sure? I feel bad. Vlad is staying at your place and you're here with me. I told you, my feelings won't be hurt if you want to hang out with him."

He pulled her close. Screw it. He wanted the fantasy, for as long as he could have it. "I'm fine. Vlad's fine, and I want to be here with you." He ran his hand along her spine and kissed her. "I love sleeping with you."

With a shy, dimpled grin, she twined her arms around his neck. "I love sleeping with you, too. It's still early, but I've been thinking about crawling into bed with you all day."

His body instantly responded. "I like the way you've been thinking."

"I was hoping you would." After kissing him, she stepped from his embrace and started for the living room, where the TV aired the evening news. "Thanks again for taking me out tonight. I had a great time. And I adore Vlad."

"I thought you would." He edged into the living room. "Can you leave this on for a sec?" he asked when she raised the remote toward the TV.

"Sure," she said as the news anchor faded, and the on-the-scene reporter filled the screen.

"Early this morning, Assistant Manager Gloria Franklin was found murdered outside the Burger Boy restaurant located at the corner of Moss Avenue and Ryder Road," the reporter began, motioning to the building behind her. The camera panned to the closed sign taped to the glass front door, then to the flowers, candles, stuffed animals and handmade signs filling the darkened restaurant's sidewalk and blocking the entrance.

"Oh, my God," Kiera gasped. "That's only a couple of miles from Liam and Bella's."

Dread crawled up Harrison's spine as he stared at the TV, at the inset photograph of the victim. At Gloria Franklin's long curly dark hair. His heart sank. This woman's death was on him. He'd had the key, the evidence to at least alert detectives to Liam, and he hadn't done anything. Vlad was right about him. He'd tried to take the easy way, had tried to save his own ass, and now another woman was dead.

"The community is in mourning," the reporter continued. "The mother of two teenagers was an active member of her church and spearheaded several food and clothing drives. According to her pastor, Gloria raised nearly fifteen thousand dollars this past Christmas, then used the money to feed and clothe the homeless and less fortunate. A candlelight vigil will be held here this evening in her honor."

"Have the police confirmed the motive of this horrific crime?" the news anchor asked.

"Other than releasing the victim's name, the police aren't commenting on anything at this time. But, I briefly spoke with the restaurant's owner, David Morales, this afternoon, off-camera. Mr. Morales had found the victim when he'd arrived to work at five a.m., and said Gloria had been stabbed. He also said he didn't think robbery was a motive because the restaurant's night deposit was still in her purse."

"Have any of your sources suggested that this murder is connected to the four others that have taken place since December?" the anchor asked, and the screen filled with the smiling faces of Carla Rodriguez, Jennette Salvetti, Wendy DeMarco, and Julie Beechum.

"Like I said, the police aren't commenting, but Tallahasseeans have been posting their theories on social media. An overwhelming majority believes Tallahassee has a serial killer living among them."

"Creepy." Kiera rubbed her arms. "Did you notice how all the women, except for Julie Beechum, have the same hair type? Don't you think it's odd that the police aren't commenting about a possible serial killer?"

Swamped with guilt, angry with himself and hating Liam for the monster he was, Harrison stared at Kiera's profile, looking for any sign that she was lying, that she was fully aware of what her brother had been doing. "Since the one woman was a blonde, maybe the hair type was just a coincidence."

"Or maybe the killer went to the wrong house? Talk about

creepy." She raised the remote. "Are you done with this?" When he nodded, she turned off the television. "This is why I don't watch the news. It's always gloom and doom, and the feel-good pieces always seem staged to me."

"You're not too cynical tonight," he said, his mind on the dead woman, on all of the victims. He *had* to be right. Liam *had* to be the murderer. Four out of five woman had the same hair type as Adeline. Adeline had tortured Liam. One of the women had the hair of a Husky on her body. Liam owned a Husky. He had Liam's fingerprint from the Dougals' house. Liam had Mel's switchblade, which Harrison assumed the bastard had used on not only the Dougals, but Carla Rodriguez and Julie Beechum. Had he stabbed Gloria Franklin with it, too? Was Liam responsible? He didn't know, but knew he couldn't keep his head in the sand any longer.

Kiera whistled, drawing his attention. "Where'd you go?" she asked.

He rubbed his eyes with his thumb and index finger. "Sorry. Someone woke me up at five o'clock this morning. Between that and the beers and burger, I'm exhausted."

Grinning, she hooked her arm through his as they walked into the bedroom. "I didn't hear you complaining about being woken up."

The lamp on the nightstand bathed her room in a soft yellow glow. The plum comforter invited him to climb in and stay forever. The dark furniture was neutral enough to fit both of their styles, and he'd love nothing more than to claim half the dresser drawers and part of the walk-in closet. But he'd have to settle with one last night in her bed. As it was, he shouldn't even be here. He should be contacting Detective Larson, the woman whose files he'd been hacking into, and telling her who killed those women.

Instead, he leaned against the bathroom door, watching Kiera pull back her hair so she could wash her face, and listening to her chatter away about the evening. After he lost his shirt and jeans, he joined her in the bathroom, snagging the toothbrush he'd brought over the day after he'd spent his first night with her. Had that really only been three days ago? Had he really only known her for a month?

Was he really going to turn her brother over to the police tomorrow?

She took the towel she'd just used to wipe water from her mouth, then ran it across his lips. "Let me make sure you're all dried off," she said, then leaned in and kissed him.

He took the towel from her and tossed it onto the counter, then backed her out of the bathroom. "And I was just thinking about how I can make you wet."

"I thought you were tired," she said as he removed her shirt.

He pushed her capris and panties over her hips. "I just got my second wind."

"I read a study that said couples who brush their teeth together were more horny than those who don't. So your second wind makes sense." She pursed her lips. "Or would that be hornier over more horny?"

God, he loved her. Everything about her. He cupped her cheeks and, even with knowing tonight could be his last night with her, he didn't have to force a chuckle. She naturally made him dream, laugh, smile and, yes, horny. "It doesn't matter to me. But if that study is right, we'll have the cleanest, whitest teeth in Tallahassee. Or would that be most clean and most white?"

Kissing the corner of his mouth, she rubbed her hand over his underwear and along his erection. "Good hygiene and grammar are important. Maybe we should study up on the subjects."

He reached behind and unhooked her bra. "Naked?"

"Absolutely," she said, tugging his underwear over his hips.

As he moved her toward the bed, he allowed himself to forget everything but Kiera. He wanted to make love to her, enjoy her body, the deep connection he hadn't known existed.

Because by this time tomorrow, it could be gone forever.

District 2 Medical Examiner's Office, Tallahassee, Florida
Monday, 10:09 p.m., Eastern Standard Time

"MORALES IS AN idiot." Detective Sharon Larson shut off the radio, popped a few pills—doctor's orders—into her mouth, then swallowed them down with cold coffee. She winced, but took another swig when the pills caught in her throat.

"I'd like to bring him in again just for being an asshole. Why in the hell would he tell that reporter about Gloria being stabbed and the night deposit? Did he *not* understand the meaning of *don't talk to the press*?" Bernadette parked the car outside of the medical examiner's offices. "Stop taking those until we get you some water. I think that coffee was from this morning."

"I'm fine. That was the last one." Sharon collected her binder. "Ready?"

"No." Bernadette opened the car door anyway. "I still don't get it," she said as they met along the sidewalk. "He kills one woman December fourteenth, kills another January eighth, then two weeks later kills two women almost back to back."

"And here we are four weeks later looking at another dead body. It's strange. Like he'd either been out of town, or something had him preoccupied."

"Being out of town makes the most sense." Bern opened the door. "It also scares the hell out of me. He could have been out murdering other women in another city or state, maybe even another country and we won't know until we catch him and dig into his activities."

They made their way to the lab, and were greeted by the ME's assistant, who led them to the office of pathologist, Dr. Keith Rolland. Since the assistant was taking them to an office rather than an exam room, Sharon relaxed. The cold, sterile autopsy room sometimes unsettled her almost as much as a crime scene.

From behind his desk, Dr. Rolland looked up at them, his dark-brown eyes surprisingly alert considering the late hour. "Detectives," he said, standing. "I'm glad you were able to stop by."

"We were on our way to meet with Dana Wong, so the timing is perfect," Sharon said. "What do you have for us?"

"As you know, cause of death was due to multiple stab wounds. Forty-three to be exact."

Bern let out a low whistle. "Excessive. If this is the same guy, he only stabbed Carla Rodriguez eight times."

"I opened up my report on Rodriguez for comparison."

"You suggested she was stabbed with a short, single-edged blade," Sharon recalled.

He nodded. "Some of Franklin's wounds were superficial, making it difficult to tell. But based on the deeper wounds, the length of the incision, I believe a similar sized knife was used."

"But that doesn't mean the same guy did it," Bern said.

"Correct. Aside from the number of stab wounds, there are other dissimilarities between the two cases. Franklin was beaten before she was stabbed."

Sharon frowned. She'd been to the crime scene that morning, but unfortunately, or maybe fortunately, the body had already been removed, and she had yet to see the victim or photos taken at the scene. Dana was supposed to supply them with pictures when they met with her after their meeting with Dr. Rolland. "How do you know?"

"Because she was stabbed in the face four times, she had a broken nose and cheekbone. There can be bruising around a stab wound, but not to this extent. Plus if she was hit after being stabbed, the incisions would likely be torn and gaping from the impact."

"So she could have been unconscious at the time of her murder?" Sharon asked, hopeful the woman hadn't suffered.

"The back of her skull was cracked and she'd hemorrhaged around her brain. I believe she was unconscious during the majority of her attack. Which brings me to the other dissimilarity, and what I wanted to show you." He handed them the autopsy diagram. "Note the markings indicating the stab wounds."

Sharon looked over Bernadette's shoulder. "The majority are

around the stomach." She glanced to the ME. "Actually, it looks like all but—"

"Twelve," Bern said, running her finger along the diagram. "He stabbed her thirty-one times in the stomach. That's insane. Was she pregnant?"

Sharon's skin crawled at the thought.

"No," Dr. Rolland said. "According to her medical records she'd had a hysterectomy three years ago. There are also no signs of sexual assault." He sighed. "Look, I've been doing this for over twenty years. Forty-three stab wounds is excessive, but thirty-one to the abdomen, to the point where she'd been nearly sliced wide open is, in my opinion, an act of hatred."

"Or revenge?" Bern suggested.

"But the husband checked out," Sharon reminded her. "The sons did, too."

"Maybe she was having an affair?"

Possible, but she didn't buy it. Not based on what they'd already learned about Gloria Franklin, and the fact that the body had been cleaned to some extent. Then again, even the squeaky clean had dirty pasts.

"We were told the body was washed," Sharon began. "With a crime this violent, if our killer was using a short blade, it had to get slippery, he had to have cut himself."

"I agree," Bernadette said. "The other murders seem tame compared to this one. Like he'd lost his cool."

"I've sent what little blood evidence I found to the lab, but it was diluted with water, so there're no guarantees they'll be able to get a DNA profile."

Bern handed the autopsy diagram to Dr. Rolland. "Forensics found cast off from the weapon used on the victim. Maybe that'll give us something."

They left the ME, then met up with Dana, who confirmed most of what they'd discussed earlier in the day. Blood spatter, position of the body and of Gloria's purse indicated that she'd been surprised by her attacker. Sharon hoped the killer had sucker-punched the woman, knocking her to the ground, the impact to her skull rendering her unconscious so she'd never felt another thing. Especially the fear, the knowing that this was it.

After Alan had died, Sharon had lain in bed many nights wondering if there was truly an afterlife, if the goodness and love that had made up her husband lived on, waiting to reconnect with her, or if the moment that bullet had ended his life there was nothing but blackness. When doctors had discovered her cancer, insomnia had become her enemy. The fear of dying, of falling into an abyss of nothingness, of her life, her soul having no meaning, had kept her awake, preoccupied. There were still sleepless nights, but she'd accepted her fate, her disease. What she couldn't accept was murder, or that there was more than one killer on the loose.

"The same guy killed all five women," she said once they were back in the car.

Bern put the keys in the ignition. "I agree. I also think it's interesting that the body wasn't remotely wet when discovered. Maybe he smartened up this time and came prepared to clean his victim." She started the car.

"So this time he planned it?" Sharon shrugged. "Could be. All the other victims were killed either in the morning or early afternoon. Gloria was killed around midnight, which means he changed up his time, too."

"Maybe he used to work nightshift, so it was convenient to hunt in the morning."

"And now he's working days?" Sharon stared out the window. "It's tough to draw any conclusions about this guy."

Bernadette pulled into the police department parking lot, then slowed near Sharon's car. "One thing is for sure, whoever murdered Gloria Franklin snapped. Those stab wounds to her stomach give me the impression this was personal."

"But was he taking his rage out on Gloria because of something she'd done to him, or was she a total stranger who happened to look like the person he really wants dead?"

Bern shivered. "Damn, that gave me chills. But I like where

you're going with it. Teens and people in their twenties tend to be impulsive. Maybe we're dealing with a son who hates his mother."

"We need to involve the FBI. I'd love to have their people look at what we have. Let's talk to Jacoby about it in the morning. I'll see you inside."

"Go home and get your rest," Bern said. "I'll work on the reports."

Sharon stepped out of the car. "Nope. I'm good. I'll grab us some coffee," she said, then headed toward the building. Her mind was tired. She didn't want to deal with the paperwork—documenting the people who they'd interviewed today, what the other units had done as part of the investigation, the evidence they currently had—and honestly had no energy to tackle it. While thankfully she hadn't viewed Gloria Franklin's body at the crime scene or morgue, Dana had showed them the photos. As exhausted as she was, Gloria's cut up, bruised and bloodied face, along with the other four victims', would only make sleep a nightmare anyway.

CHAPTER 13

"THAT WAS SOME goodbye kiss," Kiera said, as she ran her fingers along the back of his head to angle his mouth back to hers. "Now I really wish I didn't have to go to work today. But I'm off around three. So maybe we can go for a walk around Lake Talquin again?"

Harrison brushed his lips along hers, and also wished she didn't have to leave. Because once he was back at his apartment, he would set into motion the fall of their relationship. He'd been stupid and selfish, and it was time to rectify his wrongs.

It was time to send Liam to prison.

He slid his hand over her rear. "Your idea of a walk is a five-mile hike through woods, swamps and over sand hills."

"Well, if you're worried about keeping up with me, we could just meet back at my place and have sex."

He chuckled and gave her fine ass a squeeze. "I love that idea."

"It *is* rather brilliant," she said, giving him a final kiss before stepping from his embrace. "I'm excited about going out of town this weekend. Did you book the room, or do you need me to take care of it?"

"No, I've got it handled." Unfortunately he'd have to cancel those reservations. There was a good chance she'd hate him by the weekend, and a possibility that he'd be under arrest for tampering with evidence and impersonating a detective.

As they left her apartment, melancholy and regret followed

him outside. A foreboding chill hung in the air, the birds were exceptionally quiet and there wasn't a lizard in sight. When they reached her Chevy, he took her by the waist and kissed her again, lingering longer than normal.

Normal. Would life ever be normal, typical, usual? Would there ever be a time when he'd look forward to the days ahead with excitement, rather than with loathing and anxiety?

"I'll call you when I get home," she said.

He closed the car door. After her taillights had disappeared around the corner, he made his way to his apartment. When he entered, he inhaled fresh-brewed coffee and immediately went into the kitchen. As he filled a mug, Vlad stepped out of the bedroom.

"Morning," the Russian said. "Vlad just about to have breakfast."

"I don't have anything for breakfast."

"Harry have pizza. That work," Vlad said, pulling a frozen pizza from the freezer.

"Why not stop by McDonald's?"

"Vlad do not enjoy drive-thru window, or food made in one minute. Harry know this."

He did, but figured the Russian would make an exception. "I have a problem," he said, when he'd rather talk about Vlad's aversion to fast food restaurants.

"Vlad know."

"You saw the news?"

"да," Vlad said, his eyes holding sympathy he didn't deserve. "It possible Liam did not kill woman."

Harrison shook his head. "I don't believe that. I don't think you do, either."

"Anything possible."

"Look, I know what you're trying to do here, but I can't go on like this. I don't want to lose Kiera, and I don't want to go back to prison. I'd take both as long as I didn't have to live with the guilt of another murder."

Vlad put the pizza back in the freezer, then poured a cup of coffee. "Vlad can kill Liam. No one need know. Crimes will go unsolved, but murders will stop."

"I'm convinced Liam killed six, possibly seven people." He still wasn't sure about the blonde, Julie Beechum, because she didn't look a thing like Adeline. "If I let you kill Liam, that's seven families who will never get their justice. What kind of an asshole does that make me? Let's not forget that I'm having my badass assassin buddy do the job for me."

"Vlad *former* assassin."

"The answer is no."

Vlad nodded. "Why is it sometime the right thing feel wrong?"

"It's not wrong, it's what I should have done the day I found the Dougals' bodies. If you're worried about where to go if I end up back in prison, I'd prefer if you stay in Tallahassee with Mel and Cash. I trust Lola, but you shouldn't be working for her. Neither of us should have."

"Agreed. Vlad have thought about what Harry say last night. ATL, it not good for people with bad history. And Vlad have grown tired of killing." He wagged a finger at him. "But offer to kill Liam for Harry is still on kitchen counter."

Harrison half-smiled. "Take your offer off the counter. I created this mess, I'm going to clean it up...starting with Nick."

Vlad let out a long breath. "It right place to start. But Vlad think Harry too hard on self."

"I used a detective's ID, after I lifted evidence from a crime scene."

"Harry was in dark place."

"That's no excuse." He pulled his cell phone from his pocket. "I haven't had a headache or dark thoughts in weeks."

"That interesting since Harrison and Kiera have dated for weeks."

"What? You think being with Kiera helped mend my brain?"

The Russian shrugged. "Why not? Vlad aware of what Adeline and Rodney were doing. The target for psychopath drug was part of brain that hold good emotion. It what make humans care for other humans and not become Honey Badger. Harry was never like the Badger. Adeline and Rodney, their drug worked to hurt your brain, but Kiera and love make it all better now."

Vlad really needed to stop reading romance novels. "I don't even know if Kiera loves me."

One of the Russian's blond brows lifted high. "Kiera love have nothing to do with lifting the darkness from Harry brain." He rested a hand on Harrison's shoulder. "*Your* love for the woman. That the best kind of medicine, да?"

A deep ache developed in Harrison's chest and his stomach soured with anxiety, with self-loathing. Whether that love had helped lighten the darkness and trigger activity to the part of his brain that cared, that understood empathy, he'd probably never know. The only thing he knew with certainty was that he wasn't the man who'd first approached Kiera. He was better. Being with her had opened his eyes to possibilities that he'd thought could only be fantasies. He could own his own business, and have a future with a woman despite his past. He didn't have to hide in the swamps, or hide his career.

He was also selfish and a liar. Characteristics he doubted Kiera could look past, even if, by some miracle, she did love him.

"I hate to break it to you," he finally said. "But love isn't going to save my ass on this one."

"Vlad is sorry. Harry try to do right thing. The heart was good with intent."

His stomach now grew nauseous as he dialed Nick's number. "I don't know about that. My intentions were self-serving."

"Was Harry not worried about killing Vlad in sleep?"

"Of course."

"See? Vlad think Harry have heart with good intent. Vlad also grateful for lock on door," he said with a grin.

When Nick answered, Harrison held up a hand to Vlad and walked into the living room. "Nick," he began, "this is Harrison. You came to my trailer about two months ago."

"Yeah, give me a sec."

While Nick did whatever he had to do for what Harrison assumed was privacy, he opened his laptop and went directly into Detective Sharon Larson's files. He wanted to see what she'd written about yesterday's murder, and if she had a forensic report yet. Before he approached the woman, he had to give her a reason to pursue Liam for these murders.

"Why are you calling?" Nick asked.

"If it's a bad time—"

"Get on with it."

The man was making it hard for him to the do the right thing. "It's about your ID."

"What about it? Are you ready to admit you were using it?"

He opened up the photo file Detective Larson had in her profile. When he didn't see a file for Gloria Franklin's murder investigation, he clicked on Julie Beechum's. "What I'm going to tell you has to stay between us. Are you cool with that?"

"What about Lola?"

"Dude, trust me, you don't want anyone knowing what I'm about to tell you."

Nick let out a sigh. "Did you break the law?"

"Not any more than I've done while working for ATL."

"Don't fuck with me. What did you do?" Nick asked, his tone quiet, angry.

Vlad stepped into the room, reached down and took the laptop off the coffee table. "Focus," he mouthed, then walked away.

Harrison didn't want to focus on Nick, who was, in his opinion, a sanctimonious son of a bitch. He wanted to be distracted. He wanted to punish himself for not going to the police sooner by staring at the murdered victims' faces.

"Are you there?" Nick asked.

"Yeah. I'm here." He rose from the couch to stand in front of the patio window leading to the balcony. "I used your ID to find a match to a fingerprint I lifted from a crime scene."

"Was this for an ATL case?"

Nick's calm tone had him on full alert. The man should be ready to come through the phone and kick his ass. "No. It gets worse."

"Oh, Christ." The detective sighed. "Just tell me."

"You know who Rodney Archer is, correct?"

"I know his story. Why?"

Harrison stepped onto the patio and stared at the lake. If he angled his head slightly, he could see the bench where he and Kiera had sat under the pouring rain. "You don't know the real story about Rodney and what went on in that plantation house," he began. Then he sat on a folding chair and told Nick everything, leaving out that Adeline had sexually assaulted him in front of Mel, and that he was currently dating a serial killer's sister.

Nick let out a sigh. "I just looked up the Dougal case. Travis James Graham is currently sitting in Thomas County Jail for the murders of Delford and Dottie Dougal."

Harrison stood and gripped the phone. "What? They've got the wrong guy. I lifted Liam's fingerprints. His *bloody* fingerprints from the Dougals'."

"I'm not saying I don't believe you. But according to the report I'm reading, Travis is a drifter and drug addict. He has a mile-long rap sheet which includes assault, theft and arson. If you're telling me the truth, they might as well add dumb luck to the list. Apparently he tried to pawn something he'd taken from the Dougals', and the broker recognized it as belonging to Mrs. Dougal. The broker called the county sheriff, and when deputies arrested Travis, they said he smelled like kerosene and had burn marks on his clothes. Travis admits to stealing and setting the house on fire, but claims he knows nothing about the couples' deaths."

Stunned, Harrison sat again. "I figured for sure Liam had gone back to burn the house down and cover up any evidence he'd left behind. I mean, the fire happened only a couple of days after I'd been there."

"This is why I'm a firm believer in fate," Nick said. "And why

I think you should keep the Dougals out of your story."

Harrison went still. "You want to let an innocent man go to prison for two murders he didn't commit?"

"That'd be shitty. What'd be shittier is if Forrester is arrested for the Dougal murders and someone happens to notice that *I* ran his prints a couple of days before the victims' house was burned to the ground. And shittier still if someone, let's say from Internal Affairs, finds this suspicious. They could start digging into my cases."

"Stop. I know where you're going with this. It's why I've waited to call you. I've been hoping to find something else I could give to this Tallahassee detective so I could avoid trouble for you and ATL."

"It's not just me. You know damn well my partner is involved with ATL, too."

Harrison hadn't thought about Jerry Tennyson, and how this would affect him. Apparently, he hadn't thought through much of anything.

"Look, I have a conscience," Nick said. "Travis Graham is a repeat offender and deserves to be in jail for the crime he did commit, just not for murder. Let me think about how to handle this."

"I don't have time for you to *think*. Five women are dead."

"Because you fucked up an investigation. If you had come to me the moment you found out who that fingerprint belonged to, we could have arrested Forrester. Yes, I would've been pissed off about you using my ID, but the guy would've been stopped."

"And I would've gone back to prison."

"You still could. Unless you request immunity."

He hadn't thought about that. "What about you?"

"Find a way to keep me out of this," Nick said, the quiet anger returning. "Be honest and tell this Detective Larson you stole my ID, and that you don't know me. Chances are, she'll be so happy to have a murderer attached to her victims she'll be too busy kicking up her heels and gathering evidence to give to the

DA, she won't care about me or whether or not we're connected."

He rubbed the back of his head and tried to relax. "Do you think asking for immunity would work?"

"I can't say for sure. That's up to the district attorney."

"Not Detective Larson."

Nick chuckled, but there was an irritated edge to it. "Trust me, she wants to catch a killer. What you've done is nothing in comparison to seven murders."

Harrison blew out a breath, then turned when Vlad knocked on the patio door window. He held up a finger, signaling for the Russian to wait. "I'm sorry, Nick."

"I'm sure you are," Nick replied, then hung up the phone.

"What a dick," Harrison mumbled, then stood and pocketed the phone. When he slid open the door, he smelled pizza. "I guess you decided to have breakfast after all."

"No time to talk about Detective Nick." The Russian dragged him to the kitchen island, where the laptop sat on the counter. "Look what Vlad have found."

"I thought you had to be at work? And, dude, I have to tell you about my conversation with Nick. I'm not sure what to think. Part of me is hopeful, the other part of me is...who the hell is that?" he asked glancing to the screen.

"Autumn Torgenson."

Harrison stared at the young, pretty woman with long dark curly hair. "Who?"

"Julie Beechum neighbor."

Tallahassee Police Department, Tallahassee, Florida
11:20 a.m., Eastern Standard Time

"OH, MY GOD. He's right." Detective Sharon Larson stared at one of the crime scene photos, specifically at the mourning neighbor captured outside of Julie Beechum's house. "Who interviewed Autumn Torgenson? You know, the woman who got the new fridge delivered from The Home Zone."

Bernadette looked over from her desk. "I'd have to check, why?"

She scooted her chair closer to Bern's. "Because I just got a call from a man who claims she was the target, not Julie."

"What? Who was the man?"

"He wouldn't say. But look." She handed Bernadette the crime scene photograph. "Look at her hair."

"Come on, Sharon. Again, how many women in Tallahassee have dark curly hair?"

"He also said to look into Liam Forrester again."

"The guy who helped deliver the fridge?" Bern shook her head. "Let's take a step back. You're telling me a random guy called, and not only claimed the wrong woman was murdered, but who to investigate?"

"Exactly."

"Any way to trace back the call?"

"It was too quick."

Bernadette rapped her knuckles on the desk. "If it's possible that he went to the wrong house, this would link all five victims."

Same hair type. Bodies washed. "You know I believe Julie is part of this."

Bern met her gaze. "I do, too. Did your caller give a reason why we should look into Forrester other than because of the delivery?"

"Yep. Mr. Forrester owns a Husky and has a history of mental illness."

"Wow. Okay." Bern blew out a deep breath, then frowned. "Wait, how would he know about the Husky hair? That information was never released."

"Shit. You're right."

"This is all circumstantial anyway, and I don't like that we don't know who called you."

"I don't either, but I want this guy," Sharon said, disappointed, but not deterred.

Bern pursed her lips. "I do, too. So let's find out what we can about Forrester."

Ninety minutes later, Bernadette slowed her car in front of Liam Forrester's address. Sharon stared out the window toward the tall pines hiding the house in the distance. According to Leon County records, the home and six acre property belonged to Bella Johnson. When they'd ran a check on the woman, what had disturbed both her and Bern was that Bella had long dark curly hair. This ramped up their theory that maybe Liam had a grudge against the woman he lived with, and instead of taking it out on her, he was taking it out on strangers who fit Bella's mold.

"Ready?" Bernadette asked.

"Absolutely."

Sharon's partner turned down the driveway, then parked the car next to a white SUV. The house was small, but well kept. Nothing menacing. No signs that a serial killer possibly lived there. Yet.

They exited the car and made their way to the door. Liam answered on the second knock, recognition, then surprise widened his eyes. "Detectives. Is something wrong?" he asked, then stepped outside, the screen door slowly closing behind him.

"We have a few questions for you. We're hoping you'll come down to the station and talk with us," Sharon said with a smile.

Forrester frowned. "You want to interrogate me?" he asked with disbelief. "I don't understand. All I did was deliver a refrigerator. What's crazy is that it was only the second time I've done that job." He looked from her to Bernadette. "Are you arresting me?"

"No. We just want to talk."

"Then we can talk here. I didn't do anything that day, but my job."

"Do you own a Husky?" Bern asked.

"Yes. My fiancée and I adopted her a couple of months ago. Why?"

Sharon peered over Forrester's shoulder. "Is your fiancée home? I didn't see another car."

"She's at work."

"Where were you Sunday night?"

"Here."

"You never left?" Bern asked.

"No."

"And your fiancée could vouch for this?"

"Of course." He reached for the screen door's handle. "I saw the news. What happened to that woman is awful. I've seen her at Burger Boy when I've gone in to *buy* a burger. But if you're here to accuse me of hurting her, then you need to leave."

Sharon looked to Bernadette, who nodded. They couldn't arrest him, and didn't have enough to request a warrant. All they had was some random guy's accusations. But she'd rather liked what the random guy had to say, especially after they'd discovered Liam was not only schizophrenic, but that his sister had listed him a missing person last summer.

Now he was a person of interest.

"No problem," Sharon said. "You moved to Tallahassee back in November?"

"October."

"What made you leave Colorado?"

He let go of the door and crossed his arms over his chest. "Change of scenery."

Bernadette nodded. "Tallahassee's a good choice. I was born and raised here. Is that why your sister moved here, too? Did she need a change of scenery?"

Sharon studied the man, noted his ears had become red, and that his back had straightened.

"Why are you asking me about my sister?"

"Just curious. Why did she file a missing persons report on you in August with the Aurora PD?"

He drew in a deep breath through his nose. "You're a detective, I think the answer is clear. She thought I was missing."

Bern smiled. "Were you, or did you know exactly where you were going?"

"It would feel so good to take a shovel upside that bitch's head," Adeline said with a bored sigh.

He absolutely agreed and imagined the mess he'd make on the front porch. Unfortunately, he couldn't do anything about the detectives, except lie.

"Obviously my sister found me." He forced a smile. "It was all a mistake."

"Your disappearing had nothing to do with being a paranoid schizophrenic?" Sharon asked.

His ears became hot as the detectives stared at him. He was no longer that weak-minded man. That part of him had burned away and was buried in the ashes of the House of Archer. No one could know Rodney had cured him. No one could know what they'd done to him, or about the parting gift he still carried with him. But he had to tell the detectives some semblance of the truth. If, for some reason, they spoke to Kiera, they would know anyway.

"Maybe Kiera's the one who contacted the detectives," Adeline suggested. *"I don't trust her."*

I do. Shut up and let me think.

"I wasn't in therapy at the time," he admitted. "I started to have paranoid thoughts and felt I needed to leave Colorado."

"You mean like voices in your head?" Detective Richie asked.

Hating these women, the way that they stared at him as if he were some sort of sideshow freak, he once again envisioned taking up a shovel. This time to both of their heads. He nodded anyway.

"Do you hear them now?"

He chuckled and shook his head. "Detective, I went back to therapy in September and I haven't had any issues since. You might want to do your homework on the illness. Many people diagnosed with schizophrenia can live perfectly normal lives. Look at me. I'm as normal as they get. Got a house, a dog, a fiancée, an average job."

"Yep. Pretty normal." Detective Richie looked around the front porch. "But you didn't answer the question."

"No, ma'am. I don't hear voices," he said, and ignored Adeline's laughter.

"Can you take us through the day you made the delivery to Autumn Torgenson's home?" Detective Larson asked. She glanced at a small notepad. "You were called into work early, correct?"

"They have nothing on you," Adeline said. *"If they thought you killed the women, you'd be in handcuffs."*

This was true. Bella was addicted to true crime shows and he'd occasionally sat with her while she'd watched them. "Detective," he began, "I cooperated with you the day you came to my work, and I'm cooperating with you now. I understand that I probably sound like a good lead because of my mental health issues, but I didn't do anything wrong. I'm sorry, but I don't want to talk anymore."

"It was a simple question," the detective pressed.

"You have your notes, so you have your answers."

Detective Larson smiled. "Then can you walk us through Sunday night? You said you were at home with your fiancée. Can you tell us what you were doing between ten o'clock and midnight?"

"Gutting the wrong woman," Adeline said with irritation. *"Liam, tell them to leave. Don't answer any more of their questions."*

"I think I was asleep by ten-thirty. I had to be into work at eight, which you can verify with my manager." He reached for the screen door handle. "This happens to be my day off. So I'm going to get back to enjoying it."

"It's a beautiful day," Detective Richie said. "What time will your fiancée be home? We'd like to talk to her."

"If you would have killed the twat, none of this would be happening. You can't let them talk to your precious *Bella. They can't know about the miscarriage. Not after what you did to that woman."*

Adeline was right. But Bella loved him. He was sure of it. She knew about the white noise, how he needed the rope. Would she tell the detectives about that? Would she betray him and admit that he'd left Sunday night?

"She's working a double shift and won't be home until around nine."

Detective Larson pulled a pen from her jacket pocket. "Where does she work?"

"Downtown. At Cherry's."

"On King Street? I love that place. They have the best cheese-cake." Detective Richie looked to her partner. "We should go grab a bite." She then smiled at him. "Thanks for your cooperation."

"We need to leave," Adeline urged him as the detectives drove away. *"This could end badly."*

He stepped inside the house. "I'm not leaving." Everything he'd ever wanted and hadn't thought possible was here in Talla-hassee. His stomach dropped as he pictured packing his things, moving to a new city, starting over again. Leaving Bella...

Panicking over losing her, he grabbed his cell phone from the kitchen table, saw that he'd missed a call from his sister, then quickly dialed Bella's number. When she answered on the third ring, he relaxed.

"You caught me on my break," she said. "How's your day go-in'? Did you get any work done on the bathroom?"

"Don't do this, lover. Don't tell her anything. She'll suspect. She'll know."

She loves me.

"But you don't truly love her. What's the difference if you leave? You can find another one just like her. Look how many we've found here in Tallahassee," Adeline said, amusement in her tone.

She was wrong. He did love Bella. He loved her enough that he'd killed others to keep her alive. She was a simple woman, with simple needs. And she had never once judged him for being schizophrenic or for his unusual desires.

"I finished painting, now I'm waiting for the walls to dry be-fore I give it another coat." Guilt over how he'd acted toward Bella since the miscarriage had him wanting to do a few extra things for her. He'd even brought home a rototiller from work, and hoped to surprise her by having the weed-infested garden ready for planting by the end of the week.

"How's the color?" she asked as dishes clanked in the background.

"Not bad."

"Don't tell her."

"Bella, the police came here today," he said, and ignored Adeline's shouts of disapproval.

"What? Why would they do that?"

"Well, I didn't tell you this because I didn't want you to worry, but do you remember the day I was called in early to help with deliveries?" he asked. "It was about a month ago."

"Sure, what about it?"

He explained about the dead blonde woman, and why the detectives had questioned him after her murder, then told her how they'd stopped by to ask about his mental health and his whereabouts Sunday night. "They know where you work, so don't be surprised if they stop in to see you."

"What do you want me to tell them?" she asked in a hushed voice. "When you left that night you told me to keep the bedroom door locked and not to come out until mornin'. Where did you go?"

Shit. He *had* said those things to her.

"I told you that was a stupid move," Adeline reminded him.

Rubbing his temple, he rested his rear on the edge of the kitchen table. "I went out back, down by the pond. I needed more time to think and cool off. You know how sorry I am for the way I treated you that night. I was upset about the baby. Instead of taking it out on you, I should've been comforting you."

"Oh, honey. You don't have to keep apologizin' for your feelings. We just need to put this behind us and concentrate on plannin' our weddin'." More dishes clanked, along with the sounds of muffled voices. "Crap, I have to go. My break is up. I'll call you before the dinner rush, okay?" After she told him she loved him, the call disconnected.

"Either the woman is desperate or stupid."

"Shut up, Adeline," he said, and headed out to the backyard.

Ginger tugged on the lead he'd strung up this morning. While he hated to curb the dog's freedom, he was tired of chasing after her.

"I think you should hear me out on this."

He walked to the shed. "Shut up," he repeated. After finding gloves and a shovel, he started for the overgrown garden at the far right corner of the yard.

"I won't shut up," she said in a shrill voice. *"I'm looking out for you, lover. I want to keep you safe and happy."*

"No, you want me to keep killing. I can't do that if I'm in prison."

Adeline laughed. *"This is true. I do enjoy the way you feed me, lover. Which is why I still think we should leave. Something isn't right with the twat. What woman would put up with your...quirks?"*

"Quirks?" He used the shovel to dig up one of the dead bushes at the edge of the garden. "What quirks?"

"Lover, you have your twat use ropes to bind you to the bed, and then you have her climb on board and ride your cock."

"That's to keep from killing her," he said, hauling the bush to the fire pit, where red hot embers still simmered in the ash from the fire he'd made last night.

"Yes, after you've already killed another woman who looks like the twat. See? Quirky."

He watched as the dried, shriveled leaves and branches smoked before catching on fire. "No, after I've killed a woman who looks like *you*."

Adeline laughed. *"Stop. You're going to make me think you're in love with me."*

"Love? No, I hate you."

"But aren't love and hate on the same spectrum?"

Ginger barked. He turned his head in time to see his sister walking around the side of the house from the front yard, carrying a couple of grocery bags.

"Talk about love and hate. Get rid of her. I don't like it when she's around."

When Adeline was quiet, he enjoyed his time with Kiera. She

knew him better than anyone, knew how to coax him from a bad mood and how to make him smile. But when Adeline was around, he didn't like Kiera near him. He swore his sister looked at him differently, as if she knew about the hungry bitch.

"I tried calling," Kiera said as she neared. Holding the bags high, she sidestepped Ginger.

"My phone is in the house. I've been working out here most of the day." He eyed the scrubs she was required to wear for her job. "Did you just get off work?"

"Yeah. I was supposed to work until three, but my last two patients cancelled their appointments. So, I thought I'd drop off some goodies and see how you were doing?"

"No, she's being nosey and checking up on you."

"I'm fine," he said, pulling a log off the woodpile and adding it to the burning bush in the fire pit.

"I tried calling you yesterday, too."

He picked up a thick stick he'd found while cleaning the yard earlier, and used it to stoke the fire. "I worked all day."

She let out a sigh, then set the two bags on one of the chairs near the fire. "I can tell coming here was a mistake."

"After the way I treated you on Sunday, I can't believe you'd bother to come around again."

"Wow," she said with shock and heavy sarcasm. "I thought you were taking out your frustrations over the miscarriage on me. I honestly didn't think you'd meant the things you said."

He looked at her and ignored the hurt in her eyes. "Well, you were wrong."

She took a step toward him. Tears swam in her eyes. "You really wish I was dead? After all we've been through together?"

"You mean after all you've done for me, right?"

"I've never said that. All I want is for you to be happy and healthy."

"She's so fucking artificial. She just wants to make sure you're taking your medication. That's all she was ever concerned about. Why else would she follow you to Tallahassee?"

"No, you want to check up on me."

"Because I'm worried about how you're handling the miscarriage." She took another step forward, then rested her hand on his arm. "Liam, stress and you aren't a good mix. You have to make sure you're sticking with your meds."

"Again with the fucking nagging." He pulled his arm free and faced her. "You need to stay out of my business. What's it going to take for you to get that?"

"Teach her a lesson. Make it so she won't come back."

"I'm not nagging you. I'm trying to make sure you don't hurt yourself or Bella."

His temper erupted at the mention of hurting Bella. He knocked Kiera to the ground. "I would *never* touch her."

Her eyes wide, panicked, she pressed her hands and feet to the ground and started to rise. "I know. I'm sorry. I'll just leave."

"What makes you think I could ever hurt her?" Breathing hard, unable to see past the rage, past the faces of the women he'd killed to keep himself from killing Bella, the air hissed as he swung the stick. When it connected and Kiera cried out, he inhaled the sweet satisfaction of her misery.

"Hit her again," Adeline encouraged.

"Liam, stop," Kiera sobbed. "Please!"

Her cries penetrated his brain. The red-hot haze suddenly fizzled as he realized what he'd just done. Sickened, he looked to the stick, then tossed it into the fire pit. When he turned and saw Kiera climbing to her feet, mascara-tears streaming down her face, he shoved both hands through his hair and gripped his head.

What have I done? Oh, God. What have I done?

"Looks like you've solved the nosey sister problem," Adeline said.

The detectives. What if they talk to Kiera? What if she tells them the truth?

"About Mommy and Daddy? Stop worrying. That case is closed and there's no way to prove you killed them. And remember, lover, if the detectives had proof, you would be in jail."

"Kiera, I didn't mean—"

Her hand trembled as she raised it. "I'm done with you."

"Don't say that," he said, terrified he might have alienated her from his life. "You're right, me and stress don't mix. But when you suggested that I'd hurt Bella…I just snapped."

"Snapped?" Kiera shouted. "Don't lie to me. That wasn't you. I know it wasn't. Your eyes change when the voices are there. How do I know? Because I've taken care of you for over ten fucking years." She winced as she took a couple of backward steps. "You wish I was dead? You don't want me to come here anymore? No problem. As a matter of fact, you are no longer my problem. I'm no longer going to allow you to be my burden."

Burden? When she turned and started toward the side of the house, he ran after her, dodging the dog in the process. "Kiera, wait," he said, reaching for her arm.

She spun on him, and shoved him in the chest. "Don't ever touch me again. I've loved you more than anyone, even more than Mom and Dad." Fresh tears trickled down her cheeks. "I tried to do right by you, and I failed."

"You didn't. You've sacrificed so much for me."

"Don't tell me what you think I want to hear."

He stiffened. "It's true. I know what you've done for me. I know it couldn't have been easy living with me."

"It wasn't," she shouted, and gave him another shove. "But I chose to protect you and to keep your secret. The day I decided to do that was the day I created my own personal prison. I can't blame you for that. It's all on me." She wiped her face and took another step back. "I'm done with you."

"Please. Let me apologize." He rushed after her and followed her to her Chevy. "Don't go."

"What are you doing? Why are you trying to keep her around?" Adeline asked. *"We no longer need her."*

"Just stop," he yelled as Kiera slammed the car door shut and locked it. As she sped down the driveway, his stomach sickened. He'd never felt so empty inside, as if a part of him had died. God, his sister was *really* afraid of him.

"She should be."

He let out a breath, then headed toward the backyard. "Shut up, Adeline."

CHAPTER 14

Kiera's Apartment, Tallahassee, Florida
Tuesday, 3:23 p.m., Eastern Standard Time

KIERA SPLASHED COLD water on her face, then used the hand towel to remove the excess mascara from under her eyes. Her back, namely her latissimus dorsi, the large muscle below the shoulder blade, throbbed with the minor movement, reminding her of what her brother had done to her.

Her eyes burned with fresh tears. She blinked them away as a knock came at her door. Relief filled her aching body. Eager to be in Harrison's strong arms, she left the bathroom.

During the drive home from Liam's, she'd tried to come up with a way to tell Harrison what had happened. At first, she'd thought about not saying a word, then had quickly dismissed the idea. Harrison knew how she felt about Liam, and knew that her brother had mental health issues. She trusted and loved Harrison, and needed his comfort, his strength. For the first time, probably ever, she had someone to lean on, and to offer her support. When Liam was medicated, he'd been wonderful to be around, but those times had been sporadic, and she wanted a constant in her life. She needed a man she could count on in good times and in bad.

Plus, she wouldn't be surprised if a bruise had already formed. In another day, it'd be dark, ugly and hard to hide. Especially since Harrison was sleeping and showering here, and they were supposed to go out of town this weekend.

She opened the door and smiled. Harrison was so handsome, even in a graphic T-shirt, faded jeans and sneakers. She loved his smile and kind eyes. She loved him. "Hi, how was your day?"

"It's better now." He stepped inside. Once he closed the door behind him, he pulled her into his arms.

Pain shot through her back. She stiffened and inhaled sharply.

He loosened his hold. His gaze met hers as he touched her chin. "Why have you been crying?"

Her eyes misted. "I got out of work early and decided to go see my brother."

"He made you cry the last time you saw him. I don't know why you went back there," he said, anger in his tone.

"Because I was worried about him and Bella." A tear slipped down her cheek. "Now I'm just worried about Bella."

"Hey," he murmured. He cupped her cheek and caught a tear on his thumb. "What happened?"

She gripped his wrist. "Liam hit me."

His face went stony, while his eyes filled with something she'd never seen from him before—hatred. "Are you okay? Do I need to take you to the ER?" he asked, his tone quiet, angry.

"No. I'm okay."

"Did you call the police?"

"I'm not going to file a report. It's not that bad," she said, trying to hold back the tears. "He was upset and...I should have seen the warning signs and stayed away from him."

"So it's your fault he hurt you? Fuck that." His hand fell away, and he drew in a deep breath. "He's not stable. You shouldn't be alone with him, and Bella shouldn't, either."

"I know it's not my fault. He's also never done this before. I think he's off therapy."

"I don't care. Therapy or not, it's no excuse. And once is more than enough. Trust me, I know. I spent my childhood either covering my eyes so I didn't have to see my mom take a beating, or hiding to avoid those same fists."

Anger replaced the devastation of what Liam had done. She once again ached for the little boy Harrison had been, and the hardships he'd been dealt at such a young age. She fisted his shirt.

"No child should have to go through that."

"No woman should, either." He placed a gentle hand on her arm. "I want to hold you, but I don't know where you're hurt."

"My back. Just below my left shoulder blade," she said, and told him how Liam had knocked her down, then hit her with a large stick. "The look in his eyes…I've seen him clouded before. That's the best way for me to describe how his eyes would get when he was seeing and hearing things that weren't real. Today was different. For a few seconds, I didn't recognize him. There was so much rage in him…in his eyes, twisting his mouth. I've been scared for Liam, but until today I've never been scared *of* him."

Harrison turned away, but she didn't miss the anger crossing his face. He took her hand and led her to the bedroom. "Did you ice your back?"

"No. I was only home a few minutes before you came over," she said as he sat her on the bed. "You're not saying anything."

"I want to take care of you. Let me help you out of your shirt."

As she lifted her arms, she squeezed her eyes shut and fought against the pain bursting from her back. "Wow, that hurts," she said, dragging in a few deep breaths, then relaxed when he had the shirt off and her arms back at her sides. She turned slightly and tried to look over her shoulder. "How bad is it?" The agony in his eyes had her gripping his arm before he could walk away. "Harrison?"

He cleared his throat. "It's bruised. Lie on your stomach, and I'll be back in a sec with ice."

She moved to the center of the bed, positioning herself onto her stomach. She couldn't shake the way Harrison had looked at her, as if her pain made him miserable. Before she could dissect the look he'd given her, he came back into the room carrying a freezer bag filled with ice and a kitchen towel. Without a word, he sat next to her, set first the towel, then the ice along her sore back.

"What do you call this muscle?" he asked, running the tips of his fingers over the opposite muscle on her right side.

"It's the latissimus dorsi."

He traced her ribs. "He could have broken your ribs."

As the ice began to numb her muscle, she relaxed under his touch. "But he didn't."

"I meant what I said. You can't see him. Not alone."

She rested her cheek on the back of her hand and looked up at him. "I'm done with him. I told him I couldn't do this anymore. I keep waiting to feel guilty for telling him I'm finished being his babysitter, but I've got nothing but a huge amount of relief."

He lay next to her, and smoothed her hair behind her ear. "That's because you've had enough, and you're ready to live for you. You've sacrificed too much for your brother. He has an illness and he's not going to change. With the way he's been treating you, I'm worried he's only going to get worse."

"If he's not medicated, he definitely will. I should call Bella. She needs to know what happened. This honestly makes me wonder if he did something to cause the miscarriage."

"I think you should report him to the police, and let Bella find out that way."

"Could you have had your brother arrested?" she asked, her mind drifting back to the day she'd discovered Liam had caused their parents' car accident. Even now, her stomach sank with dread, with remorse. For over ten years, she'd been plagued by guilt. Would her parents have wanted her to tell? Had she let them down, or just herself?

"It's easy to say yes because I'm not you."

She grinned. "Not helping."

He kissed her shoulder. "Did you take anything for the pain? You're going to be sore for a few days."

"No. I'll take some ibuprofen later."

"Take some now. Tell me where it is and I'll get it for you."

He made to move, but she stopped him. "Stay like this with me," she said. The concern in his eyes touched her. The last person who had worried over her had probably been her mom. After spending so many years dealing with the pressure of having to watch out for Liam, it was nice to unload the burden and share parts of herself she'd kept hidden. She loved Harrison for more than that, and although they hadn't been together long, she could see them lasting. Right now, he was the only real friend she had in Tallahassee, and the only real reason she would remain here.

As that thought hit her, she realized she'd been isolated for many years. She had friends in Aurora, but none of them had really understood her daily life. That had been her fault for not letting those people into her world, and she regretted not allowing herself to trust. If she left Tallahassee, she saw no reason to return to Colorado. There was nothing there, except memories she'd rather bury.

When Harrison took her hand and kissed her knuckles, the tenderness in his eyes had her throat tightening and a few tears escaping. He laid back down, until they were almost nose to nose. "Your tears are killing me," he murmured. "I'm trying so hard to keep my cool right now, when I really want to go over to your brother's and punish him."

"These tears aren't for him, or because my back hurts."

"Then what are they for?"

"I was just thinking about where to go from here. I moved to Tallahassee for Liam."

He rubbed his thumb along her knuckles. "Would you move back to Colorado?"

"Get out of my head." She half-smiled. "I was just thinking about that."

"And?"

"I don't think I can."

"Why?"

When he met her gaze, the longing in his eyes had her heart pounding harder, faster. Fear of rejection made her breathing shallow and her mouth dry. "Because I love you," she said, needing to put her heart out there, and for him to understand that she was one hundred percent invested in their relationship.

His eyes filled with agony again, and her heart sank. She

blinked back the tears, the humiliation, and pushed onto her elbows.

"Kiera, don't move. You need to rest."

The ice had numbed her back, but not enough to kill the pain. She sat up anyway. "I think you need to leave. I'm feeling really stupid right now and would like to be alone."

He sat on the edge of the bed. "No."

"Look, I've dealt with enough bullshit today. I don't need yours. Now I'm not asking, I'm telling you to leave."

"I don't want to leave."

"Why would you stick around and make us both uncomfortable? Sorry, but that's not my idea of a good time, and I certainly don't need your pity."

"I don't pity you," he shouted, and pushed off the bed. "I love you."

She stilled. "What? I don't believe you, not when you're looking at me as if I just killed your dog."

"It's true." His eyes became intense and the longing in them returned. He walked back to the bed, reached out and touched her cheek. "I'm so fucking in love with you it makes me ache inside because I know it won't last."

Her breath caught, her chest tightened. "I don't understand. Why wouldn't it last?"

The mattress dipped as he sat next to her. "I told you I don't deserve you, and now I'm going to tell you why."

Her head buzzed with dread. She didn't want to know. She wanted to continue to live in the world they'd created.

"I trust you, which is why I'm going to tell you something very few people know." He took her hand, and laced her fingers through his. "Ah…" He cleared his throat and shook his head. "I've thought about how to tell you, and how to sugarcoat my past, but there's no easy way."

She gave his hand a squeeze. "Just say it. I'm not here to judge you."

"You might when I'm finished," he said, looking down at

their joined hands. "Everything I told you about growing up, juvie, prison…that's all true. Same with my brother being dead. You asked me if I could turn my brother over to the police, now I'm going to ask you something—if you had a gun pointed to your head and were told the only way to live was to carve a message into your brother's stomach, would you do it?"

"Oh, my God. You're as crazy as my brother." Of course she would be drawn to someone with mental health issues. She'd grown up with a schizophrenic father, and had been taking care of her equally schizophrenic brother for over ten years. She tugged at her hand. "Please, Harrison, just go."

"I'm not crazy, just ask Vlad or Mel. They know the truth. Cash does, but not the full extent."

"Why? Were they there?"

"Vlad was, and Mel knows because we used to work together for an investigation agency."

She lifted her brows. "You're a spy?" Yep, Harrison was nuts.

"No." He let out a breath. "Will you just let me talk? And please be open minded."

The seriousness banked in his eyes and in his tone, made her want to believe. Whether she would remained to be seen. But she'd listen. "Of course. I'm all ears."

"A couple years ago," he began, "Mick talked me into doing a job with him. I wanted to stay legit, but it was a struggle. Because I was a felon, I couldn't find decent work, and the lure of easy money was there. I agreed without knowing the full extent. Do you remember the domestic bombings that took place all in the course of a few days?"

"Of course. One of them happened at the Denver International Airport."

"Right. I was part of that."

Harrison wasn't crazy. He was a terrorist. "Hundreds of people were killed. This isn't something to joke about," she said, trying to pull away again.

"I had no idea who me and Mick were working for, or that we

were planting bombs all over the country. When I figured it out, I did my best to stop him. In the meantime, I watched the bastard torture and murder my brother," he said with so much pain in his voice, she hurt for him. But he didn't stop there, he continued to tell her the horrors he'd witnessed during the short time he'd been held hostage and forced to kill or be killed. His story was graphic and realistic. Everything he said had a ring of truth to it. But she'd lived with a paranoid schizophrenic. Liam had also worked with government agencies, and had helped to quietly save the country a couple of times—from aliens, from terrorists, from secret agencies.

"So after you helped save the country, you went to work for CORE?"

His chuckle held heavy sarcasm. "I've been so bent about telling you the truth, and you don't believe me. Wait until I tell Vlad."

"Your best friend and the man who was going to cut off your brother's tongue."

"One and the same." He let go of her hand and stood. "I get the skepticism."

"As you should. You don't think Liam made up wild stories that he believed were true?"

The look he leveled her with was so earnest she wanted to believe him. "I'm about to make a believer out of you," he said, then told her how last year he'd been hired to work for a secret underground agency that skirted the law and was affiliated with this CORE group. "Which brings me to why I'm here in Tallahassee."

"You're here on a secret investigation?" she asked, not to be a bitch, but for clarification. As it was, her head was spinning. Even Liam's stories were never this detailed.

He nodded. "Have you heard of Rodney Archer?"

"The nut-job doctor? What about him?"

"I was part of the team that stopped him."

"According to the news—"

"Fuck the news. It's very important that you listen to me." He sat back on the bed. "Mel and I were both held against our will.

We went in to stop them, but neither of us had been prepared for what Rodney and Adeline had in store for us. They drugged and tortured us. Their goal was to scramble our brains, turn us into psychopaths so they could use Rodney's drug to fix us."

Her head began to ache almost as much as her back. "I'm sorry, but this is too much."

"Mel will tell you, same with Cash and Vlad. Mel will also tell you that your brother was there with us."

She rubbed her temples with both hands. "Okay, I've heard enough. This is ridiculous. Liam left Colorado on an imagined secret mission. He wasn't kidnapped by some mad scientist." She dropped her hands. Needing to get away from Harrison, she scooted from the bed. "I'm not sure what game you're playing with me, but it stops now."

She pulled a baggy T-shirt from the drawer, then left the bedroom. Once in the kitchen, she pulled it on. Stabbing pain radiated from her back to her shoulder, but she didn't care. Her heart and head hurt worse.

"I'm telling you the truth," he said from behind her. "Mel and I were held in that house for less than twelve hours. But your brother was there much longer. I have no idea how much of their drug they gave him, but based on their brainwashing methods, his schizophrenia and my personal reactions to the drug, I doubt he's the same man who was dragged into that house."

She faced him. "What do you mean? Are you suggesting that the violent outburst he had today was part of a reaction to being drugged by those people?"

"Probably."

Probably? "I saw the news about Rodney Archer. I remember hearing about a couple of survivors, but they'd died."

"Liam escaped." His jaw tightened and she watched him swallow hard. "Before he did, he killed a man, and hurt Mel. Because there was no proof he existed, our agency was told not to go after Liam. And Rodney confessed."

"But you said you and Mel saw him."

"We'd also been drugged." He leaned against the counter. "Mel quit the agency to be here with Cash, and everyone else in our organization went back to business as usual, except for me. I couldn't let it go. I needed to find your brother. I needed to know if Rodney and Adeline created a monster, and if I'd end up one, too."

"Oh, my God." Her heart started to race so fast she grew lightheaded. She walked around the kitchen island and took a seat at the stool. Devastated, she closed her eyes and told herself the prick wasn't worth her tears. "You used me. You used me to get to my brother." The days and weeks she'd been with him rushed through her head. "Do you have any idea how many times I thought we were the perfect match?"

He rushed around the island, then sat on the opposite stool. "We are a perfect match."

"Go to hell." Sickened by him, disgusted that she'd allowed the man into her heart and her bed, she stood up and walked toward the front door. "You need to get out now," she said, her voice shaking with humiliation and outrage.

"I'm not finished." The misery in his eyes and the guilt on his face had no effect on her. She wanted the liar to be miserable. "Hate me all you want, but there's more and it's very important you listen to me."

"Hate? I loved you. I believed we had something great togeth-er. And the whole time you were shitting all over it." Already humiliated, she no longer cared if the tears fell. "When I first saw you, I thought you were so good looking, and I was stunned that you asked me out when there are prettier, skinnier, sexier women all over this complex. But you weren't attracted to me, you were using me, feeding me bullshit lines, and I bought them all."

She leaned against the door and stared at him. Her cheeks burned with embarrassment. She'd been played for a fool this entire time. "I believed you," she said on a bitter sob. "That day in my bedroom, what you did and said with the bikini, I believed you."

His face and eyes hardened as he reached her in several long powerful strides. "Everything I've said, everything I've done, was real," he said, crowding her, caging her. "I love you. I want to be with you. I crave your kisses and your smile. Never in my life have I met a woman like you." She gasped when he gripped her chin. "I went out of my way to pursue you to get to your brother. After the first night at the luau, I knew any information you could give me, I could pretty much get on my own. But I used Liam as an excuse to keep seeing you. Cash and Mel, they both warned me, they told me I was making a mistake and that I was going to pay for it. They were right. Because the way you're looking at me is fucking torture. Worse than any I've experienced, and I've experienced plenty."

She refused to have any pity for him, or for what he might have gone through—if his other stories were to be believed. Harrison was a liar, an admitted thief, and clearly a user. "Well, you should have listened to your friends. Thanks, by the way, for making me look pathetic."

"You don't look pathetic."

"Oh, no? It's obvious I don't have any friends here. So why not keep the ruse going and get your friends to pretend they want to hang out with me."

He frowned. "Melanie threatened to cut me because she likes you and is mad at me for dragging you into this."

"Cut you? And what are you dragging me into?"

"She has a thing for knives. Did you notice the switchblade your brother carries?"

She had a quick memory of him using one to cut the tape off a Christmas present. "What about it?"

"He took it from Mel the night he escaped the plantation house where we were being kept."

She jerked her chin from his hand and shoved at his chest. "You say Liam killed a man. Well, you know where my brother is, so I don't know why you're still here bothering me."

"I can't prove he killed that man," he said, not budging. "I can, however, prove he killed two elderly people right after he escaped. I also believe he's responsible for the five women who've been killed here in Tallahassee since December."

Bile rose in her throat. She covered her mouth and shoved past him. When she reached the bathroom, she quickly hung her head over the toilet and retched. She gripped the toilet and sobbed. When Harrison's hands pulled her hair from her face, she swung her arm, causing pain to slice through her back. "Get away from me," she said, then heaved some more. He held her hair back again, and this time she let him. At this point, she'd take false comfort over nothing at all. Because if he was right, and Liam killed all of those people, it was her fault. She could have sent him to prison after their parents' deaths. He could be there now and eight people would be alive. Those women could be with their husbands, boyfriends or children. Instead they were dead. Liam might have been the one to murder them, but she'd facilitated it by keeping her mouth shut.

She took the towel Harrison offered her, wiped her eyes, mouth and nose, then stood. Without looking at him, she reached into the cabinet drawer for her toothbrush and toothpaste. "I don't understand why you're still here and why my brother isn't in custody," she said, and began brushing her teeth.

"I told you I can prove he killed the old couple, but I don't have the evidence to pin the five murders on him."

She rinsed out her mouth. "Then how do you know it's him?"

He pulled out his phone, pressed the screen a few times, then handed it to her. "Do you know who this is?"

"No." She stared at the pretty woman with striking green eyes and long dark curly hair. "She looks a little like Bella."

"This is Adeline."

"The woman who kidnapped you? She's beautiful."

"She's an evil bitch."

The angry edge in his tone had her looking up at him. There was something in his eyes, an underlying despair that tugged at her heart. "What did she do to you?"

"Nothing," he said, but she didn't believe him. He'd looked away too quickly, blurted the word too fast. "Now look at these photographs."

She took the phone from him and immediately recognized the first woman. While she couldn't remember her name, she knew she'd been murdered in the car outside of her apartment building. As she swiped through the photos, with the exception of the blonde, all of these women eerily resembled Adeline…and Bella. A chill swept through her. "The resemblance doesn't prove anything."

"I know for a fact that the hair of a Husky was found on the first victim. I also know that all of the victims had been cleaned, which I believe connects them together."

"Again, a single dog hair proves nothing."

"Today, Vlad discovered another link. Your brother made a delivery to the house next door to Julie Beechum." He held up the phone and showed her the picture of the blonde woman. "Guess what the neighbor who received a brand new refrigerator looks like?"

"Oh, my God." She moved past him, opened up the linen closet, then pulled out a bottle of ibuprofen. "If Liam's doing this, why hasn't he hurt Bella?"

"I don't know. But I made an anonymous phone call to one of the detectives investigating the murders, and pointed them in Liam's direction."

"When?"

"This morning," he said, and when he touched her shoulder, she knocked his hand away. "If they talked to him today, then that could explain why he lost his temper with me."

"Kiera, I'm so sorry. I never—"

She left the bathroom. "Save it."

"No," he shouted, shocking her to a halt. He turned her to face him. "I am responsible for the murders of those five women. Don't you get that?" He closed his eyes and rested his forehead to hers. "I've done terrible things with a gun pointed to my head. It doesn't make the guilt go away, and I have to live with the murders of men, women and children. Every. Single. Day."

When he looked up at her, her throat tightened and her chin wobbled. He was fighting tears and she needed to be strong for him. Deep down, beyond the hurt, the humiliation, the devastating blow to her fragile ego, she loved him. And she understood guilt more than he knew.

"No one was pointing a gun to my head when I broke laws to hunt down Liam," he said, his voice rough. "Or when I told myself using you wouldn't be a big deal as long as I got what I wanted. You know what's sad? The moment I found out Liam was schizophrenic, I knew his results from Rodney and Adeline's experiment couldn't be compared to mine. By that time, two women were dead and someone had burned down the old couple's house, along with evidence your brother was there."

He let go of her. "I told you I didn't deserve you," he said, and started for the door. Gripping the door handle, he looked over his shoulder. "I never lied about how I felt about you. You're special, Kiera." He opened the door. "Stay away from your brother."

As soon as the door clicked shut, she rushed to it. Tempted to go after him, to confess the sins she'd planned to take to her grave, she quickly locked the deadbolt. Her knees grew weak. On a sob, she slid to the floor, clutched her legs to her chest and cried.

For years, she'd known her brother was a murderer. By turning a blind eye to what he'd done to her parents, and without a gun to her head, she'd allowed Liam to become a serial killer.

Harrison...he carried the deaths of so many on his shoulders, he shouldn't go through life believing he was responsible for the people her brother had murdered. He would though, because she had no intention of telling anyone what only she and Liam knew.

Hating herself, she swiped the tears from her face. And Harrison believed he didn't deserve to be with her...

PART III

"Darling? Light, of my life.
I'm not gonna hurt ya.
You didn't let me finish my sentence.
I said, I'm not gonna hurt ya.
I'm just going to bash your brains in!"
—Jack Torrance, *The Shining*

CHAPTER 15

Leon County State Attorney's Office, Tallahassee, Florida
Wednesday, 9:33 a.m., Eastern Standard Time

"DOG DNA TESTING?" Assistant State Attorney, Craig Hollis, chuckled as he entered his office. "Sorry, Detectives, but you don't have a case here."

"Of course we do," Sharon argued. "Our suspect owns a Husky. A dog hair belonging to a Husky was found on our first victim. Our suspect was also delivering an appliance to the house next door to victim number four. He lives within two miles of where our fifth victim was killed outside of Burger Boy."

"Sharon, stop." The young prosecutor slid out of his suit coat, then smoothed the back of his short blond hair. "I read the reports. Everything you're presenting is circumstantial. You don't have a murder weapon for three of your five cases. There is no DNA evidence or fingerprints, and you can't place your suspect at any of the crime scenes."

"He was right next door to Julie Beechum's house within two hours of the estimated time of death," Bern reminded him.

"Then he went back to work, correct?" He leaned against his desk. "His fiancée claimed he was home Sunday night, so unless forensics stumbles across a miracle, you again have nothing to link your suspect to that murder."

She knew trying to obtain a warrant to collect DNA from Forrester's dog was a long shot, but she'd hoped for an opportunity to at least search his home. "He's schizophrenic," she said.

"That's no basis for a warrant. And if anyone found out we'd used his diagnosis to search his place, the media—especially social media—would slaughter us." He let out a sigh as he loosened his tie. "Look, I firmly believe we're dealing with a serial killer. There are too many similarities between several of the victims. But if you honestly think your one and only suspect is who we're after, you better give me something more concrete."

A young man in a trendy suit knocked on the doorjamb. "Excuse me, sir, do you have a minute?"

Craig looked at Bernadette, then her. "Detectives?"

Sharon forced a smile. "Thanks for your time."

"He was cutting teeth when we were graduating from the academy," Bern said, once they were in the elevator. "He could've at least *tried* to get a warrant for us."

"If we could search the place, I feel like we'd find something. I still think the fiancée was lying." Yesterday afternoon, they stopped at Cherry's where Bella Johnson worked. To view the woman's driver's license photo had been one thing, but to meet her in person and see the striking resemblance to their victims had been eerie. "I guarantee Forrester called her and gave her a heads-up we might be by."

"Maybe she's working with him. He does the murders, she's the cleanup crew."

The elevator doors opened. "And the motivation would be, what? She wants to rid the city of any woman who might resemble her?"

Bern chuckled. "That's just silly."

"What might be silly is me believing an anonymous tip."

"It's not," Bern said as they made their way through the parking garage. "We've solved plenty of cases thanks to anonymous tips and informants."

"I know. The problem is I want Forrester to be our guy. I want to be done with this so we can put in a request for vacation and go on that cruise."

"We don't need to be done with this case to go on vacation. You know damn well it could be weeks, months or years before we catch another break."

"I have weeks and months, but I don't have years." She stopped at Bernadette's car. "I keep thinking about Julie Beechum's husband, and how he wanted to be her hero. You know, Alan was that way."

Her friend smiled. "I know. Troy used to be jealous of him."

Bernadette's ex-husband, Troy Richie, was a mortgage broker who made great money and couldn't understand why Bern wouldn't play the role of the good little wife...stay home, keep the house clean, spread her legs when he wasn't screwing his secretary, and raise their brat. "Troy's a prick."

"Don't I know it?" Bern chuckled and opened the car door. "Did I tell you what my daughter said about the baby's crib?" she asked once they were driving through the parking garage.

"This oughta be good."

"It is. Since her father spent three grand on a two-piece bedroom set—I'm talking crib and dresser—she said she needs me to buy her the matching changing table and glider."

"Three grand? I don't think Alan and I spent that on our bedroom set." Bernadette was such a good person, how she'd ended up spawning such an ungrateful creature Sharon couldn't understand. "What did you tell Miss Sunshine?"

"That I had two hundred dollars to spend, nothing more. Wait until she finds out about our cruise. That'll really get her going."

"I hope she lets you spend time with the baby."

"Me, too. But I'm not counting on it."

The sadness in her friend's tone didn't settle well with Sharon. She might have to pay Lauren, aka Miss Sunshine, a visit, pull out the cancer card and remind her that life was short, that her mother was someone to be valued.

"Hey, I was just thinking," Bernadette began, "if we don't need a warrant to go through trash left on a curb, or to get DNA off a coffee cup left in an interrogation room, I don't see how we'd be doing anything wrong if one of us happens to get dog hair on our clothes."

Sharon stared at Bernadette's profile. "You're a genius. Do you have two grand to pay for the testing? Without Craig backing us, I don't see how we're going to make that fly."

"I do have just the right amount. But that's for a cruise." She slowed the car. "Maybe we should try to catch her at home."

They'd tried reaching Kiera Forrester yesterday after they'd talked with Bella Johnson, but their suspect's sister wasn't home. When they'd tried calling later in the evening and received no answer, and no return call then or this morning, they'd figured they would try her at work. "If she's not here, we'll stop by her apartment again."

They exited Bernadette's car, then headed into Mercy Memorial. After checking the directory, they made their way to the physical therapy department located in the west wing. After introducing themselves to the receptionist, whose eyes widened when Bern flashed her badge, they waited in the lobby for Kiera.

"Did I tell you what Lauren and her goober husband are thinking about naming the baby?" Bern whispered.

"No. And why are you whispering?"

"It's quiet and my voice carries."

She smiled. "I'll give you that. So what are the names?"

"Archibald, if it's a boy, and Hester, if it's a girl."

"I've never met an Archibald or a Hester."

Bern let out a quiet sigh. "I guess I'm going to meet one or the other in a few months."

Sharon nudged her. "I can't wait to see you all goo-goo over that baby."

Bern gave her a big grin. "You know I'll be." She nodded toward the receptionist's desk. "Looks like the gal from the driver's license photo."

Kiera Forrester approached them, her eyes concerned, her smile wary. "Detectives?"

"Yes," Sharon said, then introduced them. "Is their someplace we can talk?"

Confusion crossed her pretty face. "Sure. My next patient isn't due in for another twenty minutes. It's nice outside, maybe we can talk there?"

After agreeing, Kiera led them out a different door and to a lovely park-like area. "I hope this is okay," she said. "How can I help you?"

"We're here to talk about your brother, Liam," Sharon began. "You filed a missing persons report on him back in August. Can you tell us a little about that?"

She tucked a thick lock of auburn hair behind her ear. "Sure. Is Liam in trouble?"

"Your brother is a suspect in a murder investigation."

"What?" Kiera's face held the shock Sharon had expected. The young woman ran a shaky hand across her forehead. "I...okay." She blew out a deep breath. "A murder investigation? Really?"

"Really," Bern said. "Your brother's last known address was with you in Aurora, Colorado. How long was he living with you?"

"Um, off and on since he was diagnosed with schizophrenia."

"That was about ten years ago?"

Kiera nodded. "He tried living on his own. There would be months of success, then he'd start skipping therapy and he'd be back."

"Any history of violence?" Sharon asked.

Kiera held her gaze. "No. He's never been in any trouble."

"Do you know why he moved to Tallahassee?"

"Not exactly. He disappeared in late August, then reappeared in early October."

"Is this typical for him?"

Kiera shook her head. "Not at all. I mean, he's gone missing for a day or two, but after checking places I know he likes, I've always been able to find him."

"Why did you move here?" Bernadette asked.

"I worry about him," Kiera said with a shrug. "Our parents are gone, and it's just me and him. I wanted to make sure he's taking care of himself."

"Is he?"

"He seems to be."

Sharon stared at the woman. "How is Liam with his fiancée? Are they having any problems?" She wasn't showing any signs that she was lying. Yes, she was a little nervous, but most people were when they were being questioned.

"Not that I'm aware. Bella recently had a miscarriage which shook them both up, but I think that's to be expected."

Bern frowned. "I'm sorry to hear that. When was this?"

"Over the weekend. Saturday."

"So Liam was home with his fiancée Sunday?" Sharon asked.

"I stopped by Sunday and dropped off dinner for them. He was there."

Anticipation rushed through Sharon. *This* was the lead they were looking for. "Okay, thanks for your time." She handed Kiera her business card. "If you ever need to reach us."

After Kiera walked away, Bern pulled her car keys from her pocket. "Notice she didn't ask about what murder we were investigating?"

"I did, but you know you can't read too much into that. She was nervous. I'm more interested in Bella's miscarriage."

"Right, she miscarries Saturday, and Sunday night a woman resembling Bella is stabbed over thirty times in the stomach. Quite the coincidence, don't you think?"

Sharon nodded. "What I think we need to do is to have another chat with Bella."

Harrison's Apartment, Tallahassee, Florida
Wednesday, 10:40 a.m., Eastern Standard Time

WHEN KIERA'S PHONE number lit his cell phone's screen, his stomach tightened with nervous energy. He answered immediately.

"Harrison," she said, her voice hushed, panicked. "Two detectives just came to see me at work. They were asking about Liam."

"What were their names?"

"Detectives Larson and Richie."

Good. They were looking into Liam. "Larson is the detective I contacted yesterday. What did they ask you?"

She quickly told him. When she came to where she'd mentioned Bella's miscarriage, an overwhelming sense of relief came over him. There was a good chance his name, and Nick's, could stay completely out of the investigation. He'd seen Detective Larson's report on Gloria Franklin and knew the woman had been brutally stabbed in the stomach. Liam was clearly unstable. His frustration over the loss of the baby could have poured over into violence against an innocent woman.

"Did I do okay?"

"Sounds like you were perfect."

She let out a breath. "This is really happening."

"I'm sorry, Kiera. Do you want me to come—?"

The phone went silent. He looked across the room at Mel. "She hates me."

"Well, honey, you knew that was a possibility."

He set down the phone, then went back into the living room and sat on the chair opposite from the couch where Mel was seated. "I know."

Her blonde hair fell to the side as she cocked her head. "For whatever it's worth, I admire you for being honest with her. You didn't have to tell her everything."

"She told me she loved me. But she loved the man she thought I was, that's not fair to her. She needed to know the truth."

"It's not fair to you, either. Did you think about that?"

"I don't know what you mean."

"You've been pretending to be someone you aren't, and trying to be someone you want to be. If Kiera doesn't love the man you are, then the girl ain't worth it."

He shook his head. "Of course you'd say that. You're my friend."

"A friend who loves you. Cash loves you, too."

He grimaced. "Please don't say that again."

"So does Vlad."

"Honestly, you need to stop."

Grinning, she scooted to the edge of the couch. "Okay, I will." She looked to her manicured nails. He'd never seen Kiera wear nail polish and absently wondered why. "Lola's been calling," Mel said, taking his mind off nails. "She's wondering if you're coming back."

"What'd you say?"

"That I didn't know, which I don't." She looked up at him. "Vlad's not talking, either. So, what's the plan?"

"I'm done with ATL. I don't want to live in a trailer, and I don't want to hack into computer systems, or break any more laws." He leaned forward. "I know things between Kiera and me are over. I can't imagine she'll stay here. If she does, I'm moving someplace else. I can't deal with seeing her and not being able to be with her." He rested his elbows on his thighs, his head in his hands. "I've been a screw-up all my life. Even when I try to do the right thing, I manage to mess it up."

"Cash screws up all the time. I still love him and think he's sexy," she said with a wink.

He half-smiled. Mel was one of a kind, and knew the right things to say, even if they made him uncomfortable.

"Harrison, I know I kinda came down on you about Kiera, but I want you to know I did that because I was worried about you. You're not like Cash, Shane or Ryan."

"You mean I'm not the badass, take-charge macho man."

"I didn't say that."

"You didn't have to. But I noticed you didn't mention Vlad."

She flipped her hair over her shoulder. "Because that crazy Russian is in a category all of his own."

"No doubt."

"What's different about you is that you don't have a problem admitting your mistakes. You own who you are, where you've come from, and where you've been. It's a sexy quality."

His cheeks grew warm as he looked away.

"You even blush. No wonder Kiera's so in love with you."

"*Was* in love."

"I suppose if I was her I'd be angry, too," she said.

"Again, not helping."

"Sorry." Mel pursed her lips. "Did you tell her what happened at the plantation house?"

He pushed himself off the chair. "I told her enough."

"Sounds like you did," she said, also standing. "I guess I'm wondering why you were honest about unknowingly working for a domestic terrorist, but you couldn't tell her about Adeline."

His cheeks went from warm to hot. He still couldn't shake the humiliation of what Adeline had done to him in front of Mel, and wasn't sure if he ever would. "I don't see the point."

"Wouldn't you want to know if a man had raped Kiera?"

He stilled. "Adeline didn't rape me. And I don't want to talk about this."

"Maybe I do."

"We've been over that night already. But you're right. If Kiera had been hurt, even if it happened years ago, I'd want to know. But that's different."

"Why? Because you're a man?" She came up alongside him. "I'm not trying to dredge up that night, but I'll be honest. It bothers me. Badly. So I imagine it has to still bother you."

"Of course it does," he shouted, the humiliation turning into anger. "There are times I don't want to see you because I get in my head and…I'm sorry, Mel. We were both victims. Can we just let it go?"

"Sure." She twirled a thick curl around her finger. "When Rodney was sentenced, I got drunk and sat on my patio and cried." With a wry smile, she shook her head. "Poor Cash didn't know what to do with me." Her smile fell. "I don't know about you, but I didn't feel any satisfaction when Rodney was sent to prison. I'm not saying Rodney doesn't deserve it. Believe me, I think the man earned the death penalty for what he'd done." Her eyes took on a faraway look as she stared over his shoulder. "Adeline was who I wanted to suffer." She met his gaze. "When I heard you left and figured you were going a little rogue, I was doin' a mental fist pump. I wanted Liam found, and you were making it your mission to find him. But when I heard how you were acting and then saw it for myself, it made me sad and angry."

"That I was pursuing Liam?"

"That you were pursuing closure."

"You make it sound like a bad thing."

She gave him a reassuring smile. "It's not, as long as you're honest with yourself and no one gets hurt."

Memories of Kiera's tear-soaked cheeks, of the bruise on her back, made his stomach twist. "I don't need to be reminded about what a jerk I was to Kiera."

"Harrison, I'm not talking about Kiera, I'm talking about you. You're punishing yourself for doing the right thing."

"I broke a bunch of laws and women are dead. I didn't do one thing right."

"And if you hadn't gone after Liam no one would know about him. We wouldn't have his last name, and the detectives wouldn't be questioning him." He tensed when she touched his arm. "Those murders aren't your fault. If you'd stayed in the Glades, and stayed ignorant of Liam's identity, those women would have still been murdered. Now, if I hadn't helped him escape—"

"You didn't know."

She held up a hand. "I'm not blaming myself. I'm also not gonna lie...I have moments of doubt and guilt. If I allow those demons to constantly stay with me, it'll destroy my marriage and me. I can't let that happen."

He admired Mel. Beneath the girly-girl exterior, she was strong and had more balls than most men he knew. She was also kind and compassionate, and he hated that she even had demons to fight. He had demons of his own, too many. They were the faces of the innocent, of his brother, of Adeline and Liam. Of

Kiera.

He cleared his throat. "No, you can't," he finally said, then let out a tired sigh. "As fun as this conversation has been, I need to kick you out and get to work."

"You're not kickin' me out," she said with a smug smile. "I was planning on leaving anyway."

"Whatever." He grinned and walked her to the door. "Hey, thanks for coming over and listening."

"Anytime, hon. Weren't you able to talk to Vlad?"

"I was, but he gave me the 'Harry should have let Vlad kill Liam' line, then he told me not to worry about Kiera 'there much fishes in ocean for Harry' or something like that."

She laughed. "I'm so glad the big goof is coming to work for me and Cash." She gave him a hug. "I'm happier you're stickin' around Tallahassee."

Even though his world currently looked bleak, Harrison was good with his decision to leave ATL and stay here. Losing Kiera sucked. It hurt and he hated himself for how he'd handled the entire situation. But Liam wouldn't be free for long. If he had to have a face-to-face meeting with the detective, and hand over the evidence he had from the Dougals, he'd do as Nick suggested and ask for immunity first. Whether he'd move from the Club depended on Kiera. Whatever happened, Vlad would not be his roommate. The Russian was his closest friend, but living with him was a pain in the ass.

He opened up his laptop, then went to the project he'd started last week. The website he was currently building was his own. The business he'd gotten up to this point had been through recommendations. Even giving clients introductory discounts, he'd made five grand this month. He could possibly double his income by advertising his company. Although still down about Kiera and eager for detectives to take care of Liam, he poured his energy into the future.

But as he worked, his mind kept drifting. If Kiera accepted him for everything that he was, would he ever tell her about

Adeline? Would it matter?

He set the laptop on the table, then leaned back against the sofa. Bitterness settled on his chest as he thought about last night. He'd been brutally honest. He'd told her things he never wanted to say out loud again. Yes, he'd hurt her. Yes, initially he had planned to use her to get to Liam. But after everything he'd dumped on her, it suddenly pissed him off that he was hoping she'd *accept* him for all his faults and all the things he'd done. He was in love with Kiera, but he was tired of searching for acceptance, for his place in the world. He was tired of constantly seeking forgiveness.

Now distracted, he closed out the file, then went into Detective Larson's reports. When he'd checked last night, she hadn't written anything up about meeting with Liam. As he glanced through her files, disappointment and frustration settled on his shoulders. There was still no mention of Liam. Based on Kiera's call, they were obviously investigating him, but to what extent.

He stared at the screen and told himself to be patient, that questioning suspects was a process, and that unlike ATL agents, real detectives followed legal protocol. But he hated having his hands tied, along with that ugly sense of impotence.

He glanced at the clock on his screen. He hated waiting…

Liam and Bella's House, Tallahassee, Florida
Wednesday, 11:33 a.m., Eastern Standard Time

BERNADETTE PARKED THE car in the empty driveway. "Hopefully she's home. I'd like to talk to her without Forrester around."

"I'd also like to meet their dog. We can't get a warrant to take a sample of the dog's hair, but if the dog sheds on me, it's not my fault."

Bern grinned. "Young Craig might disagree, but if we have a DNA match, it won't matter. We'll have probable cause."

Although Sharon was excited by the prospect of having the suspect's dog shed on her, the hair might do them little good. "It cost the department two grand when we had the dog hair originally tested, and it took about three weeks to get the results. I think we'll probably need something else to justify the DNA sample."

Bernadette stepped onto the front porch. "Why can't this be easy?"

"Because then our job would be boring," Sharon said, and knocked on the front door.

"Because spending hours filling out paperwork isn't? I should go back to patrol. I miss being first on the scene, then letting the investigators deal with the paperwork."

She sometimes did, too. But the promotion to Detective meant more pay, and more opportunity for overtime. A lot of good all of those extra hours would do her now. Between her husband's pension, and the savings they'd accrued over the years, she had money in the bank. Enough that she could've retired at sixty, and then started traveling the world. Instead of spending the hard earned money, she'd had to talk with her attorney and figure out what to do with it once she was gone.

"Maybe she's not home." Bern looked through the front window. "I'll go around the garage and see if there's a car here."

While Bern walked across the driveway, Sharon casually paced the front porch. After they spoke with Bella, they planned to interview acquaintances of their last victim. She didn't want to bother, but knew it was necessary. They could be chasing after the wrong guy. If only the random guy would call her back. She hadn't been prepared for his original call, and now had questions to shoot at him. The biggest question she wanted answered was how the man had come to suspect Liam Forrester.

By all accounts, Forrester was an average guy. He'd never been in trouble, not even a speeding ticket, and had no history of violence. And if Forrester was their killer, what had driven him to take a life? None of these murders had been sexually motivated, and these weren't crimes of passion. What motivated the killer also had her wondering how long he'd been at it. In her experience, people don't wake up one morning and decide to kill a stranger.

"There's a car in the garage," Bern called. "A blue hatchback."

Bella's car. Sharon stepped back to the door, then knocked again, this time harder. A dog barked, followed by a woman's muffled voice. When the door swung open, a cute Husky snorted and pressed its nose against the screen.

"Detectives," Bella said, breathless, her eyes wide. "What are you doing here?"

Sharon masked her surprise. When they'd met Bella at the restaurant, she'd been wearing a clunky uniform that hid her figure. Between the tiny red tube top, and shorts that were tinier than most underwear she owned, Bella hadn't left much to the imagination. She also didn't look like a woman who'd had a miscarriage four days ago.

"We forgot to ask you a couple of questions," Bern began. "Gotta few?"

Bella tucked a dark curl behind her ear. "Ah, sure. Let me put Ginger out back. She has no manners," she said with a smile.

"I love dogs, and Detective Richie has a couple of her own. Your Ginger won't bother us."

"Okay, but I warned you," she said, holding open the screen door.

The moment they walked into the small house, the Husky was dancing around their legs, wagging her tail, brushing up against their pants. "How old is Ginger?" Sharon asked.

"Almost seven months now. We're still working on training her." Bella motioned to the dated, fading sofa, then adjusted the tube top. "Please, have a seat. Can I get you something to drink?"

"No thanks, we won't keep you." Sharon sat next to Bern. "I heard Huskies are energetic."

Bella sat on the olive-green corduroy recliner opposite the sofa. "That's the truth. She's a lot of work, but we love her," she said, tapping her thigh and gaining the dog's attention.

"I've also heard they're good with children."

"Let's hope so, because me and Liam plan on having plenty," she replied with a smile. "We're gettin' married in May and want to start our family right away."

"You're smart to wait two to three cycles," Bern said.

"Wait for what?"

"To try for another baby."

"Another?" Bella frowned and looked at each of them as if they were speaking Russian. "I don't understand."

"Liam's sister said you had a miscarriage this weekend," Bern began. "We're sorry to hear that."

Bella continued to scratch the dog and look at them with utter confusion. "*Kiera* told you that? I don't know why she would."

"So you were never pregnant?" Sharon asked, unsure who to believe. Forrester's sister had been convincing and genuine. And it made no sense for her to lie about her future sister-in-law's miscarriage.

"Never. Not to get all personal, but I did get my period on Saturday night. Kiera was here then."

"Why would she think you miscarried?"

Bella shrugged her slender shoulders. "I have no idea."

"And Liam was here with you Sunday night."

"For sure." She smiled. "We're not gonna start a family until after the weddin', but we do enjoy practicing. Anything else I can help you with?"

Sharon returned the smile. "Not right now." Once she and Bern were in the car, she asked, "Why would one of these women lie about a pregnancy?"

"Yeah, it doesn't make sense. Neither did what she was wearing. I don't think I could even get my arm through one leg of those shorts."

Sharon laughed. She and Bernadette were never happy with their weight and had been on more diets and exercise kicks than she could count. "Stop it. You have a great figure, and Joe doesn't complain, right?" Bern and Joe had been dating for over three years. He was older than her by about eight years, and a great guy.

"He knows better," Bern said. "Okay, back to the baby. I tend to believe the sister."

"I do, too. So, maybe Bella really did have a miscarriage and she's lying about it because she knows what her fiancé did."

Bernadette stopped at a red light. "How would she know? And if she did know, why would she cover for him? He's not rich, he's okay looking if you're into scars...I doubt Bella Johnson would have any trouble luring a man into her bed. She could do better than a possible serial killer."

Sharon chuckled. "She could do better? Bernie, you're too funny." She opened the glove box. Using a latex glove, she plucked several of Ginger's hairs from her pant leg, then slipped them into one of the extra bags she'd brought with them. "Okay, joking aside, I agree. Something isn't right here. Either Kiera misunderstood, or Bella's lying."

"We should ask Daddy."

The sun was shining and the temperature was exceptionally warm today. She wasn't ready to spend the day inside hunched over a computer. "Let's."

The Home Zone Rental Center, Tallahassee, Florida
Wednesday, 12:17 p.m., Eastern Standard Time

"NOT THESE TWO bitches again." Adeline let out a long breath. *"I'm telling you, lover. It's time to go."*

Liam finished processing the rental agreement he'd been working on, then handed it to the middle-aged man planning to power wash his deck. "Here's your receipt. Just have it back to us by ten a.m., Friday, and your card won't be charged for an additional day."

The man thanked him, then hauling the power washer out of the rental center, nodded to the two detectives. As the women approached, the one with the short silver hair and pretty blue eyes smiled.

"Hello, Mr. Forrester," Detective Sharon Larson greeted him, while the blonde detective leaned against the desk. "How's the rental business today?"

"I was busy all morning. I haven't even had time for a break."

"I imagine with this nice weather we're having today, people are wanting to tackle a few outdoor jobs."

"I imagine so. I switched shifts and plan to leave early and finish working on my fiancée's garden." He pointed to the notepad in her front coat pocket. "You might want to jot that down in case you're looking for my whereabouts for some other crime I didn't commit."

"Aren't we sassy today," Detective Richie said with a smug smile.

"You've come to my house, to my fiancée's work, now you're bothering me at my job. Sorry, but it's getting old and starting to feel like harassment."

The blonde raised a brow. "I'm sorry you feel that way. We just had a quick question for you."

"And that would be?"

"Did Bella have a miscarriage Saturday night?"

"That twat has been a problem from the start. She's going to get us in trouble, and needs to go."

"She got her period," he replied, his mind still unable to understand why Bella would have lied.

"Because she knows," Adeline said, her voice hushed, yet panicked. *"She knows what you've done."*

Impossible.

"Don't be stupid, lover. The white noise. The ropes. The only time you let her tie you down and ride your cock is after you've fed me." She laughed. *"Like I told you, you're too predictable."*

"Then why would your sister tell us she had a miscarriage?"

"My sister? You talked to Kiera?" The bitches. He tried to hide his rage, his worry, but couldn't stop his hands from trembling. "This is definitely harassment. Maybe I should get a lawyer."

"Keep your cool, Liam. They have nothing on you. Otherwise they wouldn't be here asking you questions."

He knew this. And he knew Kiera. She wouldn't betray him,

even after what he'd done to her yesterday. If she did, she could possibly face criminal charges.

Detective Larson shrugged. "If you feel you need an attorney, then by all means, hire one."

"I will."

"Fantastic." She smiled. "So why would Kiera tell us your fiancée had a miscarriage?"

The twat has really fucked this up for us. Instead of going home to work on her garden, you need to dig her grave.

No! There has to be a reason. Bella must think she's helping me.

"Helping you because she knows you stabbed that woman in the womb? How could she know this? There's been no mention of how the Burger Boy lady died, just that she'd been murdered."

A young guy entered the rental center, and immediately walked toward the drills. "I can't speak for my sister. The next time you want to talk to my fiancée or me, you'll have to go through our lawyer." He stepped from behind the counter. "I have a customer."

When the detectives had left, and the guy had told him he was still looking, Liam contemplated calling both Bella and Kiera. He glanced to the clock on the wall. His shift wouldn't end until three. With the man still browsing, he pulled his phone from his pocket. Since Kiera was likely working, he'd send her a text.

"How do you know she won't lie to you?"

Why would she?

"As much as I don't like your nagging sister, I think your focus should be on the twat."

You're right. He pocketed the phone. *Kiera only told the detectives the truth. She doesn't know about the women.*

Adeline's mocking laughter filled his head. *"The truth? Aren't you wondering what is the truth?"*

You think Bella lied about the baby?

"Think, lover. Both of her doctor's appointments were scheduled when you were working. She didn't save the pee stick for you to see. And, after the miscarriage, she refused to go to the hospital."

Everything you're telling me can be explained. You're being paranoid.

She laughed again. *"Says the schizophrenic. Something isn't right, Liam. Bella is lying to you."*

If she is, I'll get it out of her.

The young guy approached the counter carrying a drill.

"Then what will you do?" she asked, excitement creeping into her tone.

I'm going to snap her neck. He smiled at the guy. "All set?"

CHAPTER 16

Mercy Memorial, Tallahassee, Florida
Wednesday, 2:13 p.m., Eastern Standard Time

KIERA QUICKLY FINISHED changing into capri yoga pants, a T-shirt and running shoes. As she stuffed her work clothes into her bag, she contemplated calling Harrison and letting him know she was heading to her brother's. He'd probably try to talk her out of it, or try to talk his way into coming with her. She couldn't do that to Bella.

Keys in hand, she hooked her bag and purse over her shoulder, then left the women's locker room. Even now she could hear Bella's shaky voice. Remembering the way she'd sobbed and told her how Liam had hurt her, Kiera waved goodbye to a couple of her co-workers, thanked them for covering her appointments, then rushed out the door. In the parking lot, she took her pace to a slow jog, then quickly climbed into her Chevy when she reached it.

Her cell phone rang as she was pulling out of the parking lot. When she saw Bella's number on her screen, her breath caught. Liam was supposed to work until closing and she prayed that hadn't changed. With Bella's car back in the shop, she had no means of transportation, and no way to escape. "Are you okay?" Kiera answered.

"I'm…yeah, I'm just scared," Bella said, her tone apprehensive. "Maybe you shouldn't come here. I don't want him to hurt you again."

"He's not going to hurt either one of us." Because once she had Bella safely tucked away in a hotel room, she was going to call

Harrison and suggest he contact the two detectives again. She also planned to talk Bella into pressing charges against Liam. "Are your bags packed?" she asked.

"Yes," Bella said with so much sadness her heart was breaking. The poor woman had a miscarriage and, a few days later, her fiancé had beaten her. "I don't know what to do with Ginger. I'm afraid Liam will hurt her."

"We'll bring her with us. I'm sure we can find a hotel that'll take pets."

"I…I'm so sorry for putting you in this position."

Kiera thought about what Harrison had said last night after she'd told him Liam had hit her. "It's not your fault. Liam's not stable, and neither one of us should be alone with him." She made a right turn. "I'll be there in less than ten minutes. I can have you in a hotel room within the hour."

"Thank you," Bella said, a catch in her breath.

After she ended the call, Kiera once again reconsidered contacting Harrison. At this point, she wouldn't turn around to pick him up at his apartment, but it might not be a bad idea to let him know what had happened to Bella. With Liam acting the way he'd been, and the possibility that he was a serial killer, she also wanted Harrison to know where she was heading. If Liam found out that she'd helped Bella, he might do more than hit her with a stick.

When she reached a red light, she picked up the phone, realized the battery was at ten percent and the charge cord was buried in her bag. Knowing she'd have to make the call quick, she clicked on Harrison's number located on her favorites screen.

"Hi," he answered. "You've been on my mind."

He'd been on hers, as well. Guilt still weighed heavy on her. Although hurt and humiliated for the way he'd used her, she could have eased some of the pain tormenting him. Instead, she'd kept her secrets safe and allowed him to continue to suffer.

"My phone is dying, so I only have a minute," she began. "Bella called me. Liam beat her up last night."

"What? Are you at work now?"

"No. I'm a few minutes from my brother's."

"Stop the car and turn around. Now, Kiera," he ordered her. "Call the police, but don't you dare go there."

"Liam isn't home, and Bella's already packed. I'm taking her and the dog to a hotel." She turned down Bella's road. "I'm almost there, and I'll be in and out. Trust me, I don't want to deal with my brother."

"Damn it," he shouted. "Why are you being so stubborn? I told you what he's done. Liam isn't the person you once knew."

The fear in his voice made her skin crawl with unease. "Stop! Just stop. I don't need you freaking me out. I only wanted you to know what I was doing."

"In case you went missing or something happened to you?" He swore, then released a deep breath. "What hotel?"

"I don't know yet. One that'll take pets."

"The Holiday Inn on Vine will. I've stayed there before and it's not too far from Mel and Cash's. It should take you twenty minutes to get there from Liam's."

"Thank you," she said, relieved they could go directly to the hotel, rather than drive around searching. "Can you text me the address."

"I'll do that and reserve two rooms. You can't go back to your apartment, not until he's been arrested."

I can stay with you was on the tip of her tongue, but what would be the point? She could eventually forgive him for initially dating her only to get to her brother, and understood his reasons. But now that she knew his history, she couldn't look him in the eye without hating herself, and without telling him the absolute truth.

"I appreciate that." She turned into Bella's long driveway. "I'm here. Liam's SUV isn't. Bella said he's supposed to work until closing, so we should be okay."

"Don't take your time. I'll meet you at the hotel in thirty minutes."

"I'll do my best."

"Three o'clock, Kiera. If you're not there, I'm coming for you. Don't doubt that."

Sure she could count on Harrison, she relaxed slightly. "Thank you. I'll see you then." When she hung up, she wondered who was the user now. Then she dismissed the thought. She had no one else to turn to, and she did love Harrison. When this was over, she might have to leave Tallahassee. Nothing permanent, just a short vacation to give her time to think, to process everything that had and would happen. She honestly saw Harrison in her future and didn't want to erase that. She'd also told him that she admired him for how he'd been able to grow from his mistakes. The sad thing was that, if he knew the truth, he couldn't say the same for her.

"Get your head on straight," she mumbled, parked the car, then exited. With her stomach a ball of knots, she rushed up the porch steps, knocked on the door and took a deep breath. She had no idea how badly Liam had hurt Bella and prepared herself for the worst. As the door opened, she steadied her shaky legs. Because the mid-afternoon sun was already dipping toward the back of the house, the shadows from the covered porch and interior foyer hid Bella's face.

"Come on in," Bella said in a small voice. "I just need to get the dog."

She stared at Bella's retreating back, and noticed she'd dressed in a baggy sweatshirt and sweatpants, making her wonder if she was hiding bruises. "You take care of Ginger, I'll get your bags."

Bella sniffed. "They're in the guest room. The first one on the left. If Liam came home early, I...I didn't want him to see."

"Okay. Where's Ginger?"

Bella kept her back to her as she used the sleeve of her sweatshirt to wipe her face. "In her crate. I'll get the leash."

While Bella grabbed the dog's leash, she headed down the hallway, then turned into the bedroom. She looked on one side of the bed, then the other. When she didn't see a bag, she checked the closet. Assuming Bella wasn't thinking straight, she went into the next room, the one Liam and Bella had planned to use as the nursery.

And froze.

She stared at the twin bed in the corner of the room, and pressed against the walls between the window facing the porch and the side yard. Four pieces of rope, the ends fashioned into a slip-knot, were tied to the bedframe. They lay haphazardly along the mattress which was covered with what appeared to be a vinyl fitted sheet, while a thick roll of clear packaging tape sat on the otherwise barren nightstand.

"Oh, my God," she whispered, and covered her mouth. What had happened to Liam? What had he become?

"Cozy, don't you think?"

Kiera quickly turned. Gasping, she took several jerky steps backward. "What are you doing?" she asked, staring at the gun Bella had pointed directly at her chest.

"Ensurin' that my husband-to-be doesn't wind up on death row."

Her skin prickled. Dread shot up her spine. There wasn't a mark on Bella, and she'd swapped out the baggy sweats for a red tube top and ultra-short denim shorts. She'd always thought her brother's fiancée was pretty, in a plain Jane way, but this Bella was stunning, sexy and, between the gun and wicked gleam in her eyes, deadly.

"I don't understand," Kiera said, now grateful for having enough common sense to call Harrison. She wasn't sure what was about to go down, or if her brother was involved, but she had a solid thirty minutes before Harrison would start to worry. "You said Liam beat you."

"I lied," Bella said with a mocking smile. "Get on the bed."

She shook her head. "I can't do that."

"Sure you can. Put one foot in front of the other and get on the fuckin' bed."

"No."

Bella pursed her lips. Her eyes narrowed. "Fine." She moved

the gun slightly, aiming it at her head.

"Wait," Kiera shouted, then dropped to her knees as Bella fired. Shaking and breathing hard, she looked up at the woman her brother had planned to marry.

Bella smiled again. "Next time, I'm going to put a bullet in your foot. The time after that, it'll be the other foot, then the legs...do you get where I'm goin' with this? I'm not gonna kill you. I'm gonna make you bleed."

Kiera swallowed and kept her gaze on the gun. "Why?"

"I'm not tellin' you. This ain't like the movies where the bad guy confesses what motivates him and gives some crappy confession about how Mommy did this or that to make him such an awful, evil man." She took a step forward and aimed the pistol at Kiera's head. "This is me tellin' you to take off your shoes and get the fuck on the bed."

Thirty minutes. Less than that now. Harrison would worry. He would eventually come.

Terrified, yet hopeful she'd either find a way out of this or Harrison would come for her, Kiera climbed onto the bed. The vinyl sheet crunched as she scooted across it.

"Put your feet through the knotholes, then give the rope a hard tug around your ankles."

She put her right foot through the knothole, then hovered her hand over the rope. "Please. It doesn't have to be this way."

"Tick, tock, or I'm going to put a hole in your foot." Bella aimed for Kiera's right foot. "One, two—"

"Okay," Kiera shouted, hatred for the woman burning through her as she tightened the knot around her ankle.

"Good. Now the other."

Reluctantly, she slipped the knot around her left foot, then yanked on the rope. The rough texture grated along her skin. She glared at Bella. "Now what?"

"Don't play stupid or try to stall. Take care of one of your arms." Bella gave her a taunting smile. "No worries. I'll handle the other one."

"Does Liam know you're doing this?" Kiera asked, and ignored the pain in her back as she reached for the rope. She hesitated. God, she did not want to strap herself to this bed. But as she reached for the knot anyway, she thought about Harrison, about what he'd been forced to do with a gun pointed to his head. When he'd first started talking about terrorists and secret agencies, she'd been skeptical. By the time he'd finished, she'd believed him.

Now she understood him.

Except she was binding herself to the bed to save her life, not the lives of hundreds of people and, at this point, she couldn't be sure she'd do anything to save her brother. She no longer wanted to carry his secrets, or worry he'd hurt himself or others. She wanted him gone, and the bitch he'd planned to marry dead.

Tears filled her eyes as she secured the knot. She missed the young boy Liam had once been...the fun teenager who'd kept her company on the weekends because she rarely had a date, and neither of them had many friends. That person was gone. Glimpses of him might have showed up here and there, but any more of those fleeting moments had been rare.

She looked to Bella, who, except for the gun, didn't look menacing or as if she was taking pleasure in any of this. Instead, she looked bored.

"Reach your arm toward the other rope," Bella ordered her. After she did, and Bella had made it so she wasn't going anywhere, Bella set the gun on the table in exchange for the tape. "Has Liam talked to you about a woman named Adeline?"

"No." Oh, God. But Harrison had. *They drugged and tortured us. Their goal was to scramble our brains, turn us into psychopaths...* "Who is she?"

"It's not important," Bella said as she ripped the tape from the roll. She then frowned and stared at Kiera's eyes.

Kiera turned her head away when Bella used her thumb to lift her eyebrow. "What are you doing?"

"Settin' the stage. I need you to hold still"

Instinct had Kiera twisting her head and shrinking into her

neck. Bella slapped her cheek and head a couple of times, the sharp stings didn't deter her. Hell if she would make this easy on the woman.

"Let's try this," Bella said. She bent along the side of the bed, only to quickly rise, then climb over Kiera's body, dragging the tape with her. "That should do it."

The tape arced, and as it neared her forehead, Kiera realized what was coming next. "Don't. I'll keep my head still," she shouted.

"Too late." Bella pulled the tape across Kiera's forehead, then secured it to the opposite side of the bed. She then did the same across her chin. When Bella was finished, she ripped off a small piece of tape. "Keep your eyes open," she said, and using her finger, she stretched the skin below Kiera's eyebrow upward.

No fucking way. Kiera's heart pounded in her head. She squeezed her eyes tight and struggled against her restraints.

The breath suddenly rushed out of her as Bella sat on her chest. The woman gripped her chin. "You might want to stop movin'," Bella said. "This is my first time and I'd hate to poke your eye."

Tears streamed from the corners of Kiera's eyes and into her hair. "No. Please, no," she begged as Bella secured the eyelid of her left eye open. Breathing hard, fighting the urge to blink, to arch her back and scream, she remained still. Harrison would come. He would worry that she and Bella weren't at the hotel, and he would look for her.

As Bella taped back her right eyelid, her mind raced to Liam. How could he approve of this? After all of the years, the sacrifices and secrets, how could he allow Bella to do this to her? Yesterday, after he'd hit her, he'd acted remorseful, as if he'd had a moment of clarity and had realized what he'd done and had regretted it. God, she didn't know, and couldn't understand where Bella fit into any of this.

The woman's breath puffed along her face. Kiera instinctively blinked. When the tape kept her lids secured, she let out a frustrated grunt and pulled against the ropes.

Bella smiled and shook her head. "So creepy," she murmured, and studied Kiera's eyes and face. "Amazin'. It's no wonder Liam's crazy."

He didn't know? She strained her eyes and watched Bella climb off the bed, then go to the windows and close the blinds.

"Where are your keys?"

"My car."

"I'm assumin' your purse and phone are there, too?"

"Yes."

"Does anyone know you're here? Maybe your boyfriend?"

"I called him when I left work, but I didn't tell him."

Still holding the tape, Bella crossed her arms. "Kinda convenient."

Kiera drew in a breath and couldn't stop the tears. "I was embarrassed. I thought he'd beaten you and I was ashamed of my brother. I didn't want Harrison to know."

Bella nodded and pulled more tape from the roll. "I get it." She ripped off a piece. "It was also a smart move. Because if he comes here, I'll kill him."

If Harrison came to the house, he'd come prepared. He'd claimed to work as an investigator. He would have skills, would know how to handle a situation like this. Except Harrison wouldn't know about Bella. She could trick him...kill him... "Are you going to kill me?" Kiera asked, her tongue thick, her throat tight. She had to find a way out of this before Harrison came, or at least warn him.

Bella smiled as she slammed the tape over Kiera's mouth. "Nope. Your brother will."

The Holiday Inn, Tallahassee, Florida
Wednesday, 3:03 p.m., Eastern Standard Time

HARRISON PACED THE hotel lobby, checked the time, then stepped outside. He scanned the parking lot, the busy street, looking for any sign of Kiera's car. With dread sickening his stomach, he pulled his phone from his pocket and called Kiera again. When the call rolled immediately into her voicemail, he disconnected. He'd tried her four times in the past ten minutes. She had told him her phone was dying. If the battery had run out, it would explain why her voicemail had kicked in after only one ring.

He looked at the time. Only one minute had passed, but that minute and the ones before it had his heart sinking with fear. He knew what Liam was capable of, but up until the day after Bella's miscarriage, he'd foolishly thought Kiera would be okay. Liam had never hurt her before, and Harrison had believed the murders Liam had committed were somehow connected back to Adeline and what had happened at the House of Archer.

Impatient and worried, he went to his Jeep. Instead of climbing inside, he leaned against the back end and continued to watch the street. Hoping, praying, Kiera would turn into the parking lot any second.

His phone rang. He quickly checked the screen and saw it was Vlad. "Hey," he answered. "How's it going?" After he'd spoken to Kiera, he'd called Vlad and had asked him to go to The Home Zone and keep an eye on Liam until he had Kiera and Bella locked in their rooms.

"Not good. Harry have women?"

"No." He pushed off the Jeep. "What do you mean by *not good*?" he asked, fishing his keys from his pocket and heading for the driver's side.

"Liam have left," the Russian said, his tone anxious. "Vlad arrive and go to pretend order equipment. Another man there. Vlad explain need to talk with Liam about rental, but man say Liam left for day."

Damn it. Harrison slammed his palm against the steering wheel and tried to think. But all he could see were the faces of the dead women. "I have to call the detectives," he said, shoving the key into the ignition.

"No. Do not involve police. Vlad will help."

"No way, dude. Remember, we're both going legit. You're a repo man now, and I'm a web designer. So I'm doing this the legit way."

"But police—"

"I'm trusting my instincts on this," he said, backing out of the parking spot. "The police want their killer, not me."

"Vlad could not live with self if anything happen to Harry."

"Same here, bro."

"Give Vlad address of serial kill in case."

Harrison half-chuckled. "Not gonna happen. I need to go. I'll call you."

"Harry, Vlad…it hard to say. We have done all job together. Vlad and Harry partners, да?"

"Not this time. Stop worrying and I'll call you later." Harrison ended the call. Before he exited the parking lot, he reached into the glove box and pulled the burner phone he'd used yesterday to call Detective Larson. He keyed in the detective's number, then hovered his thumb over the SEND button. He'd seen and done plenty of bad things, but he'd never purposefully killed anyone. The one time he'd been prepared to take a life, he still hadn't been able to, even in the name of revenge. He had a Glock and a knife with him. He'd been trained to use both weapons and knew in his gut he wouldn't hesitate today.

He loved Kiera, not the idea of love or the chance of finally having a life partner who wasn't a six-foot-six Russian dude. And he loved her enough that he'd not only take a bullet for her, but he'd sacrifice his freedom and go back to prison for the crimes he'd committed.

Without further hesitation, he called Detective Larson.

Tallahassee Police Department, Tallahassee, Florida
Wednesday, 3:08 p.m., Eastern Standard Time

"LIAM FORRESTER BEAT his girlfriend and sister, now I can't reach them."

Detective Sharon Larson immediately recognized the caller as the man who'd contacted her yesterday. She tapped her desk. When she had Bernadette's attention, she mouthed, "Random Guy."

"Hello," Sharon began, as Bern moved her chair closer and angled her head near the phone. "Thanks for the heads-up, but unless Mr. Forrester is a magical wizard, or cloned himself, that's just not true. We met with both his fiancée and his sister. They were perfectly fine."

"When?"

"Why don't you tell me why you're so certain Mr. Forrester should be a person of interest."

"I told you about the dog and Julie Beechum's neighbor."

"You did, but you hung up before I had the chance to ask why I would care that Mr. Forrester owns a Husky." There was a long pause, long enough for Sharon to worry he had ended the call. While she and Bern still believed Liam Forrester was a viable suspect, they were equally suspicious of the informant. "Are you still there?"

"I can explain later. You saw Bella today?"

"Yes, right before we met Mr. Forrester at his work. So you can understand why I'm suspicious and—"

"What time?" he asked, sounding genuinely panicked.

She looked to Bern, who nodded.

"About eleven-thirty."

"And Liam?"

"An hour later. My turn, do you know anything about Bella Johnson having a miscarriage?"

"Yeah, it happened Saturday night."

Bern frowned, and mouthed, "What the hell?"

What the hell, indeed. Two of the four people were lying, and she just couldn't figure out who or why.

"Can you go to Liam and Bella's?" he asked, his tone firm, but desperate. "Kiera called me and said she was on her way to pick up

Bella, because Bella claimed Liam beat her. They were supposed to meet me at a hotel at three and didn't show."

"Look, there wasn't a mark on Bella. Maybe Kiera's lying to you. Besides, if Bella was so terrified of her fiancé, she could have asked us for help, or packed her bags and left on her own."

"Kiera's not a liar, and Bella's car is in the shop. I can't explain why Bella called Kiera then, but I do know for a fact Liam hurt Kiera yesterday. I saw the bruise on her back. Maybe you just couldn't see Bella's."

Sharon thought about Bella's tiny tube top and short shorts. If she'd had any bruises on her, they would have seen them.

"Something isn't right," he continued. "I feel it in my gut. Liam's on his way home now. Can you please just go there, or send an officer to check up on them."

She glanced to Bern, who nodded. "I don't know. Mr. Forrester is already threatening us with harassment. You're going to need to give me something else to go on."

"He murdered *five* women, and that's not enough?"

"*You* say he did. Unfortunately, pointing fingers doesn't hold up in court."

"Fine. Look up Adeline Archer. When you do, look very closely at her picture. She's the reason Liam is murdering women," he said, his voice lowering with anger.

"And you know this how?"

"That's all I'm going to say. Are you going out there or not?"

"Sure," Sharon said. "We can pay them another visit."

"Good. I'll meet you there."

"Meet us? No—"

The phone went dead.

"Shit." She set the phone on the desk. "I don't know what to make of this."

"Did he say Adeline Archer?" Bern asked, opening up an Internet browser on the computer they shared with several other investigators.

"Yeah, wasn't Rodney Archer recently sentenced?"

Bern glanced over her shoulder. "Late September, around the same time Liam took up residence in Tallahassee."

"That doesn't mean anything," Sharon said, worrying it somehow meant everything. Their caller was either one hell of an actor, or he was genuinely concerned about Kiera Forrester and Bella Johnson.

"Oh, hell," Bernadette muttered. "Look."

Disturbed, a disquieting foreboding shrouding her with apprehension, Sharon stared at the photograph of Adeline Archer, the woman who had helped kidnap, drug and torture homeless men. How many? No one could be sure. Adeline Archer, the same woman who'd happened to be a damned psychopath…with long black curly hair. "Who in the hell is our random guy that he would suggest this?" She continued to stare at the screen. "If I remember, there were a couple of survivors."

"Hang on, let me look it up," Bern said, and began typing. "This article says both are deceased, due to complications from the drugs they'd been given. They died shortly after Rodney confessed." She closed out the article. "What if someone escaped and never came forward?"

"Why wouldn't they?"

"I don't know." Bern sighed. "And I question why we're even entertaining any of this."

"Because there are five dead women and someone just pointed out that four of them look like Adeline Archer, who *happened* to be a kidnapper and murderer."

Bern gave her a wry grin. "This is true. So where does Liam's girl fit? She looks more like Adeline than any of our victims."

"Bundy had a type." Sharon stood. "Or maybe Random Guy is playing us and this is just some sort of weird family dispute. If you think about it, the guy called us yesterday and also claims Liam hurt Kiera then, too. Maybe this is his and Kiera's way of getting back at the brother. I get the impression Random Guy and Kiera are dating or close friends."

"Except our caller knew about the dog hair, and pointed out

that Autumn Torgenson could've been the original target instead of Julie Beechum." Bernadette snatched her car keys off the desk. "Don't you have a doctor's appointment at five? We could send an officer to do a wellness check."

Sharon had no desire to see her oncologist. At this stage, she didn't see the point. The cancer was not only now in her lungs, but likely her brain. She didn't want the test results. There was no cure, there was only treatment. She was sick of being treated, of the side effects, of the depression that followed. She wasn't giving up on life, she was taking control of it. Because, damn it, she and Bern were going to go on a cruise. And during the trip the only sickness she'd accept would be sea sickness, not the kind that came from chemotherapy, radiation, or whatever other drugs they wanted to put into her body.

"I'm sure we'll be back in time. If not, I'll reschedule," she said, starting for the door.

Liam and Bella's House, Tallahassee, Florida
Wednesday, 3:22 p.m., Eastern Standard Time

"BELLA?" LIAM CALLED as he entered the house.

"Hey, lover," she said from the kitchen. "How was work?"

"What did she just call you?" Adeline asked, resentment in her tone.

While he rather enjoyed Adeline's bit of jealousy, the term of endearment *was* strange coming from Bella. Honey, hon, babe...those were more her style. He pocketed his keys and headed into the kitchen, then came to an abrupt halt.

"And what in the fuck is that twat wearing?"

Something incredibly sexy. In all the time he'd known Bella, he'd never seen her dressed so...

"Slutty?"

Adeline was definitely jealous. Apparently she was the only slut allowed in his life.

"Fuck you, Liam. At least I was genuine. This isn't right. Stop

thinking with your dick. Something is wrong with Bella, and you know it."

He did know there was something wrong, but had a hard time tearing his gaze away from the way that tight red top hugged Bella's breasts, how her denim shorts rode so low, if he gave them a little tug at the waist, he'd see her dark curls.

"Remember the miscarriage. Remember the detectives."

Bella smiled and approached him, a sexy sway to her hips. "I've missed you today. I'm glad you were able to get off early." She reached down and rubbed his thickening erection through the front of his jeans. "Because I've been thinkin' about all the ways I can get *you* off."

He gripped her wrist, stopping her. "Were you thinking about that while you were telling the detectives you were never pregnant?"

She held his gaze. Her eyes glittered with challenge and smugness he'd never expected from his sweet Bella. "Even then."

He caught her hair in his fist. She gasped and grabbed his wrist. In turn, he clutched her throat. "You better explain what the fuck is going on."

"Or what?" she said with a grunt. "Are you going to beat me with a stick?"

"You talked to Kiera?" He loosened his grip as guilt over what he'd done to Kiera resurfaced. "When?"

"They're all conspiring against you," Adeline said with disgust.

"Today."

He gave her hair a yank. "After you met with the detectives?"

"Ow! Yes! Stop, lover, you're hurtin' me."

"I don't give a shit. Because my sister told them about the miscarriage, and your story doesn't match, those two bitches are going to think we're hiding something. Why would you lie?"

"Because we *are* hiding somethin'."

Stunned, he let her go. "What are we hiding?" he asked with caution.

Bella tossed her hair over her shoulder, then rubbed her

throat. The corners of her mouth turned up slightly as she narrowed her eyes. "I know all about the women."

"I told you to kill the twat."

Not now. His heart beat rapidly. "I don't know what you're talking about."

"Oh, I think you do." She placed her hand on her curvy hips. "But that's okay, *lover*, your secret is safe with me."

His mouth went dry. "What secret?"

"Please don't play dumb. You killed those women. I know you did, because I cleaned up after you."

The room started to spin. He took a step back and leaned against the wall.

"You were sloppy and had no plan. That first woman in the park?" She shook her head. "I knew somethin' was up that day. Actually, what triggered it for me was the night before. I can't tell you how many times you'd get this look in your eyes that scared the bejesus outta me. A bit of lust and a whole lotta hatred. Like you wanted to hurt me. I gotta admit, it scared me and turned me on at the same time. It also made me glad I kept you around."

Her last words registered and had him coming alert. "Kept me around?"

She gave him a smile that would have been sexy if not for the malice in her eyes. "You and me are a lot alike. I wasn't sure at first, but sensed it that day you came here to pick up the carpet cleaner I rented. That's why I let you live."

"Liam, listen to me," Adeline said, frantic, her voice heavy with warning. *"You need to put an end to her right now."*

"I'm glad I did," Bella continued, and took a tentative step forward. "Now that I know what you can do, I believe we can have ourselves a good life."

"I don't understand." He really didn't. How could she know and still want to be with him? Why would she attempt to cover up what he'd done? *How* had she covered for him? He had so many questions, and yet the only answer he had was to kill her. To snap her neck and put Florida behind him.

"Let me show you somethin' that I think will help put a few things into perspective." She came closer, then placed a hand on his chest. "Are you gonna hurt me?"

"I don't know."

"Have you wanted to?"

"Many times," he answered honestly.

"Because of the white noise?"

"Don't tell her anything. Don't you dare," Adeline shouted.

On this, he chose to listen to the bitch in his head. Right now, she seemed saner than the one rubbing his chest.

"I know you're not comfortable talkin' about it. That's okay. I understand." Bella took his hand in hers. "Before I show you somethin' that might...upset you, I want you to know that I honestly love you."

"Don't believe her."

But he desperately wanted to believe. He'd fought the voices, the paranoia, the medication for years, always thinking he would forever be damned to a life of psychosis, that he'd never know the love of a wife, of a child, that he wouldn't be able to have a job, a house. With Bella, he'd thought there was a chance of stability. Even as he'd fed the hungry bitch inside him, he'd hoped he would eventually find the normalcy he'd craved.

"I love you, too," he finally said, and ignored Adeline's high-pitched screams of disapproval.

"Good. Then know that I did this for us." Bella led him down the hall. When they reached the last bedroom on the left, she stopped. She released his hand, took a step back, then reached behind and pulled out a small pistol.

When he jerked away, she smiled. "Here's the thing about a .22. When you get shot with one of these, it's not quick, and it's not painless. The bullet doesn't go through you, it lodges itself inside, festers, makes you suffer until it eventually kills you. Trust me, I know. I've tested it many times and I don't want to test it on you."

He ran a shaky hand along his forehead. "Since you know

what I've done, I suppose if you wanted me dead I wouldn't be standing here."

"My point exactly. But what I'm about to show you could go a couple of ways, lover. I'm hopin' it goes my way. Now open the door."

When Adeline remained silent, he reached for the door handle. "Why do you keep calling me lover?"

"I thought you liked it. That's what you've always told me to call you when you have me *bring out the ropes.*"

Had he? Those nights had sometimes been a blur, and his focus had always been on seeking the satisfaction he couldn't gain from killing without hurting Bella. His skin tightened with unease. "What else did I say?"

"When you were dealin' with the white noise?" Bella cocked her head and grinned. "Open the door and find out."

"Liam, don't." Adeline's voice was weak, breathless and barely a whisper.

I...I think I might need you. Stay with me.

"Go on, lover. Look what I've done for you."

When Adeline didn't answer, he drew in a fortifying breath, then opened the door. "Kiera?" He rushed forward, and instinctively went for the fucking tape holding open her eyes.

"Don't touch. *That's* not allowed."

His heart beating violently and aching for his sister, he wiped a hand down his face instead of freeing her. "How did you know?" he asked, staring at Kiera's eyes, wild with fear. Had that been how he'd looked? Grotesque, frightened?

"The white noise. You talked then, and I pieced together parts of what you said. Looks like I got it right. Based on the women you've killed, it also looks like you're still tryin' to get even with Adeline. Am I right on that, too?"

He waited for Adeline to respond, but there was nothing.

"I look a lot like her. Why didn't you kill me?"

"I planned to," he said honestly, his insides a knotted mess. Kiera didn't deserve this. She'd always been there for him. Yesterday…he hadn't meant to hurt her, just to make it clear she needed to stop mothering him, nagging him, butting her nose in his business.

"So why didn't you?"

"Because I liked you."

"Do you still like me?"

Unable to bear the terror in Kiera's eyes, the way she struggled against the ropes, he turned away and met Bella's gaze. "I don't know what to think."

"Don't you want a wife and a family? Don't you want someone who will accept you, the real you, love you for everything that you are?"

When Kiera whimpered, his eyes filled with tears. "Yes. I was so happy when we were going to have a baby."

Bella's lips shot out in a pout. "You were *too* happy."

He tensed. "What does that mean?"

"You stopped killin', didn't you? I know, because I watched you. I always knew the signs and when to watch for it. There were a few times you threw me off guard, but I still managed to help you. If I hadn't been followin' you, I would've never known to contaminate that woman at the rest area. I'll tell you, that one makes me think twice about goin' to those places. And the blonde? Good job on changin' up that one. You can't be too predictable. It made me realize I couldn't be predictable with the cleanin' part. But the Burger Boy lady…" She shook her head. "I almost wasn't gonna help with her. When you came into our room that night, I thought I was gonna have to kill you. Then I worried about what kind of mess you might make. When I saw what you'd done to her body, well, you better believe I slept with the .22 under my pillow." She cocked her head. "I gotta know, why didn't you hurt me? Why'd you tear up that woman instead of me?"

His mind was scattered all over the place, but he thought back, remembered how badly he'd fought Adeline. Remembered the grief, of how fatherhood had been stripped from him. "It wasn't your fault the baby wasn't meant to be. But I was angry," he admitted.

She directed the pistol to his head. "Then this is gonna really rattle your cage. You might even hate me."

He stared at her, remembered loving her body, loving her the best he could, along with fighting the urge to give into his darkest desires and play out exactly how he'd fantasized killing Adeline. "I know anger, and I know hatred. Other than binding my sister to a bed and taping her eyes open, I can't think of any other reason to hate you."

"We'll see about that." She inhaled. "Ready?"

He slowly nodded.

"I was never pregnant."

CHAPTER 17

K IERA WENT COMPLETELY still. Her brother was not only a serial killer, but he'd been living with a psychopath. She read between the lines. Bella wasn't sweet, and she certainly wasn't the simple woman she'd wanted them all to believe.

"But the blood," Liam said, devastation clear in his voice.

Kiera ached for him. She knew she shouldn't, not after what he'd done. But she ached for the boy she'd once known who would forever have a place in her heart.

"My period," Bella replied.

"I…Why?" he shouted, and fisted his hands.

The muscles in Kiera's eyes strained as she tried to see what was happening. "It was an experiment. I wanted to see if becomin' a family man would change you, which it did. There was no mention of the white noise, you didn't ask me to bring out the ropes, which was a shame because I enjoyed gettin' kinky with you. You were just…normal."

Liam smacked his chest with his hand. "That's all I've ever wanted."

"But that's not what *I* need," Bella said, her voice turning icy. "I kill normal guys. Desperate guys who think I'm some uneducated piece of trash they can fuck for a while, then dump when somethin' better comes along."

"What is wrong with you?" Liam asked with disgust.

Bella laughed. "Are you kiddin' me? What? Is this some sort of double standard? It's okay for you to kill women who look like some bitch who fucked with your head, but it's not okay for the little woman to knock off a few guys for some money?"

Kiera caught a glimpse of her brother's face as he paced in circles. She was fairly certain he wasn't medicated, and that her current position was the same one Liam had been in when he'd been held at that house with those Archer people. Bella was stoking the wrong fire. Her brother was a serial killer. While she'd believed most of everything Harrison had told her last night, there had been a side of her that had held out hope. That hope was now gone.

"Is that what you were going to do to me?" he asked. "Kill me so you could steal the twenty bucks I might've had in my wallet?"

"Not your wallet, your identity," Bella said as if he were stupid. "What's funny is that carpet cleaner you came here to haul away for me? I rented it to clean the blood stain out of my bedroom carpet."

"Oh, my God," Liam shouted.

"Don't judge me. You flat-out admitted you thought about killin' me." She let out a sigh. "I love you, Liam. You amaze me. You've come such a long way, and it's sexy how you can murder a woman one day, yet be so gentle and tender with me the next. I love that you want to be a good provider, and how you think about our future. I still wanna marry you, and I'd like us to have a family. But I got needs, too, and we certainly ain't gonna get rich doin' the jobs we got."

Acid burned in Kiera's throat. Bella made her sick. The devious bitch was playing on her brother's longings for a regular life. In his current state, she feared he just might go for it. And why not? Bella was accepting him, and the monster he carried with him.

"I know this is a lot to take in, but I gotta know where you stand. I can't be with a man who can't be my partner in all things."

Liam looked over his shoulder at her. "What about my sister? Was this show really necessary?"

"Well, you hate a dead woman so much, you not only chose

to live with me, who looks like her, but murder women who do, too. Like you were torturin' yourself, or maybe you can't get over the torture that was done to you. As for this *show*...I didn't know if it'd be a good idea or not. Durin' those white noise times, you were so caught up with Adeline, I thought if I act a little like her, make you realize she can be replaced, maybe we had a chance. Don't be mad for what I've done to your sister, but even you've complained that she was bossy and nosey." She let out a slight chuckle. "To be honest, I've never killed a female before. When I found out that she'd gone and told the detectives about the miscarriage, I was ready to make her my first. She could cause a lot of problems for us."

Liam closed his eyes and turned his back on Kiera. "I know she can. But killing her would draw attention to me, and I don't need any more than what I've got."

"This is where my experience with stealin' identities will come in handy, 'cause I plan on stealin' hers. Plus, the police have nothin' on you. I made sure of it. Heck, I would've let you keep believin' I had a miscarriage, but when those two detectives came by asking about the baby, the first thing I thought of was the Burger Boy lady. If those detectives believed I had a miscarriage, they could look at that as motive for you to kill her the way you did."

"What about the dog?" Liam asked.

"What about her?"

"The detectives asked about Ginger."

Liam had moved slightly, blocking Kiera's view of Bella. But she heard the frustration in her sigh. "Damn. And Ginger was all over those two detectives when they were here. How much you wanna bet one of us left a dog hair with one of the dead women?"

"Had to be you, since you're the one that came by afterward to clean up my *mess*," her brother said, sarcasm in his tone.

"Don't get smart with me." She sighed again. "One of my crime shows used DNA from the family cat to convict a guy. You know how much I love Ginger, but we're just gonna have to kill her and burn her in the fire pit. We'll get another just like her."

God, the woman was sick. And stupid. While she wasn't an investigator, she had common sense. Ginger shed like crazy. Disposing of the dog would not wipe the house clean of her hair. Investigators would still be able to link that evidence back to Liam.

"I don't want to kill my dog," Liam said, anger lacing his voice.

"I know, honey. I don't either, but we have to protect you."

He nodded. His shoulders slumped. "If you're willing to kill Ginger, then I have a feeling I know what we need to do to my sister."

Bella stepped into view. She lowered the gun and touched Liam's arm. "Does this mean you'll stay with me, be my man?"

He ran his hand through her dark hair. "I want to marry you and have kids."

"What about Adeline and the white noise? I don't want a dead woman coming between us. I also want you to know that I'm not tryin' to replace Adeline. From what you said durin' the white noise times and what I read up on the crazy woman, I don't ever want to be anythin' like her."

"Adeline *is* the white noise. The moment I realized what you've done, she's been quiet."

"What does that mean?"

"That I don't need her, not when I have you."

"You're so sweet," Bella said, happiness in her tone. "I wish we'd had this conversation a long time ago."

He chuckled. "What kind of icebreaker would you have used?"

"Oh, geez, I have no idea," she said with a half-laugh. "I love you."

Afraid she'd vomit, Kiera fought the nausea. The romantic moment between her brother and Bella had murder written all over it. If only she could have the chance to talk with Liam. Alone. She knew her brother. Even when he wasn't himself, she'd been able to reach him to some degree. He knew right from wrong, and he had to know *this* was terribly wrong. Bella had him snowed, blinded him with a fantasy that simply wasn't possible. How could he honestly expect wedding bells and the pitter-patter of little feet in his future?

"I love you, too. Now get rid of the gun," he said, an edge in his voice.

Kiera held her breath. Maybe her brother wasn't as far gone as she'd thought.

"After you get rid of your sister."

He turned slightly and looked at Kiera. His eyes were strangely unreadable and his face was void of expression. "How?"

"I don't care how you do it, I just want her gone and out of our lives. Make sure you bury her in the garden with the others. The pond water is too shallow. Trust me on that."

Outside Liam and Bella's House, Tallahassee, Florida
Wednesday, 3:39 p.m., Eastern Standard Time

THE TALL PINE trees covering the front of the property offered little cover, forcing Harrison to park the Jeep about a quarter of a mile past Liam's driveway. He checked the time. The school bus he'd ended up stuck behind had slowed him down. If the detective had left right after he'd spoken to her, she wouldn't be far behind, and he wanted to be as close to the house as possible before she arrived.

Not caring that he wasn't supposed to be in possession of any type of weapons, he quickly pulled the Glock from the lock box he'd brought with him, shoved it in the waistband at the back of his jeans, then slid the sheathed knife into his sock. Nervous, worried, he checked his surroundings, then ran into the wooded area and toward Liam's house.

As he ran, he pictured the bruise on Kiera's back, pictured the Dougals' house, the blood on the walls, on the floor and ceiling, the skulls and few bones the animals hadn't taken. He saw the women Liam had killed. Once he reached the house, he'd give

Detective Larson five minutes, then he was going inside. They could arrest him later. At this point, Kiera and Bella's safety was all that mattered. His freedom, the fantasy future he'd created in his mind weren't as important, because he couldn't live with the guilt if anything happened to them. Damn it, he knew what Liam was, and he'd waited too long to do anything about it. Now the waiting was over.

Harrison neared the yard, slowed his pace and searched for cover. Though there was no one out front, if anyone looked out the window, they'd likely spot him between the trees. A few large bushy plants framed the left side of the porch. He'd have to run across the open yard to get to them. Deciding it was worth the risk, he didn't hesitate and hauled ass. Once he'd crouched behind the leafy bushes, he took in shallow breaths to keep from going lightheaded and to regulate his heart. The gun dug into his tail-bone, the leather surrounding the knife stuck to his sweaty skin, both reminding him why it was time to quit ATL. After witnessing enough death, and seeing the atrocities one human was capable of doing to another, he wanted to be like the rest of the world, only catch snippets of how ugly humanity could be from various news footage, or posts on social media. He wanted to bury his head in the sand...tomorrow.

He peered around the bush. Kiera's car wasn't there, but both Liam's SUV and Bella's hatchback were parked in the driveway. Bella's car was supposed to be in the shop. With unease slithering down his back, and keeping low, he moved away from the porch toward the rear of the house. Ginger was a barker. If she was out in the yard, she'd alert anyone inside to his presence.

With Kiera on his mind, he edged around the corner. There was no sign of Ginger, but it didn't mean the dog wasn't romping around further back under the cover of the trees and tall grasses. A thin stream of smoke lifted from the fire pit. A shiny rototiller sat outside of the old shed, and a shovel stuck out of the ground near the weedy patch on the far right of the yard. He stepped back along the wood siding and looked to the window above him.

Based on the one time he'd been to the house, and how it was laid out, the bedrooms were likely located on this end. Holding his breath and hoping he wasn't making a mistake, he rose to the sill and looked through the open blind. He saw the edge of a bed, a dresser with framed pictures he couldn't make out, and an entrance to what looked like a bathroom. He crouched back down, then moved toward the next window. The blind was drawn.

Frustrated and wanting nothing more than to shove his way into the house, he sat on his ass and contemplated his next move. Thought about what the CORE agents he'd worked with would do, what Ryan or Shane would do if they were in the same position, then honed in on Cash and Vlad. Big mistake, because he knew those men wouldn't be sitting on their asses waiting and wondering.

But he wasn't any of those men. He didn't jump into the water without testing it first. He was a computer guy, he tested, he analyzed, he created programs that suited his needs.

A door slammed from the back. He crept that way again, and watched as Liam rushed toward the weedy area, then ripped the shovel from the ground. When he stabbed the earth, Harrison decided to risk it and try the front door. As he moved closer, the faint scent of cigarette smoke wafted from the front porch. He looked through the bushes, saw red toenail polish and sparkly flip flops.

"Hey, Tammy, it's Bella. I'm real sorry, but I can't make it in for my shift," she said, sounding tired and sickly. "I should be okay tomorrow." She paused. "Yeah, I think it might be something I ate. I've been throwin' up." She chuckled. "No, I'm not pregnant. But you might want to think twice about orderin' from Sammy's Pizzeria. Liam came home from work early complainin' he don't feel so good, neither."

Harrison rushed toward the backyard, then hesitated at the corner of the house. Detective Larson said she'd come here, but not when. Kiera's Chevy wasn't in the driveway. Oddly, Bella's car was there when it was supposed to be in the shop. He had no justification to be on the property. Bella's *not pregnant* remark was off, yet meant nothing. But if everything was fine here, why hadn't Kiera called him? He hadn't been able to see Bella's face, but if she was bruised, he'd think she would need more than one day off from work. If she wasn't hurt, why would she lie to Kiera? He'd called the Holiday Inn just before parking the Jeep along Liam and Bella's road, hoping Kiera had showed, but the clerk had said no one fitting Kiera or Bella's description had arrived. So one of two things had happened—either Kiera never made it here, or she'd never left this place. Was it possible she'd gone home and chosen not to call him? Of course, but he couldn't see her doing that, not after last night, and not based on the panic in her voice when she'd called him earlier.

Needing answers and his gut telling him not to wait, he turned the corner, saw Liam still had his back to him and was digging. After pulling the Glock from the back of his jeans, he hurried up the deck. When he reached the patio door, he held his breath and hoped to God the dog was in its crate.

He slid open the glass door, watched Bella through the front window, pacing the porch, smoking a cigarette. Her face remained shadowed, but at this point his sole focus was finding out if Kiera was here. With a final glance toward Liam, he slipped inside the house.

He quickly scanned the empty kitchen and dining room combination, then headed toward the small living room. Bella stood in front of the window, her back to him. With no sign of Ginger, he made his way down the hall. All the doors were open, except the last one on the left, and the one he believed led to the master bedroom. The dog could be crated in either room. Once Ginger saw him, her barking would alert them and he'd be screwed.

Fuck it. He was tired of living with guilt and would face any consequence so long as he knew Kiera's exact location, and that she was safe.

He reached the last door on the left. When he'd been outside, the closed blinds hadn't allowed him to see inside. Were they hiding something, or did the dog like the lights off when she napped? Ready to find out, he reached for the brass knob, then slowly turned it. The door opened smoothly on the hinges. A trickle of sunlight penetrated through a small fissure in the blinds on the side window, and formed a ragged Z on the opposite wall. Now that the door was open, he could hear Bella's muffled voice as she continued to talk to someone, and what little light was in the hallway created his shadow on the floor. If the dog was in the room, she should have barked. Taking a deep breath, eager to get in and out of the house, he stepped inside, then nearly fell to his knees.

He covered his mouth with his forearm to keep from shouting out in rage, in fucking horror, and rushed to Kiera's side. There was enough light for him to see her exactly as he'd once looked. Helpless, vulnerable, tortured. Fighting for control of his emotions, fighting to remain here—in the present—he set the gun on the bed, then reached for the knife in his sock. Mel's image surfaced anyway, but he blocked it and quickly cut the rope surrounding Kiera's ankles, then worked on the ones around her wrists. When he realized she couldn't move her head, he went to the side window, then cracked the blind slightly.

He rushed back to her side and stopped her from reaching for her face. She would want to rip the tape off her eyelids and he knew from experience that wouldn't be pleasant. "Don't move," he whispered against her ear, then slowly peeled the tape from her mouth.

"My eyes. They burn."

He'd avoided looking at her eyes up to this point, but as he removed the clear tape along her forehead and chin, he couldn't any longer. He could honestly say that, except for one person, anyone else he'd ever hated was now dead. Hatred didn't even begin to encompass the emotions coursing through him at this moment, and he wasn't sure if Liam would ever be dead enough for his satisfaction.

"I know, baby." Aching for her and wishing she'd never had to experience the terror he understood all too well, he smoothed a hand over her brow to see how much tape had been used. "I'll take it off, but you can't make a sound." He placed the tape back over her mouth. "I'm sorry," he said, then worked the tape loose.

"I TOLD YOU to kill the twat," Adeline screamed. *"I told you and you ignored me. Now you're fucked. You really know how to pick 'em,* lover. *You couldn't settle for me, or a whore to get you off. No, you had to shack up with a greedy bitch who has no regards for life."*

Laughing, he stabbed the ground. "You have no room to talk. How many people did you murder?"

"Apparently not as many as the twat. Didn't you catch what she said? Bury her with the others?"

He tossed dirt onto a pile and thought back. "I was thinking about my sister. Are you sure she said that?"

"Yes, she said that." She huffed. *"And you wanted me out of your head. Thank God I'm here. You're going to need me on this. As much as I don't like your sister, I don't think it's smart to kill her."*

"Kiera's not dying today." Not by his hands or by Bella's. "She hasn't done anything wrong."

"Please tell me you're not planning on hurting the dog. I abhor animal abuse."

He would never understand Adeline's logic. "And yet it's okay to kill people."

"That depends on why. Bella is a greedy twat. From the sound of it, she didn't take pleasure in killing however many men she'd duped into falling for her trashy ass. She did it for profit. Whereas I killed for pleasure."

"What about me? Where do I fall? I didn't kill anyone for money, and I didn't take any pleasure when I killed those women."

"That's because you didn't kill the right *woman."*

"Bella?"

"Think, lover. You were fine until you met her. She made us *hungry."*

As he continued to dig, he recalled life just before Bella. His body and mind had healed. There would be an occasional dream about Adeline, but they were usually sexual, and nothing nightmarish. He'd followed the Rodney Archer investigation with great interest, and sometimes fantasized about killing the man. But they were only fantasies. As much as he still hated the bastard, Rodney had cured him of schizophrenia. Thanks to Rod's drug, he'd become clear-headed. Focused. Eager for a fresh start and ready to put the past behind him.

What he'd done to his parents, to his great-aunt...there was no joy in their deaths, but there was also no guilt. He'd killed his aunt out of curiosity, and his parents out of paranoia, and with the absurd idea that if they lived he would not be allowed to survive outside of a mental institute. He'd made peace with his choices.

When had that changed? When had he started to resent his sister? Why had he suddenly craved power? When had the darkness crawled into his head, unleashing Adeline and the monster he couldn't always control?

Even with Adeline here with him now, everything became crystal clear. The green weeds in the garden, the tiny white rocks he unearthed within the brown dirt, the gunmetal gray of the shovel...the colors were sharp, the objects themselves severe, as if someone had outlined them all in black marker. He swore he could smell the decay of the vegetables the garden had once held, the smoldering remains of the logs and branches he'd burned yesterday, the dog shit he'd meant to pick up today. He grinned as the past four months blurred together only to come into focus on one person.

Bella.

He should have killed her the day he'd come for the carpet cleaner. By resisting the urge, by projecting his rage, his turmoil onto other women who'd looked like her, like Adeline, he'd only prolonged the torture. And he'd kept killing not because *Adeline* was hungry, but because *he* wasn't satisfied.

Just like with Adeline.

He'd wanted so badly to be the one who had ended Adeline's life, but he'd never been given the chance. Now she was dead, her ashes likely beneath the rubble of the House of Archer. While disappointment and frustration had gnawed at him, he'd healed during his stay at the old couple's house. At the beginning, Adeline had kept him company, then she'd eventually left him, only to return the day Bella Johnson had walked into the rental center.

"I should have killed her from the start."

"Bella is very bad," Adeline whispered. *"Are you going to let her tell you what to do? Who to hurt?"*

"No. I'm going to make it look like she's the one who committed the murders. Kiera will go along with it, and she knows how to keep a secret."

"How will you convince the detectives? Or explain the grave you're digging?"

He tossed dirt, filled with more white rock, to the side, then knelt. Not rock. He lifted one of the pieces and realized it was bone. "I think I just found one of *the others*," he said, using a gloved finger to sift through the dirt. When he connected with something hard, he brushed off the dirt and stared at what appeared to be a human bone. "I'll tell them Bella held a gun to my head, I wrestled it free and shot her, then saved my sister. The police will see this garden and know I had nothing to do with it. Hey, if Bella was capable of murdering these men, why wouldn't she be capable of murdering the women, too?"

Adeline chuckled. *"Brilliant, lover. I always knew—"*

A car door slammed, followed by another.

HARRISON FINISHED REMOVING the tape from Kiera's other eye,

then went to the window facing the front yard, and peeked out through the side of the plastic blind.

"Bella did this to me." Kiera came up behind him and grabbed his arm. "We have to leave," she whispered frantically. "She's killed people and knew what Liam was doing."

He didn't see that one coming.

"I gotta go, girl," Bella said, stepping into view, giving him a clear shot of…the small pistol she had tucked in the waistband at the back of her shorts.

He moved so Kiera could see out of the window. "I called the detectives and told them I was worried when you didn't show at the hotel. I can see that was a mistake," he said, pulling his cell phone from his pocket, then handing it to her. "Call the police. I'm going—"

She turned and gripped his arm. "You're staying with me."

"Fine. I parked on the road. We'll have to go through the woods to get there." He grabbed the gun from the bed, and slid the knife back in the sheath along his calf. "Liam is out back digging."

"My grave."

He looked up at her. "We can either wait it out here, or make a run for it."

The back patio door slid shut with a loud thump. Worried Liam would come to the bedroom and discover Kiera had been freed, he took her hand. "Other room."

She stopped him. "We can surprise him."

He met her frightened gaze. "I want you out of here." As much as he wanted Liam dead, he didn't want to shoot him in front of Kiera. She could end up resenting him more than she already did, and he'd rather the police handled Liam.

When she didn't respond or budge, he dragged her toward the door, then looked down the hall. Liam's shadow stretched across the wood floor at the entrance of the hallway. *Too late.* He backed her up, then closed the door and looked around the room. "Get in the closet," he said, opening the bi-fold. He handed her the gun.

Kiera claimed to know how to shoot, and he wanted her to protect herself. "Call 911." He unsheathed the knife again, then gave her a quick kiss. "I love you."

Before he could close the door, she gripped his wrist, and tugged. "Don't be a fool. Get inside with me," she said, just as he heard Liam's heavy footfall from the other side of the door.

Damn it. He did *not* want to wait in the closet like a coward. He had a knife, a bad attitude and vengeance on the brain. But he had a brain, and it told him he'd already made too many mistakes.

He closed them inside, pushed her to the far corner behind several men's jackets, then stepped over men's boots and planted himself opposite of her. The door to the room bounced off the wall. The interior of the closet was pitch black until light suddenly glowed from the crack between the bottom of the closet door and the wood floor. Now wishing he'd kept the gun, he stared at the location where the door would open first, and waited.

The light dimmed in places. Knowing Liam had to be blocking the door, his heart rate cranked up, pounded in his head. Sweat trickled down his back. His palm grew clammy as he clutched the knife. The light below glowed as it had before, then it went out completely. The bedroom door clicked shut and he let out the breath he'd been holding.

He reached for Kiera, and immediately snapped his arm back as the door was ripped from the casing. Liam shoved his arms inside. Metal hangers scraped, clothes rustled. Harrison shot his foot out, connecting with Liam's torso. The man fell back on his ass, but quickly scrambled to his feet as Harrison stumbled over boots and out of the closet.

Liam's face registered shock, then recognition. His gaze darted to the knife Harrison held. "Where's my sister?"

"We're going to go outside and talk to the detectives," he said.

"Not happening." Liam held up his hands. "I won't hurt her."

Because he'd kill him before the bastard had the chance.

Kiera's quiet voice came from behind him, and he cracked a smile as he heard her telling the 911 operator their location. "It's over," he said, and though tempted to yell out to the detectives, he worried about the gun Bella possessed.

Liam walked backwards toward the window facing the front. Harrison moved in sync, stalking him, ready to pounce. "How could you tape Kiera's eyes open?" he asked, hoping to stall Liam, but also curious. "After what they did to you, how could you do the same?"

Liam frowned and looked over Harrison's shoulder as Kiera came up behind him, the gun trained on her brother. "Is that what they did to you?" she asked. "To both of you?"

"Both?" Liam looked back to him. "You were there?"

"The switchblade. You know, your souvenir? That doesn't belong to you."

Liam grinned. "The blonde who set me free." He reached toward his back pocket.

"Don't move," Kiera ordered, the Glock shaking in her hand.

Liam froze. "Would you really shoot your baby brother?"

"Give me the gun, Kiera," Harrison said, knowing he wouldn't have a problem.

When she remained silent and still, Liam edged a little closer to the window. "Don't do it, Kiera. I need to take care of one little thing."

"AND YOUR CAR was never in the shop?" Bern asked, and looked toward Bella Johnson's blue hatchback.

Bella shook her head and, crossing her arms, stepped back toward the window that had the blinds drawn closed. "Not for months."

Sharon's stomach dropped as she stared at Bella's reflection in the glass window, specifically at the gun she had tucked in her shorts. The blinds covering the window moved as if someone had given them a hard shake. She glanced to Bernadette. They needed to get the hell out of here and call for backup. While she couldn't be sure Random Guy was telling them the truth, during the drive over, they'd called Mercy Memorial, where Kiera Forrester worked, and was told she had left early due to a family emergency.

Now Sharon wondered whose car was in the garage. Mostly she wondered why Bella had been compelled to arm herself, and who the hell was moving the blinds.

Bella looked toward the screen door, then back to them. "Is there anything else?"

"No." Sharon started toward the porch steps, not as quickly as she'd like. Without knowing what was happening here, she wanted Bella to believe everything was copasetic. "You have my card. If you hear from Kiera, would you please give me a call?"

"Absolutely. I'm really worried about her. First she lied about me having a miscarriage, now this. It just doesn't make sense."

Sharon ignored the question in her partner's eyes. Once they were in the car, she'd tell Bern about—

A gun blasted. Glass shattered.

Sharon reached for her Smith & Wesson, saw Bern do the same, and turned toward the porch, just as Liam Forrester fell backward from the window. When another man jumped on top of Liam, Bella reached behind her.

"Gun," Sharon yelled to Bern, and pulled the trigger.

The bullet hit the siding to the left of Bella's head. As Sharon released another round, Bella fired multiple shots. Sharon grunted when she was hit in the chest and stomach, then cried out when Bernadette's body jerked back several times, eyes widening with shock.

Bella turned the gun on the men struggling along the porch. "No!" Sharon knelt and fired three rounds into Bella Johnson. The bitch dropped, her legs splayed beneath her, her head resting at an odd angle against the siding that was now covered with blood and brain.

Liam let out a painful scream. When Kiera Forrester emerged from the window, a gun pointed directly at her brother, the man who'd been beating the hell out of him jumped off and staggered back, wiping blood from his lip.

"She was mine to kill," Liam shouted, his eyes wild. He swayed forward and fell to his knees in front of Bella's dead body. "Mine!"

Kiera stepped behind him. Without hesitation, she hit her brother over the head with the butt of the gun. Liam dropped. Breathing hard, tears streaming down her face, Kiera looked to the man who Sharon assumed was Random Guy, then to Bernadette. She rushed across the porch, and the man did the same.

Relieved it was over, Sharon lowered her weapon, then crawled toward Bern. Her chest and abdomen burned as if someone was sticking her with a hot poker. "Call 911," she managed, fighting through the pain.

"Already done," Kiera said, kneeling next to Bern, and smoothing her friend's bangs from her forehead.

The unknown man came alongside her. "Don't move," he said, his gaze skimming over Sharon's body.

"Are you the guy who called me?"

He nodded, and looked down the driveway. "Help is on the way."

She coughed, tasted blood and looked toward Bernadette. "Where's she hit?"

Kiera ran her hand over Bern. "Shoulder, above the hip. She has a laceration along the side of her head. Not from a gun. I think from when she hit her head on the gravel."

Sharon curled into the man. "She'll be okay, don't you think?"

"I…" He cradled her in his arms. "I do. You will, too."

"I'm dying." She sobbed against his chest. Not because the bullet wounds would likely kill her, but because if anyone should go, it should be her. Not Bernadette. She had Joe, her daughter, a grandbaby on the way.

"No," he said, his voice firm, yet shaky, anguished.

"Sharon?" Bern asked, her voice tinny, distant, dream-like.

"You shouldn't move," Kiera said. "Stop, let me help you."

Seconds later, Sharon stared up at her friend. She tried to

smile, but her lips wouldn't work. The temperature around her felt as if it had dropped forty degrees and her limbs had become numb. "Bern," she managed.

A hot tear hit her face. And she knew in her heart this would be the last person she'd ever see. That was fine by her. Her husband had died alone. She'd spent the past year agonizing over what her death would be like, and what, if anything was on the other side. Today, she'd die at a crime scene—fitting because she'd loved her career. More importantly, she'd go with her friend by her side.

"I love you," Bern said, the simple admission encompassing over thirty years of friendship.

She wanted to respond, but the words wouldn't form. They were there, in her heart, in her spirit. She closed her eyes. As she relished the loving embrace of her friend, she drifted off, dreaming of her husband.

KIERA COVERED HER mouth. Watched as Detective Richie pressed her head against Detective Larson's, and as Harrison held them both. Sirens wailed in the distance, and while Detective Richie needed medical attention, her wounds, from what she could tell, weren't life threatening.

On a sob, she tore her gaze away and looked to the porch, to Bella's dead body, to her brother lying face down. When he and Harrison had begun fighting, there'd been a side of her tempted to pull the trigger, to put an end to the burden and to give the families of the people Liam had killed some semblance of justice. Even before she'd whacked him over the head with the Glock she'd been drawn, seduced to the idea of a world without Liam.

But then she'd be no better than him.

"Are you Random Guy?" Detective Richie looked up at Harrison, her eyes puffy, her face tear-soaked.

"I called Detective Larson." He continued to hold both women. "I'm so sorry. I didn't know about Bella. I'm so sorry," he repeated, his voice thick with agony.

With utter helplessness, Kiera watched the detective's shoulders shake as she cried. Her brother was a killer, his fiancée had been no better. Because she'd tried to protect him, people were dead. She stared at the detectives and Harrison, her vision blurring with tears, her heart breaking, her soul shriveling. She'd known guilt, but nothing like this. The enormity of her choices didn't just weigh on her, they suffocated her. Suddenly lightheaded and overwhelmed with remorse, with grief, with crushing sadness, she fell forward and bawled like she'd never done in her life. For her parents, for the women, for the detectives only a couple of feet away from her. For Harrison and all that he'd suffered, and would continue to endure.

The sirens grew unbearably loud. Tires crunched over gravel, along with booted feet. A hand touched her shoulder. She looked up and met a female officer's blue eyes. While the woman asked if she was injured, Kiera looked over to Harrison whose focus was on her. The pain in his eyes made her continue to weep, especially when the other officers, their faces solemn, moved around the area, their gazes drifting to Detectives Larson and Richie.

"Ma'am, are you injured?" the female officer asked again.

She shook her head. "No," she managed. "My brother, he's on the porch. He killed women. Bella…she…check the garden. Look what she did." She rambled on, knowing she wasn't completing sentences and jumping from one thing to the next, but she couldn't concentrate, couldn't wrap her mind around everything that had happened in such a short amount of time.

A warm hand slid along her back. She looked up. Harrison's eyes were intense, filled with concern, sorrow and regret. Needing his strength, she leaned into him, then closed her eyes when he half-embraced her.

"Ma'am," the officer began, "I need you to repeat what you said about your brother."

Kiera opened her eyes, and looked over the officer's shoulders to where EMTs were lifting her brother onto a stretcher. She met the officer's gaze, and for the first time in over ten years, she could finally admit the truth. Say it out loud and with ownership.

"My brother is a murderer."

CHAPTER 18

Four days later…
The Hampton Club Apartments, Tallahassee, Florida
Sunday, 11:03 a.m., Eastern Standard Time

ONCE A STALKER, always a stalker. Harrison moved away from the kitchen window which overlooked the parking lot. In his defense, he hadn't been staring out the window searching for signs of Kiera's Chevy, he'd been cleaning out the coffee pot. But now that she was finally back from wherever she'd gone, he'd do his damnedest to get her to talk with him.

She wanted to end things between them? Fine. He understood and would respect her wishes. But before she shut him out of her life, he needed to know how she was coping after everything that had happened. He'd guarantee she'd never witnessed the deaths of two people, especially in such a brutal manner.

Or maybe he was reaching, making excuses to see her before he moved out of his apartment. Once he was gone, he couldn't casually pass her on the jogging trail or in the parking lot. He wasn't that much of a stalker.

Even though there wasn't a drop of coffee or a crumb on the counter, he wiped it down, stalling, debating his next move. Had he gone with Vlad to the Glades, he wouldn't be in this position. No, he would be dealing with breaking the news to Lola that he no longer wanted to work for ATL. He wasn't nervous about telling her, but more worried how she'd handle losing two more employees. She'd been a little shaken when Mel had left, and it probably hadn't helped that he hadn't been acting himself. Once he and Vlad were officially gone, it'd just be her and Ryan. Shane occasionally provided transportation for the agency, but between his air charter business and his wife, Beth, they mostly saw him during the holidays, or when he was able to make one of their cookouts. Barney loved being part of the team, but he was pushing seventy and preferred to tell stories while he fixed things, rather than involve himself in ATL's sometimes dangerous activities. Vlad had talked about the new dude, and he'd heard Ryan say he had a few other guys that might be interested in working for ATL, so the agency wouldn't go under without him and Vlad. Yet he still couldn't help feeling as if he was abandoning Lola.

Damn, he was tired of dealing with the constant guilt. Why should he feel guilty anyway? The investigation he'd conducted, if it had gone another way, could have had him doing time. Same with most jobs he'd done for ATL. He didn't want to live that way, and here in Tallahassee, he had a clean slate, a fresh start, a chance to make a good life for himself. And he wouldn't be doing it alone. He had Vlad, Mel, Cash, and even the guys from the garage.

Now all he needed was Kiera.

After tossing the paper towel he'd been using into the trash, he headed for the door. Without hesitation, he left his apartment. He didn't just want to know how Kiera was coping, he wanted to know if she still loved him, if there was the slimmest chance they still had a shot at something good and lasting. He'd made mistakes. He'd also spent most of his life apologizing for his choices. When would it be enough? Why wasn't *he* enough?

When he reached Kiera's apartment door, he raised his hand to knock, but didn't. What the hell had he been thinking? While he'd apologized the day he had told her the truth about him, Liam, everything, that apology might never be enough. He'd broken Kiera's trust.

The door swung open and Kiera nearly collided with his fist. She stepped back and held a hand to her heart. "You scared the crap out of me."

He lowered his arm. "Sorry. I would've called, but you haven't answered any of my calls or texts."

"I needed time. I told you that when we were leaving the police station."

"You're right." He took a step back. "Maybe you'll call me when you get back home? I need to know how you're doing."

"Come in," she said, opening the door wider. "I was actually on my way to your apartment."

Hope tried to warm his chest, but he wouldn't allow it. Not yet, not until he knew why she wanted to see him. When he stepped inside, he noticed a weekender bag on the floor. "Where were you?"

"Jacksonville Beach." She closed the door. "The day after...everything, I packed a bag, got in my car and drove east until I reached the Atlantic. I spent the last three nights hanging out in a hotel room or walking on the beach." She went into the living room, then sat on the sofa. "I needed to clear my head."

He took a seat next to her. "How'd that work out for you?"

"I don't know. I cried a lot." She looked down at her twined fingers. "I...know Liam confessed. Does this mean you won't get in any trouble?"

The pond at the back of Liam and Bella's property had been drained after investigators had unearthed the bones of four males in Bella's garden. Once emptied, the skeletal remains of two other men had been exposed, along with Julie Beechum's hot pink blow dryer. Blood evidence had also been found on Liam's switchblade. Although investigators were waiting on DNA results from that, and the family dog, Liam couldn't explain away the blow dryer. From what Harrison had heard from Detective Richie, Liam hadn't even tried.

"No trouble. Liam even confessed to killing the older couple in Georgia." Which meant Travis James Graham, the drifter who'd been charged with the Dougals' murders, would not serve time for that crime, only arson. It also meant Harrison hadn't been forced to come forward and show investigators the photos he'd taken, the fingerprint he'd lifted, or admit to using Nick's ID. "The only thing I don't think he told detectives about is what Rodney and Adeline did to him."

"I think I can understand why." When she looked up at him, he almost wished she hadn't bothered. He didn't need the pity in her eyes. "I'm sorry for what you went through."

Unfortunately, Bella had given Kiera a taste of what it had been like for him and Liam. But he'd take dealing with Bella over Adeline any day. Both women were psychopaths, except Adeline was pure evil, whereas Bella was a greedy opportunist. Bella's modus operandi had been a bullet to the head or chest of her victims. Quick and easy. Adeline...the slut might've been easy, but there'd been nothing quick about her when it had come to making her victims suffer. She'd enjoyed inflicting pain, both physical and emotional.

"I'm sorrier you had to experience it," he said. "And I'm sorry for what Rodney and Adeline did to your brother. He had no history of violence until they scrambled his brain. We wouldn't be sitting here right now if Liam had never crossed paths with them. I would never know you existed, or what it's like to love you."

Kiera hugged herself and leaned forward, hoping to ease the nausea rolling through her stomach. She'd cried so much over the past three days, she didn't think it was possible to have any more tears. While she'd been gone, she'd thought long and hard about the choices she had made, and how they'd impacted so many lives. People were dead, families were destroyed, and she'd fallen in love. All because she hadn't told the truth. How was that fair? How could something good come from a bad decision? Her eyes misted and her throat tightened. The moment Harrison had told her about Liam, she knew there was no way to move forward unless she was honest, but had tried to convince herself no good would come from sharing her darkest secret.

Last Wednesday, as she'd sat in the Tallahassee PD interrogation room, she had prayed for the right answer. While she'd waited to be interviewed, she couldn't stop thinking about Sharon

Larson, and her partner Bernadette Richie. How Sharon had given up her life to save hers and Harrison's, how grief-stricken Bernadette had been when her friend had passed. That had been when she realized the right answer had been in her heart all along. Honesty might not take away the guilt, but the truth would release her from Liam's shadow.

Harrison scooted closer and rubbed her back. "Don't," she said, sitting up and facing him. She didn't deserve his touch, not until he knew the truth. "I love you. It's almost bittersweet, you know? If we'd never met, I could keep living with lies and pretending everything is going to be okay. Instead I have to face ugly truths about myself and my brother." She drew in a deep breath and met his wary gaze. "Liam killed our parents." A tear trickled down her cheek. "The day he told me…I honestly thought he was talking figuratively. He and Mom had gotten into a heated argument that morning and Dad was rattled, so I assumed that was what Liam had meant. A few days after we buried our parents, Liam had his first psychotic break. A month later he was home with me, and I was trying to cope with losing our parents and Liam's diagnosis. That's when he confessed and told me he'd caused the accident."

Afraid of seeing the disappointment in Harrison's eyes, she looked back to her hand. "I didn't believe him at first. I thought his ramblings were due to the schizophrenia. The day I realized he was telling me the truth, was the day I betrayed my parents and everything they'd taught me. Liam was lucid then. I…looked on what he'd done as a mistake, as something he never meant to have happen, that it was the disorder, the voices. Ten months later, when I was getting ready to sell my parents' home, I found the paperwork Mom had filled out to have Liam institutionalized. It was dated the day before the accident."

She faced Harrison, met his gaze. The understanding in his eyes, the lack of judgment gave her the confidence she needed. "So you shouldn't feel any guilt about the people my brother killed. If I had done the right thing and notified the authorities about what my brother had done to our parents, he wouldn't have been free. He would have never met Rodney and Adeline, the Dougals, Bella...all of the women he'd killed would be alive. It's my fault they're not," she admitted, Liam's dark shadow dissolving and freeing her. "I'm sorry I wasn't as honest as you were the night you told me about the murders. It wasn't fair of me to let you walk out of here blaming yourself, when the guilt lies with me."

She drew in a ragged breath. "The day Liam was arrested, I told detectives I had additional information on Liam. Once I was granted immunity, I explained to the state's attorney that, ten years ago, Liam had admitted to killing our parents. Before I left town, I provided them with the paperwork my mom had filled out prior to her death. Fortunately, Liam confessed to killing them, too, which means I won't have to testify."

"Thank God." He reached over and took her hand in his. "I think you've punished yourself enough."

"With guilt? I don't think it's enough of a punishment."

"Okay, then look at it from a different perspective. You knew your parents. Would they want you to spend the rest of your life feeling guilty over something you couldn't have possibly ever predicted would happen? Especially when you weren't one hundred percent sure he was telling you the truth about the accident. Looking out for your brother, trying to protect him...I honestly would have done the same thing."

She gripped his hand. "But I knew the truth later. I could have done something then."

"Why didn't you?"

"Because I loved my brother," she said, tears blurring her vision. "He was all I had. I grew up with a schizophrenic father, saw what he went through, dealt with the stays at the hospital, the psychotic bouts. Before my dad died, he was almost normal. And that gave me hope."

"You thought Liam could be normal."

She nodded. "But from what you said about what happened to him, to you, I don't know if there's any amount of therapy that could fix him now. I have to live with that, and my decision to not report him to the police. So, again, the guilt, the blame...that's on me."

"I disagree. I don't think there's a person out there that hasn't wondered, what if I hadn't done that? There've been more nights than I can count where I've thought back to the day my brother told me about the job that was too good to be true. If I'd said I wanted no part of it, would the bastard who'd hired us have found someone else to do the job? Would all of those people still have died? Or maybe a different group would have, or maybe even more people? Would my brother still be alive? If I hadn't volunteered to be kidnapped by Adeline, I wouldn't have known about Liam. I couldn't have been there at the house to cut you from those ropes." He touched her chin. "I would have never known what it was like to love you."

Her heart hammered with hope, that maybe there was still a chance for them. "You already said that."

"I thought it was worth repeating." He moved closer. "You told me my past didn't matter to you. I feel the same way. I'm only sorry you had to deal with the weight of your choices and the burden of Liam alone. It doesn't have to be that way. We could be there for each other." He captured one of her tears with his thumb. "Could keep working on us."

She hugged him. "I want that." She kissed his neck, his cheek, his lips. "When I was at the beach, I kept thinking about us and what kind of life we could have."

"Really?" he asked, looking genuinely surprised.

"Why wouldn't I?"

His eyes clouded with regret. "I broke your trust."

"No. You stopped two serial killers." She twined her arms around his neck. "You saved my life." Her throat tightened. "You held Detective Larson as she took her final breath, and comforted her partner. You think I'm so special, and that you don't deserve me? Check yourself, because I'm incredibly proud of the man you are, and I consider myself fortunate to have you in my life." When his cheeks reddened slightly, she kissed him again. "You're humble, too. Very sexy."

He pulled her onto his lap. "So what kind of life do you think we could have?"

"A happy one," she said, straddling him.

"Here in Tallahassee?"

She nodded. "There's nothing for me in Colorado. But when my six-month lease is up in May, I'm going to have to find a new place to live."

"I sublet my apartment to Vlad."

"Why?" she asked, disappointed. She didn't like the idea of him living far from her. Because, yeah, even a five-minute drive was too much distance.

"I didn't know what would happen with us, and I didn't want you to be uncomfortable. It's not like we wouldn't run into each other here." He frowned. "Wait, why do you have to leave your apartment?"

"I'm adopting Ginger." Hoping this wouldn't be a deal-breaker, she studied his face, looking for any sign Harrison had an issue with becoming the owner of not just one, but two serial killers' dog. "Do you have a problem with that?"

"Why would I? She's a great dog. It's not her fault she was adopted by a couple of...never mind."

"Were you going to say a couple of psychopaths?"

"Maybe."

She grinned. "I was going to pick up Ginger this afternoon. Maybe you'll come with me?" After he agreed, she slipped off his lap. "Come with me. I want to show you something," she said, leading him into the bedroom.

He hesitated in the doorway. "Kiera, I want to, but I also don't expect—"

"Oh, you better expect to mess up the bed later," she said, opening up the top two drawers of her tall dresser. "Actually, we might want to before we bring Ginger home." She walked across the room, then opened up the closet door. "I need to move a few things around, but half of the closet and dresser are yours."

He stepped into the room and immediately went to her. "You want me to move in with you?" he asked, the love in his eyes a gift she would never take for granted.

She wrapped her arms around his waist. "Since you gave up your apartment to Vlad, and I'll need to move so Ginger could have a bigger place and hopefully a yard, maybe we should give it a shot?"

"I told you before, if I go anywhere, it'll be because you want me gone."

She rose to her tiptoes. "Then I guess we have quite a life ahead of us," she said, then brushed her lips against his.

Three days later…
I-75 South, Outside of Sarasota, Florida
Wednesday, 7:47 p.m., Eastern Standard Time

HARRISON SET THE cruise control of his Jeep, then reached over and touched her thigh. "You've been quiet," he said, then they both chuckled when Ginger snored deeply. "I think she's narcoleptic. She bounces around one minute, then she's sound asleep the next."

"She's a good girl," Kiera said, looking to the backseat. "Crap. I forgot to give her the flea and tick medicine."

"I took care of it this morning, right after I took her for a run, then brushed her."

"You're such a good doggie daddy."

No question about it, he was in love with Ginger. Whenever she stared at him with those adoring, pretty blue eyes, he melted.

He and Kiera had only been living together for a few days, but he knew in his heart and gut that they would work. They even talked about buying a house, rather than renting a bigger place for them to live, which he could swing. According to Barney, the new guy Lola had hired wanted to buy Harrison's trailer, not live in the agency's headquarters. If the deal worked out, that'd give Harrison fifty grand to put toward a down payment on a house.

Kiera checked the GPS setting on her phone, then let out a sigh. "We won't be to your trailer until after ten-thirty. I wish I could've gotten off work today. I wanted to get there when the sun was still shining."

"Barney stocked up my fridge with a few things and aired out the place. All we'll need to do is let the dog out and bring in our bags. There'll be plenty of sun tomorrow. Barney's looking forward to taking you out on the airboat."

"I can't wait," she said, then added, "But I heard you talking to Vlad earlier. I feel bad you didn't get to go out with your friends tonight."

"They changed plans when they found out when we were coming to town." He gave her thigh a light squeeze. From the moment she came home from work, Kiera had been acting anxious, fidgety. "Why are you on edge? Did something happen that you're not telling me about?"

"I'm not on edge, just…something is bothering me."

"What is it? If I'm doing things around the apartment you don't like, you've got to tell me. Mind reading isn't one of my talents," he said, glancing at her.

She half-smiled. "You're doing everything fine."

"But?"

"This is not a topic I've ever discussed with anyone."

Now she was starting to worry him. The last topic she'd never discussed with anyone had to do with knowing her brother had killed her parents. "Just say it. You know I'm not going to judge you."

"See, that's the problem. I feel like you kind of are, and I'm not doing it right."

"Doing what right?" he asked, now totally confused.

"Oral sex." She took his hand in hers and laced their fingers. "You don't have a problem giving it, but seem to have an issue receiving it. Last night, you, well…maybe I should drop the subject."

Sex wasn't the biggest part of a relationship, but it was very important. He and Kiera had fantastic chemistry, and he loved having sex with her. But she was right. While he enjoyed pleasuring her with his mouth, he wouldn't give her the chance to do the same for him. Each time she'd tried, he couldn't help but take a jump back in time. He couldn't stop remembering Adeline, the agony in Mel's eyes, the humiliation.

"No, it's okay," he finally said, even though he was absolutely not comfortable talking about what happened with Adeline. He loved Kiera, wanted to buy a house with her, eventually marry her and make a bunch of babies. He'd kept nothing else hidden from her, and he believed the same went for Kiera. He trusted her and needed her to understand his hang up had nothing to do with her.

But to admit...

"Honestly," she began, "let's pretend I never brought it up, okay?"

"Adeline assaulted me."

"What?" She tightened her grip on his hand. "You mean—"

"While I was tied up, just like you were at your brother's." Through his peripheral vision he caught her staring at him, and kept his gaze on the road. His face burned with humiliation, making him grateful the sun had gone down, leaving only the glow from the dash.

"Harrison, you don't have to say anything more," she said, her voice strained, thick.

He looked at her, saw the tears in her eyes, then faced the road again. "You haven't asked me anything about that time." Which had surprised him. After what she'd personally experienced, and how her brother had changed for the worse, he'd expected her to question him about Rodney and Adeline, and what had gone on in the House of Archer.

"I had a pretty good idea, and didn't want to bring up bad memories for you." She rubbed his forearm. "And I did it anyway. I'm so sorry."

"It's okay." He brought their joined hands to his lips and

kissed her knuckles. "Don't apologize or feel bad. How could you know?" And where was the anger that normally accompanied the memories of Adeline?

"Now that I do, let's just change the subject," she said, reaching for the radio.

"Mel was in the room."

She curled her hand away from the dashboard.

"Other than Mel, Vlad is the only one who knows what happened. Cash doesn't need to know, and Adeline is dead," he said, then told her how he and Mel had ended up at the plantation house, and how Adeline had tried to break him in front of Mel. When he finished, there was no embarrassment or anger, just a huge sense of relief.

"You're right, Adeline was an evil bitch. I wish you two never had to go through that. I have even more respect for you, and for Mel."

"You won't feel weird around her?"

"For something that neither of you caused? Not at all. I'm glad your friendship was strong enough to withstand what you both went through." She let out a breath. "So where do we go from here?"

"With?" he asked, glancing at her. This was probably one of the most awkward conversations he'd ever had.

"Before the plantation house, did you enjoy oral sex?"

Clearing his throat, he nodded.

She let go of his hand and rubbed his thigh. "Then maybe you need to replace the bad memory with something new?" She moved her hand toward his groin. "Something fun," she said stroking him through his jeans, making him hard and taking his mind off their conversation. "Something wild." She slid down his zipper. "Something a little dangerous."

When her soft hand wrapped around his length, he sucked in a breath and gripped the steering wheel. He checked the rear view mirror, noticed there were hardly any cars on the road, then pulled off along the shoulder. With her mouth poised above his erection, she looked up at him, the glow from the dash revealing her questioning gaze.

He smoothed her thick hair away from her face. "I love fun and wild, but I've had enough danger."

A sexy smile curved her lips just before she took him in her mouth. As she licked and sucked him, bringing him closer and closer to the edge, all he could think about was Kiera, the pleasure she was giving him, how much he loved her...and how many times he planned to make her come once they reached his trailer.

Union Correctional Institution, Raiford, Florida
Wednesday, 8:23 p.m., Eastern Standard Time

"I TOLD YOU to kill the twat."

Liam lay on the bed staring at the ceiling of his prison cell. Monday, he'd been transferred to his new home where he would spend the rest of his life, and he was already regretting his decision to confess in order to save his ass from receiving the death penalty. Death couldn't come fast enough, and he was unable to picture himself forty years from now, in his seventies and still staring at the ceiling. He didn't want to be told when to eat, what to eat, when he could shower or drag in a breath of fresh air.

"If you'd done what I told you, we would be free," Adeline continued. *"Traveling the world, enjoying life, freedom. But, no. You decided you were in love with a crazy white trash twat who probably killed more people than the two of us combined."*

She fooled everyone, he reminded her.

"Not me. I knew something wasn't right with her. What did she call it? The white noise?" Adeline huffed. *"Any woman who thinks tying up her man while he's having one of his* moments *just isn't right in the head. You mistook acceptance for dominance."*

Bullshit.

"It's true." She let out a sigh. *"I suppose this is partially my fault. You did enjoy the way I kept you tied down."*

I hated it.

Adeline laughed. *"Really? I didn't hear you complaining when I was riding your big cock."*

That's because my mouth was sealed with duct tape. Just shut up and leave me alone.

As he rolled onto his side, he looked at the empty bed across from him. His cellmate, according to the bible-thumper he'd met at lunch, had been in the infirmary for the past few days. He could only hope the guy had died there. The bible-thumper claimed his cellmate was deeply involved in the same Christian prison group he was, and that maybe Liam would like to join them. At that point, Liam had almost slammed his own head against the table to either knock his ass out or stop Adeline from laughing—whichever would come first.

He reached beneath his pillow and pulled out the letter from his sister. His attorney had brought it with him when he'd come to the prison to sit through Liam's psych evaluation. From the start, he knew there would be no chance for an insanity plea. He'd known exactly what he was doing when he'd killed the old couple and all those women. But because he'd been diagnosed a paranoid schizophrenic, he was required to meet with the prison psychologist to determine if and what type of medical therapy he might need.

Only he didn't need therapy. Rodney had cured him.

"Yes, Rodney was brilliant," Adeline said. *"It's a shame the two of you hated each other. The three of us could've been a powerful team."*

It's a little hard to think about how powerful we could've been when you're dead, and me and Rodney are both doing life sentences.

"At least we have each other. Poor Rod. He's all on his lonesome."

She was right. They had each other. He touched the envelope from Kiera, addressed to his attorney. There was no return address, but the postmark was from Jacksonville, Florida, which had him wondering if she'd already moved, or was in the process and still traveling.

It used to just be him and Kiera. Even after he'd told her he had killed Mom and Dad, she'd stuck by his side. Looking back, he should have never told her what he'd done. If he could go back and change his life, he probably wouldn't have killed his parents in the first place.

Adeline laughed. *"Liar."*

True. He grinned as he smoothed the bent edges of the envelope. *I still wish I'd never told Kiera.*

"You know my feelings about your sister. But I do admire her for the way she'd handled herself. I wonder why she didn't kill you. Have you wondered that?"

He had. If he had died, the secret he'd forced her to keep would have died with him.

"I'm also wondering about her boyfriend. How could he know what went on at the plantation house? He knew about the blonde and the switchblade."

You didn't recognize him?

"Lover, I see what you see, and remember what you remember. Read the letter from Big Sis. Maybe she can enlighten us."

I…I'm afraid to read it. She is…was the only person who gave a shit about me. Bella, in her sick, twisted way, might have cared for him enough not to kill him, but he wasn't a fool. She'd planned to use him. Just as Adeline had. Both women had been greedy in their own ways, and had planned to thrive upon the monster he'd become. Kiera hadn't. All she'd wanted was for him to be normal, and to probably know that she hadn't made a mistake by not turning him over to the police the moment she'd found out what he'd done to their parents. He'd guarantee she now regretted that choice.

His intention had never been to hurt his sister. He had wanted her to be proud of him, to make her an aunt, and had pictured his house filled with children—his, hers—during the holidays. Now Kiera would likely never speak to him again, and he would have to spend the rest of his days with only Adeline for company.

"I won't take too *much offense to that, lover,"* Adeline said, contradicting herself by sounding completely offended. *"If you'd told*

the psych doc about me, about the House of Archer, that insanity plea might've worked after all."

And let them experiment on me? Fuck that. I'll take hard time over being some quack's lab rat.

"But we could find out about Kiera's boyfriend, and where he fits into the mix."

I don't care about him. I care about never having to swallow another pill, or having a needle shoved into my veins.

His temper now burning, he sat up and opened the envelope. He unfolded the letter, drew in a deep breath, then read it.

Dear Liam,

I started writing this letter at least a dozen times, and then decided I can no longer waste my time on you. I've spent over ten years trying to do my best by you. I failed. I failed you and myself. There is nothing I can do to change the choices I've made. I can only move forward. For the first time in my life, I will move forward without you. Unfortunately, I will have to live with knowing you've killed so many: Mom, Dad, Delford and Dottie Dougal, Carla Rodriguez, Jennette Salvetti, Wendy DeMarco, Julie Beechum and Gloria Franklin. I hope there are no others.

As you know, I finally told the police that you killed Mom and Dad. I'm only sorry I didn't do it sooner. Your secret had become my burden. Over time, you had become my burden.

I'd like to think you wouldn't have allowed Bella to kill me. I will never know. Even if I can bring myself to visit you, I don't think I'll be able to believe anything you would say anyway. I suppose it doesn't matter now. What does is that you are where you've belonged all along. I'm sorry it took over ten years and the deaths of nine people to get you there.

~ Kiera

"Well, isn't she a little bitch?"
He folded the letter, then slipped it back into the envelope.

"Shut up, Adeline," he muttered, knowing he deserved much worse from Kiera.

"Who cares what she thinks? She's always been a goody-goody. We need to focus on finding a way out of here."

After tucking the letter beneath his pillow, he rolled onto his back and stared at the ceiling. *This isn't the movies. We're in a maximum security prison. Death is the only way out of here.*

Adeline sighed. *"Lover, I don't think I can last in this place. There's nothing to do. And I'm starting to get hungry. Aren't you? Don't you have the craving? Don't you want to prove to the smug bastards who put us in this hellhole that* you *are powerful? That you will take what you want? That you are unstoppable?"*

The hunger pangs were there, but what good would come from him attacking a guard or another prisoner?

"Didn't you just say the only way out of here is through death's doors?"

Not as melodramatically, but yes, he had. He could do himself a favor and commit suicide. He could strangle himself before his bible-thumping cellmate returned and tried to shove Jesus down his throat.

"Suicide? Liam, is that really how you want to go out?" She chuckled. *"I thought you had more style than that, or at least more balls. Feed me, lover."*

So I can wind up on death row anyway? Screw that. I'll only be trading one shitty cell for an even shittier one, where I could end up for ten plus years before they put me out of my misery.

"But I'm hungry now," she whined.

Too bad.

"Please, lover. Give us what we both want. If you do it right, I bet you'll never make it to death row."

A guard spoke. Metal clanked. He looked up at the guard and momentarily wondered if he'd talked aloud, if they'd heard him. "Cellmate's back from the infirmary," the man said, as two other guards came into view. "Don't be stupid."

"Don't be stupid?" Adeline mocked. *"Liam, I want you to kill*

the prick. Wrap your hands around his throat and squeeze until his eyes bleed. Do it. Feed me. Kill him. Hurry, lover. Hurry!"

His stomach seized with the pangs he'd been trying to deny since Bella had been killed. He sat up in his bed, and placed his feet on the floor. Perspiration broke out across his brow as a sense of vertigo created a wave of dizziness.

"Feed me, lover. Give in to the hunger. Take. Kill," Adeline demanded, her tone desperate, pleading.

"Don't move," one of the guards ordered, his voice tinny, distant.

Liam kept his eyes to the floor. A pair of ugly feet clad in a pair of flip-flops stopped in the center of the room.

"Take, Liam. Take from these men. I know you want to. I know you crave it. You're so hungry. Hurry, lover. Hurry!"

One of the guards bent to uncuff the metal bunching up the pant leg of his cellmate's blue prison-issued pants. Liam glanced up at his cellmate and hid a smile. The man had kind brown eyes, a crooked nose and...long dark curly hair.

As Adeline laughed, she taunted him. Screamed loud and long. Filled his head with demands he wanted to meet. Just like the day he was digging in Bella's garden, his vision sharpened, his hearing became acute. The guards stepped away, then out of the cell and, from his peripheral vision, he watched them leave.

His cellmate half-grinned. "How 'ya doin', man?" he asked, offering his hand.

Liam shook the man's hand. "Honestly, I'm starving."

"Tough luck. Breakfast ain't for a while. You'll get used to the schedule."

"Take, take! Kill him, lover," Adeline encouraged. *"Get us the fuck out of this place."*

"I'll never get used to it," Liam said, then smashed his fist into the man's face.

With Adeline cheering him on, with the man's screams filling their small cell, he pinned his cellmate to the floor and beat him in the head. The guards' heavy footsteps echoed. Other prisoners shouted. And as the man's eyes rolled back, Liam could think of one surefire way to avoid death row or solitary confinement.

"What's that, lover?" Adeline asked, breathless, as if she were on the verge of an orgasm.

"Bitch, I'm going to feed you," he said, and she groaned when he sank his teeth into the man's throat.

"What the fuck? Stop!" a guard shouted. "Open the cell."

"Oh, my God!" Another guard slid to a stop. "My God, what are you doing? Get away from him!"

Liam lifted his head. Blood dripped down his chin as he spat on the floor. "I'm feeding the bitch inside me," he said, bent his head and took another bite.

The cell doors slid open and the guards rushed inside. As he tore at his cellmate's flesh, the guards kicked and punched him, tried to pull him free. He ignored the pain, prayed for a quick death, and that Adeline wouldn't follow him into the afterlife.

Just as the heel of a boot smashed his head...

EPILOGUE

"You think it is over,
but the games have just begun."
—Jigsaw, *Saw IV*

Two days later…
Captain Stan's Animal Sanctuary & Alligator Park, Everglades City,
Florida
Friday, 7:43 a.m., Eastern Standard Time

"DON'T YOU WORRY about Polina, she'll be just fine. We keep the lake stocked with fish, so she'll be eatin' like a queen." Stan Thomas, the owner of the sanctuary, placed a hand on Vlad's shoulder. "She needs to be with her own kind."

Harrison watched as Vlad looked at the lake Polina would soon call home, then did the same. Dozens of gators, some bigger, some smaller than Polina, either moved slowly through the water or lounged along the shore.

"Polina like hot dog. What if not eat fish from lake?"

Stan chuckled. "She's a gator, not a picky Poodle. Trust me, she'll eat. Who knows? Next time you come for a visit, she might even have some babies for you."

"No more baby alligators," Harrison said, when the Russian perked up and grinned.

"Vlad know this, but would find joy in being grandpapa."

Laughing, Stan made his way toward the gate which led to the lake. "Barney wasn't kiddin'. You sure are a character." He began unlocking the padlocks. "Hell, I remember the day I sold you that gator. I was expecting to see you back here within a few weeks. You done good. Kept her healthy, and kept all your limbs." He nodded to one of his workers. "Once we get her inside, we just gotta remove the band around her mouth, and she could head on in and make herself some gator friends."

Vlad sighed, and looked to Harrison. "Right thing feel wrong."

"I know, man."

Vlad hung his head and, speaking Russian, led Polina by her pink leash toward the gate. The alligator didn't exactly act like a domesticated animal, but she listened to Vlad and had never once snapped at him. She'd never snapped at Harrison or anyone else, either, but no one other than Barney, who sometimes played gator-sitter, had gotten close enough to her when she wasn't wearing a band around her snout.

When they reached the gate, Vlad walked through with her. Harrison noticed Stan not only took a step back, but put a hand on the pistol he carried around his waist. Stan's employee had gone a step further, and had a rifle trained on Polina.

But the gator was calm and docile as Vlad stroked her head and took off the leash. "Polina будет иметь хорошую жизнь. Vlad будет не хватать его маленькая девочка. Прощай, дорогой друг," he said, removing the band from her snout.

Polina didn't move. Even after Vlad had stepped back outside the gate, and the locks were secured, the alligator remained still.

"Go find gator friend," Vlad said from the fence, and waved his hand toward the lake. He looked to Stan. "Why Polina no go? This concern Vlad."

"Just give her second to adjust." He patted Vlad on the back as he walked past him. "Hey, if you're looking for a new pet, our Bobcat is due next month. I'll sell you one of her kittens."

"It too soon for Vlad to think of new pet," the Russian thankfully said as he continued to watch Polina.

"What'd you say to Polina?" Harrison asked.

"Vlad say Polina will have good life. Vlad will miss little girl."

He let out a sigh. "Farewell, dear friend."

"I'm sorry me and Polina never bonded. I know how much you cared about her."

"It okay, Harry. Vlad understood. Reptile not warm and fuzzy like kitten."

Harrison stared at his friend's profile. "You like kittens and puppies. Why did you choose Polina?"

The Russian shrugged. "What Harry think of Vlad when first we meet?"

He thought back to the time he'd been held captive in a hotel room by the chain-smoking Russian and his Colombian counterpart, Santiago. "I think you know."

"Icy-cold killer, да?"

"Ice-cold sounds a little more badass."

The Russian grinned. "Never forget, Vlad make all thing badass." He went back to watching Polina. "Not like puppy, reptile have cold blood, it look scary, and show no emotion. This much like Vlad."

"Dude, you're not like that."

"That because Harry know Vlad. Polina much the same as Vlad. Gator look scary and show no emotion. But Vlad believe Polina feel something for Vlad."

Harrison disagreed, but wouldn't say that to his friend. He also now had a better understanding of why Vlad had chosen an alligator for a pet. In a way, Polina represented how Vlad believed people might see him. Between his huge size, his ice-blue eyes and the hardness that usually lined his face, he could understand why the man would intimidate anyone. When he'd first met Vlad, the dude had scared the hell out of him. But Vlad was a deep thinker, intelligent and loyal. And Harrison was glad Vlad had chosen to join him in Tallahassee. Life just wouldn't be the same without Vlad.

"I'm sure she'll miss you," Harrison finally said. "Stan's right, though. This is the best place for her. But I bet if you brought Polina on repo jobs, people would probably throw their keys at you."

The Russian grinned. "Vlad have thought this. But apartment too small for gator." He nudged him. "It good size for Chee-chee-wa-wa, eh?"

"You just told Stan you weren't ready for a new pet."

"Vlad lie to Stan. Harry and Vlad go legit, да?"

"да."

"That mean Vlad need legit pet, too. No wild animal for Vlad."

Harrison half-laughed, and brought Vlad's attention back to the lake. "There she goes," he said as Polina made her way toward the water."

The Russian beamed. "Vlad have much pride."

They watched Polina until they could no longer tell her from the other alligators. When tourists began to filter into the sanctuary, Harrison suggested they go. Since neither of them had accumulated much while living in the Glades, they'd rented a moving trailer to hitch to Harrison's Jeep, and planned to head back to Tallahassee in the morning. The apartment Harrison had rented had come fully furnished, and he looked forward to combining his things with Kiera's. Meanwhile, he wanted to finish packing, and cleaning the trailer now that Knox Lynden, a former Navy SEAL and Lola's recent hire, decided to purchase it from him.

"Will Kiera come for cookout at Polina's?" Vlad asked, stopping to watch the otters use the slide in their pool habitat. "Vlad would not blame Harry girlfriend if become vegetarian."

"No kidding," Harrison said, trying not to picture Liam using his teeth to tear out a man's throat. "She plans on coming. I don't know, man, I think she's relieved Liam's dead. She hasn't come right out and said as much, but I can see it in her eyes. Even her face looks more relaxed."

Vlad nodded. "Eye windowpane to soul. Vlad do not blame Kiera for relief. Serial killer is dead like Vlad say should be."

"Yeah, but to go out that way? Either the man was crazier than anyone thought, or he was desperate to die." Kiera had said that the prison guards had been forced to use excessive force before he'd finally dropped dead. The man he'd attacked had died later that night.

"Sound like little of both," Vlad said, lingering by the panthers' exhibit. "Now that Polina free, Vlad mind is on Asian Lola. Do Harry think Asian Lola okay with Vlad and Harry leave ATL?"

"I don't think she's happy about it, but I definitely think she's happy for us."

Vlad grinned. "да, Vlad think same, and happy for us."

"Me, too. I'm proud of you, man. You're going to have your own apartment and a real job."

As real a job as a former hitman could have. There might be a time in the near future where Vlad could become a somewhat legal U.S. citizen, that is if Ian Scott could get his government buddies to not only give Vlad a new identity, but amnesty. Vlad had already made it clear that he had secrets the U.S. government would like, and he'd be willing to give them up for something in return. In the meantime, Vlad would train as a mechanic while doing repo jobs for Cash and Jude, and Harrison would build his web development business.

"Vlad also proud of Harry." They stepped away from the panthers. "And Vlad happy to start another adventure with Harry."

"Yeah, ATL, living in the Glades, it was a good run. But I'm ready to see what kind of damage we can do in Tallahassee. Nothing illegal, of course."

"Of course," Vlad said with a chuckle, then threw his arm around Harrison. "Harry and Vlad like Han Solo and Chewbacca."

He grinned. "As long as you're the hairy dude."

"Vlad do not want to be known for hairy body. Maybe Butch Cassidy and Sundance Kid?"

"Didn't they die at the end of that movie?"

"Vlad do not remember. Barney have made Vlad watch too many movie at one time." The Russian frowned. "Bert and Ernie?"

"They're Muppets, man."

"Laverne DeFazio and Shirley Feeney? Thelma and Louise?"

"What?" Harrison stopped him just before the exit. "You do know those are women, right?"

"Woman with balls good enough for Vlad."

"Vlad, buddy, don't ever say that in front of the guys at the garage."

"Why? Vlad like woman with balls."

"I get it, but it sounds like…never mind. Can't we just be Vlad and Harrison?"

The Russian grinned. "That good enough for Vlad."

As they made their way out of the sanctuary, Vlad looked over his shoulder toward the lake and waved. "See you later, alligator."

Vlad, Harrison and the boys from the garage will be featured in my new Repo Men Series. Subscribe to my newsletter or like my Facebook page to find out when they'll be back!

You can also expect the start of another C.O.R.E. and Celeste Files trilogy. So stay tuned…

Other Books by Kristine Mason

C.O.R.E. Above the Law

Perfectly Twisted (Book 1)

What do you get when you mix a snake-handling reverend, a necrophiliac, a cop and an ex-con? Something perfectly twisted...

Sound like the start of a bad joke? Not to Shane Monahan. The ex-con, former Army Night Stalker and newest recruit to the underground criminal investigation group, ATL or Above the Law, has it bad for Collier County Deputy Beth Price. But ex-cons and cops don't mix, especially when this particular ex-con is looking at going back to prison for his involvement with ATL.

All Beth wants is a fun distraction from the stress of her job and law school. She thinks she's found that when she meets Shane during an airboat tour through the Florida Everglades. But Shane's a felon, a man who could destroy her career as a deputy, and jeopardize her future as an attorney. She doesn't know what to do—until dead bodies start showing up around the county.

When three abused corpses are found with snake remains inside them, the discovery brings a murderer out of retirement. The Reverend, as he calls himself, doesn't like his kills being mimicked, especially by a man who abuses the dead—after all, the Reverend does have a reputation to uphold and a congregation to scam. Now it's time to teach his copycat a deadly lesson...

Perfectly Toxic (Book 2)

What do you get when you mix a mad scientist, a psychopath, an ice cream lady and a repo man? Something perfectly toxic...

Melanie Scarlet is a knife-wielding badass who knows how to dispose of a body, and make evidence disappear. But Mel, a.k.a., the Ice Cream Lady, draws the line at one thing: she refuses to live with her husband, Cash Maddox, unless he quits the repo business that nearly got him killed—no matter how much she loves him.

To thaw Mel's heart and convince her to leave the Everglades and move back home to Tallahassee, Cash is finally ready to retire from his adrenaline-fueled job...until homeless men begin vanishing. As Mel investigates the disappearances, Cash's temper goes into overdrive when he realizes his wife has been keeping a dangerous secret from him. She's been doing more than scooping ice cream—she's a cleaner for the underground criminal investigation agency, Above the Law.

Mel isn't the only one with a secret. A scientist has created a drug that will cure psychopaths by deadening the urge to dominate, hurt and murder. To prove his chemical combination works, he uses the homeless as test subjects. He breaks and scrambles their minds, turns them into killers, then tries to fix them. But what if the scientist creates a killer he can't fix? A true psychopath he can't control? As Cash joins Mel and the ATL crew, they learn firsthand, the results could be...toxic.

C.O.R.E. Shadow Trilogy

Shadow of Danger (Book 1)

Beware of what lurks in the shadows...

Four women have been found dead in the outskirts of a small Wisconsin town. The only witness, clairvoyant Celeste Risinski, observes these brutal murders through violent nightmares and hellish visions. The local sheriff, who believes in Celeste's abilities and wants to rid their peaceful community of a killer, enlists the help of an old friend, Ian Scott, owner of a private criminal investigation agency, CORE. Because of Ian's dark history with Celeste's family, a history she knows nothing about, he sends his top criminalist, former FBI agent, John Kain, to investigate.

John doesn't believe in Celeste's mystic hocus-pocus, or in her visions of the murders. But just when he's certain they've solved the crimes with the use of science and evidence, more dead bodies are discovered. Could this somehow be the work of the same killer, or are they dealing with a copycat? To catch a vicious murderer, the skeptical criminalist reluctantly turns to the sensual psychic for help. Yet, with each step closer to finding the killer, John finds himself one step closer to losing his heart.

Shadow of Perception (Book 2)

What happens when negligent plastic surgeons receive a taste of their own medicine...?

Chicago investigative reporter, Eden Risk, receives an unmarked envelope containing a postcard ordering her to watch the enclosed DVD...or someone else dies. No Police. After Eden watches the DVD, a gruesome, horrifying surgery, she turns to the private criminal investigation agency, CORE, for help. Only she hadn't expected that help to come with a catch. Her former lover, Hudson Patterson, has been assigned to the case.

Hudson would rather have another CORE agent handle the investigation. Two years ago, he'd screwed things up with Eden...bad. And as more DVDs arrive, Eden and Hudson find themselves not only knee-deep in a twisted investigation, but forced to deal with their past, and the love they'd tried to deny.

Shadow of Vengeance (Book 3)

Welcome to Hell Week. You have seven days to find him...

At Wexman University, male students will do anything to get into a top fraternity. They'll prove their worth during Hell Week by participating in various physical, psychological and even juvenile pranks. But those shenanigans aren't so funny when pledges start disappearing. What kind of evil has stalked this small Michigan university for the past two decades? Theories range from obscene scientific experiments to grotesque satanic killings...but they're all wrong. The murdered boys serve a single purpose...the ultimate revenge.

Rachel Davis, forensic computer analyst for the private investigation agency CORE, has been itching to leave her desk behind and work in the field. When her brother Sean, a student at Wexman, is found beaten and his roommate kidnapped during Hell Week, she gets her chance. Only her boss insists former U.S. Secret Service Agent, Owen Malcolm, helps her with the investigation. Owen is the last person she wants on this assignment. She'd been secretly half in love with him for over four years, until the night he'd crushed her ego and destroyed her hopes for any kind of future with him.

For his own reasons, Owen refuses to risk becoming involved with a coworker. Now that he and Rachel are stuck working side by side to solve this perverse investigation, he's having a hard time fighting his attraction to her...an attraction he's tried to deny from the moment they met. But time is ticking. They have seven days to find the missing pledge and catch a killer. Seven days before the body count rises and the pledge ends up another victim of Hell Week.

Ultimate C.O.R.E. Trilogy

Ultimate Kill (Book 1)

When the past collides with the present, the only way to ensure the future lies in the ultimate kill...

Naomi McCall is a woman of many secrets. Her family has been murdered and she's been forced into hiding. No one knows her past or her real name, not even the man she loves.

Jake Tyler, former Marine and the newest recruit to the private investigation agency, CORE, has been in love with a woman who never existed. When he learns about the lies Naomi has weaved, he's ready to leave her—until an obsessed madman begins sending her explosive messages every hour on the hour.

Innocent people are dying. With their deaths, Naomi's secrets are revealed and the truth is thrust into the open. All but one. Naomi's not sure if Jake can handle a truth that will change their lives. But she is certain of one thing—the only way to stop the killer before he takes more lives is to make herself his next victim.

Ultimate Fear (Book 2)

When a deranged mother's grief drives her to replace her dead son over and over, obsession leads to murder...

Chicago detective Jessica Donavan will never stop looking for her missing daughter. Her obsession has destroyed her marriage, but the search is the only thing that helps keep her sane and her mind off of everything she's lost—her husband and her baby girl. When she uncovers a string of unsolved disappearances and reappearances of a number of baby boys, Jessica turns to her soon to be ex, Dante Russo, a former Navy SEAL turned investigator for the private agency, CORE, to help her fit together the pieces in this perplexing puzzle. But as Dante helps her, she realizes just how much she still craves his support—and his touch.

Dante is still in love with his wife and would do anything to have her back in his life again. He's been miserable since she left him to deal with the grief over their daughter's abduction, never understanding how much he grieves as well. When Jessica tells him about the case she's working, he jumps at the chance to take part in her investigation. He's hoping not only to save their marriage and ease his personal pain over the loss of their daughter, but to stop a serial kidnapper from taking another victim.

As Jessica and Dante work side by side, pregnant women begin to turn up missing or dead, and they start to uncover the consequences of another woman's unfathomable grief. The childless mother doesn't just want a baby. She wants a newborn straight from the womb.

And when forced to confront the dark and twisted perversion of a mother's obsession, can Jessica and Dante find their lives again...or merely more death?

Ultimate Prey (Book 3)

When the hunter becomes the hunted...who will become the ultimate prey?

CORE agent Lola Tam has two things on her mind, quitting her job as a criminal investigator and baking a frozen pie for Thanksgiving dinner without burning it. But a midnight call forces a change of plans. Her boss and future stepfather, Ian Scott, has been kidnapped from his Florida vacation rental—along with her mother. The kidnapper's plan? Drop Ian and her mom in the Everglades and hunt them like animals. Terrified for her mom, Lola takes the bait and travels to Everglades City, Florida where she's determined to end the hunt before it begins.

Ryan Monahan, former Navy SEAL turned airboat captain is used to taking tourists through the Everglades, not guiding a sexy agent on a rescue mission. After spending years dealing with a past filled with guilt and regret, he needs a little action and adventure in his life—he needs to prove he could still be a hero. What he doesn't need? Falling for a woman he has no business wanting, especially when the hunt takes a deadly turn...

Psychic C.O.R.E. Series

Celeste Files: Unlocked (Book 1)

Some secrets should remain locked in the past...

Celeste Kain hasn't had a psychic vision in two years. After being brutally attacked while helping criminal investigation agency CORE stop a serial killer, her mind repressed her clairvoyant abilities. Married to CORE agent, John Kain, mother to their toddler, Olivia, and owner of an up-and-coming bakery, Celeste has been doing fine psychic-free. Only now the dead are using her body to tell their stories again...putting her new life and family at risk.

Haunted by a murdered woman, Celeste turns to a psychic mentor to learn how to control her gift, protect her family and bring justice to the dead. But the more she digs into the dead woman's past, the further she slips into the unknown, unlocking secrets literally worth killing for. As the body count rises, it becomes clear: someone in the dead woman's family is deeply, violently *wrong*. And Celeste needs to be careful, before she loses something more precious to her than her life.

Celeste Risinski, the heroine of Shadow of Danger (Book 1 C.O.R.E. Shadow Trilogy), is back with her own series. Join her as she learns how to deal with being a wife, mom, baker and...psychic investigator.

Celeste Files: Unjust (Book 2)

Dealing with the dead is murder...

Psychic Celeste Kain has two things on her mind, relaxing for a week in Florida with her husband, John, and making a baby. But a fishing trip turns her vacation into a nightmare when she reels in the body of a dead boat captain and accidentally unleashes an evil ghost who has one thing on his mind...revenge.

As the dead boat captain haunts Celeste, she looks deeper into his past and discovers that his murderer had done the world a favor. The ghost tormenting Celeste doesn't see it that way and will go to any length to avenge his death. If Celeste won't give him what he wants, he will take over her body and use her as a weapon...to kill her husband.

Celeste Files: Unforgotten (Book 3)

Something is wrong with the children...

Seven years ago, CORE agent, Dante Russo and his wife, Jessica, faced a parent's ultimate fear...their ten-month-old daughter was abducted. With no clues, not a single sighting or trace of evidence to keep hope alive, the case went cold...until now.

When the ghosts of murdered children begin to haunt psychic Celeste Kain, she's forced to get involved in her most challenging case yet. The ghosts know who has Sophia. They know her kidnapper intimately. They know him as Daddy, and as their killer.

Using psychic visions and the clues the young spirits provide, Celeste and her husband, John, travel across the country, desperately searching for the girl and her kidnapper. The dead children have made their warning clear...find Sophia before Daddy kills again.

About Kristine Mason

Kristine Mason is the bestselling author of the popular romantic suspense trilogies, C.O.R.E. Shadow and Ultimate C.O.R.E. She is currently working on her next series, C.O.R.E. Above the Law, along with more Psychic C.O.R.E. novels.

Although Kristine has published a few contemporary romance novels, she focuses most of her energy on her romantic suspense stories, which she loves for their blend of dark mystery/suspense and sexy romance. She is fascinated with what makes people afraid, and is famous for her depraved villains whose crimes present massive obstacles for her heroes and heroines to overcome.

Kristine has a degree in journalism from Ohio State University and lives in Northeast Ohio with her husband, four kids, and two dogs. If she's not writing, she's chauffeuring kids, gardening, or collecting gnomes. Oh, and she makes a mean chocolate chip cookie!

Connect with Kristine on Facebook facebook.com/kristinemasonauthor, Twitter twitter.com/KristineMason7 or email her at authorkristinemason@gmail.com. You can also find out more about Kristine's books at www.kristinemason.net.

www.ingramcontent.com/pod-product-compliance
Lightning Source LLC
Chambersburg PA
CBHW072112250626
47159CB00007B/2410